To Save a Prince . . .

The sorcerer Yamuna stepped forward. He wound his fingers around one of the hundred braids in his hair, each one a working of protection for the emperor, or so Makul had heard. His heart thudded shamefully. "Give me the arrow," said the sorcerer, "and you will have an easier death than you should."

Makul fitted the arrow into the string.

With one swift yank, Yamuna tore the braid from his scalp and cast it to the floor, where it lay, its grey strands unraveling.

At once, Makul felt his heart laboring to beat. The world blurred before his eyes.

No. Not my eyes. I must see. He blinked hard.

Pain licked him like a flame. Weakness took his knees, and again the world blurred. *No!* He shook his head, and bent his leg under him, raising the bow high, pointing the arrow south toward Sindhu.

Mother Jalaja guide my hand.

Yamuna lunged forward. Even though Makul's eyes could not see, his arm remembered what to do. He let the arrow fly. For one dazzling moment, he saw a line of fire traced across the blackness that was his world.

With that burning image before him, and Yamuna's screams in his ears, M⁻⁻¹ fell to the floor and died.

Sword of the Deceiver

A Novel of Isavalta

Sarah Zettel

TOR®
fantasy

A TOM DOHERTY ASSOCIATES BOOK
NEW YORK

This is a work of fiction. All of the characters, organizations, and events portrayed in this novel are either products of the author's imagination or are used fictitiously.

SWORD OF THE DECEIVER

Copyright © 2007 by Sarah Zettel

Edited by James Frenkel

A Tor Book
Published by Tom Doherty Associates, LLC
175 Fifth Avenue
New York, NY 10010

www.tor.com

Tor® is a registered trademark of Tom Doherty Associates, LLC.

ISBN-13: 978-0-7653-4320-8
ISBN-10: 0-7653-4320-7

First Edition: March 2007
First Mass Market Edition: April 2008

Printed in the United States of America

0 9 8 7 6 5 4 3 2 1

This book is dedicated to my loving and supportive husband,
Tim.

Acknowledgments

This book was a little tougher than usual to get out. I'd like to thank my editor, Jim Frenkel, for his much needed assistance and patience. As ever, I also had the unflagging help of The United Writers' Group, and I'd particularly like to thank Anne Harris, who put her finger on the heart of so many problems.

Sword of the Deceiver

Chapter One

It was the season of dust.

The sky was copper with dust. Dust smeared the white cotton of Natharie's plain skirt and breastband. Dust rose in a plume from the distant road as some messenger rode pell-mell for the river bridge. Dust clung to her sweating skin; the itch and smell of it filled her nose until she could taste it in the back of her throat. The whole world was an oven and only the flies danced.

Despite this, Natharie strode joyously through the shin-high grass, her bare arms swinging and the white skirt flapping around her knees. Today was her nineteenth birthday; today Natharie would at long last be declared a woman.

Queen Sitara, Natharie's mother, followed her, all her gold chiming and glittering in the hazy sunlight. Four of Natharie's sisters, Oma, Shu, Vikka, and Rasura—younger than she, yet women already—walked with their mother, all swaying hips and superior airs. Behind her blood family walked Natharie's aunts, cousins, maids, attendants, and nurses. Anun, the rough, round, bawdy captain of the women's guards, strode with them, her voice rising in a hoarse bellow over their clear song. Even the old nun Sathi followed Natharie today, and Natharie stretched out her long legs, determined to keep ahead of them. Little Malai, Natharie's youngest sister and the only remaining girl-child of the family, took the excuse of the festive occasion and ran, only half a grinning, giggling step behind Natharie.

It was all Natharie could do to keep from laughing as her smallest sister's high, panting voice struggled to get out the words of the womanhood hymn that rose up from the glittering procession.

The grain full ripe falls to seed the earth.
The grain will grow up toward the sun.
The girl gives birth to the woman, who gives birth to the
  world.
So turns the wheel, until Heaven is achieved.

In the traditional way of things, Natharie's womanhood ceremony would have been held when she was thirteen or fourteen. Mother's had happened when she was only nine. No one could become a bride until they became a woman, and this was why Natharie's ceremony had been so long delayed. Treaty obligations written before Natharie was even born gave her, the king of Sindhu's oldest daughter, to the king of Lohit. When the old king found himself widowed, he had sent for Natharie, but her parents had demurred and delayed, for one year, and another, and still another after that.

Now, the old king was dead, and Natharie was finally free from her extended childhood. Free to claim the rights and the obligations of womanhood, and of her own home and a new land to go with it. The new king, Pairoj, waited for her to become his bride.

The girl gives birth to the woman, who gives birth to the
  world.
So turns the wheel, until Heaven is achieved.

The women of the procession were the only color in the dust-brown world. Their silks and linens made them a river of color in the pale grassland: scarlet, sapphire, emerald, silver, gold, diamond white. Even Captain Anun had laid aside her uniform for a gown of amethyst and silver. Tia, Natharie's ancient nurse, had been stitching the emerald threads onto her red cotton skirt for over a month now.

"My mistress will only become a woman once in this life," she'd said with a grin. Natharie had hugged her then. Neither one of them had been sure Tia would survive long enough to see this day. Because she had never been declared a woman, Natharie's childhood servants had stayed with her for far longer than the usual time. Now they would all be gone. That was the hard part of this day, thought Natharie. So many familiar faces and presences would be given other places, or paid their final pensions and returned to their family homes. A woman did not need the same tutors, servants, and possessions as a girl. Especially when she would shortly be sent to her husband's home. Natharie pushed that thought away. Later there would be time enough to worry about the future. Not, she told herself, that there was much to worry over. Pairoj's letters held the promise of a bright and considerate husband. After all, her mother had come from Lohit to be queen of Sindhu and found here a good life and a kind husband. She knew this must be a day of endings as well as beginnings. That was as it should be. Natharie lifted her chin and lengthened her stride. She would not go afraid. She would go with her eyes open.

Beneath her sloping bank, the sacred river, Liyoni, was low, flat, and brown. The passing boatmen were black shadows who raised their hands to the brightly colored procession as the current carried them swiftly past. She pushed her way through the chattering reeds that lined the riverbank. The dried edges grazed her skin. Warm mud squelched between Natharie's toes and tugged at her sandal heels with loud, sloppy kisses. A trio of ducks, offended by their noisy passage, burst into the air, complaining as they flew.

Natharie's mother and the other women set down their baskets and, singing still, surrounded her.

The wheel turns life to birth to death to life.
The wheel turns girl to woman to widow to girl.

Take her hand, O! Awakened One!
Open her eyes as yours were opened and lead her from the
  wheel to Heaven.

Anun the guardswoman grinned like a tigress and stripped off Natharie's white skirt and breastband. Tia crowned her tangled hair with the golden flowers. Oma, Rasura, Vikka, Shu, all of them, crowded around her and draped more garlands around her shoulders, kissing her and laughing as the bright petals fluttered down to stick to her arms and the backs of her hands. Malai hung garlands on Natharie's wrists and hugged her big sister hard. Natharie was a little surprised at the tears that came so quick and strong to her eyes as she returned the little one's embrace.

Lastly, Mother came to wrap the girdle of white chrysanthemums around Natharie's waist. Then she stretched up on tiptoe and kissed her forehead. Fate had declared that Natharie should have all her father's height. Where Mother was tiny, slender, and straight-hipped, Natharie was as tall as most men, with a broad, curving body, and arms and legs hardened by the playing and fighting she did with the female guards who looked after Mother and the concubines. There were many jokes whispered among Natharie and her sisters about . . . accommodations her future husband might have to make because of her size.

Mother stepped back to let old Sathi, the only other one here wearing white, hobble forward. Natharie held still and found that, for all her delight, solemnity came easily. After this day, her new life would begin in earnest. She needed this blessing as she had never needed any other. The challenge of her size was the least of what she had to face.

Someone handed Sathi the clay bowl of henna and jasmine. The nun raised it up to the coppery sky and began the hymn of departure in her cracked voice.

Let the way begun again be the way of peace.
Let the horizon that is seen again be seen from the calm and
generous heart.
Let the eyes be open to see Heaven and the Awakened One
and all the Blessed.

The familiar voices all took up the hymn, spinning the
words over and over again until Natharie felt dizzy. Sathi
dipped her withered fingers into the henna and Natharie
stooped down so the nun could mark her brow with signs of
tranquillity and the turning wheel of time. Then Sathi passed
the bowl to Tia, and took Natharie's hand. The ancient nun
led Natharie into the river. Boatmen called out blessings as
they passed. Natharie found she was shaking a little.

Let the way begun again be the way of peace.
Let the horizon that is seen again be seen from the calm and
generous heart.

When the water was up to Natharie's breast, Sathi turned,
grasped Natharie's shoulders, and shoved her down into the
water.

The water roared as it swallowed Natharie. There was no
time to draw in extra breath. The world below was brown
and shifting and silent. Water, sand, and silt filled her eyes
and ears. Shadows scattered and sunlight sparkled through
the brown water. Her blood pounded in her ears. She tried
to hold still, but it went on and on, and she kicked at the
sand underneath her, but Sathi held on tight. She grabbed
at the wiry fingers, trying to pry them loose, but Sathi still
held her.

All at once, Sathi let go, and Natharie shot up into the air,
gulping in deep, whooping gasps of air, and of the water that
fountained off her, which made her cough and gag and gasp
again. Sathi embraced Natharie, and led her—a woman

grown now, and still coughing gracelessly—back to shore where the other women still sang for her.

Let the new heart bring peace in the time of hardship.
Let the new voice bring wisdom in the time of darkness . . .

Natharie coughed out the last of Liyoni's waters and pushed her streaming hair out of her face. Then she froze, ankle-deep in river water, her face warm with sudden wonder.

A horse stood atop the bank. He was pure black without trace of paler color, so shining and perfect he might have been a polished statue. His mane flowed like silk, and were it not for the wind that blew it back, it would have hung down almost to his knees. He tossed his head at her, stamping his hoof as if in greeting.

Natharie's jaw dropped open. The thought flitted through her mind that her father had sent this beautiful creature as a womanhood gift. But the other women all turned as well, and they too froze like stone. Now Natharie could see that the horse was surrounded by a crowd of men. Three were wrinkled things in flowing red robes with high, curving gold hats that they had to keep clutching to prevent the wind from blowing them into the dust. Their hands were full of scrolls and gold rods and other shiny things that they kept dropping as they tried to keep their hats on. They looked like busy little brown monkeys next to the beautiful black horse. All but one. That one stood tall and stern, his great arms folded, frowning down on the world. Smaller monkeys, boys she saw now, scurried around their red-robed masters, picking up what they had dropped, dusting it all off. The red monkeys shouted and pointed and sent the boys scuttling off on new errands, to the palanquin bearers and other dust-caked servants who waited behind them, to other men in plain robes bearing tablets and styluses, who bobbed and scribbled while the red monkeys held on to their hats and shouted at each other.

The men behind looked much more imposing. They stood in neat formation, four rows of five. They wore armor that glittered like fish scales. They carried long spears and wore curving swords at their hips. Bows and quivers of arrows had been slung over their shoulders. One young man led them, his face stern, his eyes cold with anger. Not at her, she thought in the odd, slow moment of her staring at him, but at the men in red. Beside him, on a smaller horse, sat a single woman in a plain white dress carrying a white staff as the soldiers carried their spears.

They were not her father's men. All of them—the red monkeys and the soldiers, the boys, the secretaries, the bearers and that one woman in white—stared at the women and naked Natharie with the dripping flower garlands disintegrating on waist and shoulders.

A horse. Red-robed . . . priests. Soldiers. Natharie knew what she saw, and knowing made her blood run cold.

Hastinapura. They've come back.

The soldiers' leader met Natharie's eyes, drew himself up a little taller, and the moment broke. The world exploded into motion. Anun shoved Malai behind her. The women on the shore scattered, clutching the wealth they'd brought for Natharie. Mother charged forward with the red dress that should have been wrapped ceremonially around Natharie and tossed it over her to cover her nakedness. Anun shouted something. Natharie snatched up little Malai, tossed the girl across her shoulder, and began to run. Mother saw that she held Malai, and with her skirts hiked up around her knees, she ran past. Natharie heard women's screams, the boisterous sounds of men's laughter, and shrill shouts that could have only been the red priests'. She thought she heard Sathi shouting, but she could barely breathe, let alone understand what was being said. It took all the breath she had to find her stride to get Malai and herself back to safety.

Rusara, Vikka, and a few of the others had caught up with them, and they all ran together. Natharie's head spun but she had no breath for asking questions. She could only clutch at the red cloth with one hand and her little sister with the other and try to keep running.

They reached the edge of the rice fields. Laborers cried out to see their queen and her maids racing through the brown grass and only belatedly fell to their knees. A horn sounded. Men, soldiers—Father's soldiers—poured across the canal bridges and surrounded all the women.

They must know what is happening. Natharie set Malai on her feet and hugged her close, relieved that her little sister was too short of breath to ask questions she did not have wit or wind to answer.

Mother was talking fast, giving orders. Anun was rattling off descriptions and numbers to the soldiers and orders to the women's guards who arrived at a dead run with them. Behind the first flood of soldiers came a troop of bearers with a double palanquin. Mother boosted Malai into it, and Natharie scrambled in behind while Anun snatched a spear out of the hand of the nearest guardswoman to take her place beside them.

"Hurry!" Mother called to the bearers, and they did. They lurched and rocked so badly, Natharie was afraid they'd be thrown out. Poor Malai huddled on the floor, hugging their mother's knees. Mother wrapped one arm around her daughter and gripped the canopy support with the other, her face grim and her jaw clenched tight.

Natharie clutched the nearest canopy pole, suddenly, childishly incensed at what had been ruined. She had waited years for this day. She was supposed to be covered in women's finery—gold and jewels and perfume. She was supposed to be walking through the streets in her gilded sandals while the people showered her with flowers.

She was not supposed to be running from the priests of the northern empire and their barbaric sacrifice.

When they reached the dark wood and gilt walls of the palace, the gates were already open. Father, King Kiet of

Sindhu, waited there, his craggy face taut with fear and fury. The bearers barely had time to set them down on the palm-lined lawn before Mother leapt out to grab his hands.

"The horse . . . from Hastinapura," Mother gasped. "The emperor's horse."

"I know. We had a messenger." Father covered her long hands with his square ones.

"Why now?" she demanded. "Chandra has been on the throne four years, why does he send out the horse now?"

When Father just shook his head, Mother covered her face. "Ah! Why not yesterday? Why today?"

Ancient Tia had come up to the side of the litter, wheezing from the run, and was tugging at Natharie's arm. "Come chil . . . Natharie. You cannot be seen like this."

But defiance filled Natharie and she stayed where she was. Malai slipped up to her, grasping her hems.

"What's happening?" the little girl demanded. "Tell me!"

Father looked at her, and Natharie swallowed as she saw the unspoken order in his eyes. Her first duty as a woman had come. She wrapped her arm around Malai's thin shoulders. "We cannot talk of such things here."

Malai pulled back, belatedly aware of how many people filled the yard—secretaries, servants, soldiers, merchants, farmers, all sorts of people kneeling before the royal family with their heads pressed against the dusty ground, but with their ears wide open. She straightened herself up and tilted her chin up. Showing all the angry dignity an eight-year-old girl could muster, Malai turned on her heel and walked toward the doors of her palace home with her nurse fussing behind her.

Mother pressed Natharie's hand. "There will be an audience," she said, and quickly turned to Natharie's sisters and the other women.

Natharie felt light-headed. A strange buzzing filled her ears as she walked slowly, carefully to her own chamber. There, her maids greeted her with fuss and flutter and a hundred questions.

"There will be an audience," she said, hearing her own voice only at a great distance. "I must be ready."

To their credit, her women stopped their questioning. They hurried forward with basins and cloths, to clothe her properly in red and gold, to wash her skin with cool water, to comb and dress her hair and make it ready to receive the high golden cap that was her crown as eldest of Sindhu's royal daughters.

While they worked, Natharie stared out of the great arched windows leading to her balcony, overlooking the gardens, the fields, and the river beyond. She was looking along the bank for dots of white and red. She saw nothing but the roots of the white mountains that held up the sky.

Hastinapura. The great empire to the north. Natharie had been only four years old when they last came. She remembered being held in her mother's arms to watch Father as he led away the long columns of the army. Father had been gone for more than a year. When he came back, he was dusty and he stank, and he had the wound that left a white and ragged line behind his ear, but he was triumphant. He and Mother had talked a lot about treaties and other things she did not then understand. She did understand that her father had persuaded the emperor on the Pearl Throne not to bring his armies into their land of Sindhu and take her parents away.

Now, three times a year, Sindhu sent tribute up the river on long lines of flat-bottomed boats: bales of rice, great logs of teak and mahogany, chests of the gold dust that washed down from the white mountains into the streams that fed the Liyoni. All of this went to Hastinapura, where the men were so afraid of women they locked them up and wouldn't even look at them in the time of love, yet allowed sorcerers to live right in the palace with the king, instead of sending them into the forest monasteries to study and pray and keep the temptation and corruption of power away from the weak and the vulnerable.

These were the red-and-gold men who walked over their grasslands behind the shining black horse. This was the lead soldier with the cold eyes. Eyes that had seen blood sacrifice over and over again, that helped it and honored it. Eyes that looked on the land of Sindhu and saw it as their property.

Then she thought of Malai alone in her chamber, at least as frightened as she herself was, and bewildered at the wreckage of this celebratory day. When the maids finished tucking the last fold of Natharie's scarlet gown, she rose and went to her little sister.

Malai's nurse, old Seta, was finishing Malai's hair, braiding it with gold as she knelt on the floor, looking more stunned than patient still. The girl had been dressed in emerald green embroidered with golden birds. She was a delicate child, Natharie thought fondly, sadly, and she would be a beautiful woman when her turn came.

Natharie must have made some sound, because Malai turned her head. She did not speak. She just tilted her chin up again, letting her interfering older sister know that she was still angry.

Natharie was smiling; and since she was not refused permission to enter, she walked into the room. Malai smelled of sandalwood, sunlight, and sweat. Seta placed a pillow for Natharie beside her sister. Natharie knelt on the cushion and began to speak. She spoke slowly and calmly, falling into the rhythms of reciting an old poem, grateful for the distance and discipline the pretense gave her. "In Hastinapura, when a new emperor ascends to the Pearl Throne, they have a week of mourning for the old emperor, and then a week of sacrifice and celebrations for the new. At the end of this time, a black horse is sent out from the city. The horse roams where it will for a year before it returns to be sacrificed."

Malai swallowed and Natharie nodded, silently acknowledging the little girl's thought. The Seven Mothers who were worshipped in Hastinapura demanded blood for the smallest blessing, it was said. The magnificent creature they had seen was destined for the knives of the priests.

"Whatever land the horse crosses is said to belong to Hastinapura, by the will of their Mothers.

"Centuries ago, an army of conquest followed the horse, but now it has only an honor guard, as you saw. If any of those who accompany the horse do not come back alive, and with enough celebratory tribute following them, it is the land where they were last seen that will bear the blame, and the punishment."

Slowly, the meaning of those words sank in and Malai shuddered. Natharie knew what she was thinking, because she had been thinking the same thing since they had reached their home and she was able to think at all. The emperor on Hastinapura's Pearl Throne expected more tribute. Wealth. Servants.

Women.

There were always women in the tribute. Mostly servants, but every so often, a daughter of one of the high houses.

Why did it have to come today? Mother had wailed. Today, when Natharie became a woman and was ready to be given in marriage as the treaty spelled out. True, the contract had not been formally witnessed, but letters had been exchanged between the kings, promises had been made, and her name had been bound to those promises. Yesterday, when she was still a girl, she could have been the one to go to Hastinapura. Now, if a daughter was demanded, there was only tiny Malai left to go.

Nausea gripped Natharie's stomach. Only little Malai, the youngest of three daughters. Only a daughter, with three brothers who would remain in the house. Oh, no. Malai was not too much to ask. Not too much to give to Hastinapura and their bloody goddesses to prevent a war.

The thought made Natharie sick, even as she realized the same reasoning could apply to any of them.

"But we have a treaty," Malai said, invoking the word like

a magic charm. It had prevented so much, surely it could prevent this.

"We had a treaty with the old emperor," said Natharie. "Our father, and our ambassadors, say his son is a very different man." She had heard the gossip late at night, after banquets and around corners. The new emperor was not well liked. He was shiftless and lazy. The most daring, when they thought no one was listening, wondered softly if King Kiet had made the Hastinapuran treaty knowing that when the old emperor died the young one might not be able to hold the new lands. Natharie had often wished this was true, but if it was, that plan would come to fruition too late for Malai. "There are . . . complications with his rule. It may be he has decided it is time to make his authority . . ." Her mouth twisted sourly. "Well understood."

Malai stared up at Natharie, her wide brown eyes blinking for a moment. Then she leaned forward, wrapping her arms tight around Natharie's neck. Natharie hugged her back, as if she could keep her sister safe with the strength of her own arms.

"All will be right, little sister," she whispered. "The wheel turns for us, that is all."

But she did not feel serene or resigned as she spoke. Instead, she felt hard as flint and as sharply edged, and when she tilted up Malai's chin so her sister had to look into her eyes, she knew an anger so fierce, Natharie was surprised Malai could not feel its heat.

"Come, Sister." Natharie stood, holding herself with all the poise she could muster. "Let us go hear what is required of us."

Cool and graceful, Malai rose, much more a woman than the girl who ran laughing to the river, and followed Natharie to the audience chamber.

The audience hall was already full by the time they reached it. Father sat on the ancient golden throne, the three-tiered crown on his head and the ivory staff in his hand.

Mother, crowned in gold and pearls, sat at his right. Beneath the great symbol of her rank, her face was rigid and cold.

Look on her, she thought toward the Hastinapurans. *We do not fear our women in this land.*

On Mother's right-hand side, Natharie's full-blood brothers and sisters sat absolutely still, without prompting from their nurses and governors who stood behind them. All of them, even little Bailo, were arrayed in their best clothing and crowned according to their birth order. Kitum, the oldest boy and the heir, did his best to look regal, but his young face was pale. He had listened well to his teachers, and knew enough to fear the northern empire.

To the left of the dais knelt the viceroy and the servants of the throne in their golden robes and collars. The "aunties," father's four concubines, knelt below these. Their children were arrayed with them, as serious and as still as the full-blood royals. What was to come affected them all. No one would be left untouched. For once even sly, insinuating Radana looked concerned, and all the fear was almost worth it for that sight.

Natharie walked deliberately, gracefully between the throne and the kneeling Hastinapurans. She moved slowly, keeping each gesture separate and precise. She knelt before the dais and set the edge of first her right hand, then her left hand on the woven rush mat and pressed her head to them in obeisance to her father. Beside her, Malai did her best to move in time with her older sister.

Natharie counted five full heartbeats before she rose with Malai and walked slowly to assume her place at little Bailo's right hand. Natharie brushed Bailo's hand with her arm as she sat, a gesture they had used many times before, and felt him move his little finger in response. They could not hug or even look at each other in formal audience, but they could share this bit of warmth and silent reassurance.

We are all here. We are together in this.

She wished she could give such reassurance to Kitum.

As she knelt in her place on the carved platform, she was able to take stock of the Hastinapurans. Their leaders—the hard-eyed captain of the soldiers and the red-and-gold priests—knelt on the mats before Father and the throne. They all looked very proper and respectful, save one. The tallest of the priests let his gaze impatiently flicker here and there, taking in the audience hall with its golden images of the ancestors, the gods, and the Awakened One. His face grew more deeply sour with each thing he saw. His huge, hard hands plucked restlessly at the cloth of his robe where it lay across his thighs. What actions did those hands wish they could take?

The one woman who had accompanied the Hastinapurans was also there. She knelt at the back of the hall with the servants and the soldiers, her white clothing making her stand out among the vivid hues of silk and gold. Natharie felt an involuntary shiver run down her spine. She must be the sorceress who followed the prince. The rulers of Hastinapura had sorcerers accompany them wherever they went. Could this one weave some influence from where she sat?

No. If that could happen, Father would have denied her entrance. Natharie tried to remind herself that Father knew much more of Hastinapurans and their ways than she did, but the trust she needed was hard to find.

Suthep, father's wizened viceroy, thumped his ebony staff on the floor. At the same time, the great gong was struck, the deep, long sound reverberating throughout the hall.

"Kiet Somchai, Great King of Sindhu, will now hear the petitioners before him!"

The gong was struck again, and Natharie suppressed a smile. Petitioners. Very good. The deep frown on the big priest's face showed he keenly felt the insult.

The captain of the soldiers kept his face absolutely still and dignified as he made his bow from where he knelt.

"Great King, I am Prince Samudra *tya* Achin Ireshpad, First Prince and Son of the Pearl Throne. I bring you greetings from my brother Chandra *tya* Achin Harihamapad, Emperor of Hastinapura, Revered and Respected Father of the Pearl Throne and Beloved of the Seven Mothers."

Prince? It was all Natharie could do not to stare in shock. This man in plain and dusty armor, commanding a tiny troop of soldiers from horseback, was a prince? Father would not even send one of her half-brothers out with so little to mark and protect his rank.

Father nodded once in acknowledgment of the prince's statement. "You are welcome here, Prince Samudra. What has brought this honor to our house?"

The big priest flushed, clearly angered by this feigned ignorance. Natharie concentrated on remaining properly composed and calm. Malai shifted her weight, probably itchy. Natharie flicked her little finger. Malai caught the gesture and stilled.

"Great King," said Prince Samudra, seemingly unperturbed by having to state his errand aloud. "As well you know, when a new emperor ascends the Pearl Throne it is right and proper that all who receive the Throne's protection celebrate the continuation of peace and harmony by sending gifts and ambassadors." He spoke Sindishi without a trace of accent, which somehow eased Natharie's feelings toward him. She also noted that in his well-mannered speech, he said not one word about the horse, or the soldiers. This one was a diplomat as well as a prince.

Again, Father nodded. "And this we did. When Emperor Chandra took his father's place, four years ago."

The Hastinapuran prince's face tightened for a moment, and Natharie thought he might be suppressing a sigh. She found herself wondering how many times he had knelt like this, and made this same demand of other kings. Sindhu was one of twenty "protectorates," taken by the old emperor. Were all of them visited by the horse and the prince?

"Your gifts were received with great thanks," answered Samudra solemnly. "But as the great king knows, not all the proper ceremonies were able to be completed at that time."

The big priest's fingers were tapping now, showing how difficult it became for him to hold his impatience at bay. Natharie felt a cold knot form beneath her heart.

"And they are to be completed now?" Father asked.

The prince nodded once. "Even so."

Father considered this for a long, uncomfortable moment. The priest's frown deepened, although the prince remained calm.

At last, Father said, "I am delighted that the emperor is so secure in his place that he is now able to turn his mind from the affairs of state to the affairs of Heaven by which blessing each of us has our place on the wheel." Father kept his voice carefully bland. "We are happy to house and feed the pilgrims of the Pearl Throne as they cross Sindhu and, of course, they will be under the king's protection. I will speak to my generals about proper escort."

Natharie's fingers threatened to curl into fists. *He's going to make them say it. He's going to make them demand the tribute.*

"I am honored to receive the great king's assistance," answered Prince Samudra, inclining his head once more. "I fear that we may have to trespass on your hospitality for a little while longer. There are several matters which require discussion."

Now it was Father who frowned, in apparent confusion. "Can that be done? It is my understanding of the ceremony that you must follow the horse wherever and whenever the Mothers lead him."

That hit hard. The big priest was now the same scarlet color as his robes, and the prince, for a fleeting second, looked distinctly uncomfortable.

"Great King," said Prince Samudra quietly. "You and I both know what is happening. I ask your tolerance and forbearance."

"Yes, we do know what is happening," Father answered. "You are saying that our offerings and embassage of four years ago were inadequate."

The prince took the accusation without flinching, and met the king's eyes. "I would never say that, Great King. You know this."

Father leaned forward, looking down on the kneeling man. "I thought I did, Prince Samudra." He spoke softly, but his voice was pitched to carry through the hall. "But if the purpose of this so-called sacrifice is not to wheedle more tribute out of your protectorates, what is it for?"

Which was the end. The big priest shot to his feet. The golden scarf around his thick neck slithered to the floor with the violence of his motion. "Barbarian!" he shouted. "How *dare* you profane the holy mysteries! You worship a vain human who dared deny the Mothers! You sit on your gilded . . ."

"Divakesh!" The prince also stood swiftly. "Silence!"

It was too much for little Bailo. A whimper escaped him and he cringed backward into his nurse's arms. All Natharie's other siblings took the opportunity to huddle together. Natharie made herself sit still. She was the oldest. She must remain still, as still as Mother was, as still as Father on the throne. Even while the court gasped and muttered, they would be absolutely correct. Behind them and on either side, the guards had shifted their grip on their spears and their swords.

If the priest noticed any of these things, the only effect was to increase his rage. "I will not be silent!" His voice shook from fury. "You will tell this petty chief that his children belong to the Mothers as does any other thing They see fit to require of him! You will tell him . . ."

"Priest," said the prince, and this time his voice was low as the first rumble of the earthquake. "You will leave the hall at once. You will not reenter it unless I send for you and then you will only do so in proper respect for the great king."

They stood there, each daring the other with his own pride, authority, and history. Natharie risked a glance at her father, and she saw a tiny smile on his face. In that moment, she understood. Father had not been speaking to the prince at all, but always to the priest. He saw the weak link and he pressed against it until it broke.

The priest turned on his heels and marched toward the door. Before the tension could break, Radana startled them all afresh, by leaping from her place with the other concubines and scuttling forward to claim the golden scarf the priest had let fall.

"My lord?" She knelt in front of him as humble as any servant, holding the scarf up for him to take.

It was a wonderful move. It broke the terrible tension his outburst had brought. Natharie was sure she heard one of the serving women snicker.

The priest, who could not turn any more red, snatched the scarf away and left the hall. Radana bowed deeply to the king and queen and returned to her place with the other concubines, a smile of smug satisfaction on her face.

For all this, it was now the prince who was shamed and he who must act humble. Which he did, bowing deeply. This time, his forehead touched the mat.

"Great King, I am truly sorry for this outburst. Divakesh is diligent in his piety and it is my fault for not instructing him more carefully on the ways of the Awakened lands. It will not happen again, I promise you."

Father sat back, looking haughtily down his nose. "That is the man who will perform the sacrifice when it is time?"

"Yes, Great King." The prince sounded plainly puzzled.

"The horse then belongs to the Mothers and he will . . . send it to them at the appointed time?"

"Yes."

Now Father spoke with cold precision. "Given this, what did your man mean when he said my children belong to the Mothers?"

Murmurs flitted through the air. Natharie heard again the sound of shifting weight, the faint jingling of scaled armor as the soldiers readied themselves in her defense, in the defense of all. At the same time, fear bit hard into her. The priest did not mean they were to be killed. He could not. Did the Mothers drink human blood? Ima, Bailo's nurse, held him close, murmuring comfort. Natharie was ashamed of herself for thinking his nurse should sit him up straight. They could not afford to show less than perfect dignity now.

Prince Samudra took in a long breath and let it out slowly. "Great King, the priest Divakesh spoke hastily and without thought. I beg you not give any consideration to his words."

But Father would not be placated. "He spoke of my children, Prince Samudra, of my son and heir. I must consider his words, and I must have them explained."

Prince Samudra hesitated. His eyes flickered toward the princes and princesses where they knelt. For a single heartbeat, his gaze met Natharie's once more, and to her surprise, she saw pain there, behind the anger and the carefully crafted mask of patience.

Then it was gone and the prince's attention was fully on the king again. "It is our hope, Great King, that you will agree that some members of your family will come with us to reside in the Palace of the Pearl Throne to strengthen the ties that bind our lands together."

Hostages.

"Some members?" said the king slowly. "Your man spoke of all my children, the whole of the royal line of Sindhu."

For the first time, Prince Samudra's patience seemed to slip and his voice took on a brittle edge. "Again, I beg Your Majesty to overlook those intemperate words. We have much to learn from each other, your people and mine. It is my sincere hope that knowledge and friendship can be increased by this exchange."

"Exchange? What will the Pearl Throne leave here when I have sent my children to the Mothers?"

"You know full well, Great King," said the prince quietly.

He meant that sovereignty would be left. Father would be allowed to hold the throne and the name of king, if he gave up what was demanded. If he gave up Malai to the quiet prince, the white sorceress, and the hard-handed priest.

Natharie knew at that moment what she must do. The realization made her weak as water, but she understood it was the right thing, the only thing she could do to save her brothers and sisters, to keep Kitum, Malai, and little, frightened Bailo and all the others free. There was a treaty, there were promises, but she was more free than her married sisters and she could not, she would not let this burden fall to Malai.

She lifted herself up, and on her knees she approached the throne. The room watched her move in in stunned silence. She felt the weight of their varied gazes like cold stones against her back as she made her obeisance and held it.

"Great King, Great Father, I offer myself to this office."

Keep your places, my brothers and sisters. Awakened One, let them see and let them hold their tongues. Let me be the only one.

Father held his peace, one heartbeat, two, three, four. "My daughter makes a tremendous offer," he said quietly, and Natharie heard the words rasp and catch in his throat. "I do not believe any other princess of her blood has ever done such a thing before. What do you say to it, Prince Samudra?"

The sound of shifting cloth told Natharie the prince bowed. "In the name of the Mothers and the Pearl Throne, I do accept this offer."

And it was done. Natharie lifted her head and met her parents' eyes. Father looked sad, but Mother's eyes were wild. She looked as if she would jump to her feet and shout denial just as the priest had, but she did not move. She could not move. Natharie had cast the dice, and only the Awakened One now could see how they would land.

Chapter Two

The audience did not end with Natharie's announcement, nor for a long time afterward. There remained a great deal of talk: about amounts of additional goods, about times for delivery, about how and where these things would be done. Natharie could not make herself hear much of it. She did manage to understand that there were two weeks left in the horse's year of wandering. After that, the horse and its masters would go to Chirag where a fleet of imperial barges waited at the mouth of the sacred river. The company would then travel back to Hastinapura on those boats, stopping on the way to gather their promised tribute.

That meant she had about three weeks. In three weeks, she was going to Hastinapura, and she would never return.

She made herself look at Malai and Bailo. How small and solemn they looked. Then she met her mother's eyes, and even across the distance between them, she saw the matchless anger there. She cringed inwardly, but then she realized that anger was not for her. It was for the Hastinapurans arrayed before her.

What will you do, Mother? wondered Natharie. *What could you do? The only other option is war and death. You know that even better than I do.*

At last the final bows were made, and servants were assigned to show the Hastinapurans to their chambers for the night. Prince Samudra politely excused himself so that he might see to his horse and his priest. Natharie watched all this distantly. She heard her brothers and sisters murmuring her name, but she did not turn toward them. She just drifted away to her own room, aware that someone walked beside her, but not sure who it was. She knelt on the scarlet pillow before the open balcony. A soft voice dismissed the servants. The green of the garden spread before her, deep and rich on the other side of the gossamer curtains. The sun was setting and the copper sky was lit in colors of burning copper and molten gold. It was beautiful and terrifying in its majesty.

That morning she had woken believing she was about to become a woman, and next a queen. What was she to become now?

A figure knelt on the bare wood beside her and laid a long spear onto the floor. They sat together in silence, just breathing, Princess Natharie and the guardswoman Anun.

Natharie's extended childhood had caused something of a dilemma as far as correct behavior was concerned. No one quite knew what to do with her. Her studies had continued, and the temple libraries were opened to her. Her mother and the rest of the palace were inclined to allow her more freedom than a woman her age would have had, as compensation for the lack of adult standing, husband, and a place of her own. Yet they were also inclined to want her under close supervision, lest her lack of husband and place lead her to dangerous adventures that would leave them all shamed. As a result of these twin needs, she had spent much time with the women who guarded the females of the court. She had heard their stories, and learned something of their arts. Anun had always seemed to think it both humorous and wicked that a princess might be allowed to learn to fight with the long stick or to wrestle, and so took to teaching Natharie as a kind of a sly game. She was Natharie's favorite tutor and became closer to her than any of the women who called themselves her aunties.

"Anun," said Natharie quietly, without taking her eyes from the burning sky. "What have I done?"

The guardswoman blew out her cheeks. "You volunteered for a hard posting, little princess," she said. "You were brave. You should be proud of yourself."

Despite the evening's oppressive heat, Natharie shivered. "I don't feel proud."

"No one ever does when they take on such a duty, but I am proud of you."

It was a plain statement of fact, and yet it cleared away some of the fog that had settled on Natharie's mind. She could think and remember a little more clearly; what she remembered was the fury burning in her mother's eyes. "What do you think Mother feels?"

Anun's hand twitched where it rested on her thigh. "I think she will tell you herself when she is calm again."

Natharie closed her eyes and swallowed hard. "I'm sorry," she murmured, as if it were Mother beside her now.

"So am I, little princess. So am I."

The sound of cloth slipping across wood whispered through the room. Anun turned before Natharie did. A servant girl knelt in the doorway.

"Great Princess, I am sent to say that the Prince Samudra of Hastinapura has obtained permission from the great king your father to request an audience with you."

It took Natharie a moment to understand this. Prince Samudra had asked Father to speak with her? What could he have to say?

Then she remembered she was a grown woman and more obliged than before to uphold dignity and courtesy in this house.

"You will tell the great prince Samudra that I will receive him, and you'll see that tea is sent to us." She glanced at Anun. "You'll stay with me?"

Anun bowed over her hands, and then picked up her spear and stationed herself by the door.

The waiting women returned immediately. They bustled about, rolling away the sleeping mat, letting down the curtains over the dressing alcoves, and laying out tapestries over the sitting platforms, turning the room into one suitable for receiving a royal guest. They were done a heartbeat before the tread of sandals was heard in the hall and Prince Samudra was announced.

As he was presenting himself to her, it was for him to bow first, which he did, kneeling and inclining his head over folded hands. Behind him, his sorceress entered and knelt, pressing her forehead to the floor. Natharie pulled back in surprise and discomfort before she remembered herself and returned the bow. The woman straightened, but remained kneeling discreetly by the door. She dressed plainly, in white blouse and skirt and a translucent white veil to cover her hair, which had been divided into dozens of tiny braids and then pulled into an elaborate knot behind her ears and bound with red cords.

Prince Samudra also straightened. He had changed from his dusty armor into loose silks of ivory and purple. His hair was black and thick and would have hung down to his shoulders if it were not tied in a neat queue. His face was lean and fine to the point of delicacy and his deep keen eyes were set wide apart on either side of an aquiline nose. If they both stood, Natharie was certain she would be the taller. His hands, however, were hardened from, she suspected, long hours holding reins and sword, and he moved with the assurance of an experienced soldier.

"Your presence honors me," murmured Natharie politely. She tried to focus her attention on the man, but her gaze kept drifting to the sorceress. She had only ever seen one other of her kind, the nun Sathi. Sathi was old before Natharie was young, her head was shaven, and she wore only the loose robes of her order, which rendered her appearance almost sexless.

"It is you who do me honor," Prince Samudra answered. "And Hastinapura. I came to thank you for your great generosity."

Natharie meant to say "you are welcome," but the words would not come to her. She only met the prince's eyes. His pain was hidden behind walls of propriety and dignity, but it was there, and anger too. It came to her that in this time, sacrifice was being made of more lives than she had guessed.

Behind him, the sorceress sat still, her eyes humbly lowered, looking like any other courtier during an audience. Why was she there at all? What was her function? The myriad possible answers to that question sent a shiver up Natharie's spine. Hastinapuran sorcerers were not bound by holy vows as were the Awakened.

"If Hamsa makes you uncomfortable, I can have her wait elsewhere."

The words jerked Natharie's attention fully back to Prince Samudra.

"Forgive me. I am only a bit distracted." Fortunately, her waiting women's timing was as good as ever, and the lacquered tea tray was set down at that moment. Natharie was able to busy herself with the ritual of pouring the steaming drink, adding the jasmine petals, and making sure the dish of sweetmeats was in easy reach of her guest.

Should she offer something to the sorceress? The woman waited like a servant. What was her rank? Her place?

Why is she here?

Prince Samudra accepted his cup of tea, bowed over it, and sipped with an approving slurp. Natharie just held her cup in her hand, letting it warm her fingers, and struggled to hold the polite mask in place.

"I know this change will be difficult for you." Prince Samudra began again. "It is my hope you will permit me to extend my friendship as well as my protection to you. The Teacher tells that right conduct is, first of all, kind, and I hope you will find kindness in us."

That startled Natharie so that her tea sloshed in its cup. "You know Anidita's teachings?"

"Some. It was my honor to speak at length with the father abbot of Lohit's monastery."

"You have been to Lohit?" *And met the father abbot? What did your sorceress back there think of that?*

"Quite recently, to prevent a war. I met the young king, Pairoj, there. He is a man of great honor and courage."

Do you know what was promised between me and him, Prince Samudra? she wondered, but in a moment, she had her answer. "Your sacrifice humbles me," he said. "What you have done will be understood and respected by the Throne."

Natharie swallowed, but the question that surfaced in her would not be banished. "And by your priest, Divakesh."

Prince Samudra's mouth twitched. He set his moss-green cup down carefully, as if he was afraid his rough soldier's hand would shatter it. "It is a hard thing not to be able to choose one's companions for a long journey. I ask you to excuse Divakesh's fervor in serving the Mothers. It leads him to indiscretion."

Then why send him on a mission of discretion? There were two immediate answers. His indiscretion had thrown him out of favor in the Palace of the Pearl Throne, or they wished to send this single-minded devotee into a land of unbelievers to show that more than one thing would change now that the new emperor was in place.

Natharie looked at Samudra for a long moment, seeing his strangely delicate face and form. This was a handsome man, and a strong one. Had he been anyone else, had this been any other time, she would have been glad to sit with him, she realized with a shock. Sit with him, talk with him, and perhaps even flirt a little, had not Divakesh and a river of blood stood between them.

"What do the Mothers say of the teachings of the Awakened One?" She bit her tongue, but it was too late. The question was out.

Samudra smiled a little, but it was an expression of relief rather than of true amusement. "The Mothers, like the Great Teacher, say many things. One of the things they say is that the path of devotion has many branches, but they all lead alike to Heaven when the heart is true."

It was far from the answer Natharie expected. In her confusion she looked again at the sorceress. The woman sat so still and calm, but now with her eyebrows raised, breaking the illusion that she did not hear the conversation taking place so nearby. "And what does your sorceress say of the teachings?"

The prince sighed. "If Hamsa could fulfill her duties from the comfortable confines of the monastery, I think she would be very glad." Now his small smile was sad. "But I am sure you are tired. We will not stay to trouble you further. I will only say thank you once more." He bowed again and then rose from his place.

Natharie bowed and watched him as he took his leave. His sorceress—what had he called her? Hamsa?—made her obeisance silently and followed him. Natharie stared after them, her head empty of thought, and her only feeling that of confusion. She felt this must be a trap, but she could not tell what kind. No answer came, no reassurance. She could not even find any words to exchange with Anun standing at her guard's post.

In the end there was nothing to do but accept the ministrations of her women readying her for bed. She curled up on her sleeping mat, eyes open and unsleeping. Mother would surely come to her soon. Mother would know what to say, and what to do. She could be a child again for this one night, and Mother would tell her what all this meant.

*B*ut Mother did not come that night. The Hastinapurans left with the dawn and with very little ceremony. During the days that followed Natharie wept, and then laughed with her sisters. She listened to lectures and legends from her brothers about the nature of the Palace of the Pearl Throne, and the women's quarters within it. Kitum gave an especially long, solemn history, which Natharie finally ended by scolding him for presuming to teach his now fully-adult older sister. The shouting and shoving that followed left them all breathless, teary, and giggling. Father walked with her in the gardens in the evening. Anun insisted she continue long-stick practice, saying Natharie did not know who she was going to need to fight off in the Hastinapuran court. Radana and the other aunties fussed and petted her, shedding many delicate tears until she shouted at all of them and stalked away, only to return later with a correct but unfelt apology.

She spent much time in the temple, kneeling at the feet of the Awakened One, telling her beads and saying the *surras* over and over to keep down the fear that nibbled constantly at the back of her mind.

And still Mother did not come to her. Natharie strove for patience and understanding, but the anger at this absence became harder and harder to push away. It pressed close against her, making it difficult to breathe and to think as the time remaining for her to live at her home spooled up before her.

Despite the fact that she avoided her daughter, Queen Sitara was not idle during those weeks, and Natharie knew it. Even the first morning, she had begun to work for delay. Mother had tried to insist that for Natharie to travel during the dust would be to expose her many times to the breath of illness, which might at the least be lethal, and at worst disfiguring.

Mother's voice practically dripped poison as she spoke those words. Not one of the red-robed priests seemed to hear it. Prince Samudra, though, heard it plainly, and his face had hardened for all his words remained respectful.

"Great Queen, it is my charge to see that your daughter arrives safely at my home, and on my honor, it will be done."

My home. He'd placed the emphasis on those words. Natharie thought he meant to remove some of the fear the thought of the place brought down. He failed, though. She could not accept the Palace of the Pearl Throne as a place where people laughed and lived their daily lives and grew old together. This was the place she would be hostage and property and guarantor of peace for her land, her people. This was the place where strangers would put her to use, or would shut her up in a casket like a jewel, as they chose.

The moment the Hastinapurans had left, Mother had given full vent to her feelings. Though Natharie belived nothing could be done, Queen Sitara clearly did not agree. She would not dishonor her daughter's sacrifice, but neither would she accept the Hastinapurans' right to take her away. Natharie learned from whispers overheard between the palace lords and secretaries that the queen dispensed many bribes, promises, and threats, but none came to anything. There was simply no time. There was barely enough time to gather and dispatch a delegation to Natharie's intended husband in Lohit informing him that the marriage could not be completed. Natharie included a politely worded letter of regret written in her best hand, even though it took hours to get that hand to stop shaking, and returned the gold disk on which his image had been hammered. She wondered what he would think of her for this, and whether she would ever find out. She thought on the few words Prince Samudra had spoken of him. She wondered what they had talked about, how they had looked and acted side by side, and what it would have been like to be a queen in her own court, receiving the prince from her place at her husband's right hand.

Fortunately, she would not have much time to brood over it. The messenger from the sacrificial procession arrived twenty-two days after the Hastinapurans had departed, saying his masters were only a day behind.

That final night was hot, thick, and starless. Natharie could not sleep. She tried to be proud. She tried to meditate and to tell her beads, but fear kept returning. In an instant she would forget what her hands were doing and only be able to kneel and shake, feeling that the priests with their long knives were directly behind her, grinning the possessive grins she had seen on their faces in the audience chamber.

She alternately walked onto her terrace to look for the stars and lay in her bed, watching the darkness and listening to the familiar night sounds all around, trying to memorize each one to carry in her heart to her new place. Eventually, she could do nothing but sink to her knees on the terrace then, staring at the distant, golden blur that was the coming dawn.

A soft step made Natharie spin on her knees to see Mother gently enter her room. Natharie gaped, and the tears she had fought back so hard sprang into her eyes.

Mother knelt before her. She took up Natharie's hands and pressed them between her own. She did not speak for a long time. They just sat together like that, each drawing what cold comfort they could from the other.

When she could no longer bear the silence, she said, "I'm sorry, Mother." Perhaps it was as she had feared in her heart, that Mother's anger was at her, not for her. She had broken promises, jeopardized their standing with their allies in Lo-hit, made a fool of the royal house before the Hastinapurans.

"Do not be," Mother answered softly. Her voice was hoarse, and as thick as the darkness that waited outside. "You have done a brave thing, and a great thing for our land. It was my weakness that kept me away. Weakness and fear, for now . . ." She stopped, and Natharie felt herself choke. "Now I must ask you to do an even greater thing."

Mother straightened, her voice softened and strengthened all at once. "This thing came upon us because we did not know enough about Hastinapura, about the ways and work-ings of the new emperor. We have no friend in the Palace of the Pearl Throne who can warn us of how they mean to work upon the destiny of our land." Natharie realized she was breathing hard. "It has fallen to you to become that friend now. You are now the eyes and ears of Sindhu among our . . . our rulers. Can you do this?"

Natharie swallowed. For the first time since sunset, her mind felt clear. The idea that she might be able to do something for herself, for her family, lent Natharie a strength that nothing else could have.

"Yes, Mother. I will."

Mother pressed Natharie's hands again and kissed her brow. "Then rest now, my child. I will stay."

With that, Natharie was able to lie down and close her eyes. Her mother began to sing softly, a lullaby Natharie had not heard since she was a child, but that she remembered deep in her heart. With her mother's hand softly stroking her shoulder, Natharie drifted into sleep.

*T*he departure morning was as hot and hazy as the night had been. The sacred river lay sluggish and brown at the foot of the dock where Natharie stood. The Hastinapuran barges were little more than shadows, but they could be easily heard: a great drumbeat pounded and the oars clacked and creaked in their locks in perfect time as the shadow drew closer, and closer yet.

Natharie had dressed carefully in her finest silks and gold, her crown on her head. Her parents and siblings all stood behind her, all the shining symbols of royalty glimmering in the morning haze. Natharie repeatedly touched her beads where they hung from her gold belt, trying to find a way to still her chaotic thoughts as the barge approached. Her mind could not focus on what was to come, let alone relax into any true meditation. Instead, her thoughts kept straying back to the things her mother had said to her. She would not be a passive prize or treasure piece. She still had work and duty to perform. She was not made completely unmade.

Natharie and her family all held themselves straight, calm, and correct. The great drum stilled as the boat glided to the dock. The bargemen leapt onto the boards, shouting at their fellows. Ropes were thrown, the boat made fast. Natharie shook. She felt small and weak and despite the presence of her family, terribly, terribly alone.

When the barges were secured, three figures emerged from the boats. They were the Prince Samudra and his sorceress, and looming over them both, the great priest Divakesh.

Natharie could not wait any longer. There had been so much time in the recent days to imagine this man coming for her that she could no longer keep still. He would not see her cower or hang back from the path she herself had chosen. Natharie walked forward. She met the prince's eyes, and she bowed, not low, but respectfully: a greeting for equals.

In return, Prince Samudra bowed in the fashion of Hastinapura, placing his hands over his face as he did so. The salute of trust they called it.

When he straightened, he said to her parents, "Great King, Great Queen, your gift honors the Pearl Throne beyond measure. Your daughter comes now to my house, and she will be treated as a daughter should. My honor rests on this."

"Thank you, Prince Samudra," replied Father. Those were the first words she had heard him speak the whole morning. Natharie risked turning toward him, and she saw how his eyes shone diamond-bright. Behind him, tears ran freely down Anun's stony face. Mother alone stood impassive, but Natharie saw how she pressed the palms of her correctly folded hands together until her arms trembled.

Answering tears pricked behind her eyes. *Take me out of here,* she wished desperately. *Let me leave before we shame ourselves.*

She did not say farewell, not even to Malai or Bailo. She could not bear it. She had left presents and letters for all her siblings with her waiting women. Anun had her own farewell message waiting. That would have to suffice. If she said even one word now, she would break in two.

It seemed to her that Samudra understood. "Please escort Princess Natharie to her barge," he said to Hamsa.

Hamsa bowed, first to him and then to Natharie. Natharie moved slowly, making each step carefully. She would not stumble. She would not falter. She would be as poised as a temple statue even as she passed beneath the gaze of the priest Divakesh.

The deck of the barge rocked as she stepped onto it. Well used to boats, she absorbed the motion and was able to walk a straight line down its length to the curtained house that would shelter her during the trip. The sorceress held open the gauzy green fabric. Natharie stepped in, and knelt on the nest of cushions that waited there.

The sorceress let the curtain fall, and made no attempt to follow, for which Natharie was grateful. It was all she could do to sit and breathe. After a time, the bargemen began to shout and she heard the rush and thump of ropes. The drum began to beat again, and the oars creaked and strained. The sacred river's water cradled the boat, and the rhythm of the oars carried it away.

She took one, long, shuddering breath, and then another. In that moment, the curtain was jerked aside and the watery light blocked by Divakesh's silhouette.

Natharie cringed. She could not stop herself. For the first time she saw his face close to hers. He was hawk-nosed and iron-eyed with thin lips that stretched tight over his teeth as he frowned at her. She was barely able to note that Hamsa stood behind him. But the sorceress did not move and Natharie shrank back further. There was nowhere to run and nothing she could do.

He lunged, and Natharie shrieked, and Hamsa held up one useless hand. Divakesh jerked the string of beads from Natharie's belt with one painful pull.

"No impure thing is allowed beneath the shadow of the Pearl Throne." His voice was hoarse with his triumph as he clenched the beads in his great fist.

"Then why are you taking me there?" Natharie inquired.

For a moment she thought he was going to strike her. She steeled herself for the blow. Behind him, Hamsa raised her staff, her face and knuckles white.

"It does not matter what you say," Divakesh told Natharie with awful certainty. "You belong to the Mothers now. It is the Mothers who will decide your fate, and it is I who wield the Mother's sword."

Divakesh stepped back, letting the curtain fall between them. The gauze, however, was not opaque enough to prevent Natharie from seeing him throw her beads—the beads her mother had given her, which had not left her side a single day for nine years—into the sacred river. She heard the splash, even over the noise of the drums and the oars, and she saw how the sorceress just stood there as the priest resumed his seat beneath the umbrellas.

Only when she was sure his back was to her did Natharie permit herself, silently, to begin to cry.

After a long time, her tears spent themselves, and the rocking of the sacred waters lulled her to sleep.

*N*atharie dreamed.

She walked the rooms of her home, but they were empty. Not even the furnishings or the mats remained. She could not remember where her parents, or her brothers and sisters, had gone, or why she was not with them. She came to the audience hall, and it too was empty. Throne, statues, teakwood sitting platforms, all were gone. In the middle of the broad expanse of its polished floor stood a small, old man in a robe the color of the dust-filled sky. He looked up at her with eyes as dark as midnight.

"Please," she said, her voice trembling. "Where are my parents? Where is my family?"

"How can you be alone?" he asked. "It is only the closed and empty heart that is alone."

"They took my beads. They threw them in the river, and she swallowed them."

The old man spread his hands, and at first Natharie thought she saw between them a string of beautiful beads, carved of precious woods and jasper, but then the old man smiled and they dissolved, leaving not even a glimmer behind. "They took nothing at all."

She awoke in the afternoon sunlight that filtered through the gauze curtains and the sound of the rowers. She could clearly see Divakesh's black silhouette outside, but for a long moment, there was no fear, only stillness.

*A*s the daylight dimmed toward twilight, the barge was moored to an unfamiliar bank. Thick forest filled the rolling hills on either side. The voices of the animals, great and small, rang on the sultry wind. The mosquitoes, awakened early by the dry wind, hummed joyfully at the prospect of food. The great mountain that was the Pillar of Heaven glowed white and gold in the light of the setting sun that rose above the darkened treetops. The sight of it through the gap in the curtains gave Natharie an anchor for her yearning heart.

A round-faced and silent servant came and brought her a meal on a lacquered tray: rice, vegetables cooked to various colored pastes, overripe fruit, and some desiccated substance that it took Natharie a moment to realize was meat. She picked up that dish, thrust her hand through the curtains, and upended the bowl over the river. Anidita taught against the eating of flesh, and she did not feel the need to be polite, or subtle.

As she picked at the remaining food, someone rapped on the side of the housing. The curtains parted again, this time to admit Hamsa.

She made a polite obeisance. "Great Princess, I will not bother asking if you are comfortable," said the sorceress, in excellent Sindishi. "I know you are not. But my master Prince Samudra sent me to you to see if there is anything that can be done to ease the burden of your heart at this time."

A dozen replies flashed through Natharie's mind, but she remembered pride over all. "Where is your master?"

"High Priest Divakesh determined that it was necessary for Prince Samudra to travel separately."

"But not you?"

Her smile was weak. "I am a person of much lesser importance."

"What does the high priest fear I will do? Attack? Leap overboard and swim for the shore?" The thought had occurred to her. They were not yet too far from the land she knew. She might be able to walk home, or hail a passing boatman.

Hamsa shook her head. "No."

"Then what?"

The sorceress hesitated and looked down at her hands. They were callused hands, much like her master's, with splayed fingers and patches of discoloration. One nail had been torn away and regrown battered and grey. They were a working woman's hands. "Great Princess, of your courtesy, do not make me answer that question. It will do my errand no honor."

Natharie folded her own hands, which were too big to ever be called delicate, but which were at least smooth as a noblewoman's should be, even after her play with the guards. Her waiting women had seen to that. "What is your errand?"

Some of Hamsa's certainty returned to her. "To see that you are as comfortable as our rough conditions permit, and to offer you what companionship I can."

This was clearly and plainly spoken, and it would have been easy to believe it was meant in genuine kindness, either on the prince's part, or on the part of Hamsa herself, but Natharie's suspicions would not let go. "Tell me, Hamsa . . . I do not know how you should be called," she added belatedly.

"My title is *Agnidh*." She was wary now, clearly understanding Natharie was in no mood to make this conversation easy.

Agnidh. It meant fire, or the one who tended the fire. "Tell me, *Agnidh,* what would you have done if your Divakesh decided to strike me?"

It was unfair, and Natharie knew it, but if the sorceress had come to work upon her, Natharie could not give an inch.

Hamsa's reply was quiet but steady. "What I could," she said.

Natharie's eyes narrowed. Here might be a chance to find out about the one who had openly shown himself her enemy. "What does he hate? Is it myself, or is it the Awakened One?"

Hamsa looked toward the shore. In the firelight, Divakesh was nothing more than a broad-backed shadow. When she spoke again, it was very quietly. "It is not with the Mothers as it is with the Awakened One. Anidita teaches of moderation. The true and most powerful worship of the Mothers demands extremes. Divakesh is their devoted child. I have seen him dance two days and two nights until his feet bled, and he never once faltered. I have seen him work the sword until he could no longer lift his arms and his body fell to the ground. He lay there only until he could stagger to his feet and take up the sword again."

Natharie remembered his face as he snatched her beads from her, his wild eyes and his utter conviction. She could easily believe all the things that Hamsa said.

"What does he mean to do to us?"

At this Hamsa only shook her head. "I do not know for certain."

You are a bad liar, sorceress. But Natharie pinched her lips together and did not speak the thought. Hamsa looked both sad and troubled as she spoke, and Natharie felt her heart leaning toward the other woman in sympathy. That sympathy frightened her. This was a Hastinapuran sorceress. It was common knowledge their kind took no vows to control their powers. She might do anything, work any magic great or small. She might be working on Natharie this moment, and Natharie would not know.

I must stay apart. I must keep my mind clear and calm.

At this moment, however, the sorceress seemed only to be casting about for some neutral topic of conversation. Her nervous gaze fell on the overcooked, overripe food set out for Natharie's solitary meal. "My apologies for the inadequacy of our preparations," she said. "We are trying to find better food."

Anger dissolved Natharie's resolution in a single heartbeat. "Why should you care about me?" she snapped. "I am only another slave, another prize. What power do you weave over me?"

This time, however, Hamsa appeared unruffled. "The power of empathy. I too had to leave my home to serve the Pearl Throne, and I did not want to."

That startled Natharie. The sorceress's smile was small, almost shy. "Bound sorcerers are chosen by the sorcerers and astrologers of the royal family. The augurs named me while Prince Samudra was still in his mother's womb. At the time, I lived in the city of Koragi and had never left it. All my learning had been from an old woman who lived two streets from me. I was twelve. When they came for me, I screamed and tried to run away. My father had to beat me to make me go with them. My mother wept a river and my little brothers and sisters howled. I thought I would never see them again."

She wants me to ask, "And did you?" She will say she sees them every year, and writes to them often. Then she will say the service I go to is honorable and beautiful and filled with delights.

"You belong to the Seven Mothers," she said. "You belong to Hastinapura. It is different."

"Yes," Hamsa agreed. "It is. But you are not alone, even now." Hamsa bowed, and stood and left Natharie there with with one thought ringing in her head.

It is only the closed and empty heart that is alone.

But behind that thought poured a flood of questions: *Did she send that dream? Could she have done that? She is watching me. She wants to understand me. Why should she care? Is it for her magic?* The serene image of the Anidita floated before her mind's eye, accompanied by a half-dozen hymns, all with the ancient refrain. *All ignorance is as sleep. It is knowledge that creates the wakeful mind, and the wakeful mind that gives birth to correct action.*

She was supposed to be eyes and ears for her family now. If Hamsa was watching her, she would also be watching Hamsa, and any knowledge she obtained in conversation, she could find a way to use, somehow. Natharie remembered how the woman had stood silent and ineffective behind Divakesh, and she wondered at that. She needed to understand who these people were and how the power between them stood. She had lived her whole life among the schemes and plans of Sindhu's royal court. She was ignorant, but she was not naive. She could learn and she would learn, and quickly.

Anything, any game, was better than sinking into the shadows of her own thoughts.

Chapter Three

When Natharie left Sindhu the sun set in Queen Sitara's heart. She wept the day away alone in her room. At night, she lay still on her bed. Her husband sent his body servant to her, asking that she come to him, and she refused. She tried to remind herself that Kiet was Natharie's father, that he too had lost a daughter, and now he needed the comfort of his wife and queen.

And she still could not move.

In the middle of the night, she woke to the sound of bare feet pattering against the floor, and a small, warm, familiar shape wiggled into bed next to her.

"Mama, I miss Natharie," whispered little Bailo, her youngest son.

All she could do was wrap her arms around him and hold him close. She stared into the darkness, looking for someone who was no longer there.

When at last she felt sleep overtake her child, Sitara rose. Cradling him close, she gave him back to his nurse with a kiss, and then, without apology, she roused her sleep-tousled maids so that they might dress her, and sent her chief woman, Rintu, to ask her husband if he would meet with her privately. She knew, with an instinct born of long years of life and love, that he too lay awake in his room. Silent, Anun watched all this, and the queen saw approval in the guardswoman's sharp eyes.

While she waited for her answer, Sitara went out onto her terrace. Night came late to Sindhu in the summer months, and when it did come, it laid itself down thick, heavy and sultry, stifling breath and movement and setting the whole land longing for the great rains that would wash the season away. Sitara knelt on the bare wood and stared into darkness. Mosquitoes whined about her ears, heedless of the dragonflies that darted here and there, or the great bats that flapped their leathery wings overhead. The tent of fine gauze that would have given her shelter waited empty a few feet away, its platform and pillows unused.

She heard a most familiar step on the floor behind her, but she did not turn.

"Your suffering will not bring her ease, Sitara."

Kiet: her husband, a good king, a wise man, a kind father, the man whose embrace could quicken her heart and blood like nothing else in life. He moved closer. She felt him behind her, heard his breathing, smelled his scent. He laid his broad hands on her shoulders. The night turned their skin damp and despite the broad garden that surrounded the palace, they both breathed dust. Of its own volition, her hand covered one of his.

"I want to go to the forest, Kiet," she said. "I want to go to the sorcerers."

"Sitara, that is not wise. You mourn. I mourn as well. The sorcerers will not change that."

Sitara turned without standing. She looked up at her husband. "They can offer her some safety, some blessing."

Kiet sighed. "The Hastinapurans are not barbarians. She will not be ill-treated."

In the face of her husband's reasoned statement, Sitara found only anger. "She is a slave. Our child is made a slave to the Hastinapuran emperor's whim! Had I the strength, I would have killed her before it came to this."

Slowly, Kiet knelt before her, and in the dust-choked moonlight, Sitara saw the fullness of the sorrow he held back by the strength of his own silence. She saw heartbreak and grief that matched her own. "It is as it must be," he whispered.

These were the right words, the wise words, but no place in her could hear them. "Why?"

Kiet stood, turning away. He walked to the edge of the terrace, resting his fist on the carved railing. He spoke to the prey and the predators that flew together beneath the moon. "Because, Sitara, they are great, and we are small."

Why could she not go to him? This was her husband and her king. Why could she not put her arms around him, hold him and be held, for comfort, for strength, for life in the midst of loss. She felt as if she were yards away from her own body. She could not reach her hands to make them stretch out to her husband, nor her heart to will it to proper feeling for another's grief.

"We are full as ancient as they," she heard herself say. "Our spirits are as strong as theirs."

"And our army is ten times smaller!" Kiet swung around, suddenly swollen with his rage and his grief, his great hands now both made into fists.

Stop. Stop. Sitara pleaded with herself. *Remember silence. Remember wisdom.*

Instead, she met her husband's eyes. "Then perhaps we must find a greater army."

"Oh, Sitara," Kiet breathed slowly. "Be careful what you say."

He was right. She could offer no retort to that admonishment, not even as far away as she was. They must be careful. They must be as careful as the mongoose stealing up upon the cobra's den.

"We have powers we have not yet begun to draw on," she whispered. "They wait in the forest for your word."

Kiet's eyes searched hers, flickering back and forth, quickly, searching to see how serious she truly was, trying to see past the anger and the grief, down to the core of her. Sitara stepped back and drew herself up, meeting and matching his gaze, returning his silence with her own. *Look, then, husband. Understand. We must call on our own strengths, and on those of the enemy of our enemy.*

She bowed to her husband. "I will go to the sorcerers," she said. "I will go to their monastery and offer prayers for our daughter's safety."

Kiet nodded, and turned away. Sitara watched her husband's broad back for a long moment, straining to find some word, some gesture that would let him know she loved him still. But none came, and in the end she could only walk back into her chamber. She stood in the middle of her room, among all the things that were as familiar to her as her own name, and found she could not think where she was or what she had meant to do.

"Sitara."

Now she did turn toward Kiet. Now she did open her arms and he came rushing to her, wrapping her in his embrace.

Frantic with need, anger, loss, and fear, they kissed each other hard, again and again, and held on tightly as they lay down together, forgetting everything else but their need.

When they were both spent, they lay together, arms and legs and breath entwined. Kiet whispered to her, "Do as you must, my queen. Do what I cannot."

It was then she understood that she had not been alone in her thoughts. In his own room, Kiet's mind had walked the same paths as hers, but he had not known how to ask her to take part in this deeply dangerous thing. He had meant to let her pull into her grief and be protected. Was he relieved now? Disappointed? She could not find words now. The only reply she could find was to gather him close and lay her head against his shoulder. It was in this way Sitara finally found sleep.

*T*he river Liyoni was the only road to the sorcerers' monastery. Queen Sitara traveled in the royal barge beneath the carved and gilded canopy that shaded her from the sun. Twenty oarsmen sped the boat along. By night they camped on the shore, sleeping underneath tents of fine linen to keep the flies away. By day, they moved against the current to the rhythm of the oars.

Queen Sitara spoke little, and did not welcome conversation. Her ladies, who had been beside her since her wedding day, knew better than to try to coax her from her silence. She needed this time to think her thoughts. When she set foot on the shore, she would begin to act. There would be no more time for thinking once events were set in motion. She must do her planning now. She must be sure.

At twilight, she prayed. At dawn, she prayed. She counted her beads and her own doubts to the clack of the blocks beating time, and the cries of the master and the oarsmen. When the forest rose dark and impenetrable around the sacred river, she put both away. She was not going to turn back. Her doubts would serve her no longer, nor would they serve Natharie where she had gone.

Nor would dwelling on the scene that played out on the docks as Sitara left for the monastery, but her troubled thoughts returned time and again to it.

It had happened just as she lifted up one foot to step over the barge rail. An unexpected voice wailed from behind.

"Great Queen!"

Sitara turned, her heart in her mouth. Radana, chief among her husband's concubines, red-faced and in disarray, ran down the dock.

"What is it?" *Kiet? The children? Are they already paying for what I am about to do?*

Radana dropped down to her knees and took Sitara's hand. Tears shone in her eyes and Sitara suddenly wanted to shake her hard to get her news out of her.

"Please," Radana said in a small, breathless voice. "Great Queen, let me go with you."

The request was so at odds with all her sudden fears that for a moment Sitara could only stand and stare. "Radana, why?"

Radana lifted her face. Tears shone in her eyes and streaked her pale cheeks. She had not, Sitara noticed, painted that face at all this morning. It was harder, she mused, to look beautifully pitiful with great rings of kohl around your eyes and black streaks down your face.

"I fear for you, Great Queen." Radana pressed her forehead to Sitara's hand. "I fear for your peace of heart. Please, let me go with you and wait upon you."

Sitara cast a glance up the dock. Yes. There were guards and servants there, paused to listen to this drama, and she saw faces on the palace terraces. This moment provided plenty of witnesses to see how much Radana loved her queen.

Sitara raised Radana to her feet. She clasped the concubine's hand, feeling the tiny tremble there. "Radana, your place is here," she said kindly. *See, I too can put on a good show.* "The king will need your comfort while I am gone."

"But Great Queen . . ."

Sitara felt her patience straining. She could not permit anger now. Not before all these witnesses. "We all must serve, Radana, and we do not all get to choose the means of service." She spoke clearly, slowly. She wanted to be well understood by those who stayed behind. "I thank you for your care," she added, reaching out to wipe away the tears that fell so artfully from the concubine's eyes. She rested her hand on the woman's bowed head in blessing. "Go now. Let me leave while I still remember my dignity."

"Yes, Great Queen."

Sitara watched Radana turn sorrowfully and walk reluctantly up the dock, casting many a backward glance to make sure Sitara saw the tears in her eyes. For a moment, Sitara's heart quailed within her. To give Radana free run of the palace for any length of time could be dangerous.

No, she told herself firmly. *Kiet is no fool. He knows the extent of her worth as well as I do.*

So Sitara sailed on to the rhythm of the oars and the river, afraid for her home and afraid for herself, but never once turning back. The forests rose thick and green on either side. The dusts did not reach here. The rains never ceased to fall, and all was warm and green, and thick and close with life, wild and strange. It was in the forests the demons and the serpentine *naga* lived. It was to the forests the heroes and hermits went, for adventure or for enlightenment.

It was to the forests that Anidita sent the sorcerers to take them away from the danger of the corruption from their own power.

The monastery was a place of wood and thatch. The walls were made of ancient timbers painted red and carved with the hideous faces of demon fighters to warn away evil. Sitara felt their unsleeping eyes on her as she was helped from the rocking barge. The simple gates stood open wide, and the father abbot waited before them to greet her.

Father Thanom was a short, wiry man. His head was shaved to indicate his holy calling, and simple robes of saffron and burgundy wrapped his thin frame. Except on holy days, the abbot never wore any regalia that marked him as different from any of the other monks in this place. He bowed low before her, and Sitara returned the gesture, holding the pose until she felt his rough, warm hand touch her head in greeting and blessing.

"You are welcome among us, daughter." His voice was strong and deep. "Come and meditate for a while."

Sitara let herself be led across the yard toward the temple of the Awakened One, knowing that her people would be respectfully greeted and well looked after. The father abbot walked with her through the shadowed gardens, past the broad pools and drooping trees. There were no flowers here, only rich and varied greenery. The few times she had been here before, Sitara found herself with the strange feeling that the shadows were tended as carefully as the plants. The monks bowed as she passed them, and she nodded to them in return. There were no nuns in this garden. Their convent waited on the other side of the high wall; it was with them that she and her women would be housed this night.

Outwardly, the temple was a simple building; long and low, made of heavy timbers that were painted red, green, and gold. Inside there were mats for prayer, brass receptacles for the incense, and the great image of Anidita, his hands folded and his eyes closed in meditation. Like the rest of this place, this image had been carved from the forest, but it had been gilded and then robed in precious white silks. Heaps of colored rice lay in lacquered dishes on the altar between the bowls of burning incense that filled the air with the scents of precious resins.

Sitara had thought she would enter and sit, counting her beads and going through the motions of meditation as she had so many times on this journey. But as she paused on the threshold, in the presence of the Awakened One's image, she stopped, and could not make herself go forward. Never had her body felt so heavy and so weak at the same time. At last, her knees gave way under her and she dropped across the woven matting, prostrating herself.

It is anger, it is vanity. It is sin. I know it is sin, but I cannot let them keep her. I cannot leave them free to crush our land and wipe away Anidita's teachings here. I cannot.

She looked up at the Awakened One, seeing him through a film of tears. *Please, give me a sign. Tell me I am the one who will take this sin into the next life. Let my husband and my children be spared. Give them strength to stand . . .*

Stand what? Stand with her? Stand against her? She closed her eyes and the tears fell down her cheeks. This was wrong. She should have the strength to let the wheel of time turn and to accept destiny for herself and her family. But even as she thought this, she saw again the Hastinapuran priest's glittering eyes and heard him proclaim that her children were the property of Hastinapura's gods.

I do not have that much strength.

Sitara wiped her eyes and prostrated herself again. Then, shaking, she pushed herself to her knees and turned toward Father Thanom. At some point, he had knelt next to her, and waited in silence beside her through the storm of her weeping. She had an apology poised on the tip of her tongue, but the abbot spoke first.

"Is there anything you wish to tell me, daughter?"

Daughter. It had been a very long time since she had been less than "my queen," to any man but her husband.

The idea of not being who she was, of being daughter to someone again, sang to Sitara. She had meant to keep her silence. Speech was not safe, not even here. But when she peered toward the future and saw all the ways that she must be strong, she hungered for a last moment of weakness.

So, kneeling there, she told Father Thanom all that had happened when the Hastinapurans had come with their doomed black horse. She told him how Natharie had volunteered to follow them as token sacrifice, and how Kiet had not only let Natharie go, but had let Sitara go to the monastery with her heart full of hate.

Father Thanom considered all this for a long time. "Your husband wishes you to cleanse yourself, so that you may return to your duties as wife and queen."

She shook her head. "I cannot. I will not."

"Your children will miss their mother."

She turned her face away. "My children will be taken from me, one at a time, one way or another. It is already done."

"Then what do you mean to do?"

With that, the moment for weakness ended. Sitara straightened her shoulders and took up her new role, as queen and as traitor. She must show the courage Natharie had shown, and she could never falter again. "Father Abbot, I cannot tell you," she said. "I ask your forgiveness, but you are a holy man and I cannot taint you with knowledge of what I carry in my heart."

She thought Father Thanom would rebuke her, but he only said, "Will you walk with me, daughter? There is something I think you should see."

Wondering, Sitara followed him from the temple. The night was closing in fast, bringing with it the insistent song of frogs and the drone of insects to counterpoint the croaking, laughing sounds of the evening birds. The whole animal world sang, so at first it was difficult to hear the song of the human beings. Gradually, however, Sitara became aware that the thrum rising and falling beneath the wild noises grew clearer as they approached the low, plain structure before them. Unlike the other monastery buildings, this one was made of slats of wood and paper screens, in the style they used in the southern provinces of Hung-Tse. What was even more odd, she now saw, was it breached the wall, so that half of it sat in the monastery, and the other half was in the convent. Lamps were lit within, making the white paper glow golden. Smoke rose from a short, squat chimney. Shadows collected on the other side of the translucent walls, and the droning grew louder with each step until Sitara's skin began to shiver.

Father Thanom slid the paper door open slowly, releasing a shaft of golden light. For a moment, he watched whatever lay within and then beckoned her. Sitara stepped carefully through the low doorway.

Inside was a room lit to the brightness of day by four great brass lanterns that hung in its four corners. In its center sat a ring of monks and nuns whose voices rose and fell in the thrumming, rumbling chant. Through their ring of bodies, Sitara saw a mandala made of sand. Her breath caught in her throat at its shining beauty and she took an involuntary step forward to see it better.

In the lamplight, the mandala blazed like a thousand jewels. All the colors of the rainbow were in that pattern, and all the shades and hues that came when those colors blended together. It was wider across than she was tall and she could not count the rings or comprehend the details and symbols that filled the space between them. At first she thought the rings were separate, concentric circles, but as she looked more closely, she began to see they were subtly connected, one to the other, the first to the last. Each complete and separate, each bound to the other. Her mind blurred. The air before her rippled and her skin shivered in acknowledgment of a power she could feel only at the very edge of her senses. The monks' droning made the air throb. It sank through her skin and found an answering rhythm in her heart and her breath. All the holy sorcerers save one sat perfectly still, their eyes half-closed in deep concentration as they sang. One young monk held out his fisted hand, letting a slow stream of red sand fall to join the glorious pattern that stretched out between them. It seemed to Sitara that the scarlet grains trickled out in time to the endless chant.

"What is it?" Sitara managed to whisper.

"It is Sindhu," answered Father Thanom. "It is the past spiraling into the future and the future to the past, for this moment, for it will change. It is changing even now."

She opened her mouth to say something, about the beauty, the complexity, about the sound and the fall of the sand all woven together, but the abbot shook his head and pointed to the door. They slipped outside into the thickening evening. Behind them, there was no hesitation in the song, no pause in the falling of the sand.

For a moment, Sitara could only stand and gulp down the evening air, dizzy with the brilliance and power of what she had seen. Then, Father Thanom spoke softly. He did not look at her. It was as if he spoke only to the night.

"And the sorcerer came to the Awakened One and said to him, 'Master, tell us, what is right action for those whose souls are not of the three parts but are single and alone?'

"The Master said, 'Right action consists of four parts. Compassion. Understanding. Wisdom. Acceptance. Without compassion no action can be good. Without understanding, no action can be right. Without wisdom, all action is slave to ignorance. Without acceptance of consequence, there is no learning, no wisdom, no understanding, and no compassion.

" 'Therefore,' the Master said to the sorcerer, 'if you say your soul is alone and apart, seek the right action you desire alone and apart and act not until all four parts of right action are held within your hands.' "

Sitara kept her silence, uncertain of what answer she could make.

"I have spent much time thinking on that last phrase," Father Thanom continued. " 'If you say your soul is alone and apart.' Does that mean the sorcerer's soul is not a single thing as we have been taught? That we are as divided in spirit as those who cannot call the magics?"

"I do not know, Father."

"Nor do I." He sighed. "But I believe had that sorcerer

gone to Anidita and asked his question but a little differently, we would not be isolated here."

Although the night around them was warm and heavy, Sitara felt the hairs on the back of her neck prickling and her hands growing cold.

The abbot glimpsed the fear in her and shook his head. "Fear not, Great Queen. I was born to feel the magic of the world inside myself and outside, and to have the ability to weave that power to affect the world. I accept the law that those like me should have a cloistered life, where we can steep ourselves in study and prayer and act only when we may do so with compassion and right understanding. That is the purpose of the mandala, as is the purpose of all we do here. Right understanding of Sindhu."

"It is an enormous task to understand the whole of Sindhu."

A smile flitted across Father Thanom's face. "Which is one of the reasons we so seldom act, and why when we act, we do so little. It is difficult, Great Queen." His voice grew so soft she could scarcely hear it beneath the myriad of other night noises. "Not all cloistered here have patience. Their power is restless within them despite all we do. They wish for the power and the patronage they see open to those who follow other ways."

Sitara swallowed. She felt the chant behind her. She felt it in her bones. Its power crawled across her skin. What would that power do if left to itself? "No one here is prisoner," she said, because it was the proper thing to say and her frightened mind could think of nothing else.

"They are if they wish to remain in Sindhu."

Enough of fear, Sitara told herself sternly. "There is nothing I can do," she said. "The law is clear."

Father Thanom nodded as if this was not only expected, but welcome. "Know this, Great Queen: If Hastinapura begins to make . . . demands against Sindhu, there are those here who will not oppose them, and as you know, it is a difficult thing to stop sorcerers from speaking to each other should they so choose."

The monks' song, the sorcerers' song, still droned at her back, and the power of it still touched her, feather-light but constant. The queen thought of the woman in white who sat so silently beside Prince Samudra at the tables and the councils. Sitara wondered what she did in her silence and what woven power she might have borne with her. A sorcerer's workings could be secured in a ribbon, or a lump of clay. She thought of the sorceress leaving a spell behind, a curse or some thing that would break her home, break the royal line if it did not yield. She thought of her children and bit her tongue hard so as not to speak her fear.

"What do you advise then, Father?" Sitara said. *Be cold. Be stone. You cannot be weak. Not now, not ever again.*

"This is the understanding the mandala brings me. This is a time of change. That violence will come. Indeed, it must come." Father Thanom frowned, seeing she knew not what before him. Perhaps he was reading the mandala from memory. "It is the smallest act and the greatest love that will turn the wheel to peace again."

Sitara closed her eyes, her heart both weary and hard. "What good does this knowledge do, Father?"

The abbot faced her squarely. "It tells us, daughter, that it is time to act, and you have not come here to refrain from action, but to take it. I also wish to see a future for Sindhu, as she is, as an Awakencd land. I ask you to permit me to help you act." He moved closer to her. "Tell me what you plan, my queen. Let me and mine help you."

"When you tell me there may be spies in your own house? I need help, Father, but how can I trust so much?"

"Because you must give restless hands work and restless hearts a purpose, lest others do so first."

With that, Sitara made her decision. "Father Abbot," she

said. "I have a message that needs to be taken to a man in Paitong called Pakpao Kamol. Can you send one of the lay brothers?" The dedicated monks did not leave the monastery except for ceremony or strictest need.

"Of course, daughter." He held out his hand. She saw the question in his eyes, but knew he would not ask. It was this that gave her the final strength she needed. From the waistband of her skirt, Sitara took the note she had written on the barge on the previous day. She had not dared to carry it on her person from the palace. The writing was weak and wandering, not at all like her usual hand. Sitara handed the paper to the abbot. He tucked it into his sleeve without reading the direction written on it. "I would pray, now, Father," said Sitara. "And then visit my people. When that is done, you and I should speak further."

Father Thanom bowed. Side by side in silence they returned to the temple. The abbot touched her head one more time in blessing and left her there. As she knelt alone before the Great Teacher, Sitara felt her fear draining from her. All decisions for the moment had been made. All action that could be taken at this time had been. What understanding she had was in motion in the world.

Sitara turned to the image of Anidita, bowed her head, and finally began to pray.

In the darkness, outside the temple, a second figure watched Father Thanom leave on his errand, and softly stole away to the river gate, to watch and to wait and to send his own words where they must go.

Chapter Four

Prince Samudra stepped from the barge onto the crowded, noisy docks of the city of Vaudanya, the capital city of Hastinapura. As his sandal touched the tarred boards, his first feeling was one of profound relief. The year was over, and he was home. The city that had known him since his birth surrounded him. Its magnificent stone and marble was supported by terraced hills and backed by mountains of emerald and onyx, sapphire and snow. At their base waited the Palace of the Pearl Throne, shining ivory-white and granite-pink in the painfully bright light of midday. Once he entered there, he was home in truth.

A year. A year of wastelands and deep forests; a year of sleeping in shifts to keep Divakesh safe from whatever tiger or snake might be fool enough to try its fangs on him; a year of visiting the courts of conquered lands and telling threadbare and defiant kings that they must give the gifts of triumph and celebration yet again.

It had been a year without real news of home, or of the northern borders. Only the briefest of missives from the palace had reached him, and those said only that all was well and he should continue on with his so-vital work of following the horse and the high priest.

But now he was home, and soon there would be real work, fit for a prince, which would serve the land and the Mothers, and not just the vanity of Divakesh.

The docks were a blur of colors, an ocean of noise, both human and animal, and a world of stench. Shirtless men, their bodies gleaming with sweat, hoisted bales and sacks, chests and cages. Elephants lifted teak logs off the open barges and laid them in neat stacks on the shore. A man with skin so dark it was nearly black shouted at a herd of silky white goats that bleated scornfully in response. A merchant poked through a sack of peppercorns with a wooden stick while the seller fluttered and twittered beside him. Samudra found himself looking for the black horse who had been his reluctant guide for the past year. It was easy to spot the creature even in the dockside's riot of activity. It had a golden halter on now, and was tossing its great head this way and that to keep the reins out of the hands of its keepers, turning its body and stamping its hooves, looking for a way out of the crowd that surrounded it. Any moment now, it would rear and kick back. Divakesh stood to one side, shouting at the grooms and lesser priests, seemingly unwilling to come too close to the sacred, scared animal.

Samudra smiled grimly.

It got used to freedom. What will you do now, Divakesh?

Samudra was under no illusions as to who had convinced his brother Chandra to finally undertake the horse sacrifice. Samudra's only consolation was that the priest's machinations had missed their mark. What could Divakesh do to influence the Pearl Throne if he, like Samudra, was following the black horse about the countryside?

If influence was what Divakesh wanted. Samudra's thoughts turned for the thousandth time to the priest's outrage in the court of Sindhu. He'd known Divakesh to be . . . single-minded in his service of the Mothers, but that moment showed that Divakesh's devotions might run deeper and more stark than he had guessed, or feared.

Patience, he counseled himself. *I will soon be able to tell Chandra how his high priest behaved himself. Let Divakesh explain his insults to his emperor.*

A legion of clerks and eunuchs swarmed up to the tribute barges. Nominally, Samudra was supposed to be supervising this final unloading of goods, slaves, and hostages. In reality, that could be handled much more efficiently by those trained to it. He was more than willing to stand back and let them do their work, until he saw the grooms struggling through the tide of activity trying to lead Samudra's own horse, Rupak, to him. Ten days on a river barge with only the briefest periods of real exercise had left the animal in no mood to cooperate.

Samudra caught the horse's bridle and stroked the broad neck, whispering to the proud animal, reassuring him that all was right. Rupak whickered and stamped, but agreed to be calmed, and Samudra felt himself calming as well.

"My prince."

Hamsa had come up beside him. She kept as far from the horse as the crowds and goods permitted. Samudra smiled patiently. Hamsa had never truly taken to riding horseback. Unfortunately, fate did not allow her a palanquin or litter like other ladies of rank. She must stay beside him, so she must ride. "How was your journey?" he asked.

One corner of her mouth twisted up. "You spend ten days in a barge with the revered high priest, the sword of the Mothers, my prince, and then you ask me that question."

Samudra's own smile was grim. "We must all follow the steps of the Mothers' dance as they are laid out for us."

"That is easier for those who set the dance than for those who follow." Hamsa's tone was utterly bland as she spoke those words, but Samudra knew that the depth of the feeling that lay beneath them matched his own.

"You speak the truth, elder sister." He sighed, his gaze skimming restlessly over the roil of activity around them. His horse caught his mood and stamped uneasily.

"This will be the longest day," said Hamsa. Samudra grunted in agreement. Once everything was organized, there would come the procession and then the sacrifice. There would be nothing but ceremony until dusk. And for what? For a glorified tax collection.

Triumph and honor indeed.

Hamsa leaned on her staff and followed his gaze. Did she know he was looking for, praying for, a messenger? Probably. She was one of the few to know he had made his former comrade Tasham his proxy inside the palace. Tasham was to watch and wait, to influence quietly when he could, and to find a way to report in secret the instant Samudra returned.

Samudra cast around for something else to think about. Anger seethed just below the surface of his thoughts. If he gave it the barest chance, it would burst free. "How is the princess Natharie?" he asked, finally.

Hamsa shook her head. "Frightened," she said softly. "And with reason."

Samudra grimaced. "I had hoped you would be able to help her." As hard as he had tried, he had not been able to come near Natharie on the whole, long voyage. Divakesh had managed to keep them firmly apart. Samudra had thought if he had tried to see the princess at midnight, he would find Divakesh standing sleepless beside her. But he had tried his best to watch over her, and it had been a surprising relief from the tedium of the voyage to do so. She was a beauty, yes, but it was her calm, her strength, that drew his eye again and again.

"I tried," Hamsa was saying as she twisted her staff back and forth. "But . . . I fear being what I am, I gave her little comfort."

The self-reproach in those words was bitter and plain. Samudra shook himself from his reverie and touched Hamsa's shoulder. "That the Awakened lands fear sorcerers is not your doing." This was not all that lay under her words, and they both knew it, but still, she gave him a grateful glance. "She will have to be shown there is nothing . . ."

A figure in grey stopped to make obeisance before him. Samudra glanced at it, nodding reflexively, and then saw it was Lady Usha, the steward of the *zuddhanta*. They were opening the last of the long line of boats, and permitting the passengers to disembark. A gaggle of young women stood at the foot of the walkway. A few were women of rank, dressed in bright colors. Gold and jeweled brooches ornamented their hair. More gold hung from their ears. Others were more plainly dressed and sparingly ornamented.

As Samudra watched, Princess Natharie descended from her barge. She looked dazed but proud. She had not yet seen Steward Usha striding toward her, nor had she seen the gold and silver chains that Usha's servants carried.

But Samudra did. He shoved Rupak's reins into the groom's hands and started after her. But the crowd closed in again behind the steward's train. By the time Samudra had threaded the maze of startled humans, nervous horses, and heaped goods and palanquins being slowly forced into a rough line, Usha had finished shackling the servant girls together with the silver chain and was turning to Natharie.

"No," he said.

The steward turned and saw who had spoken. She dropped quickly into the salute of trust, but not before he saw her square her shoulders, ready to assert her authority in this matter.

"Princess Natharie has come to serve her land among us freely and with honor," Samudra said, raising his voice to make sure Natharie could hear him. He met her eyes, and tried silently to tell her that he had been there all along, that he would not let anything happen to her. "There is no need for this ceremony."

What is happening here? Natharie's eyes were cool, her anger plain, and the sight of it tore at his heart.

Usha looked up, saw that he was serious, and covered her eyes again. "As you command, my prince." She moved away, but Samudra did not miss the hard and appraising look she gave Princess Natharie.

Nor did Natharie miss it. Clearly, she strove to remain calm, but her nervous glance kept darting from him and Hamsa to Divakesh where he stood with the priests, casting his long shadow over the slowly forming procession.

Samudra opened his mouth, searching for something to say, but before the words could come, a hoarse shout broke over the continual noise of the docks. "My prince! Prince Samudra!"

Samudra turned. A large, shirtless man, sweat gleaming on his deep brown skin, elbowed his way through the crowd, earning shouts and curses in response. He knelt on the dock beside Samudra's horse and held up a fold of paper sealed in green wax. Samudra recognized the man as belonging to Commander Makul's household. Makul was Samudra's own battle-father, who taught him much of the art of war and the work of soldiering.

Makul? What is this? The message should be from Tasham.

Samudra dismounted to accept the message. He broke the seal and read:

My Prince,

Captain Pravan returned yesterday from facing the Huni in the mountains. He was defeated utterly and over half his men are dead. You must come at once.

Makul doa *Rahish Irashapad*

Samudra stared at the message. Disbelief and confusion assailed him. Beneath them, the anger that he had controlled so carefully all this long year broke. It raced through his blood, making his face burn as his hands crushed the unwelcome message. Pravan? Pravan had been sent to face the Huni while he, Samudra, had been sent wandering about the country collecting tribute as a coarse reminder of Hastinapura's power? Pravan returned in defeat, and it was Makul who sent him the missive that should have come from the emperor?

Blood of the Mothers! Where is Tasham?

"What is it, my prince?" asked Hamsa.

His teeth grinding in rage, Samudra stuffed the crumpled message into her hands. Without even looking back to see her reaction, he threw himself onto his horse.

"Clear the way!" he shouted to the crowd, vaguely aware that at the same time, Hamsa was calling for her horse. "I must get to the palace! Clear the way!"

Servants and soldiers, Makul's man first among them, plunged into the crowd. "Way! Clear the way for the first prince!" they cried. Conches and horns sounded. Slowly a lane began to open in the crowds and Samudra was able to urge his mount forward, with Hamsa right behind him on her brown mare.

. . . The Huni in the mountains . . . defeated utterly . . . over half his men are dead . . . These words made a drumbeat in his mind as he rode through the twisting streets. Masses of people scrambled to get out of the way. Others stood and stared to see him ride past. Samudra had never before been so tempted to lash out at the slow carters and the clumsy beggars as time and again he had to rein Rupak up short until his hastily assembled entourage could clear the way.

Over half his men are dead.

Who were the dead? Yasuf, maybe? Ojas? Even Pravan would not go to war without Tamin to head the cavalry. Who else had been chosen to fight under Pravan? Pravan the fool. Pravan the flatterer who had his brother's . . . his emperor's ear and was invited to private banquets in the *zuddhanta,* no matter how many times Samudra tried to tell Chandra the man wasn't worthy.

Why didn't I see this? Why didn't I realize that with me gone, Pravan would seize his chance? Why didn't I think?

Because I was too caught up in the insult Chandra dealt me to think on wider implications. Samudra now wanted to lash out at himself, to beat his own back until the blood flowed down. These dead, whoever they were, however many they had been, did not belong only to Pravan.

Why did I get no word they had even gone to the mountains?

Tasham should have gotten me word, or Mother. They would not have let this happen without warning me.

Which only left him to wonder why that had not happened. His anger and the fear deepened as the streets broadened, rising up to meet the palace gates.

The great timbered portals were closed when he reached them. His entourage stood before them, shouting up at the men on the walls, who shouted down at them. Samudra rode up to the gates and hollered above the babble.

"What is this delay!"

"Sir, you were not expected! You have not been . . ."

"I have been gone too long! Open the door! Do you disobey the Throne?" *I am still prince. You will hear my word!*

There was no more argument. The smaller gate to the right of the great one was pulled open and Samudra rode through into the vast green park that was the palace garden. A road of crushed shell and stone led to the inner court. Free of crowds and obstructions, Samudra was able to launch Rupak into a gallop, not caring how far he outpaced those who were supposed to prepare his way. The thunder of Rupak's hooves found its echo in the gait of Hamsa's mare, as the sorceress clung grimly to her saddle and reins, doing her best to keep up.

The inner court had its own walls, and its own gates of carved ivory. These too were shut fast. Now, however, only one man in a wealth of scarlet robes stood on the wall above. Samudra reined Rupak to a halt and stared. As fast as he had been, word had flown ahead. Asok, Divakesh's first acolyte, waited above the gates, his wiry arms folded in defiance.

"Asok, open the gate!" Samudra cried. "I have urgent business with the emperor." Where were the guards? The men on watch?

Asok made the salute of trust. "I cannot, my prince. You have not been purified from your travels among the barbarians."

"Asok, do not . . ." began Samudra dangerously.

But the acolyte shook his head. "I have my orders from

my lord Divakesh. We will not affront the Mothers by letting the impure tread in the heart of the sacred dance. Not even my prince."

"Asok . . ." Where was the guard, damn them? They were his men. Why weren't they here?

"You must be cleansed and make sacrifice before you enter the palace," said Asok as firmly and as calmly as a man saying the sun must rise tomorrow. "These are the Mothers' laws, and I will not break them. I will not of my own will open these gates."

Beneath the fire of his rage, Samudra knew Asok did no more and no less than act according to divine law. There was ritual that must be performed after an extended journey, to shed the outer world and reembrace the inner, to reweave the steps to match the rhythm at the center of the dance. To disrupt this was to disrupt Hastinapura itself and break the compact the first emperor made with the Queen of Heaven. Samudra knew this. He had done it scores of times, returning from a campaign or from some diplomatic journey at his father's side.

But Samudra also knew what Divakesh did under the cover of that law. This was payment for what had happened in the court of Sindhu. This was Divakesh reasserting his power and authority.

In thinking of the dead, Samudra had forgotten all these lesser things.

The dead, unnumbered and unnamed, the dead laid low by Pravan's incompetence and his own thoughtlessness. This truth washed away the shame brought by his forgetfulness of holy rite.

"Asok, there is no time. We are defeated. I must speak with the emperor and I must speak with Captain Pravan. We cannot delay!"

"All you say shows how polluted your thoughts have become," said Asok stubbornly. "In this, my master's rank is higher even than yours, and his duty to the protection of the emperor and the Pearl Throne even greater. No one will open this gate to you until the sacrifice is ready."

Slowly, regally, the acolyte turned, and descended from the walls, vanishing from Samudra's sight. Samudra was left before the locked ivory gates, with no sound but the garden's birds to break the ringing in his ears, and no one but the servants and Hamsa to hear him shout.

It was Hamsa he turned on, his anger blotting out reason. "What has happened here?" he demanded. "What is being done to me?"

Hamsa, who was supposed to be his first friend and best advisor, could only say, "I don't know, my prince."

"Why! You are the sorcerer, you speak to the Mothers and scry the future. Why didn't you see this!"

Hamsa bowed under his shouted words, turning her face away. Samudra regretted his outburst at once. "Never mind, Hamsa. It is not your fault." *You were sent with me. They knew they had to get you out of the palace as well.*

For a moment, her mouth moved without sound before she made the salute of trust, covering her face with her hands and bowing low before him.

In that moment of silence, he heard a new sound, a familiar sound. The clash of metal on metal, the faint shout of men's voices.

The training yard. There were exercises happening in the training yard. The guard, his men, were outside the walls.

Fool! He cursed himself and wheeled Rapuk around, riding swiftly around the great curve of the inner walls. The Mothers, their heroes, saints, and the lesser gods looked down on him with stone eyes as he passed by. He knew that Asok was right. That he had been ready to toss aside the requirements the Mothers themselves laid down for the sake of his anger . . . if that was not the sign of pollution he could not have said what was. But his anger would not ease, nor would his urgency. He had to see his brother, now. But he could not. Walls of stone and law barred his way. His anger turned inward and it felt as if he would choke on it.

The practice yard stood outside the walls because no violence was permitted within the sanctum of the Throne. It was a broad bowl of grassy ground with a few stone outbuildings for its border. Beneath the green turf waited a maze of tunnels and storerooms for the soldiers' use. One of them even ended in the vast stables. Samudra could have used that to get back into the palace, but the idea of sneaking like a thief back into his own home, and possibly being thrown out again, was more than pride could bear.

At the center of the exercise arena, men drilled closely with their spears, responding to the brusque shouts of their officers and instructors. On the far side of the rim, archers took aim at straw targets of men, or tried to shoot over false wooden walls. On the near side, Captain Pravan *dai* Vanash Itorapad, proud and splendid on his black-maned roan, watched over them all surrounded by a crowd of captains and high officers.

Samudra's hands began to shake. Rapuk whickered and danced, and the prince climbed down from the saddle. He was distantly aware that a man ran to take the reins from him, and that Hamsa slipped down from her horse to join him.

A member of Samudra's entourage ran up to Pravan, who leaned down from his horse to listen closely. Then, slowly, with great dignity, Pravan turned and looked down at Samudra. He was a magnificent sight, his armor gleaming and each detail of him just as it ought to be. No one would know that just recently he had returned in defeat, and that today he reviewed a decimated corps.

Anger, boiling and unreasoning, poured through Samudra's veins as he saw Pravan's thin, dry mouth spread into a smile.

"My prince . . ." Pravan began.

Before he could say more, Samudra crossed the distance

between them, jerked Pravan from the saddle, and threw him into the dust.

"Coward!" he shouted. "How many are dead because of you! How many!"

Pravan began to struggle to his feet. Samudra lunged forward to knock him down again, but Pravan caught Samudra's wrist, pulled him off balance, and sent Samudra rolling over his own shoulder.

Samudra came up on his feet to see Pravan crouched low before him. "You are my prince," Pravan hissed. "I owe you all honor, but no one calls me coward."

"I say you are a coward," Samudra answered, his voice steady and sharp. *And a dead man.* Pravan had struck him, the First Prince of the Pearl Throne. Pravan was dead, no matter what happened next. He was dead and he deserved to be, and Samudra would carry out the sentence with his own hands. "I call you a coward and a fool who led his men to death and saved his own skin at the cost of defeat."

Pravan charged, and Samudra, ready, dodged. The other man pivoted quickly and Samudra had time to see what a fool he was to attack in anger. For Pravan charged again, this time with his knife in his hand. Samudra stepped sideways and kicked at Pravan's ankle, sending Pravan sprawling on the grass. He leapt, rolling the other man over, until he came up kneeling on his armored chest, holding his own knife at Pravan's throat.

"You are a coward and unfit to lead men," Samudra said through gritted teeth even as he panted for air. "I should kill you here and now, and deny the emperor the chance to make that mistake again."

"Now, Prince Samudra." Pravan smiled despite the steel against his flesh. "Do you say the Father of the Pearl Throne made a mistake in appointing me to command? Do you think you could have made a better choice?"

Samudra froze and Pravan continued to smile. Samudra had just criticized the emperor. Publicly. There were at least thirty men close enough to have heard his words. Anything, anything Samudra said in answer to that question could be called treason, and a hundred armed men stood at his back, all loyal to the Mothers and the emperor. Except, perhaps, those who were loyal to him.

Samudra lifted the knife and stood back, letting Pravan rise. He did so slowly, straightening his armor and clothing carefully. Then Pravan made his obeisance, all correct and proper.

"Had I been aware my prince desired to sharpen his skills as a wrestler, I would have dressed for practice. I ask forgiveness."

Samudra's impotent rage burned so bright that for a moment he saw only red. He was aware of nothing except the knife in his hand that Pravan had not bothered to reclaim.

"My prince." Another voice, close by, startled him. His vision returned and he saw Makul beside him, also making obeisance, his face ashen grey. "I am sorry to disturb you, my prince, but there is a matter I would discuss with you. Will you honor me with a hearing?"

Samudra realized he had been holding his breath. He let it out, and took fresh air in. He tasted dust, and blood where he had bitten his tongue. "Yes, Makul, of course." Then he took two steps forward and handed the knife to Pravan. "You dropped this, Captain."

He was rewarded by the smallest flicker of fear in Pravan's eyes as the man received his knife and repeated his obeisance.

Before his rage could take him again, Samudra walked away with both Makul and Hamsa following close behind. The sorceress said nothing. What had she thought of his little display? What did it matter? She could not, would not have done anything, and yet he still felt shame that she had witnessed his loss of control. But Pravan did not deserve to live. He had taken men to die for nothing, nothing at all, and he lived in defeat without shame or loss of stature.

He did not deserve to live.

Samudra had no idea where he was going. He still could not see clearly, let alone think clearly. Makul steered their steps toward the white and saffron pavilion that would shade the men when they took their meals. It was a wise choice. Here they could talk out in the open, without being overheard by any hidden person.

Servants hurried forward with pillows and tea, and Samudra sank down to sit beside a low table. Hamsa stationed herself nearby, watching the exercises that continued below and at the same time watching for any would-be spies. Makul knelt before Samudra and poured two cups of tea. Makul was a big man, ten years Samudra's senior, and the one who had taught Samudra the science of war. The first commander pushed one of the simple white cups toward Samudra. Samudra cradled it so that warmth seeped into his palm. He sipped slowly, letting the spices spread through his mouth and linger against his palate. He soon found he could breathe, could see, could think again.

"That was not a wise move, my prince." Makul looked down into his half-empty cup for a moment. The lines care had carved around his eyes and mouth were now deep clefts. "Pravan was expecting it."

"One might think he engineered defeat by the Huni so I would attack him," replied Samudra with a bland disinterest that was the opposite of the turmoil surging within him.

"No." Makul took another sip of tea and looked out across the training field. The exercises with all their shouting and clashing had begun again. "I do not think he plotted that well."

"An interesting choice of words," said Samudra, but Makul did not reply. To elaborate on his statement now would be more than dangerous; it would be foolhardy.

Samudra longed to ask Makul about Tasham, but he held back. As much as he trusted Makul, Samudra had not told him that Tasham was his right hand inside the small domain.

This was strategy Makul himself had taught Samudra. Let no man know the names of all the spies, not even the spymaster. "Tell me what happened with the Huni," said Samudra softly.

Makul sighed and finished his tea, but he did not pour himself any more. He just stared at the empty cup.

"It was the month after you left. Pravan had an audience with the emperor. I was not invited to attend." He pushed his cup an inch to the right. "When he emerged, Pravan called the captains together and announced that he would be leading an attack against the Huni outpost in the Iron Pillar mountains."

Samudra felt his heart seize up. "But to do so they would have to take the army through Lohit Province." Unless they went three days out of their way. "I swore there would be no imperial troops on their soil as long as they kept the peace . . ."

"I know," said Makul quietly.

Just before Chandra ordered him to oversee the horse sacrifice, Samudra had been sent to Lohit, one of the lands where the worship of the Mothers had given way to the teachings of Anidita, the Awakened One. Although Anidita taught against violence, word had reached the Pearl Throne that Pairoj, Lohit's new king, had used the excuse of worship to begin a rebellion and slay the soldiers in Lohit's Hastinapuran garrisons. Samudra had been sent to the coast to stop that rebellion, and to punish the instigators. He had set off hot with righteous anger. But on the long and grueling march, his blood had cooled, and thoughts of the Mother of War had given way to thoughts of the Mother of Increase. He arrived in Lohit, marched to the capital, surrounded the city walls at a safe distance, and sent Hamsa to one of the monasteries where the sorcerers in Awakened lands were forced to dwell. She brought their father abbot and mother superior to him. Samudra gave them tea and sat with them for long hours, questioning them about the one they followed and

how he was worshipped. When he had learned what he
needed to know, he thanked them for their patience and sent
them back to their forest home, with Hamsa as their guarantor of safe passage.

Then, he had his scribes write a message using all the language he had learned from the monk and the nun. He spoke
of the importance of knowledge and the folly of acting from
ignorance, of enlightened dialogue between differing minds
and the preference of peace over war. He asked the king to
send a messenger, to speak of his grievances.

The plan met with success. First came a messenger, then
an ambassador, then the king himself beneath his umbrella
of state, to sit with Samudra in his pavilion and talk about
the havoc the Hastinapuran soldiers had wreaked on his capital, about how the priest who served the garrison said the
sons of the Mothers had the right to plunder and despoil
those who falsely worshipped a man as a god.

With the king as witness, Samudra sat in judgment on
those soldiers who survived, and leveled punishment where
it was merited, for rape, for theft, and for murder. In return,
the king paid the taxes and tribute owed and permitted the
priests with Samudra to exhume and burn the bodies of the
soldiers who had died, all with the proper rites to the Mothers. When all this was done, Samudra exacted a promise that
the taxes would continue, and that a levy of men would be
sent to the palace each year. As long as this was done, Lohit
would be left in peace and no soldiers or priests would return
there, only a clerk and an ambassador to tally the tribute.

The agreement was celebrated in Lohit's capital with the
ceremonies proper to both the Seven Mothers and the Awakened One. Without losing a single man, without spilling a
drop of blood, Samudra marched home, the province behind
him secure.

Or it had been. Samudra felt his throat close. "Tell me
Lohit violated the treaty, or tell me that permission was
sought . . ."

But Makul was already shaking his head. "Pravan marched us through without a word of warning. We took what was needed, according to custom, and some took more than that. King Pairoj had no time to resist, and Pravan left him a warning . . . that I think came more from Divakesh than the emperor . . ."

Samudra was barely listening. His word was in shreds. His peace was broken. This was why he had been sent away, so his treaty could be violated without his objection. To attack the Huni in their strongest outpost, this was the excuse, the excuse that had cost . . .

"How many dead?" he whispered.

"Five hundred," Makul answered. "Yasuf and Tamin among them."

Samudra's fists tightened.

Makul pushed his cup a little to the left. "My prince, it has long been in my mind to honor your return with a feast. Will you grace my house with your presence tomorrow evening?"

Sensing the undercurrent in Makul's words, Samudra nodded. "Makul, I would be most pleased to do so."

Makul bowed over his hands. "Until then, I expect you will want to rest, and to visit the great queen your mother, and pray in the temples."

Calm myself. Seek good advice, and keep my silence.

"I shall surely do all these things." Samudra paused and then reached out to clasp the other man's wrist. "Thank you, Makul. It is good to be among friends again."

"The Mothers themselves have surely ordained that wherever there are soldiers, my prince will find friends," said Makul. He made a final obeisance and departed, and Samudra watched him go.

"Well, Hamsa," Samudra murmured. "What do we do now?"

"We wait, my prince," she answered softly. She sounded as tired as he felt. "Until the gates open and we are allowed back into the palace. Then, we shall see."

In his mind's eye what Samudra saw was King Pairoj. He imagined that bright voice cursing his name as Pravan trampled through his few fertile fields, and heard the laughter of soldiers who have been turned loose to do as they would. He saw Divakesh standing with his great arms folded in satisfaction. Pairoj was surely no longer alive. He was not one to stand by while his land was torn apart.

He thought then of Natharie, and how he had left her, a step away from being chained like a slave and paraded through the streets as a prize. What would she think if she heard that one of the Awakened lands was treated in this way? She would surely fear him more than she already did.

Why he should care about this, he was uncertain. Perhaps he was just unwilling to think of it now when there was so much blood, anger, and fear in his mind.

"Hamsa," he said. "I need to debate with myself for a time. Will you go down to the procession and walk with the princess Natharie? I do not think we should have left her alone."

Hamsa licked her lips uncertainly. "I doubt she will find me good company, my prince."

"You are all I have here, Hamsa."

Hamsa made the salute of trust where she knelt. Then she rose and called for her horse. Samudra watched her mount the animal awkwardly and ride away. He turned his eyes from her to the walls that kept him from home, family, and truth.

We shall see, Hamsa had said. "Yes," he whispered. "Mothers help us all, we surely will."

Chapter Five

When Natharie arrived at last at the gates of the Palace of the Pearl Throne, she came kneeling in the center of a litter heaped with pearls and gold coins, one more prize for the emperor. She was dazed by long hours in the sun and deafened by the roaring crowd that had filled the streets to watch the tribute procession. As dazed as her mind was, though, she had wit enough left to wonder why Prince Samudra stood before these outer gates of his own home to greet them as they wound their way inward. What had gone so wrong for the first prince of Hastinapura?

The procession did not even slow to absorb this new addition, but continued its stately passage through the open gates. The guardian walls were so thick, Natharie felt she had entered a deep tunnel. The sweat that slicked her skin turned cold, raising goose pimples on her skin. It was the feeling of crossing into another world.

The sun dazzled Natharie's weary eyes as she emerged into the gardens of the palace.

It is another world.

Her home had gardens, and they were broad and green and well tended, but they were nothing like these carefully trimmed trees, these banks of grass and flowers descending to meet chattering brooks or groves of fruiting trees. Deer grazed here, and antelope, and pure white oryx. Peacocks strutted. Flamingos stood motionless in green ponds. Birds of paradise and vultures nested in the trees.

As the gardens she knew paled in comparison with what lay before her, so did her home. The palace she had grown

up in was a wooden hovel compared with the granite and
marble city that rose above this expance of parkland. The
sun hung low over the green mountain that stood sentry over
the palace, washing all with red-gold fire. Its windows and
balconies, arches and exposed corridors made it look more
like a web spun by a hundred thousand spiders than an edifice constructed by men.

A broad white road descended through the paradise of
greenery. Fountains splashed cool droplets on her thirsty
skin. Monkeys looked down from the trees, shaking their
heads at her passage. Birds added their voices to the flutes.
Everywhere, the scent of oranges and lemons hung in the
air. The world around them was now hushed, and Natharie
could hear the sounds of the many feet of the procession, the
hoofbeats of the horses, the bearers' grunting. Horns blew
and were answered by the sounds of drums and flutes.

The road rose, winding toward an inner wall of red stone
set with a pair of intricately carved ivory gates. Natharie
thought they would be taken into the palace now, but the procession turned aside, and instead followed the walls to a
courtyard dominated by a great altar shaped like the bowl of
a fountain. Six garish scarlet and gold shrines surrounded it.
Priests who bore the images of the Mothers split off from
the procession and circled the yard, each of them placing
one image in its waiting home. As they brought her closer,
Natharie could see that steps led up to the altar bowl and in
its center, a single carved image stood on a pedestal of red
stone. This was most likely Mother Jalaja, the one called the
Queen of Heaven. Fire burned at her feet. Gold rings circled
her wrists and ankles. Her gilded headdress sparkled with
precious stones, some of which were surely diamonds. She
had been decked with scarlet flowers. Her upraised hands
held an open lotus and a bowl heaped high with saffron rice.

But what truly struck Natharie was the Mother's staring,
white eyes. The red stone had been set with shell that left a
dark iris through which the goddess could see. She seemed

to look directly at Natharie, seeing all her defiant thoughts and her hardened heart. For a brief moment, Natharie cringed.

The procession halted. Natharie was set on solid ground for the first time in hours as the bearers around her knelt and kissed the ground. Hamsa slipped from her horse and did the same. She thought they were prostrating themselves before the goddess, but then, at last, Natharie saw the emperor.

His dais rose up in a space between the shrines and he sat cross-legged on a throne of precious woods. His skin was the color of summer wheat. His clothing was of pure white cloth that shimmered with embroidery of all colors. His hair hung in silken ringlets down past his shoulders. His crown was a cap of gold and pearls, with a single great ruby that seemed to pulse like a living heart in the sunlight. His long, delicate face turned toward the tribute procession, but she could not tell if he saw her amid the overwhelming pageantry.

At his feet sat a withered man wearing only a white breechclout about his waist. His hair was braided and bundled as Hamsa's was. Another sorcerer then. More magic for the ruling of men.

Two carved screens of light wood stood beside the throne, one on either side. Back there would be the women, the queen and her attendants, hidden from public gaze lest the eyes of others besmirch their purity.

On either side of the screens were arrayed a selection of priests, some in the scarlet robes and tall golden hats such as she had seen before, some in saffron, and some in simple white.

While Natharie took in this mighty spectacle, Prince Samudra dismounted his horse and strode to the foot of the dais. Hamsa now left her place at Natharie's side to follow her master. He knelt to his brother, the emperor, and Emperor Chandra beckoned broadly to him. Prince Samudra mounted the dais steps with Hamsa two steps behind him. A silken cushion had been placed beside the throne and Samu-dra sat down, cross-legged, straight-backed, and Hamsa sat at his feet. It seemed strange to see the prince sitting so low when he had ridden head and shoulders above others since she had first seen him.

Then, Divakesh rose from his place in the procession, red and gold and powerful. His regalia flashed in the burning sunlight. Slowly, he mounted the steps to the great altar. The wind freshened at that moment, and Natharie smelled some-thing at once sweet, bitter, and familiar, but she could not place it. Divakesh knelt before the Queen of Heaven and bowed with his face in his hands. Only then did he make the same salute to the emperor. One of the priests from the dais walked down to him, bearing something on a red pillow. This Divakesh took and held aloft. It was a sword, its silver blade broad, keen, and curving. Divakesh kissed the flat rev-erently, and a deep shudder ran through Natharie.

The emperor lifted his hand and the remaining priests and acolytes left their places. They too mounted the stairs to the altar of the goddess and made their obeisances before her. When they rose, each of the acolytes held a wooden staff. They laid the ends of these into the fire burning at the goddess's feet. Carrying their torches high, they circled the edges of the platform. Black smoke rose up into the blue sky.

Then, they thrust those torches down into the bowl below.

Now Natharie realized the scent that had troubled her was perfumed oil. The fire opened like an enormous flower. Red, gold, orange, white, and blue, it stretched out its petals until the Queen of Heaven and all her priests walked on flames and were entwined by fragrant smoke.

Now the horse was led to the altar. It was so ringed by at-tendants, Natharie could see no more than its head, and its eyes flashing white as it panicked at the nearness of the fire. But by now the the beast was held too tightly to rear. It was time. Natharie's hands missed her beads. She tried to steel herself. The goddess watched her unblinking, looking for her fear.

Somewhere, a great drum began to beat. The rhythm was slow but insistent. A brass bell joined it, ringing high and clear. The beat quickened, became a complex pattern, and Divakesh began to dance.

He danced before the Mother, now kneeling, now leaping higher. He spun, his sword flashing in the sun as it arched over his head. It was a dance of sacrifice of blood and self. The rhythm of the drum pushed its power into Natharie's blood and left her afraid. Bell and drum drove Divakesh on, whirling faster, his body moving with sure, swift precision. Natharie's heart raced. Her breath came fast and shallow. The priest's scarlet robes flowed with the movement of his dance, wrapping him in their own fire. The acolytes stood still as statues, and the sword whirled over their heads, was laid against their necks, as if it would make them sacrifices for the Mother. None of them so much as flinched, but watched the sword and the dancer with shining faces, lost in the ecstasy of the moment.

For a single instant, Divakesh stood still, the sword raised high, his face exultant. Then, the sword flashed down again, past the horse's broad neck. The beast screamed. The sword came up again. Blood, dark and rich with its store of life, fountained out across midnight hide.

A wave of nausea flooded over Natharie, leaving her sick and faint. She had seen dead animals before, but she had never seen one die, let alone one being killed. The acolytes were holding out bowls, catching the blood they'd spilled. The priest was laying the bloody sword at the goddess's feet. Now he dipped his fingers in one of the bowls and painted the goddess's face with that same blood.

The Queen of Heaven watched Natharie, and Natharie bowed her head and shook.

She was moving again, being carried forward, closer to the fire. She could not make herself look up. She was going to be sick. She was going to faint and fall from the palanquin. It was too hot. The smoke rasped against her throat and filled her mouth with the taste of sandalwood and ash.

A hand grasped her chin, forcing it upward. For a moment, she saw Divakesh frowning hard at her.

Hamsa had told her what was to come. Divakesh would paint her face with the horse's blood. With this, she'd be pronounced clean enough to enter the palace.

It is only blood, she told herself now as she looked into the priest's stern eyes. *It is only ceremony. It will wash off.*

The high priest smiled a little, and Natharie steeled herself for the brush of his bloody fingers.

"Hold," said Divakesh.

At that single word, the whole world fell silent. Divakesh released Natharie's chin and clamped his great, bloody hand around her wrist instead.

She felt the world staring, emperor, priests, prince, sorcerers, the hidden queen. She felt the weight of that terrible silence. Not even a fly buzzed. No one dared so much as murmur. Dizzy from the sacrifice, heat, and shock, Natharie could focus only on Divakesh, and his little smile.

"Let this one, polluted beyond all other measure, come to the fire."

He pulled her upright, but Natharie's legs had gone to sleep long ago, and she sprawled facedown at his feet. She lay there a moment, ridiculous and ashamed. Without so much as a grunt of effort, Divakesh swept her into his arms like a sack of wheat and strode to the Mother's pedestal. There, he dropped her again, and a cry left her, and she huddled at the feet of the goddess.

"Look on the Queen of Heaven, look on the one who danced the world into being, and who will bring its destruction when the day is good. Look on her, you who would dare elevate a mortal man to her equal, and see the truth!"

Shaking, Natharie lifted her head; she looked up at the form, magnificent and bejeweled and wreathed in flame.

"Speak the truth, little girl. See the purity of truth for all."

What is it? What does he want? The world spun. She was so sick, so dizzy. She wanted to faint, to cry, to answer, to give this man anything he wanted, just for a drink of water and an end to the blood and the confusion that roared through her.

"What is your sin? Speak before the Mothers and show how all may be made clean!"

Natharie looked up at the white-eyed goddess, and she saw the lotus and the blood and the fire that seemed brighter than the sun, and she remembered her womanhood ceremony and being held under the water while her lungs strained for air. The goddess rose above her terrible and splendid, forever dancing on her fire. She wavered in front of Natharie's vision, and Natharie seemed to see her dancing the dance they said shaped the world, and would end it, and would begin it again. In a heartbeat, it seemed she understood all.

"Speak!" roared Divakesh.

His cry broke her trance, and the world snapped back into place around her. Divakesh the man held her, and made her huddle like a slave on the hot stone. Divakesh had stolen her beads, belittled her family, killed the great horse. It was not the goddess who demanded anything of her. It was the man, and the man would have nothing at all. She would defy him though it meant her death, and the whole of his world would watch her do it.

Natharie bit her tongue against her fears, and raised her head.

The silence stretched out, a handful of heartbeats, a handful of breaths. Divakesh stared down at her, his face thunderous with his wrath, and his eyes filled with disbelief. Natharie closed her own eyes. She felt herself sway. She heard the rasp of metal. She heard the drum of footsteps and felt the breeze of passage. The drum began its steady rhythm again, the world's heart, the Mother's heart, her heart. There was no other rhythm. Fear squeezed her until she was hollow, and still she held. She was going to die. Her blood was going to paint the feet and hands of Divakesh and his priests, and she would die alone and she would be silent.

Not alone. Her heart was full and it was open. If this was death, she would meet it and there would be life again. She would not be alone.

She felt the rush of the sword. She felt the steel touch her throat, and the edge draw along her skin, felt the warmth of her own blood. The pain did not come until a long moment later, sharp and clean as the cut had been, and with it came the realization that she was alive to feel the pain, and her eyes flew open.

Divakesh was on one knee before her, his breath heavy and rasping. He smelled of sweat and incense. He smeared her blood on his hand that was already wet with the blood of the horse, and dipped his scarlet fingertips with it. Those glistening fingers stabbed ruthlessly at her face and the pain sharpened and brightened and Natharie gasped, and the priest's grin grew wild.

"The clean blood of sacrifice cleanses your pollution. The mark of the Mothers makes you Theirs, and it is by Jalaja's will you live and die, in this life and in all lives to come." Then, softly, softly, almost a lover's whisper, he added, "And your whole world will pay for your silence."

Natharie swallowed her bile. There would never be water enough to wash this mark from her. She closed her eyes and imagined her beads. In her mind, she remembered how they felt slipping through her fingers.

What are the strongest fetters?

Pride, hatred, ignorance, reliance on rite and ceremony, desire for a future life in the worlds of form.

The deeply familiar admonition ran through her, stilling her within herself, grounding her although the world still swayed around her. He would not defeat her, not even with this blood mark.

Natharie rose to her feet, smoothly, gracefully. The high priest took a step back. Natharie ignored him. She bowed over folded hands to the goddess. This was Jalaja's house, and one did not fail to honor one's hostess. She bowed to the emperor, her mortal host. She saw, very briefly, that Prince Samudra was on his feet and halfway down the dais steps. She wondered distantly what had stopped him. She turned and walked back to her palanquin, her head held high and her deportment so perfect her tutors would have been amazed. She knelt. She folded her hands and looked back up at Divakesh. The sword dangled loose in his huge hand, and for a moment she saw the stunned disbelief in him.

In Natharie's dignified repose, she knew her triumph. Her bearers lifted her up and carried her to a doorway in the shadow of the palace's white and pink wall. A horde of slaves surrounded it, stripping off the heaps of treasure as men with heavily kohled eyes and long silk coats snapped orders and made notes on tablets.

"Up, up!"

It was the grey woman—what had Prince Samudra called her? Mistress Usha?—again, snapping her fingers to rouse Natharie from the distant place her mind had gone.

Natharie was able to stand, but the strength and grace that had been hers a moment before were gone. She shook and she shuffled. The grey woman gestured impatiently toward the darkened doorway and Natharie staggered forward, following the other young women as they entered the dim corridor. Weakness made her mind swim with confusion. The change from the shining and sinister magnificence to the cramped, low-ceilinged darkness was too abrupt. The badly lit hall smelled of warm dust. They were taken to a poky, unadorned room where Mistress Usha walked around with a key and undid the shackles from the other women's wrists, passing them off to waiting slaves. Natharie sat on the floor with the others as she was told. Bowls of rice were brought, and she ate, in the light of the single, flickering lamp, never minding the strange flavors. Slaves scurried about laying out pillows on the floor. Mistress Usha pointed to a corner and glowered at Natharie. Meekly, still trembling, Natharie crept over to her allotted space, and lay down. She closed her eyes once more. This time, sleep came to her, and Natharie received it with a profound gratitude.

*T*he sun was well behind the hills by the time the horns blew their final warning to whatever demons lingered outside the palace walls and the priests made their final obeisances to the Mothers. The bearing poles were slotted into place on Chandra's throne, and the emperor was carried back inside the palace. Samudra shifted his weight as much as he dared.

What had Divakesh been trying to do? Samudra's head still swam with the shock of it. The priest had threatened the life of a member of a royal house. He had shed her blood in the middle of the purification ritual. Anger burned in Samudra like the flames at the feet of the Queen of Heaven. Anger polluted each thought, and the presence of all seven Mothers could not wash it away.

Chandra will give the orders, he told himself during the endless ceremony and sacrifice. *This is a perversion of the ceremony. Divakesh will lose his head.*

Now that the emperor had departed, the purified tribute procession marched itself into the depths of the palace where the various components would be distributed to the appropriate ministers and stewards. Samudra glanced down at Hamsa. Her face was bland but he saw anguish in her eyes. She too had thought Divakesh might kill Natharie.

Now Chandra must understand what Divakesh truly is.

Samudra's turn to depart had arrived. He got to his feet and walked to the golden door of emperors. The guards knelt and raised their spears in salute, and he and Hamsa crossed into the palace.

Beyond the door waited the robing chamber, a place of carved ivory, polished stone, and open chests. The servants moved around him at a stately pace, handing each other the various pieces of the formal regalia—the crown, the robe, the rings—to be bowed and prayed over, polished, wrapped in linen, and stowed away. As he knelt in obeisance, Samudra had an odd image of an outer shell being put into storage and his brother being left behind. There was no emperor here. The emperor was in boxes.

Chandra himself lounged perfectly at ease, a robe of purple silk wrapped loosely about him. Chandra had always enjoyed the princely life and partook deeply of its luxuries. He had not yet begun to turn fat. He was too fond of wrestling and riding for that. But a sly and lazy look could creep into his eyes, a covetous look that assessed all before him, whatever their place or birth, as if they were gems to be set into rings for his arms. Beside Chandra, of course, was Yamuna. Yamuna was always beside Chandra, as Hamsa was always beside Samudra. Always waiting, always working for the life and health of the one to whom he had been bound. Yamuna was to Chandra tutor, confidant, protector, just as Hamsa was to Samudra.

The next thing Samudra saw was that Divakesh stood there by the wall, as solid and unperturbed as any of the statues around him.

Samudra's mind slammed shut. He knelt in obeisance, trying to collect his wits. Why had Chandra not already pronounced judgment on Divakesh's outrageous action?

"No more of that, Brother," announced Chandra, laughing at the formality of Samudra's obeisance. "The ceremony is over. Give me your embrace and let me look on you!"

Samudra stood on knees suddenly weak as water. Over his brother's head, he saw the satisfied glitter in Divakesh's arrogant gaze. Samudra walked over to Chandra, and embraced him. At the hard warmth of his brother's touch, Samudra found himself looking at Chandra closely to see what the past year had brought. He wanted to find some understanding of what made the emperor completely disregard the enormity of what the priest had done before the altar.

"You look good!" cried Chandra, pushing him back to arm's length and gripping his wrist. "Strong. Your time among the barbarians and their women has agreed with you."

Samudra had to call on all his discipline not to throw his shorter, slighter brother to the ground as he had done so many times when they were still boys. As he had thrown Pravan. "Thank you, Ch . . . Majesty." *You address your emperor,* Samudra reminded himself fiercely. His emperor, and to one side Divakesh, the sword and the voice of the Mothers, with his great arms that could dispatch a bull with a single blow if the ceremony called for it, but with hands of such skill and delicacy he could draw a lotus of a dozen colored sands. Divakesh who had the power to keep Samudra out of the palace with a word and to shed royal blood so that everyone saw, and no one saw.

"So." Chandra stretched himself out on his pile of gold and silken pillows and held out one hand. A servant put a goblet into it. At a gesture, another was brought to Samudra. His throat was dry as dust, but he could not drink. Chandra, however, sipped from his cup and gave a loud sigh of enjoyment. "What news do you bring me from the outside world?"

This could not be what it seemed. His brother could not simply be ignoring Pravan's disaster and Divakesh's . . . he had no name for what Divakesh had done. Samudra swallowed and tried to find some words that would not destroy decorum. "It is rather the news brought to me that I would speak of."

Chandra sighed and rolled his eyes toward Yamuna and Divakesh as if to say, "I told you." "You heard about the Huni? It is no matter." He took another swallow from his goblet. "Pravan will get them in the spring."

At that, the fragile dam holding back Samudra's fury burst. "Pravan is a coward and a fool who squanders the lives of his men in pointless displays!" he roared. "He could not find his ass with both hands if he had a slave to guide him!" He took a step forward, hands flexing at his sides, inches from his sword, forgetting everything, thinking only of the Huni, of dead men and the treaty that had been destroyed. "You sent me chasing across the country after gold and you let Pravan destroy our treaty with Lohit and then fall down before the Huni. All so Divakesh"—he stabbed his finger toward the priest—"could make some blasphemous example of King Pairoj's rule!"

"Brother, guard yourself more closely here," said Chandra with sudden sternness.

Samudra felt his blood surging in his head and in his hands. Wasted. Wasted for nothing, lives and time, and chances . . . and this priest stood smugly beside his brother, telling him the Mothers knew what idiocies . . . "Ch . . . My emperor, why? Pravan could have brought the tribute. The Sindhu princess did not have to be threatened. Why . . ."

"Is it for a soldier to question his officers?" replied Chandra, the sly, lazy smile creeping from his mouth to his long eyes again. "Or is it to obey?"

Control yourself. Samudra was beyond that sort of control now. He spread his hands to his brother. "My emperor, who has told you I need to be put in my place? And at the cost of such dishonor?"

Something flickered behind his brother's eyes and to Samudra's shock, he found he could not tell what it was. A year, he thought again. It should not have meant that much. He had been gone for long periods before. He was a soldier. But this time it was because someone had been pouring honeyed suspicion into his brother's, his emperor's ears.

Who? Who could come between them like this? Divakesh had been with him, Samudra. Who else was there to speak such subtle lies to Chandra that he would come to believe them as truths?

Memory overtook him: of sitting on the stone steps on Liyoni's banks. Beside them their father's funeral pyre was a bed of coals and the wind wafted the heat over his skin.

"It will come, you know," Chandra had said as they sat side by side. "There are those who will try to use you to bring me down. They will say, Samudra, he is the soldier, he is the better man. Let us break the dance and set him on the throne."

"They will fail," Samudra had answered. "You are my lord and my brother. Nothing under Heaven can change that."

He had thought Chandra would embrace him then, but Chandra held his place. Only his mouth moved, shaping words Samudra could not hear.

At the time, he had thought his brother was saying "Thank you," but now with the strange light shining behind Chandra's eyes, Samudra was no longer certain.

"Why should anyone speak against you, Brother?" asked Chandra, his voice suddenly as sharp as his eyes were indolent. "Is there something I should know?"

There was a special awareness that could descend on a man during battle, the extra sense that allowed his skin to feel the blow that had not yet fallen, and move the body so that it breezed harmlessly past. Samudra felt that same awareness come over him now. He felt the coming blow in Divakesh's gaze, felt weapons hidden in the room, but he could not tell where. It could not be that Chandra held these weapons. Chandra was being used as a weapon.

Samudra understood then, with absolute finality, that Chandra had known what would happen when he sent Pravan north. He had let it happen. It might be that he even knew what would be done to Natharie at the altar.

If the emperor saw any of this new understanding in his brother's stricken face, he gave no sign. He only leaned back and turned to Divakesh.

"I had a dream last night," he said, sipping once more from his goblet.

Divakesh folded his great hands in an attitude of reverent prayer. "Speak your dream, Sovereign. I will tell you what it means."

"I stood on my balcony. In my hands were the signs of kingship. At my feet burned the sacred fire. Below me, I saw a woman. She was dressed in rags and tatters and her face was grey with ashes, but her body was ripe and full. She called to me, saying 'Chandra, Son of the Pearl Throne, Father of Hastinapura, come out! Chandra, look on me with your own two eyes!' "

The priest watched his emperor keenly. "And what did you do, Sovereign?"

Chandra shrugged. "I did nothing. I awoke."

Divakesh shook his head heavily, and Samudra thought he looked relieved. "Oh, my sovereign, that was an evil dream. The woman was a devil, the temptation of sin calling you to forswear your purity and pollute yourself by mixing with the outcasts and the blooded. The ashes were to disguise the marks of her face, and the skirts hid her feet, which you would have otherwise seen were backward, as a witch's are."

For the first time since Samudra entered, Chandra turned to his bound sorcerer. "Is that also what you say, Yamuna?"

Yamuna appeared to consider this for a long moment. "Tell me, Sovereign." Yamuna's words always sounded carefully measured, as if he thought he might be charged for their weight. "What did this woman carry with her? Besides the ashes, what decoration did she wear?"

"Nothing, save a white flower at her throat."

The corner of the sorcerer's mouth twitched. Behind him, Samudra heard the rustle of cloth as Hamsa shifted her weight. Yamuna lifted his black eyes to regard Divakesh. "Priest, do you still say this was a devil?"

"Of course." Samudra would have sworn Divakesh's

shock was genuine. "She called our sovereign to leave the heart of the dance, to forsake purity."

"Of course." Yamuna nodded. "Sovereign, what can I add to what the voice of the Mothers has told us? It cannot be other than the high priest says."

Hamsa sucked in a sharp breath, and Yamuna's gaze turned to her at once.

"Have you something to say, Hamsa?"

All attention fell against Hamsa. Her hands gripped her walking stick, and Samudra watched her wither before those other, stronger eyes. He knew Hamsa's strength, he knew her sound counsel, but he also knew she had never truly become used to court life. She was most herself, as he was, when they traveled beyond the palace walls, and even then only when she could walk rather than be forced to ride horseback. She was a creature of the out-of-doors and the wilderness. Intricacies and intrigues tired her, and, if Samudra was honest, they frightened her.

"Yes," said Divakesh, his relish of the word undisguised. "If the first prince's bound sorcerer has an insight, let her speak."

Samudra found himself wishing with all his heart that Hamsa would do so, but he knew anything he might say would only make matters worse.

Hamsa bowed her head. "No. I have nothing to say."

At which, Yamuna smiled, and his smile was sharp, and Samudra felt the hidden weapons about him again.

Chandra turned back to Samudra. "You will dine with me, Brother?" he inquired. "We must celebrate the success of the sacrifice."

Samudra felt another numbing moment of pure disbelief. The Huni were digging in on the northern border, his treaty with one of their father's protectorates was shattered, a royal woman was threatened and humiliated in public. He, Samudra, had been all but accused of harboring traitorous designs, and the emperor of Hastinapura was having dreams of devils, and Chandra had dismissed it all in an instant. No, he had forgotten about it.

Samudra managed to fold his hands and bow his head, as was proper. "With permission, my emperor, I wish to go visit our mother before she retires."

"And perhaps visit some of that pretty tribute you brought me?" Chandra laughed heartily. "A man of your martial temperament can only restrain himself so long, Brother. Go, go!" He gestured expansively with his goblet. "Take whichever of the newcomers you want. Bandhura will surely know which will best suit a man such as yourself!"

Samudra bowed his head to the floor to make his obeisance and backed away, leaving the robing room to the sound of his brother's laughter, and leaving his brother to Divakesh.

Once in the hall, he could only stand and stare at the door that the servants discreetly closed behind them. He heard the scurrying feet as others hurried ahead, to warn the various chamber attendants that the first prince would soon be coming their way. He heard Hamsa's harsh breathing beside him. He heard his own blood roaring in his ears.

"What is it you did not say?" he asked her quietly.

She hesitated nervously. Sometimes, Samudra forgot that she was older than him by almost fifteen years, and wanted to shake her like a little sister. "That was no devil the emperor saw," she murmured at last.

"What was it?"

Hamsa looked up at him, as if surprised he did not already know. "The white flower. No demon can wear a living thing, even in a dream. If that white flower was a lotus . . . the emperor saw the Queen of Heaven."

Mother Jalaja? Divakesh lied about the appearance of Mother Jalaja? No. He would not. Divakesh was nothing if not completely dedicated to the worship of the Queen of Heaven. Hamsa must be mistaken. If the Queen of Heaven had appeared to the emperor, Divakesh would be on his knees at once. Samudra found he was opening his mouth to say so, but he looked at Hamsa's face and saw how stricken she was. She knew full well she had just accused the high priest of ignorance, at the very best. At worst, what he had done was blasphemy.

And she did it outside the room where Divakesh waited on the emperor.

Samudra turned and strode down the corridor, his sandals slapping loudly against the shining marble floor. Around the corner there waited a small contemplation room, lined with alabaster vases of green ferns and decorated with bright murals depicting the deeds of the Mothers and some of the lesser gods. He turned to face Hamsa, and the doorway.

"Did Yamuna know?" he asked in the lightest of whispers. "That who my brother dreamed of was Mother Jalaja?"

For the first time, Hamsa's mouth hardened with anger. "Assuredly."

"Then why did he not say so?"

Hamsa snorted, an unusual sound for her. "You must ask? Yamuna hates Lord Divakesh."

Samudra felt himself frowning. "But then why not expose his . . . mistake? It would embarrass him before the emperor."

For this, Hamsa had no answer. Her gaze fell and her hands twisted her walking stick.

"Is it possible Divakesh could have honestly missed the sign?"

Hamsa shook her head. "I think he chooses to close his eyes."

The feeling of weapons waiting, of hidden depths in his home, closed around Samudra again. "They would ignore the call of the Queen of Heaven for fear and jealousy. That my brother is so served . . ." he murmured.

Hamsa lifted her eyes. "Yet you do not speak to him. Why not?"

Samudra rubbed his forehead. "Perhaps I too am afraid, Hamsa."

"Perhaps?" she repeated.

Samudra sighed and folded his arms, his attention flickering to the hallway. He heard nothing, felt no warning instincts wake his mind. "Now, my sorceress, you will tell me what it is I fear."

Hamsa hesitated another moment, but she did answer. "You fear having to believe the worst of your brother," she whispered. "You fear that if you speak to him any further of these things he has dismissed, he will leave you no choice."

He wanted to deny it. It could not be true. He was a soldier and he was afraid of nothing. At the same time, he wanted to take his sword and cut that fear out of himself. "Yes."

Hamsa bowed her head, humble before the bitterness she heard in that one word.

Samudra rubbed his own head. He ached. He did not want to think any of the thoughts that thronged in his mind. He did not want to speak anymore of what had happened that day. He wanted it to be done, to be gone, to be some mistake. "Hamsa, you must be as exhausted as I am. Go get some rest."

"And what will you do, my prince?"

Samudra found he could not bear to stand still a moment longer and brushed past her. "I will do as I said. I will go visit my mother."

And mother will send for her private clerk, Tasham, and I will finally finally know what has happened in my absence.

𝒟espite the turmoil within him, it felt good to walk the palace corridors again, good to be surrounded by the rhythms at the heart of Jalaja's dance, to see the cool wood, the bright gold, the polished stonework and carvings telling again and again the history of Hastinapura and the Seven Mothers. It was here Samudra felt most deeply his part and place. Here he was most whole, even more than on the field of battle, for in this place lay all that the battles were fought for.

It was said that was part of the magic of the palace. The sorcerers who oversaw its building had worked bindings of duty and place into its patterns so that those who ruled the Mothers' land would follow the Mothers' words. Samudra found himself very much wishing that were true. Such mighty magics would help soothe his anger, and restore him, and more importantly Chandra, to the right path. He needed that belief very much now.

The Palace of the Pearl Throne was a city beneath its vaulted roofs and ivory beams. There were those who never entered the world outside its walls. Indeed, some were forbidden to leave, lest the pollution of the outer world render them unfit for their office. The edifice was constructed as a series of nine rings, one inside the other, each rising higher until all culminated at the Throne's chamber.

Each ring had its own function and patterns to which it must adhere. The seventh ring of the palace was the *zuddhanta,* the women's quarters. The name was misleading, as many folk other than women dwelt there. Of course, Chandra had his suite of concubines, as their father had. These, for the most part, served out their time and went on their way to be married or to set up their houses, seldom leaving a mark or impression on the memory. The seventh ring was also, however, the place of the unmarried princes and princesses, Samudra and Chandra's half-brothers and sisters, their nieces, nephews, and cousins, and of the wives and families of highly placed servants to the Throne. It was a city within a city, and those who lived there had their own name for it. They called it the small domain.

The small domain was the place where Samudra had grown up. Then it had been in the strict care of his grandmother. As was the custom, his own mother, Queen Prishi, had taken charge only when her son Chandra became emperor. All the palace was his home, but it was these particular halls he had raced up and down as a child, these balconies he had looked out of to see the pageants and processions of the city. It was here he'd learned all the princely arts save that of war, and it was here he returned when that training and service was done. Memories flocked about him as he walked the passages between the princess's suites—of riding and shooting with his father, endless mischief with his brother and other siblings, the procession of tutors who struggled courageously to din something into his head that didn't have to do with weapons, chariots, or horses. The time his father informed him that if he didn't want to become a proper prince, he could be a slave in the wheat fields, and actually sent him down to the fields for a month to labor beside the sun-cured men who laughed at his soft hands and weak arms. After that, languages and poetry became much more bearable.

Chandra, on the other hand, had garnered much praise from his tutors by the expeditious method of discovering which ones he could bribe and what their price might be. Samudra had known, but had never told their father because his brother had wept and made Samudra swear not to.

Chandra understood people well. His langour and lack of restraint when pursuing pleasure and luxury made this easy to forget.

The center of the small domain was the queen's viewing chambers, a complex network of open rooms separated by beautifully carved arches. Each space was designed with care for its ordained purpose—for sewing, for sitting, for singing and performance, for dining. As first prince, Samudra had his private suite off these chambers, and as he could not appear before his mother dusty and unkempt after a day spent fuming and sweating at the gates, he went first to his own rooms. His personal attendants, Bori and Amandad, had, as usual, prepared all things for him. The bath was filled. Fresh robes of burgundy silk, rings of gold and garnets, and soft slippers were waiting once he was dried. They also laid out a light supper of bread, spiced chickpeas, and honeyed dumplings.

Feeling once more the proper prince rather than the rough soldier, Samudra returned to the viewing chambers. It was his mother's habit to sit in the "garden" and watch moonrise. Occupying a huge terrace, this inner garden was as carefully and lovingly tended as those outside. Tiny birds nested in its perfect trees, cats basked in the sun, and water trickled from half a dozen fountains. The whole chamber smelled of greenery, oranges, incense, and perfume. An ivory lattice-work enclosed the whole of it and was cunningly carved so that light could enter, but no one, even had they been able to climb to this height, could see through from the outside.

As he entered the dim garden, he saw a cluster of ladies sitting amid the miniature trees and his spirits lifted. Queen Prishi, his mother, his father's first wife, was a wise, quick-witted, strong woman. She had guided him through the morass of court intrigues all his life and ruled the small do-main with a firm hand. She would know what he should do.

"Brother of my heart! How glad I am to see you!"

At the sound of that voice, Samudra's hopes toppled yet again. It was not his mother who sat on the carved stone bench, but Bandhura, his brother's beautiful wife, with her flock of ladies at her feet. As he approached, she smiled up at Samudra with all seeming joy.

Samudra remembered to fold his hands and kneel with proper respect, even as the ladies made obeisance to him. "I salute the first of all queens."

Bandhura stood, took his hands, and raised him up. "Come, let me kiss you." She suited actions to words, kiss-ing his brow although she had to stand on her toes to reach it. "It is good to have you home again." She resettled herself on her bench and with a gesture had a servant come forward with a cup of wine. In the blend of silver moonlight and golden lamplight, he could see her appearance was perfect in every aspect, as it always was. Yet, Samudra had learned to watch her eyes closely. There, he could sometimes see the hard glitter betraying the flint heart within the silken queen.

He saw it there now. He also saw that neither his two cousins nor his nearest half-sister sat among Bandhura's ladies as they had when he left.

"I had not thought to see you this evening," Bandhura was saying. "You seemed so tired during the ceremony."

We will not speak of my outburst, of course. Nor of Divakesh's . . . demonstration. But tired. Yes, I was tired, and I am. "I have come to see my mother."

Her hand went to her mouth, a little gesture of deprecation for not thinking of something so obvious. "Of course." Then, she dropped her eyes, hesitating. "But, this is so . . . Brother, I must tell you . . ."

Samudra waited until he could keep the impatience from his voice. Bandhura's artifices wore on him, and worried him. "What is it?"

"Your mother, our mother, has not been well of late." She murmured as if speaking of a subject that might be thought immodest. "I fear the years weigh on her. She is . . . easily tired these days."

A fresh bolt of fear shot through Samudra. "She is ill?"

"The physicians say not." There was no confidence in the statement. "She has already taken to her bed for the night."

Samudra bowed hastily to Bandhura. "I will ask her ladies if she sleeps yet. If not, perhaps she will still see me, briefly."

Bandhura frowned. "If you think it wise, Brother . . ."

No, but I will do it anyway. He bowed once more and left Bandhura to whatever thoughts lurked behind her perfect face.

The emperor's mother, as mistress of the small domain, had her private suite of rooms at its center, which was symbolically the center of life in the palace. Her eunuch guards knelt in silence for Samudra as he slipped through the doorway, treading carefully so as not to break the silence of the shadowed chamber.

Nonetheless, a small, round woman rose up at his entry. Her greying hair was pulled back in a simple knot. Samudra

smiled. Here at last was a welcome face. "Damman. It is
good to see you. Does my mother sleep?"

The waiting woman gave him the salute of trust. This was
the same woman who when he was a child had more than
once had grabbed him by the ear and marched him to his
bath, or his bed. "Not yet, my prince, but it would not matter.
She said most clearly that if you came, you were to be allowed entry." Her eyes darted to his face for one bold instant
before she turned away. "I am glad you are home," she whispered, and Samudra's fear grew colder.

Damman led him through the open sitting rooms into the
bedchamber. Only one of the hanging lamps still burned. In
the dim light, Samudra saw his mother propped up on her
pillows, her head lolling back on the fine linen sheets she
had always preferred, and her eyes closed. Her normally
busy hands lay on the gauzy coverlet, thin and still.

His heart beating hard, Samudra knelt beside her.
"Mother?"

Slowly, Mother turned her face to him, and to his horror
he saw it was blighted by dark scabs where the skin had
peeled back. "My son," she whispered hoarsly. "I have
missed you."

She moved her hand toward Samudra and he took it gently. More scabs roughened her palm. The room was close
and warm, but her bony fingers were cold. "How are you?"

One corner of her mouth turned up in a half-smile. "I am
tired, as I'm sure the daughter of my heart has told you."

"You do too much." He made the statement on reflex. He
could think of nothing else to say, seeing her there so weak
and listless.

"Bandhura agrees with you. She has been so good as to
take many of my burdens onto herself so that I might rest
more completely." The words were mild, even grateful. Only
one who knew her very well would hear their edge.

"Surely that is what you need."

"Surely." She spoke to the ceiling now. "As you were

needed to supervise the collection of tribute. Asking you to lead the expedition to repel the Huni would have been too grave a strain as you are still recovering from the death of your father four years ago." She knew then. Sick and weak, maybe dying, she knew what had been done.

No! he wanted to shout. *No, I do not want this. I want my home, I want to lead my men and follow my brother and the Mothers.* Bitter shame filled him, but those selfish desires did not abate. "Mother . . . where are Ila and Tustia? And Saryu?"

"Ila was sent to Lady Teshama to be her head waiting woman. It was Bandhura's judgment that she should have an opportunity to make a brilliant marriage in that province. Tustia is herself married now, to the lord of Nagishi Province."

"So quickly?" Tustia was Samudra's half-sister, his closest in age and the one he cherished most.

Mother shrugged a little and pulled her hand from his to wave it upward, toward the ninth ring, where the Pearl Throne waited. "The emperor was most anxious to see to the change of administration there. The former Lord Nagishi was found to be diverting tax monies for his own use."

"But . . ." Samudra shook his head. "Tustia was betrothed to Tasham." Tasham had soldiered at Samudra's side when they were both still youths, but he had never developed a taste for war and instead settled happily into a counselor's robes. For all Samudra taunted him about a life of endless numbers and dry words, he had to admit Tasham did his work well, and cheerfully, and could be trusted utterly. That was why he had made Tasham his eyes and ears in the small domain while he was gone.

"Tasham is dead," said his mother flatly.

"What!" Although he knelt, Samudra felt his legs tremble. Samudra had always thought that when he finally married, he would take Tasham to his estate with him. That soldiers should be dead was one thing, but Tasham was only a bureaucrat, and Samudra's own age . . .

Is there anything here left to me? Anything at all?

"An accident. He was thrown from his horse and drowned in the river." Her hand moved to touch his fingertips. "I am sorry I was the one to tell you."

For a long moment, Samudra could not speak. It might have been an accident. Such things happened. The Mothers knew Tasham was no horseman but Samudra could not make himself believe that.

He leaned close to his mother and whispered, "How bad has it become, Mother?"

"You do not yet know?" His mother's cold fingers brushed his cheek. "Oh, my son, your wits have not yet returned from your travels."

Samudra looked deep into his mother's weary eyes. Then, behind them came a thump and a shuffle and Damman's voice saying "Oh, pardon, pardon, First of All Queens!"

Samudra sat bolt upright.

"Clumsy . . . !" cried Bandhura, and this was followed by a second thump that was surely Damman dropping hard and fast to her knees before the queen's wrath.

"Bandhura?" called Queen Prishi plaintively.

"Mother of my heart?" Bandhura pushed through the draperies that separated the bed alcove from the chamber beyond.

"Daughter." Queen Prishi made an effort to push herself up on her pillows, and failed, but still she smiled in open welcome. "Come, sit and stay. I was only catching my son up on the little news of our doings here."

"You should not tax yourself." Bandhura hurried to her mother-in-law's side. "I will have tea brought to you."

Queen Prishi patted her hand. "So thoughtful. Never have I been better cared for," she added to Samudra.

Samudra found he was standing, but he could not remember having moved. "What is wrong, brother of my heart?" asked Bandhura.

Samudra swallowed, swallowed outrage, swallowed impotence and fear. "Nothing, Sister, but the emperor invited me to dine with him, and I believe I must accept."

She smiled so sweetly he knew she was satisfied her mission had been accomplished. She had cut off what conversation he might have had with his mother. "Of course. I will attend our mother here while you wait upon our lord."

Samudra's mother looked up at him, her face shrewd despite all. "Was there something else you wished to say to me, my son?"

Samudra licked his lips, and wondered if he dared. *Yes. Yes I do. I must.* "Yes . . . the princess of Sindhu, Natharie, has come to guest with us. It was my hope you would grant her audience, let her know she is welcome here. She finds us very strange and is, I think, afraid." He looked straight into Bandhura's eyes as he spoke, and saw again the glitter of flint. *There, I will not speak either of what was done today. But I will wonder, sister of my heart, what you think of it, and of my lord Divakesh. I will wonder too why you do not care to let me have private conversation with my mother.*

"Of course, my son," said Queen Prishi. "If you wish it."

"Thank you, Mother." Samudra kissed her brow and tried not to feel how slack and dry her skin was. It was the skin of a very old woman. Then, he bowed to Bandhura. "I salute the first of all queens."

Before she could utter whatever pretty platitude she had reserved for this occasion, Samudra left. However, instead of turning toward the corridors and staircases that would take him to the dining hall and his brother, he found himself drifting toward the terrace garden again. Bandhura's ladies had dispersed and he was alone. He breathed in its clean, green scents, taking himself into the shadows to hide the thoughts he could not keep from his face.

When their father died, Samudra believed his brother truly mourned. Chandra stayed sleepless beside the pyre for three nights, tending the fire until it was pure enough and hot enough to receive the emperor's body. As the flames enfolded their father, Samudra saw tears falling down his brother's cheeks. During the ceremonies and sacrifices that elevated him officially to the rank their father had held, Samudra thought he looked nothing so much as frightened.

Oddly, it was that fear that had given Samudra hope that Chandra understood how serious his life had become. He prayed that the Mothers would open Chandra's narrow, frivolous heart and let the welfare of Hastinapura enter into his thoughts.

But that was four years ago, and Chandra's dread seemed to have been dispersed as surely as their father's ashes, cast into the sacred river and carried away. Chandra found the rank of emperor delightful, and quickly had decided that the empire existed to provide him with the pleasures he sought.

That was not so bad, Samudra had told himself. Hastinapura had survived sybaritic emperors before, and thrived. It would do so again. He, Samudra, could protect the empire, and there were many men of wisdom among the nobles and the high clerks. Behind them all, Queen Prishi oversaw the small domain, where the highest of the bureaucrats were trained, and where so many alliances were forged by marriage and by other, more subtle contacts and promises. Her wisdom would allow the skilled, the subtle, and the careful to rise.

His brother was who he was. Samudra had loved him and protected him. He could do so now.

But it was now clear that Chandra was being sheltered from far more than the consequences of his debaucheries. Divakesh, Bandhura, and Pravan were quickly taking hold of threads once held by better hands, and Chandra did not seem to notice.

These were not thoughts that came easily to Samudra. Chandra was the elder brother. It was his place to rule. The Mothers decreed it so. The Throne was his and he was bound by the word of the gods and the dance of the Queen of Heaven. It was Samudra's place to support his rule, to guard the land of the Mothers and protect the sacred throne with his sword.

Hamsa's question came back to him as he stared out through the lattice, watching the white half-moon where it hung in the black sky.

What will you do, my prince?

"I will go to dine with my brother," he sighed to the night. "And tomorrow I will go hear what Makul has to tell me."

And then? he asked himself.

"And then I pray the Mothers will show me what I must do next."

Chapter Six

There is Earth. There is Heaven. There is a place in between where shadows and spirit powers dwell, where the gods go to look down on Earth and see better than they can from the many heavens. It is a shifting place, a place of many truths and many lies.

In this Land of Death and Spirit, there is an ocean. The waves churn and crash, constantly changing and never ceasing.

At the edge of this ocean stood a man.

He was a small man, with slender hands and a face that was lined and patient. The wind whipped at his simple saffron robes. He held an unadorned walking stick in one hand. He faced the ocean, watching the waters as the waves rushed onto the beach at his feet and pulled back, leaving behind only the gleaming sand. He said nothing, he only waited.

Then a great rumble began. The wind blew hard and cold, whipping his robes hard. Then it was as if the horizon itself had begun to heave up and come forward. A great wave, a wall of green water as tall as the cliffs and as broad as the ocean itself, bore down upon the shore.

The man did not move.

The wave broke and the waters poured down. There was no thunder to compare with the sound. An ocean's worth of water rolled across the beach, shaking the stone cliffs, shoving boulders up one against another until the stones ground together and broke and were dragged back into the waters by the current as the ocean drew the wave back into itself, leaving behind mountains of sand and sea grass and shattered trees.

On the beach, new tide pools rippled and glimmered. The cliffs seemed to sag a little from their battering. Stones the size of houses had been buried in the sides of the beleaguered dunes.

And there was the man, drenched head to foot, loosely holding his walking stick, and waiting.

"*U*p! Up!"

The harsh voice jerked Natharie from a series of confusing and disturbing dreams. The cut she had been given yesterday by Divakesh was a thin line of fire at her throat. She looked up from her nest of plain blankets to see the grey woman standing over her. The room was still dark, except for the light of one lantern a servant girl carried.

"The queens are asking for you, Princess Sacrifice," announced Mistress Usha. "We must make you presentable."

The woman's critical eyes raked her up and down; then she turned to the tiny flock of attendants behind her. "She'll need a bath first," she said. "Get the hairdresser, the perfumer, and the draper to the bath." She glowered down at Natharie again. "Do you understand, girl? Up!"

Natharie just stared, her mind too blurred by sleep and alien surroundings to feel anger as she scrambled to her feet.

She was taller than the other woman by at least a head, but the grey woman carried herself as one who knew she was mistress of all around her, and Natharie felt gawky standing so tall in front of her. At their feet, girls and women stirred, pulled from sleep by the barking voice and yellow light. Some lifted their heads; some turned away, burrowing under their coverings, trying to find sleep again, or just hoping not to be noticed.

Remember yourself. Natharie straightened her shoulders, which had begun to hunch together. "Who are you?" The Hastinapuran words felt strange and slippery, but she would show here and now that she was not completely ignorant.

That stopped the woman. A small smile twisted her lips. "I am Usha *jai* Ruverishi Harshaela." She spoke the syllables of her name slowly, making sure Natharie heard each one. "I am steward of the *zuddhanta*. It is my duty to tell you that whoever you were outside the gates, whoever you called master, you now belong to the Mothers, the queens, and me." The emphasis on the last word made it easy to tell which of these she thought was the most important. "And you are slow, and a barbarian and you need a bath, and you will come with me unless you want me to tell the first of all queens you are also disobedient."

For a heartbeat, that was exactly what Natharie wanted. She wanted to sit down right here and make whoever followed Steward Usha drag her out. Why shouldn't she? What had she to lose?

She caught a glimpse of motion behind the steward. A girl had raised her head. She looked at Natharie, and shook her head quickly, as if she knew what Natharie thought and was warning her against it.

The heartbeat gave Natharie a moment to think. What had she to lose, but what had she to gain? To let them see her heart, her fear and her anger, this would give her nothing, not yet.

Natharie closed mouth and heart. She dropped her gaze,

folded her hands, and bowed over them. Usha grunted and turned on her heel. Her sandals sparkled in the lamplight, gold or silver, Natharie couldn't tell, as she followed. She did see the same girl who'd given her the warning. She'd seen this girl on the docks when they were all waiting to be shunted into the procession. She also was a piece of tribute, but she clearly felt neither remorse nor fear at this. Even now, this bold other smiled slyly at Natharie as she passed.

Natharie, however, was not the only one who made note of her. "You!" snapped Usha. "Since you're so eager, you can come get this one get presentable. She clearly needs help."

The girl bowed quickly, pressing her head to the floor, and scrambled up at once to join the procession that followed the steward. Natharie could have sworn her smile only grew broader as she did.

Beyond the door, the world was filled with sunlight. Breezes stirred the sultry air, enlivened with the scents of greenery, citrus, and incense and the sounds of voices. Dozens of voices. Natharie blinked and, in her first astonished glimpse of the women's quarters, barely remembered to keep her mouth closed.

"What is it like . . . inside?" she had asked her father one night when they sat together, watching the stars.

"In the women's ring?" He shook his head. "I do not know. I have never been permitted entry."

Despite her best efforts at stillness, Natharie twisted her hands together in her lap. "So, they are allowed in then . . . men other than the emperor?"

Father nodded. "His high council and advisors, other members of the family, his trusted favorites. They are permitted entry."

And surely when your daughter is there, you will be permitted entry. Natharie thought this, but never said it, because she could not bear to hear her father say "I do not know" yet again.

Now she saw this secluded place with her own eyes, and it was none of what she expected. It was larger than she had ever imagined. She had not been able to shake the image her brothers had spun, of a single chamber filled with half-naked women lounging about, eating artfully sliced melons and cucumbers. What she saw instead were small children shrieking with laughter as they played an elaborate game of tag between the plants and the pillars. Grandmothers alternately petted and scolded from their seats beneath fans of palm fronds and peacock feathers that were waved by clean and well-fed slaves. Two beardless men of middle years stood in a patch of sunlight, talking animatedly. A cluster of girls in blue and white dresses bent over their needlework under the supervision of a dried-up, bony-looking woman, who said something that was answered, to Natharie's surprise, with a fleeting round of giggles. On the other side of the court, a group of boys was gathered around a plain-robed tutor who peered at the work on their tablets of wood-framed clay. Here, he administered a word that might have been praise. There, he cuffed a boy on the ear.

She didn't know what surprised her more, the sight of all these busy activities, or the realization that the sun was well up and the place already bustling. She and the others had clearly been allowed to sleep late.

The windows were broad and numerous, but were not open. All were screened by elaborate, lacelike ivory carvings that allowed glimpses of the gardens below.

The Mothers were everywhere. They watched from the walls. They danced across the beams overhead. They stood among the plants and kept watch over the smallest growing thing.

And they watched her with their eyes of stone and paint. They watched her closely.

You are in our place now, little girl, their eyes told her. *Remember the blood you spilled to us yesterday. You too will join our dance.*

Natharie shivered and bowed her head so she didn't have to see anything but Usha's silver sandals as she was led from chamber to chamber, and at last, with a breath of cool, fresh air on her face, to the bath.

The bath was set against the mountain that backed the palace, and, Natharie now realized, formed part of its wall and foundation. It was a great stone pool on a sheltered terrace nestled into the living stone itself. A waterfall ran down the cliff face, constantly refilling the basin and watering the ferns that sprawled out of nooks in the living rock. There was yet another statue on the cliff where the waters ran down. The woman held up a bowl into which the waters fell and then spilled out the side.

Like the rest of the quarters, the bath was already busy. Several women washed themselves in the fresh water, wringing out their hair; servants, their skirts tied up around their waists, scrubbed their mistress's backs and limbs. More women and girls were busy around the pool. Nothing seemed to be done for its own sake, everything a lesson. A woman braiding and dressing a lady's hair had a girl beside her to hand her the brushes and absorb the art. Another woman, presiding over cosmetics, lectured a trio of young apprentices on the preparation and quality of ingredients. A skinny, white-haired, hard-eyed woman presided over all, rapping out sharp orders to both the girls and their tutors.

"Well?" Usha glared at Natharie. "I assume in Sindhu you know what to do with clean water."

Which, despite her resolve, was more than Natharie could stand. "We do," she replied calmly. "I was only taken aback to find that the Hastinapurans do too."

She braced for the blow she saw in the steward's eyes, but the woman only reached out with one finger, and ran its tip along the line of Natharie's cut, making her shiver with anger and fear. "One, Princess Sacrifice, and that is all I will allow. Get yourself clean." She marched away toward the door and was immediately joined by the white-haired woman, who started gesticulating so broadly her multiple bracelets slid up and down her skinny arms.

"That's Sevvi, mistress of the ewer. She has charge of the bath."

Natharie spun. Behind her was the young woman summoned to follow her. To Natharie's embarrassment, she had forgotten the other was there.

Before Natharie could form a question, the other girl pointed to the woman leaning over her pots of creams and powders. "Jula, the cosmetics mistress. Valandi, the perfumer, is with the first of all queens right now."

"I . . . how . . . ?" Natharie stammered.

In return, she got another of the girl's broad smiles. "Start learning quickly, Princess Sacrifice," she whispered. "It's the only way you won't get trampled and sold off in such a place."

"How . . ." Natharie tried again.

"I learned at my mother's knee. I'm Ekkadi," she added. She gazed around her, and Natharie saw a strange mix of envy and satisfaction in her quick eyes. "I didn't grow up anywhere so grand, but it's pretty much the same. My mother sacrificed eight sheep to Jalaja to get me here."

"Why are you doing this?"

This finally made Ekkadi stare. "Because you need a maid and I need a mistress, or *I'll* be trampled on and sold off. Come on, let's get you washed. It doesn't do to let queens grow impatient. Even you must know that much."

Her mind's eye showed Natharie her mother sitting straight and still in the audience chamber, her brow furrowing and her jaw tightening. Yes, that much she did know.

She made no further protest as Ekkadi quickly and efficiently stripped her down. The maid stood aside so Natharie could walk down the steps into the water. The water was ice cold and the shock of it made her gasp, but the sun was hot, and more than anything Natharie wanted to wash off the blood that still smeared her face. It itched, and felt as if it had leached into her skin. She knelt, ducking her head down while she scooped up handful after handful of the pure water, never minding the cold. Just get rid of the blood. Just be clean again.

Ekkadi had soon hitched up her skirts and waded in beside Natharie, her hands full with soaps and brushes she'd acquired from . . . somewhere. She was not overly gentle, except when it came to Natharie's injured throat, but she was thorough. She scrubbed all the dust from Natharie's skin and doused her repeatedly with the frigid water. When she was satisfied with the cleanliness of Natharie's body, she turned her attention to Natharie's hair, pouring a measure of perfumed soap over her and working it in well.

"So," Ekkadi said as she reached for the comb tucked in her waistband and began to pick the knots and tangles out of Natharie's hair. "Where are you from that you don't know what's going on?"

"Sindhu." Natharie tried to hold still and enjoy the sunshine, but her feet were beginning to go numb.

"Oh." Ekkadi paused in her work for as long as it took to say that word. Then she gave Natharie's hair a twist, wringing the water out. "You're an Awakened one, then?"

"I follow the teachings of Anidita," Natharie acknowledged.

"Do you really think your brother's a pig?"

"*What?*" Natharie jerked her head around, and was rewarded by her hair pulling hard.

Ekkadi shrugged and wound Natharie's hair up into a knot on top of her head to keep it from trailing into the water again. "That's what they say, that Anidita teaches that men are brothers to pigs."

She's offered me help, and I need help. It will do no good to vent anger on her. But she still could not muster a courteous reply. "*They* are ignorant liars," she muttered.

"Funny, that's what I've heard about your people. Let's get you out of here before you get wrinkled." Ekkadi sloshed to the edge of the bath, climbed the steps, and held up a towel for Natharie.

While Ekkadi dried Natharie off, the draper made her appearance. Mistress Panna—Ekkadi whispered the woman's name in Natharie's ear—was a tall woman with an unwaveringly erect carriage and a train of little wide-eyed girls following behind her in silence. The dress she wore could have graced a queen, it had so many colors and was so beautifully trimmed with pearls and gold. She eyed Natharie with a gaze as piercing as any of the goddesses. Then she gave a series of orders to the girls behind her at such a clip that Natharie could not understand a word she said. The girls scattered like sparrows and when they returned each bore some part of the costume Natharie was to wear for her appearance before her new mistresses: a breastband and pantaloons of dusky green silk; a length of blue silk so dark it shimmered like twilight, to be hung across her shoulders and belted with silver; a veil of translucent blue to cover her hair, which Ekkadi had braided and coiled so that it hung in three loops down her back; silver and amber for her ankles and wrists; and a silver collar so fine it might have been woven of silken threads rather than crafted of metal that wrapped her neck and hid her thread-thin wound. There was yet more silver to hang from her ears and to drape across her forehead.

The perfumer came next. No girls followed her. Instead, she had a trio of tan-skinned, broad-bellied, broad-shouldered eunuchs. Each bore a wooden chest, which he set down and opened. The mixture of scents that rose from them was dizzying. Mistress Valandi came up close to Natharie, staring at her even longer than the draper had, her nostrils quivering and her tongue flicking out to lick her lips. Natharie felt she now understood what a bird felt as it was mesmerized by a snake. At last, the perfumer turned to her trunks. She alone, Natharie realized, had no students and gave no lesson. She opened bottles and boxes picked from her trunk and ground and mixed these mysterious substances in her mortar. It was she herself who anointed Natharie's wrists and throat with something that smelled of musks and flowers and things Natharie could not name. They all bore cool, refreshing scents that made her think of the evening her dress was colored after.

At last, Mistress Valandi stepped back. "You may now tell the steward she is ready."

Ekkadi bowed at once and ran to do just that. Natharie stood where she was, trying to keep her composure under the weight of her new finery and at the same time trying not to lean nearer the rippling bath waters to glimpse her reflection.

Will I be so torn about everything that happens from now on?

Mistress Usha strode out onto the bathing terrace and her gaze raked over Natharie. "Come, then," she said without the least note of approval. She turned and strode back toward the heart of the quarters, and Natharie followed. She felt rather than heard Ekkadi close behind her, and she found she was grateful to know the other girl was there.

After the open chambers where the lessons and the lives unfolded, there came a broad corridor with four dark-wood doors opening from it. Each of these was flanked by a pair of kneeling slaves who held ivory rods. These in turn were flanked by pairs of black-skinned men, tall and well-muscled and hard-faced. They wore light armor with swords at their hips and carried spears in their hands. Mistress Usha took Natharie and Ekkadi up to the farthest door and bowed before it. The right-hand slave bowed in return and silently went inside. None of the others moved at all, not even to let his eyes look at the ones before them.

The door opened again, wider this time, and Mistress Usha led Natharie and Ekkadi to the queens. Natharie glimpsed two women, one old, one young, seated in a room that was opulent even compared with what she had already seen.

The steward barked at her to bow and Natharie obeyed, grateful for the chance to reclaim her wits after being dazzled by the wealth strewn about her.

"Come now, Natharie," said the old woman. Her voice was hoarse and high. "Sit up, daughter of the great king."

Natharie did. The steward had shuffled to one side, and remained prostrated. It must have been very uncomfortable. Natharie kept the smile of satisfaction from her face and turned her attention to the queens.

She had never seen two women less alike. The older of the two had ash-grey hair under her translucent veil. Her skin was sallow and scabbed. It wrinkled like cloth as it hung from her bones. Not all the draper's artifice with scarlet and gold could hide the ill health its color betrayed. Her dark eyes were sunken and her mouth shriveled tight. She would be Queen Prishi, mother to the emperor. Hamsa had told her something of the order of this place while they traveled.

The second woman was not only young, she was vibrant. This was surely Queen Bandhura, the emperor's beloved queen. Her skin was lustrous brown and her hair midnight black. Her eyes sparkled knowingly. She leaned on one elbow, her long hand lying carelessly on the red silk cushion. It was a position carefully rehearsed to look flawlessly casual. She had seen her father's first concubine, Radana, pose just so many times. This woman, this young queen, wanted to be underestimated.

"Someone, you, bring her pillows, and here is food." At the queen's word, a low table was brought forward and laid with numerous dishes, and several pots of tea. The sweet and savory fragrances went straight to Natharie's stomach and sharpened her dull hunger. "You must be half-starved." Queen Bandhura's smile seemed full of concern, but the expression did not reach as far as her eyes.

Queen Prishi coughed and a slave came at once to dab at her forehead with a cloth. "Yes. Yes. We must take special care of this one, daughter of my heart," she said to Queen

Bandhura. "My son Samudra asked after her particularly."

Bandhura's eyes glittered as they turned to Natharie, and Natharie's throat tightened so that her scab pulled, and the food suddenly smelled less appetizing.

"Please, eat," the younger queen urged.

Intensely aware that she was on display, Natharie helped herself to the piquantly spiced dishes. The bread was fresh and warm, the fruit had surely been on tree and vine less than an hour before. There were drinks of fruit and yogurt as well as the tea. All quantities were small, but there was a great variety and before long Natharie began to feel satiated.

And still the two queens watched her.

When Natharie could bear to think of something besides food, she bowed over her folded hands. "I thank the great queens. Your hospitality is all I have heard."

The old queen coughed. "As is your courtesy. I hope you can be comfortable here."

Natharie lifted her chin, modest and correct no more. She might never sit in such a place with such a moment before her. "I am sent here as tribute. I barely know where or who I am. I am told I am a servant. I am told I am a favorite. I am told I am a barbarian and a sacrifice. I am told I may never leave this place again. How can I be comfortable?"

In the stunned silence that followed her words, she saw something new in Queen Prishi. She saw steel beneath the illness. The woman was weak now, but it was not always so, and some trace of that strength remained.

But Bandhura did not let the other queen speak further. "It is of course difficult for one who has just left her home, but soon, Natharie, you will understand the delight of your new life here."

Her tone invited Natharie to play the game of courtesies, but Natharie declined. "What is to be the nature of my life here? No one has told me."

"Why, you are one of the daughters of the Pearl Throne," said Queen Bandhura, as if surprised there should be any question. "We are your family now, and we will care for you in all ways."

"I am sure my mother and father will be glad to hear it," replied Natharie. "May I write them soon and tell them this?"

"Of course. The secretaries are at your disposal." Bandhura laughed. "You did think you were a prisoner, didn't you? Foolish child."

Stop now. Stop now. If you incur her anger, you will be useless to your people. But Natharie could not stop. She could not forget the chains that Prince Samudra had only barely kept from her wrists, or the sword laid against her throat. "Can I leave?"

Queen Bandhura waved her long hand dismissively. "Should you be married to a prince or potentate in another city, of course you will leave and go to head his household."

"That is not what I asked, Great Queen," said Natharie bluntly. "I asked can I leave here, this place, these rooms, should I wish to do so."

The young queen's eyes narrowed ever so slightly, and her soft, beautiful features hardened just enough to show that her mouth was a little too wide for the rest of her face and her eyes were a little too close to the broad bridge of her nose. "The daughter of such great kings would surely not wish to contemplate so immodest and dangerous an act as to expose herself in the public street."

Natharie nodded, and returned to her pose of modesty with folded hands and downcast eyes. "Which is my answer, and the truth of my condition here. It is best that we all know it." Even as she spoke, she felt the vague intuition that the old queen approved of what she heard.

How sick was the woman truly? The scabs looked terrible, but a skin disease did not necessarily go deeper.

Another silence stretched out between them. "I believe I understand now why it is Prince Samudra who favors you," said Queen Bandhura, thoughtfully. In the next heartbeat, her voice became light and cheerful again. "It is customary for the daughters who live in the quarters to refine and educate themselves in the sixty-four arts." She paused. "You, of course, practice the sixty-four arts in Sindhu?"

"Of course," replied Natharie. The sixty-four arts were the accomplishments necessary for the education of the noble person. They included reading and writing, dance, an understanding of poetry and dramas. She doubted very much that the Hastinapuran reckoning also included the ability to sing and discourse on the hymns of Anidita. "And you here?" she added innocently.

"We know them." Queen Bandhura's too-wide mouth frowned, but only for a moment; then all was pleasantness again. "The mother of my heart is often dull in her illness. Will you, of your kindness, perhaps share with her some of the arts as they are known in the house of Sindhu's king?"

Her first thought was *I am no street performer!* But the request was phrased with courtesy, for all the queen's eyes were sly. To refuse would be to truly look the barbarian, and she had done enough to distance herself from the one she should be trying to bring close. *Forgive me, Mother. I am making a very poor start.*

She had no music, so she could not dance. She was certainly not going to sing any of the *surras* for these two. It would have to be one of the epics then. Which one?

Which could they understand?

She made obeisance as gracefully as she could, and in the proper fashion with her brow pressed against her hands, not to the floor. Then she shifted herself so her legs were tucked neatly under her and her unfamiliar twilight skirts spread out gracefully, her back straight, her face calm. She was the vessel only. She held the tale. Would she be able to speak it properly in this clumsy new tongue? She would have to.

"It came to pass in the last hour on the tenth day in the eleventh lunar month, there was born to the first wife of a great king of Ahyudar a daughter, and her mother named her

Duranai. The babe was so fair that light seemed to shine from her brow, and all stood about in amazement at the sight of her. In the morning, her nurse carried her through the gardens that she might be presented to her royal father, and overhead a great eagle flew. With his sharp eyes he spied the beautiful babe and the sight of so fair a creature made him hunger. He swooped from the sky and snatched her from the nursemaid's arms carrying her aloft in his great claws . . ."

So began the story of "King" Duranai. The story was an old one and much loved. It told of the great and wise queen who had dressed as a man and fought a war in order to deceive her enemies and free her captive husband. Natharie herself had told it many times. The gods in it were old, from the time before Anidita's coming, so they would not offend the Hastinapuran way of worship, and she felt sure the tale of a great and brave queen could not fail to please the women who listened to her, and judged all she said.

There was telling a tale properly, and there was telling it well. The words, the gestures, these were classic and needed to be presented with precision and grace, but the rest—watching the audience, seeing who was smiling, or leaning forward, and catching their eyes, adding emphasis, holding back at the right moment, pouring strength into the words at others—these were not the formal art, but they were part of the art all the same. She had learned it with her tutors, and in the barracks with Captain Anun, and in her bedroom after dark, scaring her brothers and sisters with ghost stories. All her well-honed tricks Natharie brought to bear on the queens. Natharie would for this moment force them to care. She would make them for an instant do as she willed in this one small way.

". . . and in that place she saw a miraculous thing. From the brown river water, fireballs rose. Six, eight, ten, they rose straight into the sky. They rose exploding like fireworks in a shower of sparks, and all who saw them bowed their heads and cowered and begged to be delivered from this thing. But

Duranai watched the fireballs rising from the river for a long time, then she turned to the people and told them there was no reason to fear . . ."

Natharie felt the waiting women, the slaves and the soldiers around them listening intently. One even stifled a gasp as Duranai commanded the great pit to open to reveal the serpentine *naga* beneath the earth who imparted to her some of their immortal wisdom. That was good, but it was the queens who mattered. With all she must do to concentrate on choosing her words, on the movement of her hands, on the rest of her audience, Natharie could not read them, but at least they watched, at least their attention was hers and did not stray.

When she was finished, and Duranai ascended to Heaven in a golden chariot, the old queen began to clap, but that exercise ended in a fit of coughing. Queen Bandhura merely nodded her approval.

"A charming tale, and charmingly told. It would be amusing to see her in a proper drama. Stand up, Natharie."

Here ends the façade of beloved daughter. Natharie stood, letting Queen Bandhura look at her. The queen took her time, and Natharie was sure that was on purpose, making her stand there on display. *I know what you are doing,* she thought. *You are showing your power over me. You are making me pay for speaking the truth earlier.*

"Yes, she's tall enough. I think she should be given over to our drama master, mother of my heart. It would be most amusing to see her in a soldier's role, don't you think?"

But the older queen had lain back on her pillows and was more engaged in her struggle to breathe than with the other's musings. "I am certain you are right, daughter of my heart," she murmured. "I was just thinking so myself."

Natharie glanced at Ekkadi, whose eyes were alight at this exchange.

"Yes," said Queen Bandhura with a force that indicated the decision was not to be debated. "We must make her known to Master Gauda, is that not so, Usha?"

"At once, my queen." Mistress Usha pressed her head against the floor.

Bandhura once again turned her kind and condescending smile to Natharie. "I am certain you will find studying with him an invigorating occupation. It will be most interesting to see what you learn."

"I am also sure of this, Great Queen." Natharie bowed properly over her hands. *So, this is the price of boldness. I'm to be made into a clown.* Despite her bitter thoughts, she could not help noticing that Ekkadi practically shivered with excitement where she knelt. What did the maid think had just happened here?

"Now." Queen Bandhura carefully set her features into a look of deep concern. "I fear the mother of my heart is tired and I must tend to her."

That was the dismissal. All made obeisance again but Queen Bandhura ignored them as if they had already departed. Usha gave Natharie and Ekkadi another of her glowering looks and led them back into the corridor.

"The players!" Ekkadi breathed softly as they followed behind the steward. If she had dared, Natharie believed she would have crowed. "We are so lucky!"

"Why?" whispered Natharie, not taking her eyes from Steward Usha. If the woman heard, she did not turn around.

The maid shook her head. "You really don't know anything, do you? If you're good in the plays, you'll be showered with gifts. You'll be precious, because the great ones will be able to brag when they've seen you and they'll vie with the emperor for the chance just to get a glimpse of your performance."

This outpouring was so outrageous, Natharie broke stride. "You're joking."

"No," murmured Ekkadi with complete soberness. "But that's for the greatest. Can you be that good?"

Natharie remembered Queen Bandhura's eyes. To become a clown, a player, to learn the stories these people told, and how to disguise herself before them, to build pleasing layers over her true heart. To be presented to the important and the powerful who competed for entry into this closed world. This could be a useful thing indeed.

Then, to her surprise, she found herself wondering what Prince Samudra would think of her taking on such training. She remembered how he looked at her, how often during the voyage up the river she had glanced up and seen him there, at a good distance, but there, watching her, drinking her in with his warm, sad eyes.

Would he like her as much as she danced on the stage for all to watch?

"Yes," she whispered to her maid. "Yes, I will be that good." With swift steps, she followed the steward to her new teacher.

Chapter Seven

Makul's home was in the City of Gardens, a district named for the beautiful greenery that surrounded its noble houses. The air here was always filled with the scent of flowers, even in the season of dust. Samudra arrived in princely style, carried on a palanquin with his guard before and his train of servants behind.

He had seldom felt more of a sham beneath the ceremony.

Conchs blew and the bells rang to announce his arrival, and Makul's slaves unrolled a great length of scarlet carpet so that his royal shoes would not have to touch the dust of the garden path. Hamsa walked behind him, her usual plain white dress replaced by a garment of pearl silk with a translucent veil for her hair.

Ahead of them, the doors had been thrown wide open. The chief servants and attendants lined the path and made obeisance as he passed. Makul stood just inside the doors to greet him with the salute of trust and usher him into the small but elegant room where his people brought tables and cups, and jars of wine and nectar. Hamsa settled in a corner, a discreet distance away from the men. Her status as sorceress removed the necessity of a screen, but courtesy required a separate table and separate servants for her needs.

The two men drank and Samudra spoke of small matters with his battle-father: the harvest, the health and well-being of families and men they both knew, or points of philosophy. The meal was brought—dishes of spiced meats or vegetables, warm breads, crisp, filled dumplings, rices of various flavors, fresh fruits, and delicate sweets. While they enjoyed all these things, they compared lines of poetry and refought several famous battles.

Samudra was glad of all the delay. It gave him a moment to be calm and to forget. All the day, he had walked the corridors feeling like a stranger in his own home. He attempted again to visit with his mother, but Damman had turned him away. Every eye seemed to be on him and no glance was friendly. His thoughts had run in circles around his mind. His rage had begun to burn brightly once more and his control of it was weakening. It was good to have distraction, especially when found with the man he trusted above all others.

At last, the dishes were cleared away and pots of tea were brought. Makul nodded to his chief servant and the man responded by ushering all the others from the room and closing the doors behind them.

As he had the day before, Makul filled Samudra's cup. He glanced at Hamsa, as if wondering whether it was safe to allow her to hear their conversation, but caught himself and settled back onto his pillows. "Now, my prince," he said. "We are alone and as safe as I can make us. For this moment, we may speak."

Samudra had so much he wanted to say, the words threatened to choke him. Although they were alone, Samudra still lowered his voice. "Does Bandhura collaborate with Divakesh, or does she lay her plans alone?"

Makul bowed his head. Samudra was startled to see the first streaks of grey in his battle-father's thick hair. "It is my belief they work together, but that they have separate aims. Bandhura's goal is the absolute security of the emperor's rule. Divakesh's is the unchallenged reign of the Mothers."

"How can either of them see these things as threatened?"

Makul looked at him, and his eyes were thoughtful. "You truly do not know, my prince?"

Samudra sat back on his heels. Divakesh . . . Divakesh was drunk with his power. It had happened to better men, it should not shock him that it could happen even to one so devout. But Bandhura? What made her so sick at heart?

He thought of the day he had first seen Bandhura. It was as she had been carried into the small domain ready for the marriage ceremony. He himself had been struck by her beauty. Chandra had smiled to see her, his eyes lazy and covetous.

She had from the first been scrupulously polite and eager to please. His mother had remarked several times on how shy and deferential she seemed.

Seemed. She had always seemed happy to see him, and glad to speak with him, especially when their conversation concerned Chandra. Chandra's health and well-being were always of minute concern with her. She had teased and coaxed Samudra in those early days to tell story after story about his brother.

He had been pleased that Chandra should have such a careful and solicitous wife, and he had been pleased when Chandra told him she was to be elevated to the position of first of all queens.

Was it after that the changes had come?

"Why would Bandhura set her hand against me?" His

whisper had become a croak. "I have always been a friend to her. She knows I am loyal to my brother."

"You are," replied Makul. "But then you came home with the Lohit treaty, and those who were less than loyal began to look at you differently."

Those words sank into him, and his frozen mind broke open. Samudra found himself on his feet. "Who are these men? Who speaks against my brother?" he shouted, and Hamsa hissed a warning. Samudra ignored her. If there were those who plotted against the Throne, he would have their names shouted so loudly Mother Jalaja would hear them in Heaven.

Soldier that he was, Makul remained calm in the face of Samudra's sudden fury. "If I named them now, my prince, what would you do?"

"You know what I would do, Makul!"

"Then I will not speak."

So black was his rage that Samudra's first instinct was to reach for his sword. Then, he saw afresh that it was his teacher, his battle-father, his friend, who knelt before him, his face utterly dispassionate. Samudra sank back onto the pillows, his hands suddenly weak.

It was not until Samudra knelt that Makul spoke again. "I will tell you this much: Queen Bandhura knows there are those who speak your name with longing. She may even know who some of them are."

Samudra lifted his head, now utterly bewildered. Nothing was as it should have been or as it had seemed. He wanted to run in terror as he had never run from an open battle. "How would she know these men?"

"She has servants, and she has spies. As first of all queens, she has much wealth and favor to dispense as she sees fit. The small domain is sheltered from the world, but not apart from it." Makul explained this slowly, patiently, as he had done when outlining the fine points of strategy and logistics to the young Samudra. Impatience flared in Samudra, and its sparks threatened to ignite his anger again, but this time he held himself in check.

"Why does she not tell my brother?"

Makul took a long drink of tea and set the cup down. "Because she wants your downfall first."

Think. Think. See the situation for what it is, not what you want it to be. "Because without me, these men have no hope," Samudra said slowly, a stupid child, picking out letters and forming them into words. "And may be picked off at her leisure. It is only around me that plans may grow." *It will come, you know . . . those who will try to use you to bring me down.* "If I am gone there also remains no risk the emperor would hear my voice more clearly than hers." Memory came then, of what Makul had said to him the day before by the exercise yard. *The Mothers themselves have surely ordained that wherever there are soldiers, my prince will find friends.* Samudra understood that Makul not only knew who these men were, but he knew their councils.

Makul was one of these men.

I should strike off your head, Samudra thought dazedly. *I should have you taken in chains to those below the palace who will make certain you tell all you know before you die.*

Samudra looked directly into his Makul's aging eyes. "She cannot believe I would have a part in such plans, or that I would stand between husband and wife."

"I do not know what the first of all queens truly believes. I only know what she has said, and . . ." For the first time, Makul hesitated. ". . . that the emperor has willing ears, my prince."

"No," said Samudra flatly. "That I do not believe."

"That you must believe."

Samudra could no longer sit still. He rose and paced across the floor. Hamsa watched silently from her corner. He had not forgotten her, but neither had he spared her a thought. His head was too full, too confused. If his mind was reeling, what turmoil was inside her, she who hated and avoided all palace scheming. He looked toward her worried face now, but did not ask what she thought. "I know my brother," he said aloud to them both. "If I know nothing else, Makul, I know Chandra."

"Yes, my prince," murmured the old soldier.

Makul fell silent then, giving Samudra's troubled thoughts plenty of time to grow and bloom within his troubled mind. He knew Chandra. He knew Chandra hid his true heart and thoughts behind the sybaritic show. He knew Chandra could be easily frightened, and fear could turn him vicious.

He knew that in Chandra love was seldom stronger than jealousy.

What did Bandhura know? For all she and Samudra had talked so often, she had seldom volunteered any story of herself. He had not been resident in the *zuddhanta* for more than a month at a time since their marriage. There were the campaigns against the Huni and the care and work to keep the new protectorates together while his father lay dying . . .

Samudra knew that the Palace of the Pearl Throne was a place of plots and many kinds of poison, and that the heart of these machinations was the small domain. He had grown up wary of those who smiled too broadly or watched too closely. His mother had taught him the intricacies of politics and the secret world, not just beneath the Pearl Throne, but wherever there was a court. He thought he had learned so well. What he had not learned was to be wary of his own kindred. His father and mother had lived as twin spirits, the one ruling the outer world, the other ruling the inner. He and Chandra had grown up loving and hating each other as full-blood brothers will. Their half-siblings and cousins had all been content with their places, as their mothers, all well provided for, had been. That Divakesh had turned his eye against him, Samudra, was hard, but at least it was comprehensible. That Chandra had, on the word of his wife, decided Samudra was dangerous was not to be imagined. Nor was the thought that Makul had listened to the words of men who thought that Samudra might turn traitor . . . This was poison. Samudra should not even contemplate it. He could not.

He needed to get out of here. But to do what? What advice could he seek against all he had heard and understood here?

It was then Samudra remembered Chandra's dream, and Divakesh's assessment of it, and Hamsa's.

He turned.

"I must go, Makul. I thank you for your hospitality."

Makul did not seem in the least surprised. He made the salute of trust. "As you will, my prince. Your litter will be readied."

Samudra smiled. "I think I will walk a little, my friend."

That did startle the old soldier. "My prince, that is not wise."

"I know, but . . . I need some air, and I need to think." *To think, to pray, to walk a fool's useless path before the weight of this all crushes me.*

"If that is what you want, my prince," Makul murmured.

"No, but it is what I need."

Makul once more gave him the salute of trust, and Samudra touched the top of the man's greying head, in thanks and in hope. Then, with Makul watching anxiously behind him, the prince walked out into the dark courtyard, out to the very edge of the pool of light the lanterns made. Hamsa followed him every step of the way, and when he halted and turned, she saluted him briefly, and stepped back.

Without a word Samudra removed his golden cap, his arm rings, and all but one of his finger rings. He handed these to Hamsa for safekeeping. As he did, he met her eyes. For a moment, he saw what she would be if she were not so constantly worried. In another life, she would have been beautiful, without the lines of strain on her face, and the work and workings that gnarled her hands. He had done this to her, and she had done this to herself. For a moment, he envied his brother the company of Yamuna, who was flush with power, and who did not doubt.

And who did not tell Chandra that it was the Queen of Heaven who called on him in his dreams.

"You are not going to insist on going with me?" he inquired of her.

He saw regret in the way her face tightened, and something of fear. "I do not think I can, my prince." She looked into the darkness. "This night is for you."

She knew what he meant to seek in the darkness, and as ever, kept her counsel. He should find some way to thank her, some way to help her, but his tongue would not move, and in the end all he could do was walk away.

The city at night was a strange and shifting place. Lamps and torches made pools of light to show doorways that were themselves black as caves. Everywhere was the smell of life and death, dust and heat. Scents of jasmine and sandalwood advertised the houses where women waited. Spices told of foods for sale. The sweet and sour smell of fermentation wreathed the wine shops. Dogs barked. Voices lifted in song, in shouts, in the endless, rapid cadence that said hard bargains were being driven in the shadows. The stars and the moon looked down on it all, spelling out their omens for the bright-eyed astrologers to read.

It was a rare thing for Samudra to walk the streets of the outer city, alone. There was freedom in it, and also danger. He did not fear the thieves and footpads. He trusted in his own ability to defend himself. Nor did he fear the pollution against which Divakesh stood such stern guard. Hamsa and the priests she trusted would take care of that as needed, as they always had before. What he feared was less certain, closer to the fear of shadows and reflections in dark mirrors. Out here he was beyond his place, with none of the protections of his role as prince and commander. Out here he was a man only, and that was a thing he'd had little time to become used to.

Where to seek the Queen of Heaven? The temerity of the question made Samudra smile. She had appeared to many heroes in innumerable guises: flower, fire, tiger, snake, all these shapes were hers, as well as queen, warrior, priestess, dancing girl, whore, and, if Hamsa was right, beggar. Should he go to her temple and pray? He could have stayed in the palace and done as much. Go to a house of women? He smirked. There, he was far more likely to find the dirt and demons Divakesh feared than Mother Jalaja.

In the end, Samudra directed his steps toward the river. If the Palace of the Pearl Throne was the heart of the Mothers' dance, the sacred river was its soul. If Mother Jalaja waited anywhere, it would be on Liyoni's banks.

The air grew dense with the smoke wafted on the breeze. Here, the smell of death and fire was constant, reminding him of battlefields, and of the night he had stood on the steps with his brother, his father's ashes smearing his face and hands. He had felt so weak as he said his final farewells and Liyoni bore his father away. Suddenly he recalled how Natharie looked as she lifted her chin to Divakesh's broad sword, her face white and sick. He had known then she felt loss as he had, and knew what it was to have to face her own death. Like her, he also now knew what it was to find home and the future to be hostile and foreign lands.

Perhaps that was why he had thought of her so frequently since he had returned.

The river flowed black and silent, a serpent of night cutting the city in half. The funeral pyres burned brightly on either side. The priests chanted, their voices becoming one soaring hymn to all the gods in Heaven. Broad steps led down to the water. Depressions had been worn in their surface from hundreds of years of feet making the descent he did now. Samudra saw the naked forms of bathers as they rinsed themselves in the shining waters. It was a common thing for astrologers to advise their clients to bathe in the sacred water by the light of this moon or that, to rinse off their sin and bad luck.

Perhaps I should bathe, or drink.

A hiss and a beam of light on his hand made Samudra turn from the river. Behind him flickered a sputtering oil lamp, giving off just enough light to show a ragged tent. A woman swaddled in greasy, colorless robes sat beneath the battered canvas. A stick with a snake's skin wrapped around it had been planted in front of the tent, the traditional sign for an astrologer.

Smiling to himself, Samudra approached the rickety shelter. The woman looked him up and down, her eyes gleaming. No doubt she saw the one gold ring he still wore on his hand, and used it to weigh the wealth hidden in the purse he had concealed beneath his tunic.

"Come forward, my son, come forward." She beckoned with a bony hand. "What question plagues you this night?"

Samudra squatted down until his eyes were level with hers. "Tell me, mother, where will I find the Queen of Heaven?"

To his surprise, the crone didn't even blink. "She is not here tonight."

Samudra rested his arms on his thighs. She spoke so solemnly and so plainly, he found he did not know what to say.

"Did you expect her?" The ancient astrologer cocked her head.

Samudra shrugged. "I hoped," he said honestly.

She turned her head so that she regarded him archly from one eye. That eye caught the lamplight, causing a single star to burn within its depths. "But it was not you she called, was it?"

Samudra felt his jaw drop open. The crone just smiled, and straightened her bony shoulders. Was it only his surprise, or was she younger than she had seemed at first?

"What do you know of it?" he demanded.

Her smile broadened and opened, revealing a row of stained, sharp teeth. "Ask another question, Son of the Moon. You have so few left."

Samudra swallowed. The chants and the pyre smoke swirled against his back. His heart beat slow and heavy within him and his throat threatened to close around his words.

"What is my place on the wheel?" he croaked.

The woman sighed and shook her head. Her hair was white beneath her ragged veil, but still streaked with black. "That is the wrong question. You know your place. You are the second son. You are the protector and the defender. You are keeper of sword and honor. Yours are the snake's eyes, not the lotus."

"But I do not understand what that means!" cried Samudra, plaintive as a child. His dignity was lost, and his home, his sense of self and place. Here he was only a man, and he knew nothing, nothing at all.

"Oh, my son," breathed the woman. "You hide so much from yourself. You are a master of deception and yet you do not know it." She stood, and Samudra saw he had been wrong. She was not old. She was young and straight and strong, and her robes were not tattered at all, but whole and rich, and it was only the ashes of the sacred dead that made them grey. "When you are ready to speak from who you are, we will talk again."

She walked away, leaving her ragged tent and her lamps and her sign, vanishing into the darkness down the steps to the sacred river. Left behind, Samudra stood slowly, staring at the dusty street where her footsteps had fallen, for behind her she left a trail of bloody footprints. Samudra bowed at once, until his forehead pressed into that scarlet dust.

This was not the sign of the Queen of Heaven. Jalaja left lotus petals behind her. The bloodied footprint was the sign of Vimala, the Mother of Destruction.

Who also bore the name and aspect of A-Kuha, the Deceiver.

You are a master of deception, and yet you do not know it.

Samudra shook. Cold seized hold of him, and yet he felt sweat trickling down his brow.

He turned from the tent and the river and the sign of the goddess. As he had never done in battle, Samudra fled. He ran through the streets without seeing them, instinct alone guiding his steps, his breath coming in frantic gasps, tears stinging and blinding his eyes and his fearful thoughts blurring in his mind.

When at last he could run no more, he collapsed against a stone wall. It was cool against his sweating skin and strong enough to make up for the weakness that had seized his legs and allowed him to keep upright.

He had come out seeking the Queen of Heaven, but the Queen of Heaven would not speak to him. He could not even find Indu, the Mother of War, to whom he had dedicated his life. The Deceiver had called him her son. Samudra leaned his head back until it rested against the wall. He had striven to be honest, to be honorable in word and deed. He wanted to pray, to pray for the grandest sacrifice of all so that any other of the goddesses would hear him and speak comfort to him, but even as he thought this, he quailed. Mother Destruction, Mother Deception, Mother of Snakes and of the ever-changing moon, was merciless to those who rejected her. But why, why would she choose him? He had never been any of hers.

And yet . . . and yet . . . while he played the dutiful prince and soldier, in his bosom he harbored doubt, and even revulsion. He had questioned what his brother had become. He had defied orders in battle, only to achieve greater victory, true, but it was defiance still, and unless he was forced to, he had told no one. Only Hamsa knew, and she knew only because she had seen what he had done, not because he had spoken openly, like a true man.

Samudra pushed away from the wall. Steady now, he walked the last of the way to the palace. The streets around him widened, and the number of people fell away until he was alone once more. This time when he came to the gates, he only looked up at the watchmen when they called the challenge. He did not know what they saw in his eyes, but whatever it was, this time there was no talk of pollution or delay. They only hurried to open the side portal and let him in. He crossed through the gardens, raising his hand to guard his stained brow from the fine sprays of the fountains carried on the night wind. He did not wish the blood of the goddess to be washed away.

He climbed up the wide stairs to the eighth ring of the palace, the place where the emperor lived. No one challenged him. No one stopped him. The guards parted as he approached and dropped at once into obeisance.

The imperial bedchamber lay at the center of the ring. The night servants, all of them mutes, waited in the outer chamber, alert for the slightest sound issuing from beyond the gauze curtains that sheltered the imperial bed. Even these guardians of the emperor's comfort kissed the floor as Samudra strode past them. He pushed aside the curtains and saw the rumpled sheets, and the two bodies lying beneath the covers.

"Brother."

But it was Bandhura who sat up, pulling the sheet up around her. She looked at him for a moment. Then, gracefully, deliberately, she rose from that bed, drawing on a pale robe that billowed around her as she walked toward him, but not before Samudra saw her body, full and perfect in the silver moonlight.

"What is the brother of my heart doing here?" she asked softly. Her bare feet made no sound on the carpets as she approached him.

"I must speak with my brother," Samudra told her bluntly.

"Our sovereign sleeps, as you can see. What matter will

not wait until morning?" Her words were mild, but her eyes were sharp, especially for one who should have just awakened from sleep. Samudra had a sudden image of Bandhura lying awake beside Chandra, waiting. But waiting for what? Did she know he had left Makul's house on foot? How had that word come to her?

"It is a matter between him and me, sister of my heart." He did not try to keep his voice down. Chandra stirred on his pillows.

"For shame, Brother!" Bandhura slapped Samudra's arm lightly. "A soldier should know restraint. Whatever you have to say, it can wait for the morning."

"No," said Samudra flatly. "It cannot." He stepped to the side. "Brother!"

Chandra rolled over. He blinked heavily and looked about him. When he saw his wife and his brother, he pushed himself up onto one elbow.

"What in all nine hells is this?" he demanded groggily.

Samudra brushed past Bandhura, feeling the heat from her angry glower as he did, and stood beside his brother's bed.

"Come with me, Chandra."

Chandra squinted up at him. "Where?"

"Out of here."

"What do you mean?" Chandra scratched his scalp.

"Come out into the streets." Samudra pointed toward the doorway where the servants crowded, crouching in the shadows, uncertain of what to do. "The Queen of Heaven is looking for you."

Chandra stared at his arm. He blinked again, bleary-eyed. "What in the Mother's name are you talking about?"

"Your dream. Divakesh lied to you. It was not a devil. It was Mother Jalaja who called you."

Memory and comprehension came slowly to Chandra, but they did come and the look on his face shifted from confusion to annoyance. "Don't be an ass, Samudra. Why would Divakesh lie?"

"I don't know." *Another lie. I do know, but I can't speak here. These are things that should not be, not here in the heart of all things.*

Chandra sighed, shoving his stringy locks back from his face. He propped himself up on both elbows now. "So, how came you to be a dream interpreter?"

Samudra knelt. He caught his brother's gaze and saw the disbelief, and the boredom. "Because I left the palace tonight. I went to the streets in your place. I met Mother Vimala there."

Chandra grinned at him, fierce and lascivious. "Brother, whoever you met, I want some of what you had to smoke with her."

"Chandra, I am not lying to you." He put all the strength of the truth he had in his voice. "Brother look at me." *See what I have seen. See the blood and the dust. See these eyes of mine that have looked at the Mother of Destruction and Deception.* "The Queen of Heaven is calling to you. You are surrounded by liars as we are surrounded by walls. Chandra, Brother, I am asking you to trust me in this. Please, come with me." He held out his hand. *Show the queen you trust me, that all her effort has been for nothing. Please, Brother.*

Chandra stared at his hand, and for a moment, Samudra saw something flicker in his eyes. It was the fear, the fear he had seen beside their father's pyre when Chandra realized he truly would sit upon the Pearl Throne.

Then, his brother collapsed backward onto the bed and rolled over. "Take him out of here."

Samudra stood, slowly. He was shaking again. Bandhura's hand was on his arm. "Brother of my heart . . ." she began sternly.

Samudra did not wait. He left his brother to her, and descended to his own place below, entering his own rooms without remembering anything of the route he took to get there. He saw nothing clearly except his brother lolling on the silken bed, and Bandhura standing over him, her robe covering the nakedness she had so deliberately exposed a moment before.

"My prince?"

Hamsa stood before him. Had she been here all this time? Of course she had. She would not rest with the other attendants in comfort at Makul's. She would come at once to the palace, and stay awake until he returned.

But Samudra did not answer her. He went out to his balcony. He wanted fresh air on his face. He wanted to see the stars, and the moon, which was his sign, a white half-circle amid the diamonds of the sky.

"My prince," said Hamsa again, sinking to her knees in front of him. "What happened?"

He hung his head and touched his brow. The blood of the goddess had dried, and came away on his fingers, as a prickling, rusty powder. In slow, halting, wondering words, he told her all that had occurred, outside and inside.

He rubbed his fingertips together. "I should kill myself."

Hamsa took his hand, stilling his fingers. "No, Samudra."

"Yes, Hamsa." He looked up, past her, to the silent moon. "The Mother of Destruction is come to me. If I stay in the dance, I will bring down the world with me."

"That is not what she said."

"That is what will happen." He turned back to her. "If you dare say that is what must happen, that I must break the ways of my fathers, I swear upon my eyes, Hamsa . . ."

"Samudra." Hamsa cut him off with a sharpness rare for her. It made him truly see her for a moment. "I don't know why Mother A-Kuha came to you," she admitted. "But I do know this." She stabbed a finger toward the world beyond the walls. "The Mothers do not speak to the ones they mean to destroy."

She spoke so strongly and with such conviction, Samudra found he could not help but believe. After a few moments, he whispered, "What do I do then?"

"I don't know this either, my prince." She bowed her head. "But understanding comes with time. You know the art of waiting, my prince. Wait now. Watch. Discover your enemy and the enemies of Hastinapura. When you know their names and faces, you will find the way to defeat them."

Softly, Samudra spoke his final fear. "What if the enemy is my brother, Hamsa?"

Hamsa swallowed hard, but she lifted her face and met his gaze. "It changes nothing, my prince. Nothing at all."

Samudra felt his face harden. "No," he said. "I do not accept that. It changes all." He stared out at the moon, which waxed and waned, changing each day and yet remaining always the same. It was a sign both of constancy and inconstancy, so it was birthed by Mother A-Kuha.

The Mother who claimed him from her brighter sisters. How could he resist the claims of a goddess?

A new idea came to him, blossoming in his mind like a black and beautiful lotus. What if he did not appear to resist? Even a goddess could be swayed by appearances. The epics and histories told of it happening many times. What if he pretended to dance Mother A-Kuha's dance, but only in the service of Mother Jalaja, who was honor, and Mother Indu, who was victory? After all, one did not fight a cunning and deceitful enemy with the same tactics one used against a man of straightforward honor.

Lives would be lost. Precious lives. Dear lives. He would be spoken of as a traitor . . . but there might be a way yet . . . and when that way unfolded, he would reaveal whose son he truly was.

He lifted his eyes to the star-scattered heavens. With resolution came hope, and the warm, close weariness that would bring sleep. Hamsa watched him and he knew she worried, but she would understand; when she saw what he brought to pass, she would understand. So would the world, and the Mothers who watched over all.

So, eventually, would Chandra.

* * *

*B*andhura, first of all queens of Hastinapura, stood at the foot of her husband's bed and watched Samudra vanish into the shadows. She glared at the servants crowding in the doorway. They kissed the floor and returned to their darkness and waiting.

"Bandhura . . ." murmured Chandra groggily.

"I am here, my husband." Bandhura shed her robe and lay down beside her lord, cradling his body against hers, stroking his arms and his brow lightly, soothing rather than exciting, whispering words of gentle sleep and rest in his ears.

After a few moments, his breathing grew deep and regular again. She lay there for some time, making sure he was far enough gone into sleep that he would not miss her warmth. Her ladies silently wrapped her in enough layers to satisfy modesty, and she walked into the outer chamber.

"Bring me the high priest Divakesh," she said to the nearest mute. The slave kissed the floor and hurried away, still bent so his head would not rise higher than that of the queen.

She settled herself into a nest of pillows, arranging her skirts automatically. Divakesh gave no sign of noticing female beauty, but his eye for incorrectness was keen.

The high priest himself entered silently a few moments later. He knelt and bowed over his hands to her, his eyes lowered, all motions proper, but they were hollow forms. He did this because he must, not because it was right. Bandhura had come to understand this shortly after she became Chandra's first wife. Chandra did not seem to notice, and Bandhura had decided it was best to keep this knowledge to herself, for a while.

"It is time we spoke truth together, Lord Divakesh," she said.

Divakesh assumed a kneeling position before her, his eyes cast toward the floor, but she saw the swift flicker as the priest dared look at her for the swiftest instant. "Yes," he replied after a moment's consideration. "Perhaps it is."

"Do you know what happened to Samudra tonight?" She never assumed Divakesh lacked information day or night. She felt it safer to overestimate his abilities than the reverse.

"I know he left the palace, and returned in agitation." Divakesh's eyes flickered to hers again.

"He came here. He told my husband to obey the dream he had and leave the palace with him."

Divakesh's glance darted at once to the curtained bed, where the emperor still sprawled safely asleep.

"The prince was, as you say, in a state of great agitation," Bandhura went on. "I am most concerned, Lord Priest, and I would know what measure you take of the prince."

Divakesh remained silent for a long moment, choosing his words with care. "It is in my mind that your brother-of-heart Samudra will try to leave the palace, to take war to the Huni on our northern borders."

"Is this not a thing to be desired?"

"It may seem so, Majesty, until one looks closer. Then, one may perceive what it truly means for Samudra to be out and among the soldiers whose might protects the Pearl Throne from all harm. He will have daily contact and conference with men who are surely impure. For him to speak with them in a familiar fashion, as he is often known to do, is to allow pollution into his heart, and theirs."

Bandhura's eyes narrowed. "Pollution?"

Divakesh nodded. Behind his eyes seethed a ferocious anger. He did not see her now. He saw something else entirely, and Bandura realized she knew what it was. He was looking at the tall Sindishi princess with all that boiling anger, the one who had made him look like a fool as he tried to break her on the altar, the one who, if reports were to be believed, was already a fair way toward insinuating herself into Samudra's impervious heart.

"Pollution," said Divakesh again, and his great fists tightened. "Such as might blind a man and keep him from seeing how the Mothers have set things in their proper places. The low and impure will see a man of might before them, and they will forget the true pattern of the dance. Such is the way of those who are imperfect in their understanding. It is best that they are kept far from such sights."

Now it was Bandhura's turn to sit in silence, turning his words over in her mind. "Lord Divakesh, do you in truth believe Samudra will try to bring my husband down?" She spoke the words coldly, practically. She had done her best to weaken Samudra, to drive Chandra from him, not because she believed that the first prince was disloyal, but to render him useless to those who were.

"Samudra burns," said Divakesh. "His place on the wheel is as the bars on a cage. Whether the Mothers or demons speak to him, he will listen, and soon. Witness his fascination with the heretic princess, Natharie."

Ah! So, you are worried about our Princess Sacrifice. Bandhura suppressed a smile. "He should have been kept here where he could be watched," she murmured, to see what Divakesh's answer would be.

"And what, my queen, would that have done?" asked Divakesh mildly. "He would have gone to fight the Huni himself, or it would have been seen that he had been deliberately held back by the emperor's distrust. Had Pravan defeated the Huni, we would perhaps not have had to speak these words between us, or if Samudra had been allowed to go but had been defeated . . . but even then . . ." He made a great show of sighing deeply. "The smaller princes place great faith in Samudra, and they would have felt his defeat to be the fault of the emperor, not of Samudra himself." Slowly, Divakesh raised his eyes to look directly at her. "And, were Samudra to die, Mothers forfend, I doubt that faith would be transferred to Pravan, say, or . . ."

"Or to their emperor," Bandhura finished for him. "Yes. I know it well."

Few understood that she truly loved her husband. She loved the beauty of his body, and the fragility he struggled so hard to keep hidden. She was proud to be his haven in loneliness. His devotion to her, even over his other wives, went straight to her own heart. Samudra gave himself out as an honorable man, but honor did not chafe at its place. Honor served. If the prince's honor was true, he would not wish his brother to be other than what he was. He would do all he could to strengthen and support his emperor.

"You will speak to the emperor of this?" she asked, her voice and heart both stony.

Divakesh bowed over his hands. "As I have before, but I believe in the charity of his heart, the emperor will not believe his brother guilty of the final treachery. This speaks of the purity of his being." Divakesh's eyes glittered as he spoke the words. "It is in my heart that it is you, first of all queens, who must stand against Samudra for the emperor's sake, as you have so often before."

Double meanings. Double meanings, even now when they needed to understand each other most clearly. Bandhura felt her mouth harden. One day, the high priest too would have his reckoning. Despite his ascetic practice and constant prostrations, his own heart was far from pure. She wondered what he really saw when he looked on Natharie and what he wanted from that tall Sindishi woman.

"Thank you for your words, Lord Divakesh. We will speak more soon."

Divakesh accepted this as his dismissal, bowed once more and backed out of the chamber. Bandhura stayed where she was, facing each unpleasant thought that passed through her mind in order to discern which might be true and which were merely her own fears.

Samudra will not harm you, my husband, she vowed in her silent heart. *He will not harm either of us.*

*   *   *

*F*rom his chamber beside the emperor's, Yamuna looked through the slit he had made in his door and watched the high priest leaving the queen's presence. He stepped back from the door, wondering what had been said. Bandhura had a talent for court life, and was, to the surprise of all, fiercely devoted to her imperial husband. She would guard him like a tigress, watching her prey from the shadows, stalking for as long as necessary and waiting in patience for the precise moment to make her open attack. He could not have asked for a better queen, even though her trust of him was only partial, which spoke to the woman's intelligence.

It did mean, however, that Yamuna must keep his own plans that much more closely hidden. No matter. He had carried his own secrets close before the woman's grandmother was born. He could carry them a while longer.

Compared with the rest of the palace, Yamuna's chambers were spartan. Only a few plain and graceful pieces of furniture adorned them. What made his chambers unusual was that they held one of the few locked rooms above ground in the whole of the palace. This was Yamuna's own treasure-house, and no hand but his could open the ebony door.

He stood before the door and undid the red ribbon that held back the grey braids of his hair. He had woven the ribbon with his own hands and his own skills. He threaded it through his fingers in a particular pattern, reaching within and without to call the magic, to enliven and awaken the weaving laid in place so long before. He laid his hand against the warm wood of the door, and the door, which had no handle, bar, or latch, opened.

Inside it was utterly black. Yamuna retied his hair, lit the three hanging lamps, and closed the door. Around him, the lamplight showed a workroom that might have belonged to an apothecary, or a maker of inks. Low, stained worktables stretched out on the floor. Bundles of herbs, dried plants, roots, and chiles hung from the ceiling. The walls were lined with shelves, and the shelves were lined with jars—great glass bottles as brilliant as jewels, small alabaster jars sealed with colored waxes, jars of onyx and obsidian, jars of carnelian and jade and jasper, jars wrapped in straw plaits, jars carved with elaborate runes and signs that not even Yamuna could read, and jars of plain, dull clay.

Yamuna lifted down one of the smaller jars. It was a graceful, curving vessel of red clay impressed with a pattern like a closely woven rope wrapping around it. Setting the vessel beside him, he opened one of the wooden boxes on his worktable. Inside the box were a number of small trays, each containing a different colored earth.

Yamuna spread a square of white canvas on the floor and sat down cross-legged before it. It was difficult to work with temporary or impermanent substances, but he had honed that skill over his long life, and he used it now. He drew it up from his blood; he drew it down from the air. Sharpening the focus of his mind and eye, he dipped his hand into the colored earths and sprinkled them onto the canvas to make his patterns. Colors wove together in a complex circle, layer upon layer absorbing the magic he brought, shaping it and binding it.

When all was ready, he turned to the clay jar and opened the lid. He reached inside and brought out a delicate, braided ring of black hair. This he laid in the center of his carefully prepared circle.

From that ring, a shape unfurled like a bird's wing. It was a woman in simple white clothes, her hair divided into a hundred braids and tied back from her dark, worried face with a red ribbon. Had there been any to see, they would have sworn that the sorceress Hamsa now knelt in before Yamuna. Only the most observant eye would have noticed the fine hair bracelet around her wrist among the silver bangles that were her normal decoration.

Satisfied, Yamuna nodded. "Now, Hamsa, tell me all you have said to your princeling regarding our dearest emperor this day, and all that he has said to you."

The image lifted its dark eyes and spoke, clearly and smoothly, a teller relating a well-rehearsed tale, and Yamuna sat in silence and listened. As he watched her, Hamsa's shape watched him with eyes sharp and keen. He wondered then, as he sometimes did, how much this shadow saw.

It did not matter. She was his prisoner and would never be released. So, Yamuna listened, and the shadow spoke, as she must, and watched, and waited.

Chapter Eight

Pakpao Kamol knelt before the chief of the Huni, and was grateful courtesy prevented him from looking directly at the chief's face.

Pakpao was a spy. He had been a spy inside the court of Sindhu and outside it since he was a boy of twelve. He had faced men who could kill him with their bare hands, and he had faced men who, with a word, could make him vanish from the earth. Never had Pakpao been in the presence of a man like this. Tapan Gol was not a man who moved rashly. This man stopped and considered all he did, especially in matters of war. Anger would not sway this man, although he clearly had the capacity for great anger. Greed would not drive him, although he surely desired riches. He was a man who used himself like a spear. Tapan Gol was a weapon, perfectly controlled and therefore perfectly deadly.

It was this that made Pakpao truly afraid.

Tapan Gol was a broad man with a thin line of beard outlining his jaw. His black mustaches hung down well past his chin. His eyes were hard and keen, like the naked swords of the men who stood behind him, like the arrows in the quivers of the women who stood guard outside. For all the Huni had sacked dozens of Hastinapuran towns, Tapan Gol displayed none of the spoils in his weather-stained tent. He sat in a simply carved wooden chair, and drank from a wooden noggin. His lacquered armor was in excellent condition, but clearly it had seen hard use, for its gilding and ornamental colors were chipped and scratched.

"These are the words of the great Tapan Gol," said the black-coated translator who stood beside the chief. "Why would the king of Sindhu send embassage to me?"

"He does not, Great Chief," said Pakpao. "I am sent by the queen."

The translator relayed this to his chief. Tapan Gol sat silent for a moment, he then spoke. His voice was thin for such a big man, and nasal in tone. *Such a man should have a stentorian voice,* thought Pakpao. Then he recalled some of what he had heard of Tapan Gol's deeds. *Such a man does not need to use his voice in order to be heard.*

"The queen must have great faith in this little man," said the chief. Pakpao spoke his language and many others well, but this was the sort of knowledge he was accustomed to keep to himself. When he had trudged up to the perimeter of the encampment, he had spoken only Sindishi to the guards, and the officers, and finally the chief's watchful translator. "With such as this to serve her, what could she want with me?" the chief mused.

His translator nodded and turned again to Pakpao. "And what could the queen of Sindhu want with the mighty Tapan Gol?"

Here came the words that would change the world. Pakpao did not hesitate. He was a servant only and he would do his duty.

"The queen wishes to say that if representatives of the great Tapan Gol came to Sindhu they would be sheltered and treated with honor, no matter what their numbers or where their errand took them."

The translator relayed these words faithfully and Pakpao risked a glance up at the Huni chief. Tapan Gol's brows had lifted the slightest amount. "I wonder if the king knows his woman plots treason? Probably not. Husbands seldom know these things. Ask him why she's willing to do this."

"The great Tapan Gol wishes to know why the honorable queen would extend such hospitality."

It was the mark of an experienced man to be able to stretch out a believable phrase. Most likely, this one had stood at his master's side for many years. Probably at least as long as Tapan Gol had been harassing the Hastinapurans. He was much trusted as well, or the chief would not be so careless with his words. Pakpao found himself wondering if this slender, black-coated man was more than just a translator.

"My great queen would extend this hospitality because she believes Tapan Gol's aims and hers to be the same."

Tapan Gol folded his arms. "I want to put an end to Hastinapura and grow rich in the bargain," he told his translator. "What does this queen want?"

"The great Tapan Gol bids you speak more plainly," the translator said to Pakpao.

Pakpao licked his lips and considered. Perhaps this was a moment for simple honesty. "The great queen, my mistress, has been offered grave insult by Hastinapura and wishes to see their destruction."

The chief nodded. "Pride. So. Something we may all understand." He stroked his chin with one finger. "What do you think of this offer?"

Much more than a translator then. You hide your strengths, and your true mind, Tapan Gol. "I think it is a great risk, but it may bring great gain," his man answered.

Pakpao kept his gaze on the carpet and made sure his expression remained slightly nervous, as would be appropriate if he did not understand a word being said.

"I agree." There was a smile in Tapan Gol's words, and it

sent a shudder up Pakpao's spine. "We have known our time must be soon, and we have only lacked the route for our attack, and here it is. This may be our best chance, or it may be the Hastinapurans have allied with the Sindishi to trick us. So. I will take a boat with this man to meet his queen, and we will not give them a chance to change their minds."

"And if it is a trick?"

"I will kill this one first. Especially as he has understood every word we've spoken here."

Tapan Gol got to his feet in one fluid motion and left the tent. Pakpao prostrated himself, and closed his eyes.

Great Queen, he murmured deep in his heart. *What have we done?*

*R*adana, chief concubine to the king of Sindhu, lay beside her lord and master. A single lamp burned low next to her bed, bathing them both in an equal measure of golden light and shadow. The act of love was finished between them, and Kiet was drifting toward sleep. He had sent for her every night since the queen had left for the sorcerer's monastery. Every night she had lain beside him, soothing him, satisfying him, giving him her company. Today, she had finally received the last message she had been waiting for.

Tonight, she would turn the tide of her own fortunes.

Radana let out a long sigh as if from her heart, and rolled away from Kiet's side. Her motion stirred him from his deepening languor.

"Radana?" He leaned over her, stroking her shoulder. "What is it, my little heart?"

"Nothing, my lord. Nothing," Radana murmured, but she sighed again, letting the sound catch in her throat.

The king kissed her ear playfully. "There is something. Come, my lover, tell me what saddens you." With a gentle touch, he coaxed her to roll over.

She let herself be pulled close, but she kept her head bowed. "It is not sadness."

"What then, Radana?" She felt his smile as he kissed the top of her head. "I would not have you lacking in any comfort. Come, tell me what is in your heart." He shook her just a little. "Your king commands it."

So be it then. Radana bit her lip. "My lord . . . it is fear."

"Fear?"

Now Radana looked up to let the king see her shining eyes. "I fear for you." She laid her hand on his chest so his heart beat against her palm. "For us."

"What could you fear?" he murmured. His voice was a little careless, but his strong arm pulled her closer, protective.

Radana took this as a good sign and snuggled yet closer, curling in on herself to appear small and frail beside him. "I . . . fear the queen."

"The queen is safe where she is." Kiet patted her shoulder indulgently. "The father abbot and the others will not permit her to come to harm."

"No, I do not fear *for* the queen," said Radana, letting her voice drop and fill with reluctance. *Be careful how you play this part, woman. This is where you gain or lose all.* "I fear her."

"Do you fear she will be jealous of us?" Kiet laughed a little. He was still in his part as lover. Kiet enjoyed that part. It let him set aside his burdens as king, which, after all, was Radana's purpose. "It is not in her nature to begrudge me your company."

"No . . . my lord." Radana sat up, wrapping her arms around her knees and hugging them to her. She did not look at him, but lowered her voice to a whisper. "I fear the queen is disloyal."

All the gentle lover's indulgence left the king between one heartbeat and the next. "That is not possible."

Radana was ready for this. She pressed her brow against his shoulder, moving her body close, letting breast and leg rub his. "I knew your heart was too good for you to believe betrayal. But, my lord, she . . . it grieves me . . ." She met his eyes again, pressing closer still.

"What is it?" snapped Kiet. "What have you heard?"

Radana turned her face away for a moment, looking into the deep shadows beyond the pool of light where they lay, as if making up her mind what to tell her lord and lover. Then, she straightened her shoulders and faced him squarely, her eyes dipped just enough for propriety. "Great King, Queen Sitara has sent your spymaster into the northern mountains to meet with the Huni."

Radana watched fear settle over the king, and saw how that fear turned slowly to anger. "Who told you this?" he croaked.

Radana crouched down, huddling in on herself there on the bed. "My king, my love, do not be angry with me. I beg you." She squeezed her eyes tightly shut so that when she looked up, they would be shining with tears. "A cousin of mine is one of the royal bargemen. He is loyal to you, my king, and very frightened, he learned of this and brought me word at once so that I could bring it to you."

The king stood, wrapped in the light quilt, and put his back to her. He walked to the edge of the lamplight and stood there for a long moment, contemplating the darkness beyond. Radana stayed as she was, hardly daring to breathe. She was so close, so close. Now that Kiet knew of the queen's treachery, Sitara would be cast aside. Sitara would die and Radana would be queen. It only required a moment more. Just a moment more.

Kiet hung his head. "I wish you had not told me this."

Triumph sang in Radana's heart. "I am sorry, but I was so frightened for you, and for your daughter who is in Hastina-pura's hands. I could not permit the queen to bring the wrath of Hastinapura down on you when I knew I could prevent it."

"Yes, Radana." He touched her shoulder fleetingly. "You have acted as you thought best."

She captured his hand, kissing its back. "I would never see harm come to you when I could prevent it, my love." She pressed her cheek against his palm. It was so warm. Soon she would move it further down her body and remind her king how much she had to give him.

He ran a thumb along her jaw, looking deeply into her eyes. "It pains me to now have to place a guard on you."

"What!" Radana cringed backward, but the king had her by the shoulders and his grip was strong enough to hurt.

"You cannot tell anyone what you know, Radana. Not now. I am sorry. Guard!"

A soldier entered the sleeping chamber at once, and made obeisance. "Take Lady Radana to her room and arrange a guard for her." There was no regret or hesitation in the king's voice as he spoke. "She is not to leave the palace, not even as far as the gardens. No one at all is to speak to her. Is that understood?"

Again the soldier bowed. He turned his stern eyes upon Radana.

Anger blazed in Radana, but she crushed it down at once. She made obeisance meekly, and on her knees she departed her king's presence, letting her hair fall in a curtain before her face, in case some hint of the fury in her heart showed through. Kiet knew what his queen did! He had known Sitara's errand when she left, and he permitted it.

Fool! Fool! she cursed herself. *You spoke too soon! You should have learned more before you acted, found a lie if the truth would not do . . .*

If the truth would not do. It sank in then, as she reached the private chamber her rank as chief concubine granted. The guard slid the doors shut behind her. This also was the truth: The king himself wanted war with Hastinapura, and Radana knew this secret, and he had let her live.

For how long? Radana knelt beside her own sleeping platform. She bit her lip in true consternation this time. When the king had time to reflect, Radana might find old Anun or one of the others entering her room bearing sweet dumplings laced with poison for her to consume, supposedly of her own free will. It was the death so often reserved for high ladies who offended.

But a king mad enough to try to make war against Hastinapura might be mad enough to leave me alive. She twisted her hands together. A single bead of perspiration slipped down from her brow. *I might yet succeed.*

And if I live long enough for the Hastinapurans to come? Her mind's eye showed her the king lying dead in a welter of blood, and of all his women thrown to the soldiers of the Mothers. Fear took her. She trembled so violently that she fell down on the woven floor mat, unable to do anything but shiver as if overtaken by a raging fever. This was why the king had turned from her. This was the intensity of the madness that had taken him.

How could she owe any loyalty to a mad king? This realization allowed her to collect herself. She sat up, composed once more. Had he stood beside her, she would have tried her best to help keep Sindhu, and him, strong. She would have done anything. But in his madness he had turned to his equally mad queen. No. She owed him nothing anymore.

Now that she was able to think more clearly, she considered the details of her situation, allowing her gaze to slip this way and that, taking in what had changed, and what had not. One of Anun's women surely stood outside the door, and she could see two others through the screens opening onto the long terrace. Watching them, she thoughtfully fingered the wide sash that tied her skirt.

Radana's mother had been a concubine in a lord's house. She had never risen to wife, but she had taught Radana all the arts that had kept her close to the king. She had also taught Radana all the skills she might need to know in case those more pleasant arts failed.

Obedient to her mother's wise tutelage, Radana kept a certain mixture of resins and powdered roots about her person at all times. She had never spoken of it to anyone. A time might come, her mother had warned, when she might have to take the mixture herself. More likely, though, she would have to slip it to some rival. Radana narrowed her eyes at the guards who stood so straight and so watchful outside her terrace doors.

Radana laid herself down on her sleeping platform, and when sleep did not come, she composed herself to wait, folding her hands and breathing softly, evenly. Much of a concubine's life was spent in waiting, so she found it no hardship. Eventually, the night waned and the slanting sunbeams of morning crept into Radana's room. She rose and stretched and washed her face in the moss-green basin of fresh water that had been left ready for her. The guards held their poses and their posts without seeming to waver. They were tired now, and thirsty. They would be relieved soon, and their replacements would stand there through the long, hot day. By evening, they would be ready to fall at once upon whatever food might be brought to them.

Now her hope must be that the privileges of rank would still be observed.

They were. The room's inner doors opened, and Radana's maid was allowed to enter, followed closely by one of the female guards. The maid set a lacquered tray of bowls in front of her mistress and bowed. Her eyes said she longed to speak, but she had been warned. Radana touched her servant's head. The maid removed the bowls from the tray one at a time, placing them on the low table. She made obeisance once more. As she straightened, Radana stopped her with a touch. She took two gold bracelets off her arms, slipped them onto the maid's wrists, and then embraced her tightly. Radana pulled back, still holding her maid's hand, wiping her eye as if wiping away a tear. The maid looked over her shoulder at the guards on the terrace. Radana nodded her head, patting the maid's hand in reassurance.

Her maid gave Radana a final bow, and left, the packet of poison tucked securely in her hand.

Radana sighed at her meal, and when the doors closed, she began to eat heartily. She would need all her strength for the long journey ahead.

Chapter Nine

In the Shifting Lands that are the Land of Death and Spirit, a small man stood at the edge of the ocean, his walking stick held loosely in his hand, and waited.

Slowly, the ocean began to churn. The waves left their ordered rows and splashed into chaos, their constant roar breaking and choking. The green waters boiled and a great stench arose, covering the shore like a fog.

The man waited.

The roiling waters darkened and steam billowed up to turn the sky white. A mighty howl poured out of the sea as if from the heart of the earth itself. The waters parted and from their depths rose a crowd of demons: foul monsters with red scales on their skins and tongues that wagged down to their knees. Black claws clutched deadly spears and black bows. Their quivers held arrows of snow and fire. Their leader, who was crowned in gold and had five gold rings in each of his ears, swung a curved sword over his head and roared out his battle cry.

Wading through the raging waters as if they were no more than a field of grass, the demons charged toward the small man, who did not move. The demons saw how still he stood and they laughed, making the air around them shudder.

The demons' leader set his misshapen, taloned foot on the shore. In answer, the man pursed his lips and blew out one silent puff of air.

Demons fell flat backward, like reeds under the monsoon's blast. As they cried in horror, the waters swallowed them whole.

The man stood on the shore while the waves washed away the demon's single footprint, and he waited.

"*P*rincess Natharie, will you please repeat your speech?" Master Gauda sat cross-legged on the floor of the performance alcove. He was a broad and well-fleshed man, as eunuchs frequently were, but his bulk was muscle hardened by long hours spent practicing the physical aspects of his craft. His light, resonant voice was as trained as his body. It rolled out over the heads of the young women and girls appointed, like Natharie, to learn the mysteries of Hastinapuran drama.

"Speak slowly this time, Princess," Gauda went on. "Remember to think on the measure of the phrase. This is poetry, not a screed from a drunken astrologer. The rest of you"—he glowered at the semicircle of students who sat before the practice stage—"watch her movements. Confidence is the essence of presence, even more so than precision." He clapped his hands once. "Begin."

Natharie suppressed a sigh, and did as she was instructed. She would accomplish nothing if she threw down the flimsy, false spear she carried and cried out to the drama master that he was a fool and a master of meaningless show.

If nothing else, it passes the time. It had been twenty days since she arrived in the women's quarters. Twenty days to learn the boundaries of the "small domain," and to learn how small they truly were. Since her first day, she had seen Queen Bandhura or Queen Prishi only through clouds of attendants. Her appointment to the drama master meant she spent most of her time here in the performance alcove, or in the library learning the pieces he set for her. This schedule severely limited her opportunities to watch and learn anything that might be useful to her own people, and Natharie was beginning to chafe against the constraints of her new life. The thought that she would grow used to it in time offered no consolation at all.

Natharie pushed these distractions aside, drew herself up straight, planting her feet shoulders' width apart to imitate a masculine stance. She lifted her hand (Let it soar, strong. You are an eagle here, not a sparrow.), and began. "Will war come down upon us? War is thunder and it is lightning." She tried to make the unfamiliar words ring. Her Hastinapuran was good, but she had learned the court tongue and this was the poetic dialect. It was ancient, and even more slurred and slick than its modern counterpart. How was she supposed to be precise when the language itself sloshed together and dropped its own consonants? "War is the rain and the great wave." *Spread your hands wide. You're talking about the sea.* "War is the time when we will prove what men we are, worthy to look upon . . ."

Just then, Prince Samudra stepped around the chamber's filigree archway. At the sight of him, Natharie's concentration broke and the phrase died in her mouth. Master Gauda opened his mouth to rebuke Natharie for faltering, but then his sharp eye caught the reason for her break. He dropped at once into the proper obeisance, as did all the other students. Natharie was the last to kneel.

"I hope you will pardon this interruption, Master Gauda," said Samudra politely.

"Your presence is never an interruption, my prince," Gauda replied at once. "How may we serve?"

"I was hoping to steal away your student."

At this, Gauda demurred. *We must, after all, play the scene correctly,* thought Natharie impatiently. "She needs her practice, my prince. It would not do for such natural talent to grow complacent." Natharie warmed to the compliment. Whatever her feelings for the place she was in, she had come over the past weeks to understand that Master Gauda truly was accomplished at his craft, and that he did not give praise where he did not feel there was merit.

"I will bring her back within the hour, I swear it." The prince was looking at her. Natharie could feel it. She kept her own gaze directed at the floor, modest and correct. They were still on stage, after all, all of them.

"I would never deny my prince anything I can provide." From the corner of her eye, Natharie saw Master Gauda bow once more. "You are excused, Natharie."

Natharie bowed over her hands to the drama master and stepped off the low stage. Hands folded and head bowed, she walked beside the prince. She was coming to know the corridors, and had little need to lift her gaze to check her way. The prince preferred the terrace garden to any other place in the women's quarters to sit and talk. They had done so almost daily since she had come. Not that they ever spoke of anything important. They talked of the poetry she was learning, a little of the past, and how that past differed in the histories and in the epics.

"You will forgive me for tearing you from your lessons?" he asked. Parrot words. He repeated them each time they walked this route.

"Of course, Great Prince." She searched for something new to say. "But I do not know that Master Gauda will."

"He is dedicated to the art. It is what makes him great." There was some thought behind those words, and memory. Good. It would make the conversation falter less.

"How did he come to be here?" she asked. It would not hurt to know more about her tutor.

"My father saw him perform as a boy, and he was so

impressed, he offered him a place in the small domain." The terrace garden opened before them, as far as such a confined place could open. Children had been sitting at lessons here and were hustled away by their tutors and nurses. The prince gestured to the stone bench, and Natharie sat down. At least here there was sunlight and the smell of growing things. She had been able to sit here and see the rains. Now that their season had come, they had poured down for weeks without stinting, washing away all the dust of the world, spilling out the silver that would again bring the green.

"I see," she said, because she needed to say something. The air here was cool, damp, and fresh. There was no rain now. It was one of the few days during the time of the rains when it remained dry, if not fair. The winds blew outside, scudding the clouds across the sky, piling them into mountains. It was as if the world were being allowed to breathe for a moment, but it would not last. If she correctly read her small glimpse of sky, the rains would begin again with nightfall.

"You are still mystified as to why any would be glad to enter here." The prince's words startled her out of her abstraction and Natharie felt herself blush for a moment. She was falling behind on her part.

Restlessness and homesickness made her dare a little honesty. "I am perhaps more naive than I care to admit. People make many choices that mystify me."

Samudra gave her a half-smile. "Should I perhaps say that as I have traveled the world so widely I will explain all such mysteries to you?"

Natharie looked long and silently at the prince. His delicate face was drawn, as if he had not been sleeping well, and his bright eyes were dim and distracted. What care weighed on him? Then, she noticed Hamsa was not following him today. In fact, Natharie could not remember if she had seen the sorceress on any of these little walks. Since they were in the women's quarters, Hamsa probably did not have to be near to protect or advise her master.

It was this thought that made Natharie understand what she saw in the prince's face. Prince Samudra was lonely.

"I begin to believe there are many things you would like to explain to me," she said softly.

"That, Great Princess, is a deep truth." He sighed, shook himself, and tried to assume a pleasant expression. "Tell me, Princess Natharie, if you were in your parents' home, how would you pass your time?"

You want me to draw you out of yourself, Great Prince. "I might sail a boat on the lake or river. I might swim. I might spar with one of the women guards open-hand or with the long staff. Perhaps I would go out shooting. I have a good eye with a bow. I might ride horse or elephant, with or without a groom. If it were a special occasion, I might be called upon to supervise the disposition of a banquet and prepare with my own hands five different kinds of sweet worthy to present to kings. Then I would sit with the lords of the land and speak of law and history, in their own languages. Were there merchants visiting the palace, I might help value silk, jewels, and spices, and do some of the bartering."

The stunned look on his face gave her a moment's odd satisfaction. "You were permitted to . . ."

"I was kept in childhood for ten years longer than was customary while . . . certain political matters were settled." Now it was her turn to give him a mirthless smile. "As I was not a woman with my own house and children, I had to be kept occupied." A crowd of memories took her, sights and scents, the cool, secure presence of Anun, of her family, of sunshine and the river, so much life and activity. She pushed them down with difficulty. She must now keep her pride and countenance.

"I did not realize," said Samudra.

"No." She thought about how he had watched her with those warm, lonely eyes, always looking but never coming near. Did she want him near? She had him now. Why did she try to drive him away again?

Natharie realized it was because she did not know for certain what he did want, and that somewhere, deep within her, she wanted those eyes to see not just a pitiful hostage. She wanted him to see the whole of her, and to keep looking.

But for now, Samudra looked around the garden. Perhaps for this moment he saw it as the prison she did. "You have good reason to be angry with me," he murmured. "With us."

He did understand. At least he tried, and Natharie was sure the attempt was genuine. She opened her mouth to say she had come of her own will, or something similar, but the words were never spoken. Cloth rustled and the many voices of the main chamber beyond went silent, causing both her and the prince to look up.

"Brother of my heart!" Queen Bandhura and her flock of women crossed into the garden, her face full of glad surprise that did not shine in her eyes. Natharie knelt at once. "How lovely that you are here." The queen took Samudra's hands and beamed at him. "And I see you take it upon yourself to help entertain our Princess Sacrifice." She gestured for Natharie to stand.

"Princess Sacrifice?" repeated Samudra.

"It is how she has come to be called, since her arrival." Queen Bandhura's smile grew even wider to show what a merry joke she thought it was.

Samudra's demeanor, however, remained perfectly sober. "I am not certain I care for that nickname."

"What could be the harm?" The queen settled onto the nearest bench, arranging her skirts, even as her ladies arranged themselves around her. "I'm sure our princess does not take it amiss." She turned her brilliant smile to Natharie.

"You do not think it flirts too closely with blasphemy?" Samudra folded his hand.

"Why, Brother, you have never cared for such matters." Bandhura was watching him more closely, no doubt searching for what he hid behind his placid expression.

"Indeed," the queen continued. "The high priest has considered, I believe, that you also flirted too closely with blasphemy."

"I know this." To Natharie's surprise, the prince humbly hung his head. "I am trying to mend my ways."

"You shock me, Brother!" exclaimed the queen. *And you are not the only one,* thought Natharie, who was at least as surprised as the queen pretended to be.

"When did you come to believe you needed to change?" Bandhura asked. "You have always been so certain of yourself."

"Since I returned I have seen how many things have changed." *You're very ready with that answer, Great Prince,* thought Natharie. *How long have you had it in mind?* "I came to understand that the dance continues, and I was a fool to try to hold still. Now, forgive me, Sister," he bowed his head, "I swore to Master Gauda, I would return Natharie to her lessons, to which I believe you set her." He made the salute of trust and then bowed formally to Natharie, who returned the gesture. As they both straightened, their eyes met for a single heartbeat.

You're lying, she thought toward him. *You're using me as part of that lie. What are you doing, Prince Samudra?*

But he gave her no hint of an answer, returning her to the study of the ancient dramas, and letting her wonder what new drama she was being used to ornament.

*R*eluctantly, Samudra left Natharie to Master Gauda and walked down the corridors to his own room. Hamsa was, as always, waiting for him. His sorceress looked affronted, but he could not help that. She'd been right all along. Her presence was just one more reminder to Natharie how distant this place was from those she knew, and he did not wish the princess to feel uncomfortable or awkward with him. He wanted . . . he was barely prepared to admit what he wanted from her, especially when he was using her so shamelessly.

"What now, my prince?" asked Hamsa, without any trace of the hurt that showed so plainly in her eyes.

"Now I go flatter Captain Pravan," he answered quietly. He looked at her, willing her to understand, and not to make him ask her aloud to stay behind.

Hamsa caught his meaning, but was not, it seemed, ready to let him go easily. "Samudra, what are you doing?" she murmured.

"What I must, Hamsa."

He watched the struggle for acceptance of this within her, and watched her lose it. Softly, plaintively, she asked, "How can I help you?"

But Samudra shook his head. "You cannot. The Mother who has claimed me as her son must help me now." He turned away, and then turned back. "Wait. There is something. You can tell Makul I will meet him at sunset, in the stables. Tell him it should look to be by chance, you understand?"

Hamsa bowed her head, in acquiescence and, he guessed, to keep him from seeing the expression on her face. He let her have her privacy and walked away.

I'm sorry, Hamsa, but there is no place for you in what I do now. This is intrigue, the worst kind of plotting. You would be lost here, even more than I am.

Samudra made his way down the broad stairs out to the gardens and the practice yard. As one of his tasks these days was overseeing the rebuilding of the chariot and cavalry corps that Pravan's defeat had left shattered, Samudra had had plenty of time to grow familiar with that rash commander's ways. He would not be hard to find. This was the time of day when Pravan liked to consult with the officers under him, sometimes sitting with them through the midday meal so they could hear what he thought about what they'd said.

The winds blew briskly outside, full of the wet scent of rain. The ground was soaked. Down on the practice yard it would be churned to mud. This was a good time for practice, because the yard so clearly imitated the conditions men would meet with on the battlefield. Samudra liked to get the men out on such days and let them learn of this. This much, Pravan had not undone.

Samudra raised his hand to Makul, who was drilling new soldiers and their new horses in tight formation down on the muddy green, but did not beckon for Makul to join him. He knew his battle-father was frowning at this, but he had other things to do before he and Makul spoke.

Pravan, as Samudra had expected, sat in the shade of the dining pavilion with his officers ranged before him. Several were hardly more than boys. These looked up at their commander with bright eyes. Samudra took note of those whose names he did not know. There were many new young officers, here and outside. Pravan had been seeing to promotions among his own ranks, and had not bothered to introduce the new men to Samudra. Among other things, Samudra would have to take the measure of these new officers, before their loyalties became too fixed. Pravan could become an epic unto himself if permitted to warm to his favorite themes of glory and honor in war, and the young and unblooded could all too easily be drawn into worship of such speech.

Samudra's entrance was, of course, quickly noted. All the officers stood and bowed, raising their hands to touch first their hearts and then their brows in the soldier's salute, which Samudra returned, while he looked straight at Pravan. "Captain," he said.

"My prince," Pravan said warily as he straightened. "I . . . had thought you engaged elsewhere."

"I was, but I am here now, as you see." He laughed a little, and those before him dutifully joined in.

"I do see, but . . ." *You are suspicious, as well you should be,* thought Samudra while Pravan struggled to find appropriately courteous words. *We haven't met since I threatened to kill you, and you threatened to have me executed for treason.* "Is there something you need of me?"

Samudra folded his hands behind his back and pasted a look of surprise on his own face. "I came to consult with you."

That plainly startled the other man. *Good. I need you off-balance early.* "I . . . Very well. You are dismissed," Pravan said to the officers. As they scattered, he gestured to his own seat. "Will you sit, my prince?"

Samudra took the proffered place. Tea was soon brought and Pravan served him. Samudra took the cup with polite thanks. "I have been remiss since my return, Pravan." He spoke as if they were exchanging nothing more than mild pleasantries. "I have not asked you once what you saw in the north. Analysis of defeat can be even more effective than that of a victory." He raised his teacup and sipped, watching the other man over the rim.

Pravan blinked rapidly. "All these things are well known," he demurred. "What would you have me tell you, my prince?"

Samudra raised his brows. "The truth, of course, Captain," he said, deliberately misunderstanding. "Tell me what happened."

Pravan bowed his head. "Very well." He paused a moment, ordering whatever thoughts he had, and, Samudra was sure, setting aside more than a few suspicions. Wind battered and slapped at the pavilion around them and the clouds turned the light pale and grey. "I do not believe it was the fault of our men that we were unable to rout the Huni . . ."

Samudra sat and listened to the litany of excuses and reordered events. He kept his expression interested, while he worked feverishly to dig out the small nuggets of truth in the self-serving account Pravan spilled. What quickly became clear was that Pravan had decided the Huni had no talent for subtlety and no patience. He had engaged in a full-force assault of the Huni's position, judging that they would not be able to resist immediately running out to join so bold a battle. Instead, the Huni had responded intelligently.

They drew themselves deeper into their protected position. Waiting until Pravan and his men wore themselves out, they crept around their flank and attacked with all the ferocity for which they were famous. Even Pravan's active imagination could not disguise the fact that it was the sacrifices of the other officers and the desperate bravery of the men under their command that allowed any Hastinapurans to escape at all.

All this Samudra drank in like bitter wine. Each word was a blow to him, but he took them all and held his face still and made no more reply than a nod of encouragement in appropriate places. He did note that not once did Pravan mention Lohit or what had happened there. Perhaps he believed Samudra had not heard. Perhaps he believed Samudra had been warned to say nothing.

And so I have. In a way.

When Pravan's tale came to a close at last, Samudra set his cup down. "Thank you for your account, Captain. There is much here to think on before we plan the next attempt. Will you sit with me tomorrow at the midday meal so we may look at the maps and make our decisions?"

Samudra watched the shock take hold of Pravan at the phrase "our decisions."

Yes, look at me. Have I accepted that you are to have command of the armies in my place? Or am I playing a game with you? We all know I do not play such games. So, what am I doing?

"It would be an honor, my prince . . ." Pravan hesitated. "Who else shall I summon to sit with us?"

"Whoever you think best." Samudra unfolded his legs and stood. "I have been gone a year, after all, attending to sacred duty. You know better than I who are our ablest remaining men." He smiled, showing his confidence. *Let's see who you bring. I would know each one of your favorites by face and by name.*

Pravan gave the salute of trust. "All shall be as you say, my prince."

"Very good." With that, Samudra took his leave, strolling out of the tent toward the exercise yard. In the bowl of the practice yard below, hooves thundered and weapons clashed. Down there, Makul was drilling the new men in combat techniques, pitting them one against the other. His voice rang out, incomprehensible at this distance, as he shouted instruction, encouragement, admonition. Samudra's hands itched for the touch of clean steel, for the feel of leather reins in his fist, for speed and noise and heat, for all the things he understood. He turned and hollered to a boy groom who was hurrying past. "My horse, boy. I will ride down and teach these children how it's done!"

For an hour, or two, he would fight and sweat and swear and take the measure of his men. For an hour he would ease his heart and be himself.

He did not look back as he strode down the hill toward the yard. To look back would be to see Hamsa and to think on what he had just done and what he must do next. If he thought on that now, his heart would burst for fear and anger. If he was right, Pravan would be on his way to the emperor. He would tell Chandra all that Samudra had said and done, and then . . . And then they would see to whom Chandra took that word.

Mother Indu help me. Mother A-Kuha, accept this as my offering to you and do not turn your darker aspect toward me.

But if either goddess heard the prayer, she remained silent. Samudra marched forward alone.

Chapter Ten

Bandhura, first of all queens of Hastinapura, sat behind her screen in the small audience chamber, listening to the men beyond the folding wooden screen with its delicately carved latticework. Bandhura chose her screens as carefully as she chose any item of her wardrobe. She had some of ivory and gilt, glittering with gems that drew the eye, reminding all of her unseen presence in the room. The one arranged before her now was a beautiful but more humble creation, something that could more easily be forgotten.

She sat cross-legged on her scarlet pillow. In front of her, Chandra, emperor of Hastinapura, Beloved of the Seven Mothers, lounged on one elbow, listening with alert ears and lazy eyes to young, eager, hopeless Captain Pravan. Bandhura could see him only by turning her head and peering closely through the screen. Every so often, Chandra would throw Bandhura an ironic or amused glance, and she would answer with a smile. Pravan never noticed. He believed he had his emperor's undivided attention.

"The time is perfect, Majesty, and Prince Samudra is willing that it should be so. There are but a handful of days before the rains cease. This time the Huni will fall beneath your might and there will be none to oppose you!"

Chandra glanced toward Bandhura, and pretended to stifle a yawn. She frowned at him and he smiled in return.

"Very well, Pravan," Chandra said. "I have heard you. It may be time to do as you say. You will be informed of my decision."

Pravan was adroit enough to recognize a dismissal when

he heard one. He made his obeisance and backed out of the room. The servants closed the great doors behind him, and Chandra flopped down on his divan, letting out a great, gusty sigh of relief.

Smiling at this boyish display, Bandhura came out from behind her screen. She stretched herself out beside her husband, running her hand lazily, lovingly, up and down his chest.

"So," said Chandra to the ceiling as much as to her. "My brother has decided to stop avoiding Pravan."

Bandhura shrugged. "While you keep the commander in your favor, there is not much else that Samudra can do."

Chandra captured her hand as it wandered over his heart, holding it close. "Do you think he understands? That I can and will show preference to others if he does not keep his place?"

"I know it grieves you, my lord, but it must be done," answered Bandhura softly. She leaned over him. "Samudra cannot be permitted to drown in his own pride."

"Mmm." Chandra sat up abruptly, causing Bandhura to roll aside. He was looking to the past, seeing something she did not. Bandhura frowned inwardly. She did not like it when Chandra's thoughts were hidden from her.

But his mood changed swiftly, and his bright smile returned to his fine and handsome face. "Well, what say you, my wife? Shall I give my brother what he most desires and send him off to face the Huni?"

Bandhura pushed herself up into a sitting position, considering carefully before she answered. Despite Chandra's demeanor, this was not a light or an idle conversation. "My husband, I of course know nothing of war and in all things your will is mine, but I think you should not send Samudra away just yet."

Chandra turned more fully toward her, his eyes half-lidded. It was an expression he used when he too wished to be underestimated. "And why is that, my wife?"

The queen chose her words with precision. "I think your

brother has undergone a change of heart, recently. I believe it may have been facilitated by the princess of Sindhu."

"Ha! Divakesh's least favorite. That would be enough reason for Samudra to want her, I suppose." He looked shrewdly at his wife. "You think this is more than a soldier's dalliance?"

"I think it may be." She had to tread carefully. There were so many things she was not ready to bring to Chandra yet. To hand him something half-formed could be disastrous. Chandra's touch was not a gentle one.

"Speak plainly," he said. His attention was already waning. "I want no riddles from you."

"I wish I could speak plainly, my husband, but I am still only wrestling with riddles myself. It may be your brother is in love . . ."

"Good!" shouted Chandra with genuine joy, smacking fist into palm. "Finally! A crack in that stone heart of his!"

". . . or it may be that the princess is . . . acting for the Awakened lands."

One muscle at a time, Chandra's face fell, into cold seriousness. "A spy?"

"Or a secret ambassador with an offer to our prince." *Consider this thought, husband.* "It may be no accident that she returned with him."

This made Chandra go very still. It was in his stillness that the emperor was the most dangerous. "My brother swims in very deep waters."

"It may be nothing," Bandhura said quickly. Chandra needed to be worried, but not overwhelmed. Samudra must live a while longer yet. It would be no good if all the flies were not trapped. No good at all. Samudra and the flies must fall together, and they must be seen to fall by all those in power. It must be clear and unmistakable that Chandra was not to be challenged, and that Bandhura, first of all queens, was his first and best guard. "It may only be that my care for you is such that I start at shadows."

"Find out for us, my wife. We must know."

Bandhura bowed her head over her hands. "I will, my husband, do not fear."

"I do fear, Bandhura," he whispered. "I fear so much I think sometimes the palace will fall in from the way my soul shakes." He lifted his gaze to meet hers. "But I fear nothing at all from you."

They were words to melt the strongest heart, and Bandhura could not stay away as he spoke them. She slipped to his side and kissed him, slowly, lovingly, as she knew he liked, and he kissed her back with the deep passion that was always so much a part of him. For propriety's sake, she should have stopped, drawn back, reminded him of modesty, but she did not want to. She wanted his touch, wanted to feel his need and soothe away his fears. So she let herself be pulled close, running her hands along his body, along arms and thighs, kissing, laughing, teasing, tempting and giving in to temptation.

There in the audience chamber he took her, and she gloried in the taking and the giving, in his love and need and her own intertwined in a dance older and greater than even the one the Mothers knew.

When it was over, they lay together, lazy in their contentment, their clothing in disarray, their hands that had been so eager moments before idly smoothing each other's hair back into some semblance of order.

Chandra ran his fingertips over her exposed breast. "I would visit this prize of Samudra's," he said, drawing her silken band back over her breast and smoothing it down. "See if she is worthy of my brother."

"Then it must be arranged, my husband." This time, Bandhura did move his hand away, pulling herself backward. "Remember, however, you are promised to meet with the overseers to ride out to the Amarin palace and review the construction. I believe they have gone to great trouble to make sure you would be well received and entertained through tomorrow." She smiled knowingly.

Chandra sighed. "Oh, yes. I suppose that should be done." He sat up. "It would not do to have my builders stealing from the imperial coffers and returning shoddy work. Will you come?"

"Thank you, husband, but I have some dull administrative matters that have already been put off as long as possible." Bandhura also sat up, ordering both clothing and hair, pulling her polite dignity back around her. "So, if you are ready . . . ?"

Heat brightened his languorous eyes. "For you, my wife"—Chandra put her finger in his mouth, and drew it out slowly, tasting it, enjoying the light in her eyes—"I am always ready."

She pushed him backward, and laughed as he rolled over his own shoulder as neat as any acrobat. "Go now, my husband. Be emperor. Let me deal with the small domain."

Chandra climbed to his feet. "Be sure to send my love to my mother. I will come sit with her on my return."

He spoke lightly, and Bandhura was content to let it be. "I will do so." Chandra seemed to believe that his mother was somehow immortal, and had never bothered to find out how ill she truly was. Possibly he could not bear to do so. No one but she knew how his father's death had cut him to his heart. The possibility that his mother might also die soon might well be more than he could bear.

She watched him stroll from the room, clapping his hands for his servants, who were doubtless already busy fetching water and fresh clothing for their master. Before he left the room, he had forgotten she was there, already thinking on his next adventure, his next pleasure.

Shaking her head, Bandhura made her own retreat behind her screen. The Palace of the Pearl Throne was not one labyrinth as many people thought; it was several, all of them intertwined. Because the queens must preserve modesty and purity at all times, they had separate doors and separate secret stairs that led from the small domain to the few other places they might properly go, such as the emperor's audience and bedchambers, the throne room, and the temple ring. They were narrow, these stairways, almost as narrow as the servants', but the builders had never forgotten these were for the emperor's wives, and they were made of inlaid teakwood. Cornices held golden statuary and oil lamps and the walls were lavishly painted with modest household designs, and some not so modest as well, reminding the queens of that which was their most sacred duty.

Chandra had not yet given her a child, but Bandhura was not worried. She saw the Mothers' pattern clearly. First she must make him safe. It was then that their son would be born and raised to glorious manhood, becoming one of the greatest of all emperors.

Bandhura smiled. Her life was like a dream to her still, for it was only in dreams or legends that a marriage such as hers to Chandra could happen. Bandhura brought nothing to the marriage. She had nothing to bring. She was a concubine's daughter, born to servitude. She had never lived anywhere but the small domain. All her training, all her mother's hope had been to make her daughter acceptable to some minor official, perhaps to an advisor to the Throne itself. Mother did not aim higher.

But Bandhura grew up watching the young prince Chandra. He was handsome and he was quick. He laughed frequently and he loved all that was beautiful and luxurious. She watched his feats in the wrestling ring from behind screens and saw the lavish rewards he gave to those he defeated. She saw him at his father's side, absorbing all that slender, sickly man had to tell him. The old emperor had no fire in his eyes, no sharp edge to his smile. All that was given to his eldest son.

How her heart had burned the day Chandra looked at her and saw her fully, not as another little girl, but as the woman she was. When he had declared his love for her, she had not believed it, but as time went on, they grew closer. It was she he sought when his mercurial heart fell into anger or despair. She held him when he wept in rage and fear over his destiny. She applauded and celebrated with him when he won his races, or left his opponents bleeding on the practice field. It was she he kissed and loved deeply when he was pleased with her music and her singing.

Even then, she had trembled in disbelief when she stood before the Pearl Throne and heard Divakesh call out her name as the first of all queens. Her knees were so weak she could barely mount the dais and kneel before her husband, placing her hands between his feet. His hands were warm as he raised her up, and his eyes were full of love and that magnificent fire as they placed that first carved screen before her so that none could look on her save her husband, lord and emperor.

Chandra loved her. He trusted her as no one ever had, and no one would injure him while she could prevent it.

In more ways than one, Bandhura was grateful for Queen Prishi's illness. She had known from the first that if she could not rule the small domain, she could not look after Chandra's interests with the diligence such vital matters required. Queen Prishi did not like her, not well, not at first. Indeed, the elder queen had done her best to keep Bandhura on a leash. It would have grieved her greatly to have her husband's mother poisoned, but she could not let the old woman keep power, not when it was so clear the unnatural woman favored Samudra over her eldest. Thankfully, the Mothers saw this too, and brought her illness down hard on her. The physicians all agreed she would not live another year.

It did not matter how long death was in coming. The Mother of Destruction had put Prishi to one side and left Bandhura free to work.

She emerged from the narrow, winding stair into her own airy chamber. Her ladies were there waiting for her. They seldom accompanied her out of the small domain, unless it was a state occasion and she required an entourage. Although she enjoyed having noble women in service to her, she had never grown entirely used to it, and she knew better than any that each of them might harbor ambitions of her own.

"I need to speak with Lord Divakesh," she said to the colorful gaggle.

"Please, Majesty," piped up little Dani. "Queen Prishi wishes to see you."

Bandhura sighed and looked down at her rumpled state. She was not embarrassed. The emperor's hot blood was famed. But Prishi's needs could be inconvenient. It would not do to neglect her, however. The one thing the old woman could still do was complain to her sons, and that Bandhura could not afford.

"Very well, come, get me washed and dressed so I may go to her."

The daughters of the noble houses swarmed around her, removing her soiled clothing, washing, powdering, painting, scenting, taking and receiving jewelry until Bandhura was freshly clad in topaz and sapphire silk. Her hair was looped into neat braids and her throat, ears, arms, and ankles were all decked with pearls. Now she might go soothe whatever her mother-in-law's pet might be.

When Bandhura entered the old queen's room, Damman, as usual, did not fully hide her anger. The woman had better hope her family would take her back, or that the old queen had left her well provided for, because her time in the small domain was limited to the span of Prishi's fading life.

Prishi herself had been moved to a low couch on the terrace, where the cool air generated by the pouring rains might ease some of the fever her long illness brought. Indeed, she looked almost lively today.

"Ah! Daughter of my heart!" she called in her rasping whisper as Bandhura approached, bowing her head humbly. "There you are. I was so worried."

"What could worry you, mother of my heart?" Bandhura

plumped Prishi's pillows and held a cup to her perpetually dry mouth, that she might sip the tangerine juice.

"I saw an omen, daughter, an omen!" She clutched Bandhura's hand in her scabbed claw. "I saw a great fish swimming through the rain. It swallowed up two dragonflies. They were my sons. I am sure of it!" The force of her words half-lifted Prishi off her cushions.

"There, Mother, calm yourself." Bandhura pushed her back down, gently but firmly, and gestured to Damman to come running with rosewater to cool her brow. "It was a dream, not an omen. A nightmare of your illness, that it all."

"No, no." The old queen shook her head back and forth. "It was an omen, an omen."

Movement caught Bandhura's eye and she saw the eunuch hesitating in the doorway with Lord Divakesh, massive and proud behind him. Priests of the Mothers were one of the few classes of men who were allowed access to the small domain. Many lewd jokes passed among the ladies and boys about how the priests used and abused this privilege, but no one told those jokes about Divakesh.

Bandhura smiled. The high priest had excellent timing. "Here is Lord Divakesh, Mother. He will tell you the meaning of what you saw."

The high priest came in and made his respectful, abbreviated obeisance. He listened seriously while Prishi repeated her babble to him. He closed his eyes for a moment, as if seeing what she saw. When he opened them, he said, "It is as the first of all queens told you, Majesty. It was a dream. But it was a dream of good omen. It means that the power of Hastinapura will soon put an end to two of the bright enemies that threaten her."

Prishi's cloudy eyes searched the high priest's face for a frantic moment, as if looking for a reason for disbelief, but even Bandhura could see nothing but utter seriousness in him. Slowly, the old queen began to breathe more easily.

"Yes, yes, that must be it. Thank you, Lord Divakesh." Prishi closed her eyes and coughed a little.

"You should sleep now, Mother," said Bandhura.

At this, Prishi's eyes flew open and again she grasped Bandhura's hand, her sharp fingers digging into Bandhura's flesh. "You will not leave me, Daughter? I am afraid. I . . . you will not leave me."

"No, no, if you do not wish it." Bandhura extricated herself delicately. She had had a great deal of practice at the maneuver. "I will just sit over here with Lord Divakesh so our talk will not disturb you."

"Yes, yes." Prishi nodded, her eyes already closing. "Thank you, Daughter. You care so well for me. So well . . ." and her words trailed away as the fever sleep took her yet again.

Bandhura leaned over and kissed her mother-in-law's forehead, ignoring as usual the glare of her servant woman. Her own servants clustered to follow her, but she waved them all back to the doorway. She did not wish an audience for the conversation she was about to have. She walked over to the bench at the edge of the latticed terrace and beckoned Lord Divakesh to follow. The rains beyond the ivory lattice made a solid silver curtain. Bandhura could understand how old Prishi believed a fish might swim past the balcony.

But this was no time for whimsy.

"How may I be of service to the first of all queens?" Divakesh stood before her, and she did not bother to ask him to sit. Divakesh resented efforts to make him comfortable, regarding them all as temptations.

"Lord Divakesh, I wish to speak to you about Princess Natharie of Sindhu."

Divakesh nodded. "She is watched, my queen. It will not be long before I have proof that she still practices her blasphemies and she will fall under the Mothers' judgment." There was no bloodlust in his voice, as there might be in a man of lesser devotion, and certainly there was no anticipation of triumph. There was only the cold certainty of the killing sword he wielded so efficiently in service of the divine.

And what will he do to me when I speak? Bandhura marshaled her courage. Chandra would not permit this one to harm her, however much he feared the high priest's words. She was safe. "I ask you spare her."

"Why should I do that?" It was as if she had asked him to stop his own heart from beating. "She corrupts the heart of the dance."

Yes, yes, but there are other considerations here, my lord. "We spoke before about Prince Samudra. I see now that Natharie is the key to reaching him. It is through her I will be able to bring his dealings into the open."

These words drew only cold anger from Lord Divakesh. "You would conspire against the one the Mothers chose to protect the Throne?"

Bandhura felt a moment's chilling doubt. Had she misjudged her moment? "Never," she said firmly. "Unless I knew he had already broken the dance."

That took Divakesh aback. He folded his great arms and for a moment he watched the rains, as if he might read the Mothers' purposes there. "You have proof of this?"

"None I can take to the emperor." She clasped her hands together, assuming an admiring look. Divakesh acted as if he were immune to human flattery, but she did not believe any man was that strong. "You have taught him that the devotion and duty to the Mothers is the most important of all things, but when he looks at Samudra, he still sees only his brother." She leaned forward, head a little turned. *See how I am ashamed, Lord Divakesh. See how I am afraid.* "While this remains true, your lessons about the dangers of the Awakened lands will not truly reach him. But I too have my eyes and my ears, Lord Divakesh." She twisted her hands, pleading now. "Give me time, let me take this pollution onto myself before it reaches the emperor. I promise, Natharie

174 *Sarah Zettel*

will be laid low, and she will take Samudra with her. When that happens, Chandra will be free to be the true servant of the Mothers you and I both know that he is." She looked up, her eyes wide and blinking fast. *See me, my lord. See the devoted daughter before you. Think about the advantage of having me do your work for you.*

Lord Divakesh considered these things for a moment, his expression rock-hard and inscrutable. "It may be you are the instrument of the Mothers. It may be she was brought here for you to show your faith, and that was why I could not reach her." He said this more to himself than to her, as if trying the idea on for size. Then, he nodded. "I will wait then, First of All Queens." She opened her mouth and he held up one finger to interrupt her. "But not long. Each day the threat to the Throne and the dance grows darker and will be more difficult to remove."

In that we are in perfect agreement, my lord. Bandhura stood and took his hand, pressing her forehead to the tough, scarred back of it. "I thank you, Lord Divakesh. I will not fail you, nor the Queen of Heaven."

The high priest touched her head in blessing and Bandhura let herself smile toward the rain-silvered evening outside. Night would come soon, and the night showed so many new things.

What Bandhura did not see was that on her couch, Queen Prishi, who had overheard each and every word spoken between queen and priest, also smiled. At last, she fully closed her eyes and slid into sleep.

*E*kkadi hated going down to the temple ring. The great temple of the Mothers was the first ring of the Palace of the Pearl Throne so that the Mothers might be the foundation of all that was done there. If the small domain was a maze, the temple was a massive labyrinth. Within its winding corridors, each of the Seven Mothers had her own great shrine, and here too waited the great central temple to all of the Seven and the dance that was theirs. Besides this, scores of priests and acolytes were housed in the first ring. The library there was the greatest in all Hastinapura, holding texts that were over three thousand years old. Always there were scribes and scholars at the copying tables, transcribing, translating, repairing, or memorizing. The ring had its own kitchens, its own laundries, and its own storehouses, for the wealth of the Mothers could not be allowed to mingle with baser golds and jewels.

The journey here was bad enough on the holy days, when she was marched down with all the other women of the small domain to watch the sacrifices and hear the hymns. Mother's breath, she had thought Princess Sacrifice was going to faint at the sight of the blood, and she'd had to hover behind her the whole time.

That was bad, but it was worse coming down on her own when Natharie had finally gone to bed. Her lamp was low and guttery, and the servants' stairs and passages were steep, dark, and cramped. Where the stairs were not stone, they creaked, and no matter what the hour, there was always someone rushing in the other direction to bump into her and curse her for being slow and stupid. *For your business is so much more important than mine.* Ekkadi was, however, careful to keep her curses to herself. She did not want one of these others to have any cause to remember her. She certainly did not want them to wonder why she took these stairs every night after most of their masters and mistresses had sought their beds. The lowest servants could talk. That was something her sisters had drilled relentlessly into her before she had been brought here. Mother might think sacrifice was the way to advance her children, but Ekkadi's two older sisters had much more practical ideas about how one's position could best be secured.

Next to all this, lying to the guards was nothing. She was a maid and might come and go from the protected confines to fetch her mistress any little thing, though she might not have managed quite so easily if she was not also carrying love letters from one of the boy clerks to his darling. What he used to bribe the eunuch who let her move about so freely, Ekkadi did not know and did not want to know.

After the narrow stairs and the winking guards came the vast, empty corridors between the temple spaces, and these were the worst of all. Her way was dogged by the never-ending thump and brush of feet she could not see. The priests' dances never completely stopped. There were dances for each hour, for each sort of weather, for peace, for war. Dances to keep all in their proper place, dances to keep emperor and empire strong. There were holy sorcerers in those dances, weaving their spells with their steps. The enormity of it made Ekkadi feel even smaller as she stole along the polished corridors. She kept her lamp close and shaded with her hand, showing no more light than she needed to. It was good to hide her face, but in truth, she did not like seeing the white eyes of the Mothers whose likenesses decorated the walls. What she did could not be wrong, not all of it, for it was at the command of the high priest, but she still did not like to look at them.

When Ekkadi reached the northernmost corridors, she came to the place she liked least of all. The priests did not have rooms in the palace; their rooms were cut from the mountain itself. A plain archway took her from the edifice raised by man and magic into one raised by the Mothers. The squared-off corridor was as elaborately carved and painted as the others, but here the very air was different. It was always cold, damp, and hushed. She could not hear the dancers anymore. She could not hear anything but her heart and the slap of her sandals on smooth black stone. Here, the carvings of the Mothers were very old, and very confusing. Other figures stood level with them, a thing that she had never seen anywhere else. Ekkadi counted curtained doorways until she came to the fifth on the right, and rapped her knuckles against the stone. "Lord Divakesh?"

"Enter."

Ekkadi pushed aside the plain saffron cloth. Divakesh's private rooms consisted of three cells—one for sleeping, one for washing, and the one she stood in now, for sitting or studying. The furnishings here were more spare than those in even the lowest servant's room. The only extravagance was in the niches. Dozens, maybe even hundreds of small, regular alcoves had been carved from the mountain's stone, and in each one stood a statue of some aspect of the Queen of Heaven. Some were plain red stone. Some were solid gold, flickering in the light of Divakesh's single oil lamp. Some were crystal, others obsidian or alabaster. There was even one small blue image that Ekkadi was sure had been carved from a single sapphire.

Surrounded by the greatest of all the Mothers, the high priest knelt before a block of stone carved to serve as a table. On it was spread some scroll. Though he was dressed in a simple burgundy robe, his presence lost none of its power. He certainly lost none of his understanding of who he was compared with his visitor. He did not even turn his head to look at her.

Despite this, Ekkadi set down her lamp and made obeisance. It would not do to disregard propriety before or, indeed, behind this man.

"It is very late, Ekkadi."

"Forgive me, Lord Divakesh." Ekkadi remained crouched on the floor. "But the princess sometimes does not sleep well and she sits in the gardens for a while."

Carefully, patiently, Divakesh lifted up one leaf of the scroll before him and laid it aside. "The Mothers make her days longer so she might see them more clearly."

"It must be as you say, Holy One," murmured Ekkadi humbly. The stone was cold and bit at her knees. She shivered.

"What of her and the prince? What did they speak of today?"

"Not much, Holy One." She wished he would turn around and give her permission to stand, but he didn't, so she remained where she was, and recited as much as she could remember of Natharie and Prince Samudra's latest meeting.

When she finished, Lord Divakesh finally lifted his head. "You heard, but you did not understand." He turned, but not to face her, to face the niches in the eastern wall. He watched the likenesses of Mother Jalaja with an expression that made Ekkadi think of nothing so much as a despairing lover. "It begins. She tells him of her polluted life, making him see it as pure and good. He falters, Ekkadi." The high priest shook his head slowly in resignation. "I knew this would come when I first saw how he looked at her. She seems so fair, young and brave. She is enough to make mortal man forget the greater sight of the Queen of Heaven. For that, though, the prince will fall." A shudder took Ekkadi, although she tried to repress it. The priest's sharp eye caught it. "You tremble at this. You should."

"Yes, Holy One." *I tremble because this place is cold, Holy One, and my feet hurt and I've been running about all day after the one you're so afraid of.*

The high priest rubbed his thick, blunt fingers together, like a merchant rubbing a coin. "She did no more than what you've told me? She spoke not a word of the corrupt teachings? Think hard."

Ekkadi furrowed her brow for what felt like a reasonable length of time, and then shook her head. "No, Lord. Nothing. I'm sorry. I am trying."

"You are. You are a good daughter." He touched her head in blessing, and Ekkadi could not suppress another shudder. "Make your obeisance, and take your reward. Remember, as soon as she speaks of the teachings of vanity to the prince, you will come to me at once."

"Yes, Holy One." *She could recite Anidita's words from beginning to end for all of me, Holy One. But you or she will win this game, and I will be standing beside the victor, who-*

ever it is. She turned to the wall of deities and kissed the cold, smooth stone of the floor before it. Then she backed away still on her knees. Divakesh remained where he was, contemplating the hundred images of Mother Jalaja in front of him. The look on his face was that of a starving man. It was raw, and terrible in the strength of its need. Ekkadi shuddered again, and shuffled back as quickly as she could.

Beside the doorway waited two small gold rings, and Ekkadi slipped them onto her smallest finger. Coins would raise suspicions if she were found with them, but new jewelry had many plausible explanations.

Lord Divakesh was already back to his studies and Ekkadi took her leave in silence. Hurrying, she left the mountain cells for the temple. Again, the distant rhythm of the holy dancers whispered in the air around her. She was already perspiring from the heat, and her weariness made her think with longing of her narrow pallet beside Natharie.

But caution ran strong in her and it turned her weary feet down one of the side corridors.

The temple doors were of course shut tight, but there were smaller shrines beside the great teak doors. Ekkadi stopped before the one that showed the woman with the sword raised high in her hand. Skulls and pearls girded her waist, and she had one eye shut and one eye open. A snake twined her shoulders and whispered in her ear, and another wound around her ankle.

It was the Mother of Destruction, but with one eye open. Those who thought she slept would be deceived.

Ekkadi put her lamp down. She made the salute of trust to Mother A-Kuha, holding the posture for ten slow breaths. Then, she slipped one of the little rings off her hand and laid it beside the goddess.

Mother, I am following your narrow path. I beg you, walk before me and clear the way, for without you I will surely fall.

She kissed Mother A-Kuha's foot and stroked the snake

that twined around her ankle, and then retrieved her lamp. As quickly as she could without blowing out the flame, she trotted toward the servants' stairs. It would not do for Natharie to wake up and miss her maid. She might say something important.

Ekkadi smiled to the darkness, curled her hand tight around her remaining ring, and hurried on.

Chapter Eleven

Agnidh Yamuna was receiving petitioners.

Hamsa stood in the threshold of Yamuna's spartan chamber, watching. Looking a strangely ascetic emperor with his white breechclout and bare head, he sat on his woven mat behind an unadorned table. The court before him was a mismatched and ragtag gathering. Men and women both stood before him. Many had been baked rich brown by the sun. Wind and rain had tanned their skins to leather. Their clothes were simple, even ragged, their hair bundled into braids that were the mark of a sorcerer. Some carried staffs as she did. Some carried no more than begging bowls. The smell of unwashed bodies was strong and sour.

These were the sorcerers of the Pearl Throne. Not Divakesh's holy sorcerers, these were mendicants and ascetics who walked across Hastinapura. These and hundreds like them were eyes, ears, and hands of the emperor's bound sorcerer. Every ten days he met with those who had made the trek to the palace. They came to him to deliver news of what they had seen and done, and what they had left undone. Yamuna heard them all with patience and serious demeanor. When he chose to dispense orders, it was with a sentence or two at most. No one questioned him; no one dared. She certainly never had.

The great difference, Hamsa decided, between his court and his master's above was that Yamuna had no advisor beside him. He could have surrounded himself with a hundred willing and experienced voices, or with a court of sycophants had he so desired, but Yamuna sat alone and issued his rulings without aid, consent, or compromise.

Each witness stepped into the carefully drawn circle which was said to remove falsehood from the tongue. Hamsa had never been certain as to the exact extent of its powers. Knowing Yamuna, she knew there were surely some hidden compulsions within it, but no one was permitted to study it closely, at least no one who spoke with Hamsa.

Hamsa remembered the first day she saw Yamuna. It was also her first day in the palace. The two sorcerers who had brought her weeping from her home to this room flanked her. Yamuna had been sitting in the same pose he held now, and he had looked up at her. Hamsa remembered how small she felt looking into those black eyes. She had never seen a face so devoid of emotion. He had nodded and said, "She is the one."

And that was the end of it. As she had matured, Yamuna had remained a distant figure. After she was bound to Samudra, she was left to others to be tutored. She saw him frequently, of course. He stayed as close to his master as she did to hers. Because she was the prince's bound sorcerer, however, she was not directly under Yamuna's command. This meant she was not required to attend spectacles such as the one before her now, a fact for which she was profoundly grateful. Yamuna with his remote, implacable power terrified her. He terrified her because he could lie to his master about the Mothers themselves, and no consequence came of it.

Hamsa could barely conceive of lying to Samudra. The binding ceremony was strong, as it should be. Sorcerers could be corrupted, just as other mortals. It was right that they not be permitted to harm those they were meant to protect.

If only the binding could prevent me from harming him through sheer lack of skill. Hamsa bit her lip.

Yamuna was now hearing from a bone-thin woman who clutched her begging bowl as if it were a charm against the one who sat before her. They were afraid. Every last one of them was afraid of the power and the knowledge of this man.

If any of them even knew her name, not one of them would fear Hamsa. At best, some might pity her. The bitterness of Hamsa's heart seeped into blood and mind. Why had she been chosen for this life? Why was she not left to her village, to be midwife and healer and have four braids in her hair and a string of lovers who would age and marry and leave her to her solitude and her useful work? Or let her wander between villages with her begging bowl, performing cures and pronouncing the fortunes of newborn children. Anything so long as she could have been free, not tied to a life she could not live.

Samudra was in danger, and he turned to her less and less in his time of trouble and she could not blame him. What skill did she have, what foresight or understanding? In battle, it was his skill and not her workings that kept him safe. Her auguries were as certain as a dice toss, and the palace was no more her home than a stable.

Why had he not been given a sorcerer like Yamuna? Yamuna had been born in the reign of Chandra's grandfather. He was old, even as sorcerers reckoned their lives, and he understood the heart and soul of the Pearl Throne. He had been bound to three generations of the emperor's family and each passing year brought him more power, and more jars for that collection of secrets that so enriched him.

Mothers, why do you not let me go? Let a stray arrow find me. Let Samudra have someone who can do him some good.

She rubbed her head. Despair did nothing but breed more despair. That much she did know. She no longer had the luxury of wailing to the heavens about her misfortunes. Not after yesterday evening.

Samudra had spent the long, sultry afternoon on the practice field, wearing himself out against new soldiers and old comrades. He fought with sword and spear and, when his horse at last needed a rest, on foot with fists and knives. No one else seemed to think the prince's burst of activity strange. The few fair days between the first and second rains were not to be wasted. What Hamsa knew that the others did not was that Samudra had been trying for many days to work his courage and his mind up to some goal. He had not yet told her what it might be. She knew it involved Makul, and that was enough. A clandestine meeting with him could only mean Samudra walked closer than ever to the idea of rebellion. He did not believe she was strong enough to be part of the plotting. Very well. She must accept that, but it did not mean she must remain passive. There were too many threads in the palace for one hand to hold them all.

Hamsa watched as a new petitioner made the salute of trust and walked the straight path that led into the bespelled circle. He was a small man who walked on tough, bare feet and wore a loose blue shawl that looked as if it served as blanket and shelter as well as clothing.

"What is your word?" asked Yamuna. No chamberlain spoke this question for him. No secretary wrote down his rulings. There would be no witness who was not here at this moment and no record for those who came after to learn from.

Perhaps he does not believe any will come after.

"Master Yamuna, I come from the city of Nadeen. There I told the sorcerer at the palace I was your representative, but I was still made to wait a full day before Master Avreshin and his people would see me."

"You spoke in my name?"

"I did, Master."

"Vasna." Yamuna spoke the name mildly, and a woman

who the years had made grey gave the salute of trust. "You walk next to Nadeen?"

"I do, Master." Even if she had not been going that way before, she surely would now.

"You will tell Avreshin that he is summoned to me, and we will learn what he has done to inspire such a bold attempt."

The whole gathering bowed at that, and over their bent backs, Yamuna looked directly at Hamsa. She flinched, but managed not to look away. She knew he had seen her fear, but nonetheless it gave her some small comfort.

She expected one of two things. Either he would turn back to his business or he would summon her to the circle. She was ready for either. But instead, he regarded his assemblage once more and said, "That is all for this time."

Without any hesitation or question the sorcerers knelt to make their parting obeisance. They left in twos and threes, saying little. Most chose to depart separately. Everyone knew Yamuna watched who left with whom, and association could later become dangerous.

Hamsa felt obscurely reassured to see all the varied shades of fear displayed by her compatriots who walked the roads. It made her feel less of a coward.

When the chamber was cleared, Yamuna beckoned her forward, and she came. She gave the salute of trust. As she did, she noted without surprise that the wheel that had worked so powerfully on the assembled sorcerers had already vanished from the place where it had been drawn.

"How does our prince?" Yamuna did not invite her to sit, and she made no move to do so.

"He is upset about the destruction in the north." Which was true, as far as it went.

Yamuna tilted his head to the side, feigning regret. "If he had carried out his orders instead of playing at making treaties, he would not now know this disappointment."

Hamsa made herself meet his gaze and hold it. She did

not tremble and that too was a small victory. "As ever, Yamuna, your words are wise and full of piety."

Yamuna's bright eyes narrowed. "Why have you come here, Hamsa? You have never done so before."

"Because my prince is in need."

Yamuna nodded and for a brief, bright moment, Hamsa thought he might understand. "The good of Hastinapura is what consumes us all."

"Consumes." It took all of Hamsa's strength to stand where she was, to keep her hands loose around her staff, lest Yamuna see her white knuckles. "It is an interesting word. It means so many things."

For a long moment Yamuna did not answer. When he did, his voice was mild. "Do you talk to me of rhetoric now, Hamsa?"

"Would such as I speak of matters of diplomacy to such as you? Never." *He will see. He will know there is another reason. He will know I want to be close to him for what is to come. My prince has not thought about Yamuna and how many ways he might disrupt a rebellion.*

Or support one.

"Sometimes it concerns me that you do not clearly understand these things." Yamuna leaned back a little. It was as relaxed as she had ever seen him.

"I know my place."

"No, you do not," Yamuna answered flatly. "You never have."

Anger, weak but palpable, flared in her and gave her boldness to speak words she had not carefully considered. "Do you now instruct me?"

"I have undertaken to instruct you many times, but you seem to care nothing for such lessons."

"When the student does not learn, is it the fault of the student or the teacher?"

Silence fell, thick and deep, so that Hamsa was sure Yamuna heard her heart thunder in her chest. Its beating threatened to shake her apart. She was a fool, she should not be here, she should have stayed in the small domain and tried to speak to Queen Bandhura.

At last, Yamuna nodded slowly. "Perhaps you are right. Perhaps you and your master require more direct lessons."

The mention of Samudra touched her and she found the piece of lion inside that was true and would not fail, even if her skills deserted her. "Do you threaten my master now, Yamuna?" *He knows. Oh, Mother of Mercy, he knows.*

Yamuna leaned forward and she looked into his eyes, and she saw . . . nothing. There was no reflection, no human expression. There were only dark holes that dragged at her spirit and threatened to swallow her whole. "Do you believe you could stop me from doing anything I wish, Hamsa? Do you truly believe you have the power?"

Hamsa licked her lips. Her mouth was dry. Her knees were ready to buckle. "I have no illusions of my power."

"Neither have I, Hamsa. Do not forget, I am the one who augured your place here. I know who and what you are. Your dance holds no surprises for me."

Breathe. Loosen your hands. You must stand here. You came, you must finish your errand. You must do that much. "My skills, or the lack of them, are not what I came to discuss."

"What is it then?" Yamuna folded his hands, at complete repose, ready to hear and consider anything she said.

Speak the truth. It is what you came to do. "You know so much of me, you know I do not play the palace games. This may be weakness, but there it is." She gripped her staff tightly, her pretense at strength beginning to crack. "I do, however, know that there is no love lost between you and the high priest."

This drew a small, thin smile from Yamuna. "There are very few whom I love, Hamsa."

"So why do you support his lies to the emperor?"

Fire sparked deep within Yamuna's dark eyes. "Ah, you

noticed that. Very observant of you." He pursed his lips. "It is strange, is it not? Our high priest wants nothing so much in this life as to look upon the true face of the Queen of Heaven, and yet he doesn't know her when she does come."

"But it was not Divakesh she came for," said Hamsa, refusing to be distracted. "You claim you want to teach me. Here I am for my lesson." She gestured broadly, surprised to find that both hand and voice had steadied. "Why allow the emperor of Hastinapura to remain ignorant of a summons from the Queen of Heaven herself?"

Yamuna pressed one finger to his lips, considering. "And if it pleases me to tell you, what will you do?"

"Wonder if you might have found . . . a different way to serve the Throne, if not the man who holds it," she added with a bow.

His mouth curled into another of his thin smiles. "A reasonable reaction, Hamsa. Why would a mere bound sorcerer play a game against gods and emperors?"

"Especially when his power is dependent upon theirs."

Without warning, Yamuna sprang. Hamsa saw only a blur of motion, and knew only that her staff had been snatched from her hand and that she was now on her knees. She felt the press of wood against her neck. Yamuna stood over her, bearing down on her with her own staff. "I am dependent on no one! No one!" he cried. "The emperor rules by my power, and mine alone! It is by my doing that he has no rival, that he has a wife who rules the small domain at her pleasure! The high priest stands by my whim only. The Mothers themselves stand only because I have not yet chosen to stretch my hand out to Heaven, but that will come in its time. Do not forget that, little Hamsa. Do not forget it for one moment."

"No." Hamsa gritted her teeth until her jaw ached. She dared make no other movement. "I will not forget."

The staff lifted from her neck as Yamuna stepped away. Hamsa dared to look up and she saw his eyes softened with a terrible benevolence. "Be glad of your weakness, Hamsa. It keeps you and your master alive."

She stayed kneeling. She was not sure she could stand. Her blood now seemed like dust in her veins.

"Not yet." He bent down close. "First you will listen to me and you will listen with care. I want one thing from you, Hamsa, and one thing only. It should be easy for you. You will assist your master in all things. He is doing exactly as he should, and I would have him continue. You will support him in every way possible, and you will remember that my eye is on you. If I see you try to dissuade him from his chosen course, I myself will level your doom. Do you hear me, little one? Do you understand?"

"Why are you doing this? I came here . . ."

"I did not ask that. I asked do you understand?"

"I understand."

Yamuna held out her staff and she accepted it, laying it down and then pressing her forehead to the floor. Then, hearing him return to his seat, she dared to stand, dared to turn, and made herself walk away.

She walked down the corridor and down the stairs, back to the women's quarters, back to her own rooms. She found the way by instinct, rather than by conscious thought. Her servants fussed as she entered the room, but she waved them both away. Alone, she knelt before the small shrine where Mother Jalaja and Mother Daya, the Queen of Earth, danced. It was only then, under the protective gaze of the goddesses, that her mind seemed willing to dare thought again.

Yamuna was mad. That was what three hundred years of service had done. It had driven reason from his mind and replaced it with the illusion of power so great he thought he could topple the Mothers themselves.

But was his measure of his own power only illusion? The blasphemous thought made Hamsa tremble, but she could not escape it. No one knew how great Yamuna's workings were, or how many secrets he hoarded in his jars and boxes. And what he had said was true. The emperor had no rival. Samudra had always been too loyal, too honorable to take that role. Bandhura did rule the small domain, even though Queen Prishi still lived. And the Mothers had chosen Divakesh.

Hamsa remembered when the old high priest had died. He had been a mild man much given to study and to prayer, and seldom seen outside the temple confines. This had suited Chandra and Samudra's father well. When his ashes had been given to the sacred river, the other priests had lit the great fire in the inner temple. Only the imperial family and the bound sorcerers had been in attendance. Hamsa had knelt behind the boy Samudra while his mother tried to keep him from fidgeting. There, the priests had begun to dance. It was a great dance, leaping and whirling, stooping to kiss the floor before each of the Mothers and leaping up again to turn and throw up their arms in praise of the creation, in wonder and delight at the gifts of Heaven that the Mothers showered on them all.

They danced until their feet bled. They danced until they began to falter. They danced until they fell. The last one who remained standing before the mothers, perfect in body and devotion, would become the high priest. None had been surprised that it was Divakesh, who was so strong and so sure of himself that even as the last rival fell beside him, utterly spent, he had not missed a beat but only stepped over the man's fainting form to stand before Mother Jalaja and meet her gaze.

She thought there was nothing but pure love and devotion that could make such a display.

But what if there was something else? Hamsa straightened up. Magic could sustain strength. A spell, properly worked, could give an exhausted man the extra breath and will to carry on with his task.

Could Yamuna, who thought himself such a maker of

kings, have perverted the ritual by which the high priest was chosen?

Then, slowly, another cold thought stole into her mind.

If he dared subvert so holy a rite, what else has he done?

Hamsa bit her lip. She needed to know what Yamuna had done, to Samudra, to the emperor. He would never tell her. She would have to try to take what she needed from the past itself.

Hamsa had a second chamber, curtained off from her living quarters. A sorceress needed a workroom. Hers was spare. The low tables were clean. The chests were plain and unlocked. She had no great trove, like Yamuna. She had not had time or leisure to craft lasting tools for her own use.

Time, leisure, or skill. She knelt in front of one of her plain chests. Inside were lengths of cloth and rolls of brightly colored ribbons. She selected a red ribbon, a blue one, and one that was pure white. She filled a simple clay bowl with water from the ewer in her sleeping chamber and brought it back to set before her shrine.

She knelt, and took several deep breaths to calm herself and focus her mind. Then, she picked up the ribbons and laid them across her palm. Carefully, tentatively, for it had been a long time, she reached both within herself and without, to draw the magic down, to draw it up, to bring it to her, to shape and to bind.

She knotted the three ribbons together and swiftly began to braid them with a delicate touch. They could not be too tight or the vision would not pass between them. She breathed over the braid she formed, letting it trap the exhalation, the words, the wish she formed.

Show me the workings of Yamuna. Show me what he has done that touches upon the prince, Samudra. Show me.

Show me.

Gently she looped the braid around the clay bowl. Earth, air, water, future, past, she tied the ends of the braid together to bind them all.

Show me.

Show me.

Hamsa gazed into the bowl, seeing the flicker of the rain-filtered light in the pure, clear water. Water compassed the world. Water always was and always would be. Water fell from Heaven and welled up from Earth. Nothing could be hidden from water.

Show me.

Hamsa gazed deeply, focusing her mind and her power. She breathed, full and deep. She looked at the clear water and felt the thrum of her power, and she saw . . .

Nothing.

Hamsa blinked. She looked again, and she saw . . . nothing. Nothing at all. She held herself, her mind open wide. She focused her breath, stilled all thought. There was only the working, the weaving. She felt the magic pulse in her blood and her sinews. It was all. There was nothing else.

There was nothing. Nothing at all.

Hamsa's concentration wavered, and then it shattered, and there was nothing in front of her but a braid of ribbon and a clay bowl of water.

Slowly, Hamsa stood. Her legs were perfectly steady. Like a woman in a dream, she walked from her chamber into Samudra's. The prince had a private terrace, open to the sky and the rains. She pushed back the doors and walked out onto the terrace. The rains drenched her at once. Their roar filled her ears. There in the rain, Hamsa buried her face in her hands and wept, loudly, fully. No one would hear. No one would listen to her.

Why me! She lifted her face to Heaven, letting the rain mix with her tears. *Mother Jalaja, do you care so little for your son that you must send him a sorcerer without power? You who oversee all the work that we do, why can you not tell me what my purpose is!*

Rain filled her eyes, nose, and mouth, until Hamsa

coughed and realized she could drown. *I should drown. I should throw myself from the cliffs.*

But she could not. Cowardice or pathetic courage, she did not know which it was that took her back indoors. Her woman clucked and fussed and dried her off. Hamsa suffered her ministrations in silence. Then, when she was dressed and dry, she stretched out on her bed. She stared at the remains of her spell on the floor. The world was drifting away. She could not move. She closed her eyes and let exhaustion take her.

*H*amsa dreamed.

She dreamed she walked through her home village, past the low hovels on paths of packed dirt. The cows looked up at her, swishing their tails. Goats bleated. But there were no people. She was the only human being. The rest were monkeys.

Monkeys quarreled on the roofs of the houses. Monkeys groomed each other in the doorways. Monkeys chittered in the trees, eating fruits and nuts, and dropping the rinds down to the dirt with soft smacks.

Hamsa stared at all this, her feet walking without her mind giving them any direction. The monkeys who looked up at her with their wrinkled faces and black, beady eyes did not scamper away. They screeched at her, as if to say, "What are you doing here? This place is ours!"

She found herself at the temple, the one building of stone in the village. She mounted the steps, certain she must pray for understanding. But when she mounted the steps, she saw that the image of Mother Harsha, the Queen of Increase, to whom the village was dedicated, was not there. Instead there was a gnarled wooden throne, and on it sat a great monkey, a black creature with a white beard and bright, terrible eyes.

The monkey drew back his lips, exposing his teeth in a

horrible, yellow grin. "So, you come here. You think to come back you will find the way forward?"

"I . . . don't know," stammered Hamsa.

"Don't know! Don't know! Don't want to know! Don't believe!"

"I do believe!"

"But what? Eh?" The monkey stretched out his long arms, the black hair bristling. "This is what you believe! Belief in emptiness and chattering! Belief that Hamsa is alone, all alone!" He threw back his head and laughed, a high, shrieking noise that pierced her ears like arrows.

Hamsa wavered. She wanted to kneel, but something told her it was important she remain standing. "Where do I go?" she whispered.

She did not think the monkey could have possibly heard her, and yet it did and the shrieks of laughter fell away. The creature leaned forward, its wrinkled hands grasping the arms of the throne. "It is not for you, the middle way, little sorceress. You have lost that chance. If you wish to truly be able to aid your prince, it is only the last sacrifice that will bring the blessing you need."

Lost?

"Lost!" The monkey leapt to his feet. "Lost! Lost! All lost!" He jumped up and down, thumping against the wooden throne. "Lost in tears and in wailing. Lost in the helplessness you believe in so deeply."

Hamsa bowed her head before his anger. "It is too late then."

"Eaaagh!" screamed the monkey. "You do not listen!" He pounded the arms of the throne with his black fists. "She listens only to the blackness in her head. Who put that blackness there?" The monkey swung down from its high seat and scampered up to her, leaning down, putting its leathery, bearded face so close to hers she could see nothing else. "Who doused the sacred fire inside you, *Agnidh*? Hmmm?"

"I don't . . ."

But that was not right either. The monkey swung away, throwing himself back onto the throne. "Take this one away! If she will not hear, what is the good of speaking!"

All at once, Hamsa was surrounded by a throng of monkeys, black, brown, white, crawling with lice and fleas, all screeching, jabbering, hooting. They lunged at her, grabbing her, pinching her. They pulled her hair and laughed as she screamed. The weight of their bodies toppled her to the floor, and all she could do was scream and scream and scream . . .

Screaming, she woke. She pushed herself upright, panting. She was sweating, her heart pounded, and her throat was raw. Her room was dark except for the light of a single wick burning in the oil lamp that hung overhead. All around, she could hear the rush of the rains, but in her mind she heard the echo of the monkeys laughing and screaming in her dream.

And of their great king speaking to her. *You do not listen! She listens only to the blackness in her head. Who put that blackness there?*

Still gasping for air, Hamsa rose. She lit a second lamp and with trembling steps she walked back to her workroom. There were the bowl and the brightly colored braid as she had left them before the shrine of the Mothers. Hamsa knelt. She set down the lamp. Its light flickered, turning the clear water golden. She touched the braid, tracing it with her fingers.

Lost. Lost in the helplessness you believe in so deeply.

Hamsa swallowed the voice of nightmare, and drew her magic up. She drew it down from the air, out from the rain, and up from the earth. She touched the braid, reweaving it in her mind, breathing out the voice, the omen of the dream that still filled her head and trembled in her soul.

What has he done to me? What has he done to me?

There was nothing. Nothing but the reflection of gold light on water. There never would be anything else for her.

Hamsa gritted her teeth. *No! I will not be made blind to myself. I will see! I will!* She reached, stretching mind and soul until she felt they would break.

On the water, the light stretched out, becoming a net of threads, like a spider's fallen web. The shining threads wove together, binding to become colors, to become images. And Hamsa saw.

She saw Yamuna alone in his chamber, surrounded by his vessels of secrets and of power. He sat cross-legged on the floor, one simple red clay jar open before him. His eyes were closed and his skin was slick with sweat. His lips moved, shaping and reshaping words she could not hear.

Through the wall flew the shape of a bird, a great brown vulture with a thick, curved beak in which was held the shape of a child. The vulture landed before Yamuna, and carefully it set the child down. Neither vulture nor child cast any shadow. These were not flesh. These were shadows, essences. The vulture bowed his great head and faded away like smoke, leaving the child shape alone before the sorcerer.

The child was a thin girl in country clothes, and Hamsa knew her at once. She could not look on her own self, her own spirit, and not know her.

Slowly, as if it gave him great pain, Yamuna opened his eyes. He looked on the shape of the girl, and smiled. He said something else. The child Hamsa had been made obeisance to the sorcerer, turned, knelt, and crawled into the jar.

Quickly, Yamuna's hand reached out and slapped on the lid. His clever fingers molded a ring of red wax around it, sealing it tight.

"NO!" screamed Hamsa, and spell and vision shattered and she was in her own darkened workroom again. She turned away from the gazing bowl and was abruptly and violently sick.

"*Agnidh* . . . ?" Her sleep-tousled serving woman stumbled into the room and saw. "Oh!"

She helped Hamsa to her bed, brought her water to wash, a fresh breastband to cover herself, and wine to drink.

So that was what Yamuna had done. He had not moved against Samudra, but against her. He had taken part of her soul, divided her spirit like that of mortal woman, and trapped part of her in that jar so she could never be whole. Without that wholeness of spirit that was unique to sorcerers, she could not feel the invisible powers, could not be fully rooted in the world to fully affect it with the shaping of wish and will.

Why was she so weak? She had been made weak, years ago. Why could she do nothing? Because she was bound and prevented.

Hamsa swallowed. She was trembling. She clasped the goblet of wine her woman had brought. She drank again, trying to steady herself.

So. Now I know. I know what I should have known before. But what do I do?

Mother of Mercy, what can I do?

All the night, Hamsa sat in the darkness and listened to the rain, and tried to think, but the only thing that came into her mind was the words of her dream.

. . . . it is only the last sacrifice that will bring the blessing you need.

Only the last sacrifice. But when should that sacrifice be made? And how?

But there were no answers to that question, or at least none Hamsa was permitted to know.

*W*hile Hamsa slept, Yamuna sat before the image of Hamsa and smiled at the words he had just heard. "Poor little Hamsa. You do try so hard, but now you know you can never stand against me. Your strength was mine as soon as I knew your name."

He gestured, and Hamsa's shadow made its obeisance to

him. But then it looked up at him for a moment with its intense, dark eyes, and he saw a spark in them, a spark that was so very like the spark of life and power that came to a sorcerer before he made a working. It gave him pause. Then and only then did the shadow fade from his sight.

It was only after a long and careful examination of the wards and seals that Yamuna was able to put the soul jar back on its shelf and walk away.

Chapter Twelve

In the Land of Death and Spirit, a small man in saffron robes waited on the ocean's shore. The waves surged in and rolled out uninterrupted, filling the air with their rumble and roar.

Presently, on the dunes that rose behind the man, two red-brown ears pricked up from behind the thin sea grasses, and then a black nose thrust itself into the open, clearing a small space for one bright green eye to peer down.

Nothing else happened for a long time. Satisfied, the fox who owned ears, nose, and eye trotted down the dunes. She came up to the man, who did not glance down to acknowledge her, and sat on her haunches beside him, staring out at the restless, green waters.

"She will not come, you know," said the fox after a time.

The man said nothing.

"She holds you in greater contempt than even myself. I am a danger, but you are an upstart."

The man said nothing.

The fox scratched her chin vigorously for a moment. "She may send a great wave to wash you from her beach. Or a flight of demons, if she's very angry. I've seen her do such things. It would not be pleasant, and it would last a very long time."

Still the man held his silence, his gaze never shifting from the green ocean waves. His hand held loosely to his stick and he did not move.

"Mmmm . . . I see. She's already done that. You wear it well." She looked out over the ocean for a time. "She might just decide to truly ignore you. You could be standing here for a thousand years, to no end at all."

The fox swished her tail back and forth, scattering small flurries of sand. "Do you know, I think I like you, man. I find I wish you luck."

The fox left him then. It was only when she was gone that a small smile appeared on the man's face.

He continued to wait.

Queen Sitara of Sindhu returned to her home as straight-backed and composed as when she had left it. Her brood of children greeted her at the docks surrounded by their aunties, nursemaids, tutors, and bodyguards. Sitara quickly saw who was missing from the gathering. Radana was gone; so was Captain Anun.

So was the king.

Sitara hugged her children and went with them to the rain-freshened gardens to run about for a precious little while and hear all about what they had been doing while she was "meditating" at the monastery. She cuddled Bailo on her lap and marveled at how much he had grown in these few weeks.

She gossiped with her waiting women and the concubines, but when she asked about Radana, they all turned their faces away and refused to speak a word. Fear, formless and nameless, began to grow inside Sitara, but she held her peace. She would have this moment with her family. All other concerns could wait for just one afternoon.

At last the swollen orange sun set over the trees and the

insects took up their night songs. The hot wind blew, bringing the scents of fresh water on its back, letting all know that the break in the rains was done and the second rain would begin in the night. Sitara ate her evening meal with her children and saw them all to bed. They seemed to have accepted their sister's departure, talking of her as if she had gone to get married, speculating a little nervously of when they might hear from her and what she might be doing now. They were, after all, children of the royal house. Even little Bailo knew his destiny was to go and do what the land and their dynasty required of him. She had left Lohit to come to Sindhu because it was required. Left Lohit, and had lived that much longer because she had. And because word of her home's rape had come to her, she knew why it had to be so. She had to live so she could die bringing vengeance for her brother, for her old parents, for her mountain home that had fallen to the greed of the Mothers and their bloody sons.

By the time she turned her footsteps to her husband's private chambers the lamps and torches were lit. She sent a servant hurrying ahead to ask for proper permission. If Radana had somehow managed to displace her in her absence, it was best that she observe formalities at this time. They would be a buffer against fear, against rage.

When she was given permission to enter, she found Kiet alone, kneeling before the golden image of the Awakened One in its shrine against the eastern wall. Sitara entered softly, but Kiet still heard. He turned and rose in one smooth motion. She remained motionless, her heart beating hard at the base of her throat. Kiet looked older than when she had seen him last, his face more serious, more sad than it had been even a few short weeks ago.

But he spread his arms to her and Sitara ran forward to be swept into his strong embrace, to receive his kisses and return them willingly, holding him as close as her arms could draw him.

For a long moment they did nothing more. She had been mother before, now she was wife. The king and queen could wait just that much longer while she pressed her cheek against Kiet's broad chest and heard his heart hammering within and felt his arms enfold her, stroking her back gently with the touch she knew so well.

But, at last, he did pull away, and, oddly and suddenly formal, they knelt together on one of the broad platforms, tea and the sweetmeats the servants had discreetly placed cooling beside them.

"What news do you bring me, Sitara?" Kiet asked her.

She met his sad, serious gaze. It was the time to speak openly of what she had done. "The Huni are coming. The rivermen will bring them. Their chief will come when he is sure this is no trap."

Kiet nodded. "We will receive them."

"And while I have been gone?"

"Radana has gone to Hastinapura. She carries news of what you have done."

The words dropped into Sitara's mind like a stone. She had expected Radana to attempt betrayal, but of the ordinary variety, seeking power and prestige while her watchful queen was away. This . . . this treason had been so unlooked for, Sitara could do nothing but sit and stare. "Did you pursue her?" she asked, ludicrously. She only wanted to force her mind into motion again.

"Yes. Captain Anun is still behind her, but there has been no news for over a week. It is likely Radana has slipped across Hastinapura's border by now."

Be calm, Sitara warned herself. *You set this thing in motion. You cannot refuse to accept its consequences now.* In anther moment she managed to say, "It is just as well."

He went on doggedly, as if he lacked the power to stop his flow of words. "If she is able to reach the palace with her news, if she is able to find someone there to listen to a woman alone, the Hastinapurans will come and come swiftly, and we will not have the Huni growing idle and greedy while we shelter them."

Sitara sat with him in silence, forcing herself to think, to consider the different possibilities. If Radana lost herself in the streets of Hastinapura, nothing changed. It was of no moment. If she did reach the Pearl Throne, and she was believed . . .

Her husband took in several deep, ragged breaths, attempting to stay calm. "They will kill Natharie."

This was what had weighed behind Kiet's eyes. This was what made him old.

"I know," she said quietly.

Anger and disbelief swept across Kiet's features. She could read his thoughts plainly. *You did this. You did this knowingly.* "You would kill your daughter so easily?"

"And how will she live among the Hastinapurans?" she demanded. "How long before they force her to swear devotion to their Mothers just to stay alive? Or force her into some degrading service or marriage? This way she goes free into the next life and may begin again." *They slaughtered my brother. They destroyed my old home on their way to the Huni. I will not let Natharie be held by them. I will not let my hands be bound by them!*

Kiet sat there for a moment, his eyes blank, his brow furrowed. Then, he drew his hand away. "Prince Samudra swore she would be respected."

"Prince Samudra!" Sitara spat the name. "Prince Samudra is his brother's tax collector! If he had true power the priest never would have behaved as he did! And you cannot tell me, Great King, that word of what happened in Lohit has not reached here yet."

When Kiet turned away, she saw that it had. When word came to the convent, she had stayed there for the three days of mourning, going without sleep and without food, weeping for her family, and for her daughter whose only protector was a fallen tiger.

"I might have stopped this thing but for that," she whispered, not knowing for certain whether she spoke the truth. "But without him, there is no safety for her, and I will not leave her to their priest. Not her, not you, not our other children or our land." She drew herself up. Tears ran freely down her face, but her voice remained true and strong. "If you believe otherwise, husband, kill me now. Send my head to Hastinapura and say you have punished your unnatural queen's treachery."

Slowly, Kiet knelt once more before her. "How can I do this when you were only doing what I could not bring myself to do? Understanding what I could barely begin to contemplate?"

She wanted to believe this, but even as the thought rang through her mind, she felt another presence in the room and she turned her head to see Anidita's image, watching all she did from his place in the east. "Is there forgiveness for this?"

"I do not know," said Kiet harshly. "But there will be revenge."

And she took his hand again and held it for a very long time.

So, the Huni came down the sacred river to Sindhu in ones and twos. They came on the barges by night, watching the rivermen watch the moonlit waters. They came by day in fisherman's dress, or with the traders, their horses hobbled and drugged so they would not panic, and at the same time would look too dispirited for any to be interested in buying when the boats put into shore.

When they reached the city, in ones and twos they came to the palace. The king took their horses and put them in his stables. He took their weapons and put them in one of several warehouses that he set his own men to guard. The Huni just grinned and let him do as he pleased.

At night, the king and queen, both grim, both cold, looked

out over the place that had been their garden, but which was fast becoming a foreign garrison. Side by side, they thought on the disaster of Lohit and vengeance for their child, for all their children, in order to keep themselves brave. The empire might try to take faith and sovereignty, as it had taken their daughter, but this time they would not go willingly. This time they would fight.

For now, there was nothing to do but wait until their chieftain decided how to begin the war.

Chapter Thirteen

In the Land of Death and Spirit, the small man waited beside the rolling ocean. Above him, the sunless sky was clear and filled with light, save for a single grey point on the far horizon. While he watched, the spot swelled and darkened, becoming a great cloud rushing forward as if to engulf the shore. Soon it became clear this was not one cloud, but many shapes.

If the crowd of demons that had risen from the ocean was horrible, these creatures were even more fearsome. Demons there were, armed with cruel, curving swords and spears that dripped yellow blood. With them flew the sagging, swollen shadows that were the ghosts of those who had died in illness. There were nightmares from the heavens and the deep earth. Death, the Last One, flew with this multitude beside the princes of Hell.

In their midst flew a great chariot, stained with the mud and blood of a hundred wars. Its horses had manes of fire and black hooves that struck sparks from the air as they galloped forward. A woman held their golden reins. She was tall and proud. Skulls and pearls girdled her waist, serpents made a mantle for her shoulders. She drove her terrible chariot with one hand. In the other, she held a sword stained black with the blood of the world.

The closer the multitude of destruction came, the lower it flew, until at last it skimmed the tops of the waves, rushing forward to the lone man on the shore. As his calm eyes met the golden eyes of the goddess, the man bowed deeply, giving the salute of trust to the queen who approached.

She pulled on the reins, bringing her great steeds to a halt. The serpents coiled into a nest about her throat and shoulders, hissing in their own language, one raising his head above the others and turning bloodred eyes upon the man, watching for the least sign of danger or disregard. The woman herself dismounted her chariot, tucking her sword naked into her girdle. She waded through the edge of the waves, coming to stand before the man. Behind her, the great swarm waited, alert and watching.

"So," said the goddess, looking him up and down. "You are Anidita."

"I am, Lady Vimala," he replied as he straightened. "You honor me with your presence."

One of the snakes hissed its disdain. The goddess folded her arms. Blood stained her hands and rubbed ochre streaks onto her brown skin. "I thought you might ignore me as well."

Anidita blinked. "Please, if your sister believes I have ignored her, tender my humblest apologies. I have attended most carefully to every message she has sent me."

Vimala's mouth twisted into a wry smile. "She would disagree. She sent me to dispatch you."

The man spread his hands. "It is within your power, Mother of Destruction."

"Yes, it is." She looked down her long nose at him. On the waves, the demons and the terrors were restless, stamping in the water, rattling their spears against their shields. The goddess glanced disapprovingly at them, and all melted away onto the wind, leaving only the rush and roar of the waves behind. "But I myself find much about you intriguing, and I would talk with you before you are wiped away."

"Then may I suggest we sit?" Anidita gestured toward the empty sands.

"Certainly." And the Mother of Destruction sat with the Awakened One on the golden sands. A gentle wind blew across them and picked up the scents of jasmine and death.

Mother Vimala rested her elbows on her thighs. Two of the snakes slipped down her arms, coiling around her wrists, flicking their tongues in and out to taste the air and the words spoken there. "Tell me, Anidita, what is it you want?"

"Help for two caught up in your lands."

"That is what my sister thought." Her cheeks puffed out in a sigh and the snakes around her shoulders coiled closer, as if to soothe her. "She is most annoyed. They are sacrificed to her."

"They are living beings, and they do not willingly follow her ways."

"They are hardly innocents, these two you are taking such pains over. They do not walk your road either. The girl, in fact, is falling fast from your path."

"Nonetheless," he replied simply.

They sat in silence for a time. Then, one of the glittering serpents lifted its head, whispering low in Mother Vimala's ear. She stroked her advisor, settling it back with its brethren on her shoulders. "You've made my sister very angry."

"I have heard this."

The goddess's golden eyes glinted. "I find it all rather amusing."

"I do not do this to amuse you, Lady Vimala." For the first time there was stone beneath Anidita's soft voice.

"No, but despite that you have succeeded. There are many points on which I and my sister differ, but challenging her . . . it is not something any of us may lightly undertake." She tilted her head sideways, examining him from this new angle. "What would you say, Anidita, if I took up your cause?"

Anidita bowed with deep respect. "I might thank you, but I fear in my weakness, I would wonder why you would do such a thing, as I am, as you say, an upstart, before you as well as your sister."

She nodded. "It would be a fair question. Let me put it to you this way. She does not like change, my sister, even when it is clear that some part of the dance she set in motion has gone quite wrong. Sometimes it is for me to show her the way to that change." She smiled, and behind her eyes were memories of many a gleeful and bloody change. Anidita saw this, and did not flinch from it. "The prince is mine already, although he seeks to put me off. What would you do if I took the girl as my own to match with him?"

Anidita raised his brows. "There are many who would say you are a most unsafe guardian, Lady Vimala."

She grinned and her teeth were dark and sharp. "So I am."

Now it was the Awakened One's turn to sit in silence, and his silence was as strong as thunder and unyielding as the mountain. At last, he said, "Do you swear then, Lady Vimala, that Natharie Somchai will be under your protection?"

"I swear that she shall come to no harm from me or my sisters, and by none of us will she be claimed as sacrifice. What harm she brings through her own actions, that is as may be."

Anidita nodded. "I accept this." He stood and gave the salute of trust once more. "Thank you, Lady Vimala." He picked up his walking stick, and with an unhurried step began to make his way back over the dunes through the waving grasses.

Vimala watched a long time, smiling, until he was lost to her long sight.

Then she too was gone.

*N*atharie was in the terrace garden when Ekkadi came barreling up to her, scattering a clutch of children who had been making up a new and complicated game of marbles and counters. It was evening. The rains had ended. Sunlight slanted in long beams through the latticework and the air was sultry and fragrant. Natharie had been puzzling over a new passage Master Gauda had set her to translating, more than half her mind occupied by wondering if the people here celebrated the rain's end. At home they would be dancing in the gardens tonight, and there would be fireworks.

"Mistress!" cried Ekkadi, exultant. "You are to go to Master Gauda at once!"

Natharie opened her mouth to ask why a summons from Master Gauda should cause her maid to become so excited. Then she realized this abrupt summons might not have originated with the drama master.

Ekkadi saw the realization dawning in Natharie's eyes and nodded in confirmation. "The emperor wants to see you."

Natharie swallowed and got to her feet, leaving the book where it was. "We are to perform?"

"No, just you. Hurry!" Ekkadi ran ahead, forgetting her role of dutiful maid. Natharie followed, a little more slowly, trying to calm her own nerves. It was stupid to be nervous. She had sung and danced for kings. She wanted to be presented to the emperor, to come once again to Queen Bandhura's attention. Despite her continuing conversations with Prince Samudra, she had learned nothing useful about the ways of power in Hastinapura. She was chafing in her patient role of student at the hands of the exacting Master Gauda and longing to begin her true role.

Despite these thoughts, her palms grew damp.

The drama master waited for her in the dressing chamber, a screened alcove off the main chamber. It was lined with chests and bundles of props, some precious antiques, some only battered playthings. Except for his servants, he was alone. None of the other students were there.

"What is happening, Master?" The title had become a reflex over the past weeks.

"What could be happening?" Master Gauda snapped back, but she read in him a mix of pleasure and worry. "There are dancers and poets aplenty for His Majesty's entertainment but he'll have nothing but Natharie of Sindhu." He glared at his four kohl-eyed servants. "Out! Ekkadi, help your mistress dress, and quickly."

Ekkadi was already lifting off Natharie's outer dress. Red trousers and a shirt of glittering scales had been laid out beside the dressing table. While Ekkadi worked, Master Gauda dipped his fingers into the cosmetics boxes, painting Natharie's cheeks with the required designs. Weeks of chiding held Natharie still under his ministrations.

"You'll be doing your piece from *The Adushtan*. It's your best." He turned to pick up a stick of kohl.

"But I thought . . ." Master Gauda had planned that Natharie's first "public" performance was to be for Queen Bandhura's birthday celebration in two months' time. "As it was the queen who asked you be trained to the art," Master Gauda had said.

"I also thought we had until the first of all queens' birthday." Master Gauda grabbed Natharie's chin in his meaty hand to hold her still while he drew the accent lines around her eyes. She could do this herself, but evidently he did not feel she was proficient enough in that area. "But our emperor is not noted for his patience."

Ekkadi handed Natharie the balsa-wood spear and placed the brass helmet on her head. The maid's eyes were shining and her hands were shaking. Natharie knew what caused

Ekkadi's excitement. To her, this could be the beginning of Natharie's fame. Fame would bring a raft of presents from those who liked her face and the display she made. Some of those presents would of course find their way to her clever and steadfast maid. Perhaps some of the men she pleased would as well. Ekkadi had mentioned this as an offhand possibility and Natharie had to stop herself from shaking her head. In Ekkadi's world, these things were the reward for constant service, and Natharie was in no position to judge.

A man's voice floated down the corridor. "Come! I would see this new favorite of my brother's!"

Natharie gripped her spear hard, her impatience flaring suddenly into anger.

I am not a mountebank or a concubine.

Master Gauda tapped her chin with one hard finger. "I know what you're thinking, my princess," he said sternly. "When will you remember that here you are whatever they say you are?"

What I let them think I am. But she bowed her head in acknowledgment of the drama master's words.

Master Gauda walked around her, twitching a fold of scale-covered cloth, running his thumb along her cheek to blend her makeup more smoothly. She endured the touch and tried to calm the maddened beating of her heart. "You'll do," he said, and then he leaned close, whispering in her ear. "Remember what you have learned so far and remember your pride, Princess Natharie. You will conquer."

Her eyes briefly met those of the pale eunuch and she found herself wondering how he knew what was happening inside her. His smile was small and he stepped forward, gesturing imperiously for her to follow him.

Natharie raised her spear in salute, and then she did follow. The corridor to Queen Prishi's suite seemed to have shortened. Almost before she had chance to draw breath, they were in the old queen's private chambers. Thankfully, she remembered to kneel at once, bowing her head to the floor, waiting for her moment. Master Gauda knelt down in front and to the side of her, also making proper obeisance.

"Up!" cried the man she'd heard before. The emperor Chandra. "And out of the way, you old eunuch. Let's see this girl!"

The shuffle of cloth told her Master Gauda had obeyed. Then he began to speak in his clear, precise voice: "And it came to be that the Golden Prince, the Sun's own son, the great Adushta was separated from his beloved, and none of his strength of arms could return her. All the mighty birds of the air, the eagles and the vultures had joined in friendship to search the world for her, but all Adushta could do was wait, and as he waited he spoke of his love, enumerating her virtues and lamenting their separation."

This was her cue, and Natharie lifted her head. For a single moment, she could see her audience. Queen Prishi lay on a litter heaped with pillows, with her women arrayed about her. The emperor lounged across a sea of pillows, practically in Queen Bandhura's lap. There was Divakesh, his butcher's arms folded in front of him. Why was he here? Yamuna the sorcerer knelt behind his emperor, watching all with bottomless black eyes. Two men, strangers to her, sat beside the imperial party. One was old with a shock of white hair and skin that hung in folds on his neck and spotted hands. The young man beside him, who was trying not to look too eager at this treat, shared the old man's hawklike nose and wide-set eyes. His son perhaps? And two more; a dandy of a man in purple silks with broad shoulders and covetous eyes. Beside him, another, older man, calm and collected in his bearing, his clothes more plain, his eyes alert, and studying her closely.

The moment was over. She must recall her part. She must speak the words of Adushta and dance his dance.

Remember your pride, Master Gauda had said. Natharie remembered well, and she began to speak.

"How shall I speak of what is lost to me? How shall I give tongue to what the gods themselves look on in wonder?"

She knelt, bowing her head in despair. She rose, striding in her anger, thumping the butt of her spear on the floor, throwing out her hand, clenching her fist, crying to the heavens. This speech belonged to the Golden Prince, Hastinapura's second emperor, who defeated the wild men of the forest who had killed his father, and in so doing secured Hastinapura's peace for a thousand years.

The patterns she had to walk were formal and strange to her. She had been told repeatedly the angled, stylized steps made part of the greater, subtle weaving of the play. Master Gauda had been drilling her hard to this. He drilled everyone hard. Natharie was constantly surprised by his unflagging energy. He, in turn, was astounded at how quickly she came to master the Golden Prince's dance. She did not tell him about the staff and empty-hand practice that she had learned during her extended childhood, and the fact was, there existed many similarities between the dramas of the Hastinapurans and the dramas she knew. Her skill as a storyteller enabled her to learn these poems. She even recognized some of the stories they enacted. But where in Sindhu, players told straightforward stories through staged song, the Hastinapurans wove many stories together in their dramas, with long asides of historical poetry. She could dance and she could speak, but the greater symbolic melding of the two that was absolutely necessary to the epic remained beyond her with her few weeks of this training. Still, she could pour herself into the words, even when she glimpsed the leer on the emperor's face. Her own loss, her own impatience were still raw, and here she could give vent to them. It kept her whole, for it gave her a safe way to show what she must keep hidden, the pain and the anger, the threats and the fear.

How much does Master Gauda know? The thought cut through her concentration and she hesitated for a broken heartbeat. ". . . How can I look again at her eyes when I have failed in my first duty. Ah! What man am I that I cannot keep my beloved safe? What gods conspire against me?"

She knelt, her head bowed, one hand clutching the spear, ending the piece in the same pose with which she had begun. Her heart was hammering, her mouth was dry, her hand was shaking. The ringing in her ears was so loud, it took a moment to hear the applause that her imperial audience scattered toward her.

"Excellent!" cried the emperor. "They breed them tall and bold in the southlands. What did you think, Tarish?"

A lighter voice, it must have belonged to the young man, answered. "I have never heard the piece performed so well, Your Majesty. You honor us by allowing us to hear it."

The emperor guffawed. "You've taught your boy his manners, Pankaj, very good. I think we'll soon see what he has left to learn!" He laughed again at this jest, and the others joined in, the men a little nervously, Natharie thought.

She was beginning to wonder what she should do. She had not been dismissed, but she was not being addressed. She could not stand, but crouching here like this was becoming increasingly uncomfortable and the sweat was trickling down under her false mail shirt. At the same time, she wanted to listen, to find out who this man and his son were and why they were nervous.

"And you, my Lord Divakesh?" croaked Queen Prishi. "What do you say?"

Natharie heard the rustle of cloth. A shadow fell across the floor, and she saw two broad feet shod in gilded sandals come to stand in front of her.

"Look at me."

Natharie looked and saw the high priest staring down at her as stern as any angry god. She said nothing. The emperor, the queen, the strangers, all in the room were watching her. She kept her hand on her spear and tried in her heart to keep from wishing she could raise it up and strike him down.

Anger. Ignorance. These are the strongest fetters. Why did her heart doubt that in the face of this man?

"I say she does not yet truly understand what the Mothers have in store for her," he said in a tone that was more mild than any she had yet heard him use. "But she will soon."

Natharie swallowed. The healing scar at her throat tightened.

"Oh, have done with Divakesh," called the emperor. "Let the Mothers take care of their own business tonight!"

The high priest turned toward Emperor Chandra and bowed. "We are at the heart of the dance here, even in quiet celebration we cannot forget that, nor can we allow a canker within that heart, or surely it is we who carry out the Mothers' will who will be punished for it."

She could not see Divakesh's face as he spoke, although she desperately longed to know who his eyes sought out with that speech. But she could see the emperor clearly, and she saw his half-drunken merriment drain away into naked fear.

"So, Lord Divakesh," said Queen Bandhura swiftly. "What would you have me do? Scourge her? Have mercy. Should I forbid her access to the dramas for the crime of being born where the Mothers meant her to be?" There was some strain under her words that Natharie did not understand, as if she were willing Divakesh to comprehend something beyond her words. "The girl is far too amusing to waste on embroidery or bath salts, or the virgin's dance. Do you not agree, my lord Tarish?"

The young man bowed where he sat. Despite this, Natharie heard his voice clearly: "If I were able to have my will, she would be locked away from all eyes save mine."

At this, the emperor let loose another laugh, and took another huge swallow from his cup. "Natharie, you have made a conquest! Be careful, Tarish. You will have to fight my brother for her! Where is my brother?" He looked about as if expecting Prince Samudra to appear.

"Ah, my son, did I forget to tell you?" said Queen Prishi weakly. "He sends his regrets that he must be late. He will attend you before the evening is over."

The emperor's eyes narrowed. Perhaps he was not so drunk as he appeared. "He's been mysterious since his return, my brother, and brooding." Then a benevolent smile spread wide across his face. "We must take greater care of him." The emperor turned his eyes upward to his wife.

Queen Bandhura smiled in return and smoothed Emperor Chandra's brow with her palm. "I myself will see to it, my husband. What he needs is more time in the company of his favorite to soothe his troubled spirits." She winked broadly at Natharie.

"Well, he should suffer a bit for his inattention." The emperor's smile grew mischievous. "Tarish, you will escort Natharie back to her rooms. Natharie, show the boy the terrace garden on the way. It is most lovely in the sunset."

Natharie eased herself back onto her heels so she could stand more gracefully. She did so in time to see that the young man, Tarish, had gone white in the second before he made his obeisance before the emperor. His father, puzzled and not entirely pleased, made the salute of trust. Then, Tarish stepped up to Natharie and made the salute to her.

Divakesh watched it all, his face thunderous.

Which is something, I suppose.

Awkward and uncertain, Natharie passed her spear to Ekkadi, who had come up behind her. She modestly folded her hands and cast her eyes down, acting the polite lady beneath her glittering prince's garb and stylized makeup, and waiting for Tarish to join her. Neither of them dared to glance back at the grinning emperor as they walked out into the corridors. Tarish remained silent beside her, doubtlessly feeling at least as awkward as she did. His presence was like an itch she could not scratch, and she was less sure than ever what to do.

Tarish cleared his throat. "You are from Sindhu?"

"I am."

He nodded. "It is a beautiful place."

That startled her. "You have been there?"

"A few times. My father is a great builder. He says that to properly understand the art it is necessary to see how the great palaces and temples are made elsewhere."

They came to the garden terrace. It was well past sunset now, and the sky outside was black. The moon peered through the latticework, leaving silver light and shadows all across the tiled floor. Ekkadi quietly directed lesser servants to light two of the oil lanterns, then shooed them away.

Natharie walked to what had become her customary bench beside the lattice, peering out at the waning moon. "You do not sound as if you enjoyed your travels."

Tarish shrugged. "I am not an adventurer. It is the pleasures of home and the city that call to me." He smiled as he said it, which spoiled his attempt at assuming a jaded expression.

"You do not find always being in one house dull?" The moon was bright. Above and around shone the diamond stars. It was the first time she had seen them since the rains began. If she cocked her head just so, she might be able to make out some of the constellations, and perhaps see the glint of the river, flowing down toward home.

"Home would never be dull were it graced by such as yourself."

Keep your mind on what you're doing! Natharie bowed her head, and hoped Tarish would take it for maiden's bashfulness. "You flatter me."

"I mean what I say."

"Then . . ." She lifted her eyes to his. *The boldness here makes an appealing contrast,* said Master Gauda's voice in the back of her mind. "I thank you for your kindness."

His smile was broad and his eyes both surprised and pleased. She found herself suddenly sorry that all this innocent gallantry was not being spent to better purpose. She turned back to the moon and stars until she could muster a smile. *Be pleased with your lover!* Master Gauda barked in her mind. *He has risked much to be here with you! You are modest, not dead!*

"What good fortune brings you to us this evening?" The words rang clumsily in her ears, but Tarish gave no sign of finding the question strange.

"The emperor and my father must discuss the progress of his new palace in Amarin. Or, the lack of it." Tarish grimaced.

Natharie managed a look of concern. She reached out and touched Tarish's arm. *You are the first link to the outer world I have found. Speak with me, please.* Tarish blushed, and laughed. "It will be settled soon. There was an accident . . . My father believes that we should use freemen for the building. He says free artisans are better at their crafts and work harder. But . . . the emperor is in a hurry, and while he was on his inspection tour, the work went late, and a rope snapped, and a beam fell. We lost ten men, and many of the others refused to continue. Father came to explain this to the emperor, and the emperor has told him to use slaves and bound craftsmen if the freemen will not work as they are bid . . ." He shook his head. Natharie left her hand where it was for a heartbeat, and then eased it forward. Now her palm lay across his forearm, which was warm and well shaped, she noted. This boy had done work in his life. "Father should not have come," Tarish whispered. "Everyone knows how the emperor is . . . he should have gone to Prince Samudra. He is a diplomat even more than he is a soldier. Everyone knows . . ." The boy shook himself. "I'm a fool," he said, remembering where he was. "I should not be talking about such things with a beautiful woman here beside me." He covered her hand with his.

Natharie drew back reflexively. Then, remembering herself, she reached up and took off the helmet, shaking her hair down and letting it cascade across her shoulders.

"Will there be trouble for you over this?" She set the helmet aside, silently hoping Ekkadi would not dart forward to retrieve it. But her maid had an excellent sense of these things, and stayed in whatever shadow where she had installed herself.

"This?" His fingers edged toward her hand again, and she caught his eye, with what she hoped was a warning glance, and he smiled. "Oh. No. My father will do as he's told. You do not win the freedom to create great things if you do not have the trust of your patron, Father says. He has been a lifetime earning that trust. I hope the freedom comes before his time ends." He shook his head again, and went on, striving for lightness and unconcern. "The men will grumble, perhaps a wall will be knocked down in protest, but in the end they'll do as they're told."

As do we all.

An idea came to Natharie, straight out of the epics she had been studying so diligently. She turned to fully face the boy in front of her, who was clearly not used to palaces or the women who dwelt there. "May I . . . tell you what I would like very much?" she said softly.

"What is that?" She saw plainly, his imagination was already flying ahead of himself. He too, of course, read the poets.

"Would you . . . could you . . ." She made herself hesitate, and blinked her eyes shyly. *Natharie, don't play this too heavily.* "When you have gone, would you write to me?" If she began receiving letters from an admirer, no one would wonder if she was seen occasionally scribbling down lines of her own. She could send Ekkadi out to deliver them, and if Ekkadi occasionally slipped down to the docks with an extra missive in her hand . . .

She feared Tarish would be disappointed with this simple request, but instead he smiled and bowed graciously. "It would be my deepest honor. You must be lonely here."

"It is very different from my home, and sometimes it is hard." These were the first true words she had spoken to him, and she felt a stab of guilt for it.

"Then allow me to ease your days, my lady." He boldly took her hand and bowed over it. "To hold further conversation with you, even through my poor lines . . ."

The shadows moved, and they both looked up to see Prince Samudra standing in the archway, watching them.

Tarish dropped at once into full obeisance. Natharie found herself cursing inwardly for a long moment, before she remembered she should do something similar, and knelt.

The prince paced forward, his arms loose at his side. For a moment, Natharie thought he was about to reach for knife or sword. Ludicrous. He was unarmed, but the thought was there nonetheless.

"Hello, Tarish," said Samudra.

"My lord prince," answered the boy, with no more than a tiny tremor in his voice.

"I believe your father is wondering where you are." The prince spoke in a voice of absolute neutrality.

Tarish was naive, but he was not slow. "Then, with your permission, I will go take my proper place beside him."

"You have my permission."

Tarish made the salute of trust, mustered his dignity, and beat a decorous retreat from the garden, leaving Samudra standing in the silver moonlight, a lace of black shadows over his face and form. Natharie kept kneeling, with no idea what might happen next, only trying not to be afraid.

"Please, get up."

Natharie did. She watched him. The prince held himself stiffly, looking both more awkward than Tarish, and more dangerous than the boy could ever hope to.

"I apologize for my lateness. I was . . . arranging an important meeting."

Natharie suddenly felt very tired. She hoped bitterly that Tarish would not decide on the prudent course and fail to write. She needed the letters, and the rumor of a liaison. It would deflect all other rumors. With all these thoughts and hopes, she did not have room to think up a neutral answer. "Why should you apologize to me?"

Samudra seemed to consider this, and had no answer, except to sigh. "I came to see how you were," he said at last.

"And what did you see?" *No sense and no mercy. Collect yourself, Natharie. You think you need that boy? How much more do you need this man?*

The corner of his mouth quirked up. "Young Tarish overreaches himself."

Natharie's heart beat hard once. She found she could not stand anymore, and abruptly sat down on the curving seat. The leaves of a fern tickled her wrist. "Then it is true. You do consider me yours." *Be quiet, be quiet, Natharie. You are still on the stage. Remember your part, remember your lines. Put your feelings to work.*

Samudra was a long time in answering, and when it came, the answer was soft. "No. You are not mine. You belong to no one here."

Anger, useless at worst, dangerous at best, flooded her heart. All she could remember now was Divakesh standing before her. His threats rang in her ears. "You seem to be the only one who believes this."

"Except for yourself," said Samudra immediately.

"For the moment." She thought on Divakesh's anger. So many threats lay under his words. She had learned enough to dissemble for the boy, if not the prince; when would she be able to dissemble for the priest? How long before she would want to? He was the one who threatened her family, her land, all she held sacred.

Stop. Remember where you are now, this moment.

Samudra took one step closer. "No one will take the freedom of your heart," he said softly, urgently.

There were many things she had thought to say. She had meant to ask whether he now considered her impure for allowing a man to look on her in lust, as happened in so many of the Hastinapuran epics. She wanted to ask if he intended to tell his mother to keep an even closer eye on her. But those words, meant to be coy and hard, dried up in her heart as she looked at his face. He had come forward and stood in a patch of moonlight, and despite the tracery from the lattice, she could see him plainly, and she saw his honesty and his old pain, and one other thing.

Desire. He looked on her and he wanted her. She had seen the look in other men's eyes in other times and other places, but never on one who had the power to put action to their desires. New fear shook her, and she took refuge in a more familiar anger.

"Tell your priest Divakesh that no one owns me."

His face went still. The desire, the loneliness drained from his eyes, replaced by a kind of angry disbelief. "Is this what I am to you?" he asked hoarsely. "Divakesh's ambassador?"

Natharie swallowed, and the line of old pain on her throat warmed. Why did she connect this man so closely to Divakesh? Why could she not stop thinking of the high priest every time she saw the prince?

She knew the answer. It was not because she believed the prince his servant, but because she knew the prince hated him too. She had known it from that first day when he had rebuked the man publicly, from all the times she had sat and talked with him, and from the pain she saw on his face now, at her words.

"No," she said softly, honestly. But as she looked at the strange hope this single word sparked in the prince's demeanor, a new question rose in her heart. *What is this man to me?* She could not believe he was only a tool, a way to make herself useful to her homeland. She welcomed him in a different way but she had resisted putting a name to the feelings that warmed her when they walked, when they spoke, or when they sat in a comprehending silence. She was afraid of what name might come to her. That fear made her angry, and that anger made her put him close beside Divakesh in her thoughts. "I spoke hastily. I ask your understanding."

"I know what Divakesh said to you," he murmured. "I am sorry. I also ask for understanding. What Divakesh teaches . . . it is not what I was taught."

"But he is the head priest of your house."

"I know, but how that came to be I do not know." He sighed. "When I was a boy, my teacher in the laws and lessons of the Mothers was a man named Ayan. He said that the dance held many patterns within it, and that no thing could be without its opposite, including worship of the Mothers. Because the worship, the teachings of others posed questions, of the right way to live, the right way to conduct oneself, and without questions, how could there truly be answers?"

It was so close to some of the *surras* Natharie had grown up with, she found new reason to stare. She swallowed.

"So what will you do about it?" she asked, keeping to the topic she herself had chosen with difficulty.

"There is little I can do. My . . . the emperor says Divakesh will stay where he is."

Natharie lapsed back into silence. She stared out the window. She could see the river's glint, a little, like a star in the distance.

"It is hard to find you must dance steps you cannot control," said Samudra softly. "I know this very well, and I am sorry."

"We speak of the wheel where I come from. It turns for us all, and we must follow."

"I know. We also speak of the wheel as well as the dance."

What is one of the strongest fetters? Ignorance.

Conscience pricked at Natharie, and she found she could give no answer to him but an honest one. "You have been kind since I was brought here, and I thank you. Forgive me that I cannot return your kindness."

At these words she saw his face tighten as the inner pain gave way to nothing less than naked sorrow. If pride permitted, she was certain, he would weep. That realization startled her so much, she reached out instinctively, resting her fingertips against his wrist.

"What wounds you so?"

His skin was warm, and even touching him so lightly she could feel the strength of his arm. The warmth that rippled through her then was not the matronly concern she had felt a moment ago at his hurt. This was the warmth that came from companionship after isolation, the warmth of weeks of polite conversation denying to herself that this man with his delicate face who she had wanted for her enemy was handsome, kind, honest, brave, and lonesome as well.

"I am trapped, Natharie," he whispered, looking down at her hand where she touched him. "Tomorrow I must betray . . ." He stopped. "Tomorrow I must do the one thing I did not believe I would ever do." He brushed her fingers with his own, almost disbelievingly. What did he feel? She felt heat and gentleness and desire. She wanted this touch in this moment and she wanted more. The sudden strength of that desire frightened her and repelled her, but at the same time she did not want it to leave her.

"I am sorry," she said, and she was. He had an honorable heart. He did not deserve this pain. Did he?

"It is my hope . . ." His whisper was faint. He continued to stare at their hands as if mesmerized, as if by moving he would make this dream of a touch vanish forever. "It is my hope that when this thing is done, I will be . . . able to be a better friend to you. Perhaps even I will be able to send you home."

Natharie said nothing for a long moment. She could not look at his sad face, so she looked out to the night. A moment before, her heart would have burst with rejoicing. Now, with all this strange and sudden feeling swirling through her, she almost felt she did not deserve to return home. Her punishment—her reward—for not moving her hand when she had ample opportunity to do so, for savoring this lightest touch of his fingertips, was to stay here with him forever.

Low over the horizon, she saw a single star hanging separate from the multitude of its brethren higher above. It was so clear, so pure. It shone over all the world, whether any was there to see it or not. It was bound to follow its course through the heavens, unfaltering across all the ages of the world, and yet, and yet, it still found its way to shine, to guide the wise, and to give its portents to those with eyes to see.

"You have always been a good friend to me, Samudra," she said, and she meant her words.

Samudra bowed over his folded hands. "Thank you, Natharie."

He left her then, and Natharie stayed where she was for quite some time, looking at her star and trying to understand the slow changes beginning within her, and she thought about desire.

She was unmarried, and had officially been a child for a long span of years, but she was not ignorant, nor was her body unfeeling. She knew full well what the tightness inside her meant, and why her eye might linger here and there when a man walked into the room. She knew why she smiled and she blushed and she made sure her feet and hands were clean and that she was dressed just so when she went out walking.

Lord Tarish had looked at her with his wide, boyish eyes, and his handsome face. There had been a moment there when she thought, why not give Tarish what he wants, at least a little? Why not find out what that touch is and what it does? She would never be married now, not to a true husband. Why should she not take what she wanted and what she could use? Others meant to make use of her here, why shouldn't she make use of herself first? There was much to be gained from the careful application of such touches, for the rustlings in the dark. She had not grown up next to a suite of concubines without noticing this much. If it would give her a hand over her captors, why not?

She had thought, *Because it would change me. It would make me into something I am not, and am not ready to become.*

But now she knew that was not the deepest reason. She did not go to Tarish because she did not desire the boy and did not wish to play at desiring him. She wanted the prince, with his dark eyes and his measured words, his pride and honor. She had found so much to hate and fear in this place. Was it truly possible she had found something to love?

No thing can exist without its opposite. It was one of the teachings of Anidita. And, it seemed, of the Mothers.

She could reason herself out of this. She could sit here until she once again came to understand that Samudra was her enemy and she was nothing more than prize and prisoner to him. But having found relief from the coldness that had surrounded her for so many days, she found she did not want to return to it. This warmth might be false, as false as the armor she wore and the smile she had given Tarish, but for tonight at least she would be fully the actress and play a part with herself. Tonight, she would believe she was in love and beloved.

Natharie sat beneath the light of the stars, closed her eyes, and let herself believe.

Chapter Fourteen

"You made a conquest last night," murmured Ekkadi.

The maid was laying out Natharie's breakfast as she spoke. The sun had not been up for more than two hours and the story of Natharie's appearance before the emperor was already winging its way through the small domain, with some startling additions. The common rooms were full of life and chatter as was usual for the mornings, but this time a large number of the women and older girls were casting knowing glances in her direction.

My fault for eating alone. This morning, she had shunned company, taking a seat in one of the small side alcoves. She did not feel capable of gossip this morning, nor did she want comments on how distracted she seemed. She needed time to order her thoughts, and her heart.

Natharie picked up a piece of flat bread and tore it in two. She looked at it in her hands. Suddenly, her mouth was dry and her stomach did not seem willing to receive food. It was not the gossip that disturbed her. She knew it for the vapor that it was. It was her own feelings that robbed her of appetite, for the warmth and despair of the night's dreams of love had not left her with the sunrise. "I would not call what happened last night conquest."

"Everyone else does." Ekkadi grinned and plucked half the bread out of Natharie's hand. She used it to scoop up a sauce of mango and tamarind, and folded it quickly into her own mouth. As she chewed, she eyed Natharie owlishly. "And I know what I saw. It is good work, Mistress. You have not one, but two men at your feet." She leaned closer and whispered. "Did Tarish make any promises? Did the prince see him kiss you?"

"No one kissed me." She set the bread down. "No one did anything." *Yet.*

"Disappointed?" Ekkadi's grin grew saucy enough that she ducked her head to hide it. "Patience, mistress. You'll be rich, and then you'll be married. If you continue this way, it won't take long." She set the last dish into place, made obeisance, and hurried away.

Natharie stared at the food laid out before her. *Eat something,* she instructed herself. *Master Gauda is not going to care you had a late night. You need your strength to face today.*

As if summoned by her thought, the drama master appeared in the archway of the viewing rooms. He crossed the busy chamber and came to stand over her.

Natharie dropped the bread and made to stand up. Master Gauda waved at her to keep her seat and knelt comfortably beside her. Ekkadi made her obeisance and withdrew to a discreet distance, settling down with a small cluster of other maids, doubtless to catch up on any gossip she'd missed in the past hour.

"You performed well last night, Natharie," said Master Gauda, smoothing his coat skirts fussily across his thighs. "I am pleased."

"Thank you, Master Gauda." She was grateful for those words, whether she should have been or not.

"There are some of the classical movements that you are still stumbling over," he went on. "But we will be training those today."

"Yes, Master Gauda." There was something he was not saying. She could feel it, and her unease returned. "Will you eat something?" She spread her hands toward the nearly untouched breakfast.

Master Gauda picked up a pastry, examined it critically for a moment, and bit it in two. "There is one point in the drama I think you should be more clear on, however," he said.

Natharie waited.

Master Gauda looked at the remaining half of his pastry. "Be careful of Ekkadi," he murmured, and popped the morsel into his mouth.

For a moment, Natharie was not certain she had heard him correctly, but he looked at her so steadily with his perfectly made-up eyes that doubt vanished.

To keep herself from glancing toward her maid, Natharie held up a dish of sugared fruits for the drama master. "She is . . . ambitious, I know that."

"She is cunning, and sharp enough to cut you." He picked

up a slice of candied orange, examined it for perfection, and ate that as well. "You are dancing a complex dance here, Natharie of Sindhu, and of all the ones who might use you, she is the one I most fear." He spoke casually, his voice low, but conversational, his face bland, his attention seemingly on the next orange slice.

Natharie bowed her head, setting the dish down, turning it slightly. "Master Gauda," she breathed. "Forgive me for this question, but, why would you care?"

The old eunuch smiled softly and leaned toward her, his finger raised to emphasize his point. "Because it is only the empty heart that is alone."

Natharie's fingers tightened on the edge of the dish until she was afraid she might shatter it. Master Gauda stood and brushed his brocaded coat straight once more. "I will expect you shortly, Natharie. We have much to do today."

He left her there, and she didn't know what to feel. Part of her was elated, part of her was only stunned. Master Gauda followed the Awakened One? Was it possible? With Divakesh so set on wiping out the teachings?

She was not given the leisure to contemplate any of these things. Ekkadi came hurrying up to bow before her. "Mistress, the first of all queens summons you."

Now what? Natharie thought, forgetting for an exasperated moment that she had hoped to bring herself back to Bandhura's attention. *Collect yourself.* Natharie took a quick sip of tea to moisten her mouth. Then she followed Ekkadi to the queen's suite.

Queen Bandhura—resplendent in her luxurious green and gold skirts and translucent emerald veil—was just settling herself before her own wide spread of breakfast dishes: fresh fruit, saffron rice, warm bread, pastries of nuts and honey. The rich scents did nothing but send Natharie's stomach roiling.

Collect yourself, she thought again sternly, and she made obeisance to the queen.

"Good morning, Natharie," said the queen. "Come, sit here." She patted the pillow beside her.

Natharie sat where she was bid, and noticed that no other lady sat beside the queen. There were only serving women here, and they were kneeling as far away as the room allowed, save for the one who poured Natharie a cup of red nectar and handed it to her.

"Thank you, Majesty." Natharie took a sip. Pomegranate juice, sweet and fragrant.

"I was most anxious to speak with you this morning. It seems you have made quite a conquest."

Natharie dropped her gaze modestly. "So I have been told, Majesty. My lord Tarish is . . ."

The queen laughed, gently mocking both the words and the modesty. "Is a boy, and you know it well. No, no. I refer to the brother of my heart."

Natharie swallowed hard, and the queen laughed again, far less gently this time.

"Oh, I know, I have been calling you his new favorite since he came, but I was not certain. He is a soldier, after all, and such as he are light and quick with women, when they choose women at all." The queen leaned back on her pillows, and plucked a slice of orange out of a dish. She ate it in silence, watching Natharie. Awkwardness began to give way to anger, and Natharie welcomed it. Anger banished fear and gave her the will to act.

"I have brought you here to make you an offer, Princess Natharie."

Natharie's head jerked up. It was the first time the queen had used her title. Bandhura's face had lost its teasing merriment and was now calm and serious.

"You hate your life here. You hate your confinement. I can give you some measure of freedom."

"Why would Your Majesty allow such . . ." Natharie searched for the appropriate word. "Immodesty?"

"Because you are the first who has deeply attracted the

Prince Samudra," the queen answered frankly. "It is of concern to me what he says and what he does." Bandura's eyes were hard. Her voice and attitude were open, but those eyes were closed. She was not telling all. "I want you to tell me what he says when he is with you, and perhaps from time to time I will give you a question or two to put to him in the course of your conversation. In return, I will send you on this errand or that. I fear it will have to be in disguise. Master Gauda and your clever maid will be able to help you there. You will be able to learn the city, and pass the occasional letter to your people at the docks."

Natharie felt the blood drain from her cheeks. The queen laughed, hiding her mouth behind her hand. "Oh! Look at the child! She's gone white. Of course you are spying for your father." The queen selected another slice of orange. "And I am prepared to help you do so, if you help me."

Despite her shock, Natharie's wits did not quite desert her. "Why would you trust me?"

The queen smiled. She peeled the orange section with quick, clever fingers and laid the peel on a separate brass dish. "Because you are spying for your father, and because I know this, I can have you killed at any time without giving cause for war." Her voice was completely matter-of-fact, even cheerful. Natharie's heart froze, and then started beating frantically.

"But you do not need to fear me," the queen went on, "as long as you serve me well." She looked at Natharie owlishly. "Indeed, in time, you would make an excellent wife for my lonely and wayward brother."

You do not need to fear me. The words echoed through Natharie's mind. *Oh, yes I do, because you care nothing for me and will abandon me as soon as it suits you.* Natharie sat in silence. It was not that she needed to think. There was nothing to think about, but she needed to get her voice under control. When she was sure she could speak without stammering, she bowed over her folded hands. "Of course, I will do my best to serve the great queen." *Which queen, I will not say.*

Bandhura nodded. "You are of a sound and sensible mind." She sat up, studying Natharie with her hard eyes. "But are you clever? You'll need to be. Well." The queen shrugged. "We'll find that out soon enough. But come, my dear, you've eaten nothing. I must go see to the mother of my heart. I'm sure she'll wish to join us. Ekkadi, see that your mistress eats something."

Queen Bandhura got up to leave and Natharie made her obeisance. When the queen was gone, Ekkadi came at once to Natharie's side. Natharie grabbed her maid's hand hard and squeezed it. Neither of them made any sound, and Natharie stayed as she was until she could make herself loosen her grip.

"Ekkadi, what's going on?" she breathed. "There's another game under this one."

"Not necessarily. This once, it could be as it seems." The maid leaned forward and smoothed Natharie's hair and veil. "It could be they just want the prince watched before they decide whether to kill him."

She's sharp enough to cut you, Master Gauda had said. He was right. "Whether or when?"

Ekkadi sat back on her heels. "That I don't know yet, Mistress."

"Can they actually mean to make me his wife?" All the warmth that had come with his touch, with the thoughts of distant, secret love drained away before the idea of a marriage arranged by Queen Bandhura for her own purposes.

Ekkadi considered this carefully. The greed in her eyes was tempered by her stubbornly practical turn of mind. "It could be. It would be a way of humiliating the prince as well as keeping a spy permanently with him."

"Yes, it would, wouldn't it?" murmured Natharie, ducking her head. Anger flared again, for herself and for Samudra. This time she was unsurprised at her own feelings. The prince had honor, the prince knew justice and sympathy. Whatever else he might be, these things made him better than the queen who would use him and bring him low if she needed to. "*Aiy-ah.* Every day this gets worse."

"Take those words back, mistress, before it truly does," said Ekkadi sharply.

Although she should not give way to such superstition, Natharie suddenly felt the Mothers' eyes looking sharply at her.

"It is too late," she answered.

"Yes." Ekkadi was flat on her face kissing the floor in her obeisance a bare instant before Queen Bandhura glided back into the chamber.

"There. We have at last gotten my mother into her bath." For a moment, Natharie saw a flicker of distaste in Queen Bandhura's eyes and she stowed away that sight very carefully.

"Now." The queen sat down again, again arranging her skirts neatly, which seemed always to be her first order of business. "At the time of the midday meal, the brother of my heart has arranged to meet an old priest near the queen's fountain. You will find a way to listen to them. You will tell me all you hear and all you see."

Natharie stared. She had told herself a thousand times that she would never again leave this place, that she must become resigned to her crowded, ivory cage. The fact that she was suddenly being ordered outside was difficult to comprehend.

"You must learn to stop goggling, Princess Natharie," said Queen Bandhura sternly.

"Majesty." Natharie struggled to pull her wits together. "How am I to get into the gardens?"

"That is clearly part of your task, my child. You may go now."

A test. I am being tested to find out if I am a worthy servant. Natharie made the expected obeisance and took her leave, Ekkadi trailing behind her. She said nothing as she walked slowly down the corridor and she could feel Ekkadi's impatience thrumming in the air.

Games, games, games. Games of religion, of conquest, of empire and blood. She knew such games. They were as much a part of the history and life of Sindhu as they were of Hastinapura. Natharie had come prepared to play. She had not, however, in her most frightened imaginings thought she would be playing for the queen and against the man for whom love was blossoming in her battered soul.

If all stayed as it was, she would truly be Queen Bandhura's pawn. That would not do, not for the tenth part of an hour, let alone for a lifetime as Samudra's wife and jailer.

She thought of the look of distaste on Bandhura's face when she spoke of Queen Prishi. Then she thought how the old, sick queen had played the game too, and survived for such a long time. There was something under the veil of her eyes. Did she know she was hated? Did she still have allies? Would she welcome one more?

Queen Bandhura wanted Natharie to be her spy and scapegoat. What might Queen Prishi want?

Another question: What did Queen Bandhura want of Queen Prishi?

Natharie paused in her stately progress back to her proper place. "Ekkadi?"

"Yes, mistress?"

"Do we know how long the old queen has been ill?"

Ekkadi did not even pretend to demure. "Almost two years. All the doctors agree that she won't last for another one. But then, they said that last year as well, apparently."

"And how long has Queen Bandhura been in charge of the small domain?"

"Since Queen Prishi's health began to decline."

Of course. "Ekkadi, listen carefully." She did not forget one word of what Master Gauda told her, but she must trust Ekkadi this far. There was no one else. "You must find me some gardener's clothes, and quickly, and tell Master Gauda I need to see him in the library at once."

Ekkadi bowed. "And what will you do, Mistress?"

No farther. It is enough that you know I am doing something. "Don't ask that, Ekkadi. Just go."

Worry briefly creased the maid's brow, but she gave the salute of trust and hurried away.

Natharie stood alone beside the ever watchful figures of the Seven Mothers and all their heroic children. *This time you cannot have cause to censure me,* she thought to them fiercely as she retraced her course. She kept going, the sound of her sandals on the marble floor faint in comparison to the drumming of her heartbeat. *Even you cannot approve of the murder of one of your own.*

Queen Prishi's chamber was not empty. She had known it would not be. The rooms of kings and queens were never deserted. But at least with Queen Prishi at the bath, the number of servants was small. A few girls and two old women went about their various tasks—shaking out silks, setting clutter in order, fanning the air, and sprinkling fresh rosewater to cover the scents of illness that the heat only increased.

Natharie set her face into a bashful smile and hurried in.

One of the servants, a puffy-faced woman with round hands looked up, a rebuke ready on her tongue. When she saw Natharie, she swiftly made the salute of trust instead.

"Forgive me," Natharie said to the older woman. *See, I know we're all servants here.* "The great queen sent me for some of her salts."

That startled the maid. "Sent you . . . ?" She blurted the words out before she was able to catch herself.

She dipped her eyes before the servant. *See, I know I'm speaking of a most delicate matter.* "Yes. I think her eyesight is not so good today. Is there something to bring her comfort for that too?" *Be earnest. You care. She's been good to you.* Once more, Master Gauda spoke clearly in the back of her mind, guiding her deception.

"Ah, my poor queen," sighed the woman. "The Mothers call her to the next life and we are left with that . . ." She stopped herself again. There was a clear reason this old woman was still doing nothing more than tidying rooms; she clearly had difficulty guarding her own tongue. That was good to know. "The doctors have given her an ointment. One more ointment. I tell you they are near useless, physicians, as bad as the sorcerers. If they can't save her life, what good are they, I say?"

She had a good deal more to say as well, but she seemed content to mutter it to herself as she walked away. Natharie hurried to the alcove that was the old queen's dressing area. One of the ways in which a slow poison might be best administered was to put it into something the victim used daily, and, by so doing, have them poison themselves. The array of bottles and boxes on the low tables, however, was bewildering. Each was a little work of art, sparkling with color and gilding. Most were covered with artful writing describing their contents and its benefits. She scanned the sparkling vessels, trying to bite back rising panic. Which one? What if she was wrong, and the poisoner did carry the compound on them?

Which is the greatest risk?

The one I'm running now.

She tried several of the jars, and found powders and perfumes and ointments. She smelled them carefully and tasted one or two, and found herbs and spices, and in one something she was fairly sure was urine and betel, and truly wanted to know which physician prescribed that for the queen so she could be sure to never let him touch her.

This is madness, she said to herself, setting that box down quickly. *At the very least, it is a jump of reason large enough to land you in the ocean.*

Then her eye lit upon a box with a lid decorated with vermilion and saffron. Such colors were used to anoint the brow for special occasions.

She saw the signs of luck drawn there, of health, and

longevity, all woven together, and something else, weaving in and out between the letters. She looked close. Weaving in and out, a serpent. A sign for wisdom. She looked again at what seemed to be a smear of the red ink. No, not a smear. The serpent's hood was spread.

A sign for poison.

She picked up the box, and opened the lid. Inside was yet another bright, white ointment. She sniffed. Jasmine and roses. For the complexion then. She dipped one finger in it and put the tiniest dab on her tongue.

Sharp, bitter, metallic. Wrong.

She closed the box. Could poison be absorbed through the skin? Yes. She'd heard of such things in the histories and in the ghost stories the guards told. She thought for a moment to tuck the box under her skirt, but there was no time. The maid was returning. She all but dropped the box and snatched up the nearest jar.

"Here, for my mistress's eyes," the maid said, handing over the gilded box to Natharie. Natharie took it with thanks, and wondered if only one of the medicines and cosmetics was poisoned. "She will not want to take it, but you must try to persuade her. She likes you, mistress. If you remind her of your connection to the prince she may do as you say."

"I will do what I can," answered Natharie honestly, and she hurried away.

If she is questioned, my story will not last a dozen heartbeats. Natharie's throat was dry, and she had to ease her grip on the jar. *I've moved too soon. I should have waited until I was sure Queen Bandhura trusted me.*

But the memory of those hard eyes and that careless laugh made her shake herself. *For that, I would have waited until the moon fell into the ocean.*

Natharie held herself to a walk as she moved down the corridor. Her ears strained for the sounds of hurrying footsteps, for the cry of the maid behind her, or the guards in front of her. The Mothers watched her from their places on the walls and on the beams overhead. What did they see? Did they understand that in this she meant to help?

Help who? Help how?

The enemy of my enemy is my friend. It was not a saying the Awakened One would approve of, but she had heard her father use it more than once, and she knew it to be true. At least, it could be. At least, a little, at least for a while.

It was better than playing Queen Bandhura's game alone. It was better than being turned against Samudra.

The library was no more empty than the queen's chamber had been. A dozen or so of the scholars, scribes, and bureaucrats that inhabited the small domain knelt before the reading tables. Their students and assistants sat beside them, or scurried to the shelves to fetch this book or that scroll. One or two glanced up at Natharie, and dismissed her. She had become as much a fixture here as they.

The great epics had their own alcove, and she went to it at once and selected the soft edged copy of *The Adushtastra*, kneeling down and opening its pages. She had barely found the page she needed when Master Gauda's shadow fell across her.

His face was bland, as it always was. She bowed her head to him, student to teacher. She swallowed.

Let me be right. She prayed as he knelt. *Let me not be mistaken in him.*

"I have a question, Master. I cannot seem to correctly translate this phrase." She pointed at first one word, and then another. *Why have you taken such care of me?*

The old eunuch frowned, then he smiled. "You are forgetting your grammar," he scolded. "You are not looking at the key element of the phrase." He turned a few pages back. "Now, follow along from here." He pointed at another word, Natharie bent over the page and read.

Awake.

He understood then. Now came the great question. He had worked hard to keep his own secret. Would he risk it for her?

Gauda was watching her steadily.

"I understand," she said, sitting back on her heels. She made her decision. "But what about this phrase here?" She pointed at a random set of words. "Doesn't that alter the larger part?"

As Gauda bent to look, Natharie murmured, "Master Gauda, can you get a message to the old queen for me?"

He paused long enough for worry to stab Natharie's heart. "I will do what I can," he whispered finally.

Thank you. Whether she was thanking her teacher or the Awakened One himself, Natharie was not sure. "You must tell her she is not ill. She is being poisoned by her daughter-in-law."

Gauda stared at her. "Are you certain of this?" he asked hoarsely.

Natharie nodded. "I found the poison in an ointment with her cosmetics."

For the first time, Natharie saw Gauda lose control of his own expression, and the anger that came over him was more fierce than she would have thought one of his kind could know. "I will tell her," he answered casually, his voice still wholly under his command. "And you? You have no time for this important duty?"

"I go to spy on her son." Natharie's mouth twisted into a wry smile. "It is well, Master, that you have taught me how to play farce as well as drama."

He returned a sour grimace. "We will see which this becomes, child." Then, in the lightest of whispers: "Anidita watch your steps."

She bowed as he rose and left her there, staring at the manuscript she had no concentration left to read. Once again, she had cast the dice. Now she had to wait to see how they would fall.

Anidita himself would not be able to help her if she lost this new throw.

Chapter Fifteen

The midday heat put an end to the training exercises. Samudra dismissed his men to eat and to rest until the relative cool of the afternoon. Pravan invited him to share his noon meal, an offer Samudra declined, although the smug look in Pravan's eyes as he did so left him coldly angry. Makul also suggested he come sit and talk, but that was only a show of politeness, and Samudra turned him down gently. It was just as well. At this time he did not want to look too long into Makul's eyes.

He tried once again to tell himself that there was nothing dishonorable about this subterfuge. What he did now was a simple matter of outflanking the enemy. It was a well-used and honorable tactic of war. The only difference was it must be done with words and with quiet deeds rather than with sword, bow, and chariot. Samudra removed his practice armor and handed it to his men-at-arms. He accepted the damp towel and vigorously wiped his face and scrubbed his head. Deception went hand and hand with honor in any battle. Mother Indu was Mother A-Kuha's sister. This was just another kind of war. That he loved his enemy meant nothing. In this much, Hamsa was right.

When he looked up, Hamsa was standing at the pavilion's entrance, as if summoned by his thought. She made the salute of trust and gave a small, tremulous nod in answer to the question in his eyes.

Good.

He had sent her ahead to make sure the gardens were clear of uninvited witnesses. He rubbed his eyes. He must find a

moment to speak with her. She seemed so . . . frightened
was the only word for it. She hunched her shoulders constantly as if to shield herself from prying eyes. It was hard,
he supposed, to believe your master was part of a rebellion.
He needed to tell her what was truly happening, lest her
worry for him give the game away.

He got up as the men around him made their obeisances
and walked out of the tent. The sun blazed down and the air
was sultry. Makul saw him from where he sat with some of
the older men; so did Pravan, who, hopefully, thought he
was retreating in continued despair over the emperor's preference for a preening upstart. Pravan was planning an expedition to try to face the Huni once again, and he had not told
Samudra. He had told the emperor, though, and everyone
knew it. Samudra had needed all his strength of will to keep
quiet. Even thinking about it made his anger flare and
brought the sweat out on his brow as he walked through the
cool green garden under the shadows of the trees and the
blossoms.

The queen's fountain stood at the heart of the gardens.
The first emperor's wife ordered this constructed here, although she had died before she could see it completed. In the
world of lush color, it was pure and black. The obsidian that
made it had been brought from the farthest of the southern
islands, as had the three sorcerers who shaped it. It was a
lacelike sphere. Inside, three great birds spread their wings,
shading and protecting those who came to the fountain's
rim. The water flowed down from the stone on which the
birds sat and into a basin. The obsidian was blacker than
night and yet at noon grew hot enough to burn the unwary
hand. More than once Samudra had wondered at its contra-
dictions, and how many of them were intentional. The birds
were caged, yet ever watchful. Lifegiving water sprang from
dead stone. That which was black blazed with bright heat.

Samudra stood gazing through the brittle beauty of the cage
to the birds within. He heard the sound of a gardener's shears

in the distance. Someone pruning tree or bush, maintaining the garden's perfection. Each thing in its place, each thread a part of the pattern, a step in the dance. Samudra's mind drifted back to all that Natharie had told him of her life in Sindhu. Part of him wondered if this was why the kings of the Awakened lands were so weak as to break their own vows against violence. They had no one to guard the heart of their world, as the queens did the small domain. Part of him wondered if he was even asking the right question with such a thought.

Part of him was remembering Natharie's touch on his wrist. He knew the act of love. There was no soldier who did not. He had known it willing and he had, to his shame, known it forced. He knew how it seared and blinded, and made a man lost to himself. But he had never known its tenderness, its intimacy. He had never lain down beside a woman who cared for his heart, as well as for his place, his purse, or his strength.

Samudra shook himself. *Why am I thinking of this?* It was a thought for the future, and right now the future was as distant as the moon. There was every chance he would die for what he did next.

He cast about for something else to think of and saw Hamsa also was contemplating the fountain, leaning on her staff as was her habit.

"What are you thinking?" he asked, partly to distract himself, partly because he was worried for Hamsa. These past days she had been silent, even for her, and her eyes had the hollow look of one who had been denied sleep.

"I am wondering how they found contentment with their place," she said, nodding toward the birds. "And yet still kept the fierceness they need to be good guardians."

Before Samudra found an answer to that, the scuff of sandals on the crushed stone of the path turned him around. A man in priest's robes approached. His back was stooped and he carried a fringed umbrella low over his head to shield himself from the sun.

And to shade his face from casual glances so idle eyes might not realize this was Commander Makul who walked up to his prince and made the salute of trust.

"Thank you for coming," Samudra said softly. He scanned the gardens all around with his soldier's eyes, all his senses sharp. He saw the gardener whose shears he had heard before straighten up with a basket of cut greenery balanced on one hip and slowly walk away. Hamsa took note of his watchfulness and understood the reason for it. She circled the fountain, strolling easily, as if stretching her legs, but in reality taking up a post opposite his own, so she could clearly see the side of the garden that the fountain blocked from his view.

"Did Pravan see you leave?" Samudra asked the man beside him.

"He may have seen, but I don't believe he marked it much." Makul grimaced his distaste. "He was too busy holding forth among his favorites."

"Yes," sighed Samudra as he gestured for Makul to take a seat beside him on the bench. "It is a pity some of those have fallen under his spell. There are a few who might make good soldiers, if they were given a good officer."

"We still have good officers among us," replied Makul mildly, but the reproof was plain.

"I know, I know. But for how long?" There was no need to mask his bitterness. Already he saw it, how senior men looked to Pravan, aware of his place in the emperor's esteem. Older men, wiser men, were beginning to defer to him, despite his recent fiasco in the mountains, and Pravan was taking note of each and every one of them.

Makul sighed and set aside his borrowed umbrella. He ran his hands through his hair. "You could end it in a heartbeat, my prince."

"Not in a heartbeat, Makul. Not anymore." Samudra stood. He could not be still. He needed to move, to try to escape from his words even as he spoke them. "Perhaps if my eyes had opened before the horse sacrifice . . . but now it is too late. Now there are only hard roads left out of this disaster."

He faced the fountain and folded his hands behind him. He did not look at Makul. He did not want to see the older man's face as Makul asked, "What is my prince saying?"

Samudra bowed his head. Shame weighed him down, shame and necessity, and neither left him the luxury of silence. "I am continuing the conversation we began in your home."

He heard the hiss of Makul's intake of breath.

"What has changed my prince's mind?"

The sun was so hot. It beat on Samudra's head and made the sweat trickle down his neck and back. It made yet another weight for his thoughts. The gardens around them were still. The trees seemed to wilt a little, despite the canals and channels that ran with water for them. Even the servants were allowed to take their rest and shelter now. The sun was too strong for bystanders and spies.

And need it too strong for you to be distracted from your purpose. You must speak.

"Pravan is planning another raid on the Huni," he said. "He speaks of it to the emperor."

Makul spun the umbrella in his thick, calloused fingers. The filigreed thing looked ridiculous in his big hand, but Samudra envied the other man its shade. "I know. I was not sure you did."

"How could I not know?" He snorted. "The barracks are full of it, and if none will speak to my face, I do still have ears, Makul."

"Are you doing this because Pravan has the emperor's favor?"

Now Samudra could turn and face him. These words he could speak with all the fervor of his heart. This was nothing less than true. "I am doing this because men are going to die, Makul. Good men. I am doing this because if my brother tries to rule by either the sword of war or the sword of sacrifice, Hastinapura is going to fall!"

Makul bowed his head. He seemed smaller now, shrinking in on himself as Samudra had never seen him do before.

"Pravan is a fool with dreams of glory," Makul said softly. "Divakesh is using him to root out the teachings of the Awakened One. He's frightened the emperor somehow."

"Chandra fears too much, Makul, he always has. I think Divakesh has told him that the Mothers will take the empire from him if he is not diligent enough in protecting their worship. He would believe that . . ." *He saw how the demands of ruling wore our father down, sickened him, killed him. Oh yes, my brother would believe the Mothers would strike him down the same way.*

Makul turned his face away. It was near blasphemy what they were now saying and even a man who harbored treason in his own heart might blanch to hear it spoken from another's lips. "It is not only them," Samudra went on. "You were right. Queen Bandhura is certain I am plotting against the emperor. She conspires to push me further and further away from my brother's trust and affections." He gazed again at the caged birds with their hooked beaks and sharp claws. "If I do not move soon, it will be too late."

Samudra knelt at Makul's feet as he had not done since he was a boy. "My battle-father," he said. "Do not let it come to this. Understand, I beg you, that this is what I must do, although it tears out my heart. Do not leave Pravan and Divakesh to rule my brother."

Makul looked at him a long time. Samudra saw understanding come to the old soldier, then belief, and last of all acceptance.

Makul bowed his head. His free hand plucked restlessly at the borrowed cloth that covered his legs. Samudra noted that the hand shook very little. "I am sorry it must be this way."

"So am I, battle-father," whispered Samudra. "Oh, so am I."

"You know I have spoken of these matters with other men?"

Samudra nodded, his throat too tightly shut for speech.

Makul nodded. "They will be most pleased if I say you are ready to speak with them."

Samudra swallowed, but his voice remained hoarse. "Will you tell them this?"

Now it was Makul who turned his face away. "If my prince desires that I should, I will."

Samudra laid his hand on Makul's shoulder. "I do not desire it, Makul, but it is what is required."

Another silence fell between them. Samudra wondered what Makul was thinking and then was glad he did not have to know. But the strength came back into the old soldier's face and his bearing straightened. "Your wisdom is great, my prince. May the Mothers guide your steps."

Samudra stood, backing away, wishing with all of his soul that there was something he could say, some way to speak of love and duty, and the harshness of the dance of sacrifice that was the true heart of being soldier and prince. But there were no words for this. "Go now, battle-father. I thank you."

Makul bowed once more and turned, becoming the old anonymous priest who had taken a stroll in the gardens and now must return to his duties at the temples.

Samudra watched, breathing hard as if he had just finished a race, his hands clenching the empty air over and over. Makul knew. He knew what Samudra was truly doing, and yet he would follow him anyway. Samudra wanted to howl until the heavens split open. He wanted to face down all the Mothers and demand to know why, *why,* this must be the price of Hastinapura's safety. He wanted to call Makul back and say he would find another way.

But he did not move. He stood where he was and watched his battle-father walk away.

So consumed was he with his own pain, he did not hear Hamsa slip up behind him.

"My prince," she whispered. "We are overheard."

Samudra froze. "Where?"

"To the right, down the slope, beneath the stand of bamboo."

He let his eyes wander in the direction she indicated. He saw it now, the patches of white and tan between the green stalks and stems. He nodded and touched Hamsa's shoulder, then made a gesture of dismissal. She walked away toward the palace, and he made as if to sit down again.

Then, Samudra lunged down the slope, snatching up the spy by the shoulders and hauling him to his feet. At first, he saw only a gardener, ludicrously clutching a basket of pruned greenery and flowers. He was about to let go from sheer relief, but then his eye saw what his mind could not at first take in.

Princess Natharie looked at him from under the wound cloth of the gardener's plain turban. Samudra was so startled he stumbled a step backward. She, in return, drew herself up straight, making no attempt to hide or to flee, or to explain.

It was Hamsa who spoke and her voice was utterly shattered. "Great Princess, why are you here?"

Natharie also backed away, giving herself the space that such dignity as might remain to her required. "You know that, *Agnidh*. I am here to listen to the prince's discourse with that . . . priest."

The hesitation told him she had indeed heard what was said. Anger and incomprehension tore through Samudra. "Who sent you here?" he croaked. He could not stop staring. A woman of royal blood, here she was for anyone to see, anyone to touch or take, dressed in a loose smock to keep off the flies and with ragged, much-used sandals on her feet. How could she do this to herself? What was this woman?

She must have seen all this in his face, but she offered no apology, not even with her eyes. Instead, she offered a flat statement. "Queen Bandhura sent me."

"Bandhura? Bandhura is using you?" *Bandhura did this to you?*

"Yes."

He could not look at her. He could barely stand to be beside her. After all that had just passed between him and Makul his nerves were already stretched taut. After all he had thought and dared to believe about . . . this woman before him, how could he begin to confront her this way?

"Why would the first of all queens send you here?" Hamsa found the words that had eluded him.

Natharie gave a small, mirthless laugh. "You cannot guess, *Agnidh*?"

Samudra hung his head. He looked up to Heaven. He saw the black glimmer of the queen's fountain and the burning blue of the sky and the silent green gardens in the glare of the midday sun. He saw everything but an answer he could understand. "Why would you do this?" he cried.

Natharie did not flinch. She did not even blink her eyes. "Because she offered me freedom and threatened my life."

"She *what*? How?" Samudra felt the blood drain away from his face, and from his heart. He looked across to Hamsa. Hamsa had gone white.

Natharie sighed. She toyed with the flower stems in her basket. "Does it matter?"

"Yes, it matters!" Anger, so familiar, so useless flooded him. Anger at her, at Bandhura. Anger at himself for not having prevented this, all of this, every last wrong, broken, treacherous event that now surrounded him. Anger at Mother A-Kuha for driving him to this place with her riddles and her bloody, bloody dance.

Into this storm of anger, Natharie's voice dropped like iron. "Samudra, what matters is that you have caught me, and I have heard what you said to the man in the priest's dress."

He folded his arms, the anger churning through him stirring all his arrogance. What was Bandhura thinking, sending such a woman out to spy on two soldiers? "What is it you think you have heard?"

Natharie smiled as she read the thoughts, but the smile was grim and without triumph. "I have heard that you are pretending to join a rebellion in order to bring it down. I also know that Queen Bandhura will use that pretense to denounce you to the emperor."

And Chandra will listen. Not even drowning beneath his anger could Samudra pretend his brother would do otherwise. "Will you tell her?"

"I must tell her something."

"You can say that you failed."

She shook her head. "No, I can't."

"Why? Pride?" Samudra regretted the tone more than the words as soon as he had spoken.

"No."

"Then why?"

She did not answer him and his anger flared again. "Do you know what the penalty is for one of your rank leaving the small domain? If your judge is feeling generous, you will only be beaten with bamboo strips until you fall unconscious. If not, you will be trampled to death." *See, now I have power over you. If no one else ever hears me again, you must hear me now!*

But again, Natharie made no answer and Samudra felt himself tremble from the fury and the fear and the love; yes, the broken and disappointed love that tore at his heart.

"Why did you do this to me?" he whispered, unable to hide his anguish any longer.

In response, Natharie's face went hard as stone. "That question is unworthy of you, Samudra."

And she was right. Again. Samudra watched his hands as they curled into fists. *You are not a boy. You are not a vain and foolish child. You are a man and you are a prince, and you are here with this woman. She is who and what she is and you must face it all. All of it, Samudra, not just what you wish you could see.*

Samudra bowed his head, gesturing his apology. "No it is not unworthy of me, it is unworthy of you. Natharie . . ." Her name caught just a little in his throat. "What will you do?"

She bit her lip, glancing back toward the white walls and ivory gates of the palace. *What is in your mind, Natharie? What is in your heart?* "I will return to my mistress, and I will tell her what I saw. I think, however, I did not hear every word correctly."

Samudra lifted his head. Hope that pierced almost as deeply as anger within him. "You will do this for me?"

She nodded. "My home needs you strong, and if you will not . . . if you cannot be emperor, then you must be the emperor's sword arm, not this Pravan, and most of all not Divakesh."

It was as if the sun rose in his private darkness, and by that light within he was able to see past his own danger and his own fragile schemes. "Bandhura will have yet more power over you."

He had thought he would see her tremble, but instead, Natharie smiled once more, and this time that smile was sly. "Perhaps not."

He cocked his head toward her. "There is something else?"

She nodded, but before he could ask what this something else was, she asked, "Samudra, will you trust me?"

He looked into her eyes for a long time. Was it only her beauty that he saw there? It was beauty enough to bring any man to his knees for her. Did he truly see her heart? She had courage, but she was also capable of subterfuge, and perhaps better at it than he. Was she lying to him with those eyes now?

It seemed to Samudra that his next words would change the whole of the dance, for good or for ill, and change it forever. "Yes, Natharie," he said. "I will trust you."

"Thank you," she whispered, and he knew she understood

how grave this was. "I hope it will not have to be for long."

He wanted to touch her. He wanted to take her into his arms and kiss her and do so much more, to take his comfort in her beauty, even as she was in the clothes of a slave, her strong, fair face bare to the harsh sunlight. "I must let you go before you are seen."

"Yes." She bit her lip again. She reached into the basket and pulled out a branch of scarlet blooms. "Take these. If anyone wonders, you can say you were speaking to a gardener about the best tokens to bring me to show your affections."

He stared at the delicate flowers she laid across his palm, and then looked up at her, and this time he knew the ache and the conflict he saw in her was real, because he felt its echo within his own breast.

"Take care, Great Prince." She made obeisance as a servant would, then, resting the basket on her hip she left him, heading toward the shadow of the palace walls without once looking back.

"Take care, Natharie," he whispered. "Take very great care."

Then there was nothing to do but turn and walk the other way.

*N*atharie forced herself not to run across the gardens. She trudged. She was a weary laborer, going home to get out of the sun. The gardeners had a barracks to themselves, dug out of the earthen berm by the palace's inner wall. Its turf roof was as carefully tended as the rest of the garden. Unless you knew the location of the narrow stair down to the doorway, you would pass the dwelling by.

Inside it was cool, but dark as a cave. The floor was packed dirt and the walls were glazed clay. By the light of the hearth fire, Natharie picked her way between the sleeping bodies of the gardeners, snoring and wheezing away the

middle of the day when it was too hot for any but madmen
and spies to be out. It was the old woman who dozed beside
the cookstove who had let Natharie stash her other clothes
here. They were actually Ekkadi's clothes. The woman had
believed Natharie's story that she was a maid of the small
domain come to deliver a love note to the prince. She would
probably entertain all her confederates with the story tonight.

But all she did now as Natharie crept past to retrieve her
bundle was open one knowing eye and wink. Natharie
winked back, snatched up the pile of borrowed clothing, and
slipped out the door as quickly as she could. Although the
foot of the stairwell was open to the sky, it was about as private as any other place she would find outside the palace.
She quickly shed her soiled and sweat-soaked gardener's
clothing, and wrapped herself in Ekkadi's simple servant's
garments. She left the others outside the door along with the
silver ring she had promised the old woman, and ran up the
steps.

The inner walls of the palace had a number of small doors
in them for those who had no business coming and going
through the grand gates as if they were the emperor. Each of
these was guarded, of course, but at times some of the
guards were more sympathetic to errands of love and mischief than others. Ekkadi, naturally, knew which these were
and fortunately, Samudra and Makul's conversation had not
lasted past the time for shift change. Natharie was able to
reenter the palace as easily as she had left it. She tried not to
count how many men had now seen her come and go. She
felt absurdly exposed. Already, she was becoming used to
the idea that modesty required that she be closed away.

*And it's only been a few months. What will I be after years
of this?*

She bit her lip, remembering Samudra's blunt recitation
of the penalties should she be caught. *If I have years yet.*

She emerged from the dim and dusty servants' stairs to be

surrounded once more by the opulent confines of the small domain. She hurried at once to the library. There, Master Gauda knelt beside a figure wearing ruby-red silks and sliver veils and made a great show of dunning an ancient text into her. It was Ekkadi, but to the casual eye, she could be Natharie, as long as she was sitting down. Without a word, they retired to the dressing alcove to exchange their costumes and assume their proper stations in the world. With that, all was done and she could breathe again.

No, not quite yet.

"You had better let the first of all queens know we're back."

"Of course." Ekkadi strode away, head bowed, the picture of the humble, obedient maid. Natharie in her turn started back toward the library. She wanted to talk with Master Gauda about Ekkadi, before the maid returned—about how to build a defense against her, just in case he was right, just in case she was the hidden knife.

This place bristles with knives. I am a knife myself. Whose knife are you, Drama Master?

But she had not yet reached the filigreed archway when another servant stepped up to her. It was Damman, Queen Prishi's woman.

"My mistress the queen mother bids you attend her, Great Princess," she said.

Natharie swallowed. She had not expected this, not yet, and the timing strained the rest of the careful deceptions she had piled together today. She would have to make do. She could not refuse Queen Prishi.

Swiftly, she took her leave of Master Gauda and hurried down the corridor.

Queen Prishi's chamber was a place of shadows even at midday. The curtains about her bed were sheer, but layered, creating a close twilight that stank of illness and old roses. In the dim light, the old queen was little more than a wrinkled bundle of silk in the middle of the great bed.

The waiting woman knelt by Queen Prishi's head. "The princess Natharie is here."

Natharie knelt. Had the queen fallen asleep?

No. She stirred and opened her pale eyes. "Ah," she sighed. "Very good. Come here, daughter." Her scabbed and withered hand lifted from the blanket and waved Natharie forward. "I would have you soothe me with one of your tales."

"Certainly, Majesty." Natharie took her cue from the waiting woman's nod and settled herself on the other side of the queen's pillow. "What would you have me tell?"

Very, very softly, Queen Prishi said, "I would hear how you came to find my poison."

Natharie's heart thumped. She glanced at the waiting woman. The queen saw the reason for her hesitation. "Have no fear of Damman. She has known when to keep her mouth closed since she was four years old."

I wonder if Ekkadi would take lessons from her? Natharie nodded in acknowledgment. "It is in the vermilion and saffron box, in a skin cream. I don't know exactly what it is, but . . ."

"The venom of the green snake mixed with antimony," the queen answered.

Natharie stared.

"I made it up myself. You see, my dear, you were wrong about who was poisoning me. I have done this to myself. Damman administers the dose every night."

Incomprehension choked her. Natharie stared again at the queen, and then at the placid Damman. "Why?" she finally managed to say.

The queen smiled weakly. "Ah. Now, there is the great question. Tell me, why did you believe it was my daughter-in-law who made up this special medicine for me?"

Natharie swallowed hard and groped for words. The smell of sickness pressed closer and the hairs on the back of her neck prickled as fear crawled across her skin. She could only find the truth. "I have seen the way she looks at you. She is contemptuous of you. It was upon your illness that she gained her power. I . . . know how such things may happen."

"In your own home?" inquired Queen Prishi.

"In history, it has happened," answered Natharie stiffly. There were rumors from the concubines' quarters when she was still young, about how one lady in particular had met her end, but she was not going to tell the old queen that tale.

Fortunately Queen Prishi seemed to accept her answer. She let her head drop back onto the pillow. "It is a good guess. It fits the facts as they can be seen by those with a will to do so. I am only sorry you are the one who made it."

"What?" Natharie's fear grew colder.

"Nothing. Nothing. This . . . I am tired and not so careful as I should be sometimes." A glance passed between mistress and maid and Damman lifted the old queen with great care, pushing several pillows underneath her, so that Prishi could look at Natharie more easily. "Why did you decide to tell me? You can hardly love those of us who keep the keys to the small domain."

There were a hundred answers Natharie could give, ninety-nine of them lies, which she felt sure the queen would sense. So, she once again gave the truth. "For the prisoner, the character of the jailer makes a difference. I would rather have you hold those keys than Bandhura."

"Very good, very good." The queen smiled a little, and the smile was not pleasant. "You could have said for love of my son, and then we would have both known what you want here."

"And what would that have been?"

"Power, of course. For yourself or for your family, it would not have mattered."

"And since I did not say that?"

Queen Prishi sighed. "Since you did not, I will perhaps prove that I have finally become an old fool, and I will trust you with a few important things." She waved at Damman again, and this time the woman handed her mistress a cup and helped her to drink. The queen swallowed, coughed, and swallowed again. "Your first question will be why am I poisoning myself?"

Natharie nodded. She could not help but cast an eye toward the doorway. She need not have worried, she saw. Two straight-backed figures knelt there. More trusted women, but not as trusted as Damman, for they were kept out of earshot.

"I take poison to keep myself alive," said Queen Prishi. "Can you understand that?"

Natharie thought, and, slowly, understanding came. Bandhura wanted power, that was quite clear. To rule the small domain, she would have to be rid of Queen Prishi. Those hungry for power seldom waited for Death to come of his own accord. If Bandhura believed Prishi was wasting away on her own, she might find a patience she did not otherwise possess.

"She would know if the illness were feigned," Natharie murmured. "And she would act."

"Very good." The queen took another swallow from her cup and then waved Damman back to her place. "It has the additional advantage of making senility quite believable, which makes people careless of what they say in front of me." She touched Damman's hand. "Even the best of women cannot lurk in every doorway without rousing suspicion."

Damman put the cup down and folded her hands. Her face was hard as she watched Natharie, looking for signs of betrayal perhaps. *Here is one who will kill if it becomes necessary,* Natharie thought. Years of fear and treachery had made Damman knife-sharp.

Sharp enough to cut you. Master Gauda's words came swiftly back and Natharie shifted her weight uneasily.

"So," said Queen Prishi. "Now you know what you know. What will you do?"

Natharie shrugged. "What can I do? I had thought to help you, but you clearly want no help."

"Did I say so?"

Natharie lifted her gaze. The old woman was smiling again. Her teeth were stained and brown and in the flickering light they looked like fangs.

"I have watched you and Bandhura. That's why I brought you here. She's using you for something. What is it?"

"She wants me to spy on Prince Samudra," answered Natharie flatly. "I believe she hopes I will one day be able to kill him, should she find that necessary."

"Why does she think you, a follower of the Awakened One, would commit murder at her word?"

"Because she offers me . . . certain freedoms, and she knows certain facts."

"Ah. Yes." The queen sucked the hollow of her scabbed cheek. "That would be a good bargain. She would have been an excellent merchant, my daughter-in-law." She seemed to realize what she was doing and stopped. "I'm sorry. For me the little habits of beauty have given way to little grotesqueries. It makes the illusion more complete."

Master Gauda would be fulsome in his praise.

Queen Prishi grimaced a little, perhaps at Natharie's silence, perhaps at her own pain. "Has it commenced, this spying?"

"Yes. Your son met with a man in the gardens today. I was sent to hear what they said."

"And what did they say?"

Natharie did not miss a beat this time, but told Queen Prishi all she had overheard. The queen blinked twice. "And what will you tell Bandhura?"

Natharie was ready for this question, and recited for Queen Prishi the lie she had readied as she ran up the servants' stairs. Repetition would help her keep the details straight and she must keep her details straight. An actor's memory is a liar's memory, Master Gauda had said at one point. Natharie found herself wondering how much he had known then.

Queen Prishi closed her eyes, her face creased with private pain. "Well done," she murmured hoarsely. Beside her, Damman only knotted her fingers together. The endless fussing and fluttering, it seemed, was part of the deception.

"So, Natharie, we know our parts? You will continue in your game with Bandhura, and from time to time, you will be sent for to help soothe me to sleep. I fear you will have to put up with me petting you and making much over my son's favorite."

"I will manage, Majesty."

"Yes, I expect you will. I have a warning for you, though, Princess. Keep your own moves simple. You are doing well, but you are a novice only. Bandhura has played for her life since before she came to power."

"I will not forget."

"Good. Now, a last question." Queen Prishi opened her eyes and turned her head. Her expression softened as she looked up at Natharie, and Natharie wondered what she was seeing. "What do you truly think of my son, Samudra?"

Caught off guard, Natharie felt a blush rise in her cheeks and she groped for some polite ambiguity. *Truth,* she ordered herself firmly. *Tell her the truth. You have gained her trust, do not throw it away.*

She had opened her mouth to speak when she heard the unmistakable thump of someone dropping to the floor, and her head jerked up in time to see the first of all queens stealing softly into the bedchamber. Bandhura's eyes glittered as she saw Natharie sitting there beside her mother-in-law, and for the heartbeat before Natharie made the proper obeisance, she saw the hunger showing openly on Queen Bandhura's beautiful face.

At that same moment, all sign of strength fell away from Queen Prishi, and she was no more than a sick and frail old woman impatient with her pain and bed.

"Daughter of my heart," she said with weary brightness. "So kind, so thoughtful. I need your hands on my brow, daughter. Natharie is a wonderful teller of tales, but her touch is too rough for my poor head."

"Of course, mother of my heart." Bandhura came forward, graceful as always, and settled herself beside Prishi's bed. With skilled fingers she began to rub the old queen's temples and forehead. Prishi let out a gusty sigh and closed her eyes.

Understanding it was time to depart, Natharie made obeisance and slipped away. Ekkadi hovered by the threshold, wringing her hands together nervously.

"What happened?" she whispered. "Did you tell her about the poison? What will she do?"

What will she do? "I don't know," she answered. "Upon my life, I don't know."

Ekkadi opened her mouth, but Natharie waved her to silence. With her maid behind her, she returned to the viewing chambers as calm and collected as she could. All round them buzzed the life of the small domain—the gossip, the study, the children's games, and the endless, endless lessons. The children, protégés, and wives of the greatest of the great empires, were all so carefully sheltered and guarded from the outside world, and given no protection at all from each other. The cruelty of power and politics was concentrated here in this ivory-framed heart.

"Mistress," hissed Ekkadi.

Natharie realized she was standing and staring, and a number of the old grannies on the benches were beginning to stare in return. There'd be questions later from her fellow students. She blinked and forced her mind back to what she must do now. She smiled shyly as if nothing was wrong, and tossed greetings to those she knew, and promises for another game to the cluster of perfumer's apprentices from whom she'd won four ear bangles last night. The small domain's women were for the most part much less serious about their gambling than the women in the barracks she had visited with Captain Anun. Natharie had to play carefully, so as not to win too often.

Natharie reached Queen Bandhura's private chamber, and looked about in confusion when she was greeted only by one of the lower serving women.

"I was summoned by the first of all queens," she said. "Or so I was told."

In perfect timing, Ekkadi bowed her head, prepared to take the blame for doing her duty like a good maid should.

"Then please sit so you may await the queen's word, Princess." The serving woman bowed and stepped aside, as Natharie hoped she would, and she settled herself onto the pillows laid out for whatever guests the queen should wish to receive in her perfect jewel box of a room. The fine curtains screened her from casual view, but the babble of voices was constant. Natharie had not known silence during the daytime since she arrived. The stillness of the garden had been both a tremendous blessing and a little disconcerting.

Queen Bandhura was not long in coming. She sailed into the room, ignoring all obeisances including Natharie's. "Will that woman never die?" She bit the words off, and rearranged her face into her usual pleasant smile. It was as smooth and practiced a motion as the one she used to adjust her skirts every time she sat down.

A word and a gesture sent all the waiting women scattering to the far reaches of the chamber, including Ekkadi who could not hide the disappointment in her eyes. *She must be bursting for the news.*

"Now, Natharie." The queen folded her hands gracefully in her lap. "What did you learn today?"

So much beauty, so well protected, and Natharie had no defense against her. None at all. "Much, Great Queen, but . . ." She demurred.

"What?"

Say it. This is the truth that will hide the lie. She swallowed hard and let her face show her fear. It was not difficult. "I was seen."

"You let yourself be seen?"

"I . . . it was the sorceress. I underestimated her watchfulness."

"Underestimated Hamsa?" Bandhura's laugh was short, and it was cruel. "Your expectations must be low indeed. What happened then?" The words were gentle, and Natharie felt her skin twitch along the thin line where Divakesh had laid his sword against her throat.

"I told him . . . I told him it was because of a bet." Gambling was a much-loved occupation in the small domain. Riddles, dice, dominoes, chess were all played for undignified wagers. Samudra, who grew up in these halls, would know that.

"A bet?" Bandhura watched her through narrowed eyes, her face a mask of calculation that nonetheless showed all the woman's burning intelligence. "Yes, yes," she nodded finally. "It's believable at least. Do you think he accepted this?"

Natharie bowed her head, her fingers fiddling with a wrinkle in her skirt. "He seemed . . . flattered, I think."

"Did he?" Natharie glanced up to see the queen lean back on her pillows, as relaxed as a hunting cat in the sun, and as watchful. "This may yet work to our advantage. I am pleased to see you have a sharp mind, Natharie." For once, it sounded as if she truly meant her words. "It will serve you well and you will find reward from it. Now, what was so urgent that Samudra had to meet a priest at the height of midday?"

"He was talking about Lord Divakesh."

"Ah. And what was the nature of this conversation?"

"He wished to know how Divakesh was regarded among the priests of the Mothers. Whether he was held in esteem by those under him, or whether it was only his association with the emperor that held him up."

The queen's brows arched. "And this priest was not scandalized by such blasphemy?"

A court is a court, whether it is of men or the gods. "He

did not seem to be. He seemed to think that Divakesh was feared more than loved, but that there were some among the higher orders of priests who might be induced to weaken his authority."

Bandhura considered this for a moment. "Were names given?"

"No." Natharie bowed her head once more. "I am sorry, Great Queen." *See, I am taking my part most seriously.*

"It cannot be helped, not at this time," she added, the hint of warning very clear in her words. "So, Samudra seeks to dethrone Divakesh. Well, he might. It could be the prelude to many other things." She paused, and directed her piercing gaze fully toward Natharie. "You must have been pleased to hear this."

Natharie shrugged. It was time to return to the truth, to fully frame the lie. "Should I deny it, Great Queen? I have no affection for Lord Divakesh."

"It is best to be open about such things, with me, at least." Bandhura reached over and patted Natharie's hand. "We must be great friends from now on, you and I. We must be seen together often, so that these little conversations will arouse no suspicion."

Here came the greatest risk of all. Natharie took a deep breath. "Perhaps not, Great Queen. Prince Samudra does not trust you."

Bandhura cocked her head toward Natharie, amused once more. "He does not? Clever of him. But it is all the more reason for me to take you under my wing, child. You see, it will make him feel all the more protective of you, as he must save you from his sly sister of the heart." She laughed, a bright, merry sound that made the skin at Natharie's throat itch. "Go now, child. Back to your games. I'll send for you again soon."

Natharie made obeisance and left the private room, pushing aside the curtain and inhaling the air of the outer chamber with the feeling of someone who had narrowly escaped drowning. Her knees were shaking and her hands were weak and she felt she must soon sit down or she would collapse.

But you survived. You survived and she believes. You have won that much.

Now all that remains is to do it again, and again, and again. Bile rose in Natharie's stomach and she swallowed hard against it. *Help me, Anidita, for without your eyes I am going to be lost in this maze.*

But there was nothing to do but pull on her mask, even as Bandhura did, and walk into the sunny viewing rooms, calm and happy for all this little world to see.

Chapter Sixteen

Beyond the Shifting Lands wait the homes of the gods, the Heavens and the Hells. They are part of the Land of Death and Spirit, surrounding it, permeating it, and yet as separate from it as the worlds of flesh and mortality. They are great cities, forest groves, whole worlds of splendor and glory, distinct from each other with their own borders and their own guardians.

It was to the edge of one Heaven that Vimala, A-Kuha, Mother of Destruction, the Deceiver, drove her chariot. She had scarcely reined in her terrible steeds when the gates of the shining city opened. Her serpents hissed a warning an instant before the form of her sister and queen flew toward her. On wings of lotus and terror, Jalaja, the Queen of Heaven, hurled herself against her sister with the force of thunder that rocked the world around them.

"Traitor!" *she screamed, and her curved sword clashed down. Vimala danced backward, her own blade flashing to*

block her sister's blows. Her arm was cut already by the first assault and divine ichor dripped down.

"Calm yourself, my sister!" cried Vimala as their swords clashed together yet again. Her steeds hissed warning, but she only retreated.

"What right have you to steal what is mine!" cried Mother Jalaja. She burned like lightning, like ice. She was all the wrath of injured destiny and the vengeance of generations, and even Vimala hesitated before her might.

"I stole nothing." She made herself say as she backed away yet again, trying to put herself out of range of the sword of the goddess. "The girl Natharie was never yours."

Jalaja circled her sister, less frantic now, but no less angry. "She came to me of her own will."

"She came to your lands. Not one threat of your sword on earth has been able to make her yours."

The Queen of Heaven only snorted at this, but she did not raise her sword. Not again. Not yet.

"You mince words, A-Kuha. You irritate me."

Vimala made her gamble, recklessly, ready for bloody consequence, as was her nature. Her serpents pressed close about her throat and shoulders, ready to shelter her from the wrath to come. "I am not surprised." Vimala smiled. "If the girl had truly been yours, I would never have been able to make this bargain Or . . ." She paused, as if considering carefully. "Do you say the power of your word and your due sacrifice is so small?"

"What are you doing, Deceiver?"

Now Vimala made her answer in earnest. "Showing you what you should have seen these long years before, Sister. We are ill-served within our lands."

"These lands are mine. If you share in them, it is at my whim."

At this, the Mother of Destruction bowed her head. "So it is." Her lowered eyes glinted with all the strength of will and steel. "It changes nothing. You are ill-served."

"By you, my sister." The words were flat, and bitter as poison.

But Vimala only shook her head slowly. "Oh, no, Queen of Heaven. In me you have a great friend, although you will not see it."

"Now you say I am blind?" Jalaja raised up the sword. Her wings of divine war spread out behind her.

"And deaf," answered Vimala mildly.

"I will strike off your head!" Jalaja swung the blade down. Vimala, ready, skipped backward, and still she felt the heat as its edge brushed past her shoulder. Her serpents hissed loudly, their mouths gaping and their white fangs bared.

"And then what?" Vimala said, her grin showing her own sharp teeth. "Who will take my place? What blood will you yourself lose as you shed my blood?"

But Jalaja shook this off question. "You overreach yourself, Sister. For all your clever words, you too are ill-served. The one you claim for your prince will not break the pattern of the dance. His vows to Indu and to me will not leave his heart."

"I know." Vimala sighed. "He is a stubborn one. So, we are even in our misfortunes. I propose we settle it with a wager."

With that, she had her sister's attention again. The divine blade was still as Jalaja's eyes narrowed. "What wager?"

And so I have you, my sister. The Queen of Heaven loved to gamble as much as any mortal queen, and her sister had known this since they came into being. "As your champion has failed your test . . ."

"It is no true test. The emperor is not my true champion."

Vimala let out a short sigh, as if giving into her sister's stubbornness. "Then let it be this way," she said. "Put forth a test for your priest, any sort you choose. If he responds in honor and true faith, then the order he maintains is upheld. All remains as it was before, save that you may then strike off my head for my insolence. But if he fails, I will set forth a test for my prince. If he defeats the temptations set before him, then you acknowledge that he is worthy to be emperor."

"What are you doing, Vimala?" whispered the Queen of Heaven.

Her sister, her other self, her enemy, her counselor, spread her hands. "What I must, Jalaja. Whether you will it or no, these are my lands too, and my servants and I will not leave them as they are."

"And if your prince wins? What forfeit do you claim?"

"The Pearl Throne. It will become right and proper within the dance that Samdura sit there."

They stood still before each other, these two. They were great as the sky, small as sand on the shore, they were all things precious and base together, they were beauty and terror, wisdom and foolishness, all at once, all together, all separate. They were each distinct and they were one being indivisible, and they stood outside the worlds and inside the heart and they watched each other. In another place, at the same time, in other aspects they danced together on a green sea, churning the waters, the infinitely complex pattern creating the new day, and still at the same time they stood here, caught in each other's game.

Perhaps not even they understood the mystery and paradox of their selves. It simply was as it must be.

The Queen of Heaven lifted her sword hand, and the blade at once became a white dove that flew into the air above the shining city. "Very well. It shall be as you say." Now it was her turn to sigh, cocking her head thoughtfully to one side. "I think I shall regret your death."

"Save your regrets until my head decorates your belt." Vimala shook her hips, rattling the skulls that hung from her girdle. Then she raised her blade and held out her free hand to her sister. The Queen of Heaven took the proffered hand and locked her gaze with the Mother of Deception.

Slowly, the two began a new dance, and beneath them, the world turned.

* * *

*W*ith the grey light of dawn, Radana arrived at the docks of Hastinapura. Most of the way she had been confined to the filthy hold with the rats and the stinking cargo of eel guts and medicinal reed bulbs which were the boatman's stock and trade. She could see the light through narrow chinks in the deck, however, and she had learned to tell, by the feel of the motion of the boat and the shouts of the family above, when they pulled up to a dock.

She had carefully selected a family boat, so as not to have any man or men try to take payment in kind from her. She still had her wits, and a knife beneath her skirt, but she did not want to have to waste them on such foolishness. The wiry, naked-breasted woman who ran her man with a sharp eye and sharp tongue was more than willing to take the two gold anklets to see that Radana arrived in secret, and unmolested. It had, however, been a painfully slow voyage. No amount of persuasion or extra payment could convince either the woman or the man to miss a single one of their regular stops along the way, where they traded and gossiped, drank and left offerings for the next stage of the journey. It was excruciating, but it was worth it. If the family was even questioned by the king's men, Radana had no notion of it.

And to undo the king's madness, I can be patient.

She told herself this over and over again, until it became a part of her meditations.

Now, overhead, she heard a heel thump three times on the deck. This was the all-clear signal they had arranged. Even these ignorant river travelers knew a human could not live days at a time without air. The signal was followed by a thump and shuffle and the hatch was thrust aside, sending a shaft of dim light down into the dark hold. With it came a host of sounds, incomprehensible voices of humans and animals, the creak of ropes and the crack and thud of heavy burdens.

Radana clambered up the splintered ladder and gazed out for the first time at the river port of Hastinapura.

Her heart sank. She had expected it to be large, but the rumbling river of human activity surging around the docks was deeper and broader than she had ever imagined.

The riverwoman elbowed her in the ribs.

Radana yelped, and came back to herself in an instant as she saw the woman holding out her dirty, calloused palm. She did no more than grunt, but her meaning was plain. She wanted payment and she wanted Radana off her boat.

Very well.

Radana handed over the ankle rings she had promised. With her chin high, she stepped from the boat onto the tarred dock. She kept her gaze straightforward and proud as she walked forward. She was noble and she was strong. She was not a river scrap of nothing.

The bluff worked. Porters and traders made at least a little room for her. She needed to find a bath, and a place she could hire some honest bearers and a palanquin. She could not arrive at the Palace of the Pearl Throne alone and on foot. Through the shifting mass of heads, shoulders, and animal torsos in front of her, she could glimpse the narrow, dark streets that led away from the open docks, and she shuddered at the thought of what waited in there.

"Well then, here's a pretty lady a long way from home."

The creaking voice startled her, but Radana managed not to jump. She turned slowly, with all the dignity she had learned in Sindhu's court, and looked down. There, in the meager shade under a pile of rice sacks, crouched a withered old man. He wore nothing but a breechclout about his skinny hips and his iron grey hair was divided into countless braids, bound back in a greasy cloth winding.

"Not so far as that, father," she answered, the Hastinapuran words feeling light and slick on her tongue.

But they were comprehensible, because the old man

grinned, showing filthy and broken teeth and answered, "You think not?"

You will not make a victim of me, old man. "You are a sorcerer."

That only made the old man grin more broadly. "I am, pretty lady, and my sorcerer's eye," he tapped his temple with one scarred, horny finger, "sees you are in want of guidance."

Don't look at the streets. Don't show indecision. She kept her haughty expression fixed, but only barely. "Anyone who served me honestly would find himself well rewarded."

With surprising speed, the man leapt to his feet. "Then permit me to be your guide." He bowed, moving like a spry boy, for all his face was as wrinkled as a walnut. "Where are we going, pretty lady?"

"To the Palace of the Pearl Throne."

That made him pull back, but only for a moment. "Ha! Pretty you may be, but they are a cage of beauty there." He waggled his finger at her. "What makes you think they'll open the door for one more bird?"

"Does it matter to you?" Radana answered with a small shrug. "Take me to the proper gate, and you will be paid, regardless of what happens afterward."

He shrugged broadly. "As you say then, pretty mistress, but first, I must have new clothes."

"Why?"

"Pretty mistress, look at me." He spread his arms wide to make sure she missed no detail of his emaciated self. "You are lovely but I am not. I cannot walk among the gardens of the noble and the blessed."

"Beggars and sorcerers are holy." She said it as a delay. She was silently adding up the jewels she had brought. She had only so much gold with her. Palanquins and bearers cost money, and she must pay for her own bath and some fresh clothing of good quality . . .

"This is my city and I know the rules of its streets, pretty mistress." He spoke simply, without the wheedling, greedy tone she knew well from the lesser sort of merchant. "Do you want to go to the palace? Buy me new clothes."

It made sense. If he was a cheat, he was a good one. She could not be led to a palace by a beggar. Stranger that she was in this place, she could see that much. "Very well, father. You will have your new clothes. And you will help me hire some honest bearers and a conveyance."

"Of course, of course: A pretty lady cannot arrive on foot. You are most perceptive. Come, mistress, come." He grinned again, bowing and sweeping out his hand toward the dark alleys of the city. "I will show you all."

*T*hey did not arrive at the Palace of the Pearl Throne that day. The sorcerer, whose name was Madhu, insisted that by the time they acquired all they needed and made their way through the streets, it would be late in the evening and the gates would be closing. So, Radana spent the night at a hostel for female pilgrims. The place was crowded with strangers but clean, and in the morning she was still unmolested and in possession of her gold. After she broke her fast with bread, spiced rice, and oranges, she and Madhu began their journey through the streets of the city.

Radana was absolutely beggared, but at least she had put on enough of a show that none of the soldiers in the streets challenged her right to pass between the great stone houses of the wealthy, the noble, and the gods. She was clean, scented with sandalwood, and wrapped in Hastinapuran style in rose-colored silks. The hired palanquin was painted green and trimmed in silver with a cloth of silver canopy to provide shade from the sun. The bearers wore matching trousers of bright blue. Madhu led the way, his ebon walking stick held before him. He now wore a coat, trousers, and slippers of pure white. His greasy headcloth had been replaced by a neatly wound cap of madder red.

The Palace of the Pearl Throne seemed to grow out of the mountainside and Radana clasped her hands together when she saw its gleaming stone walls and intricate carvings, the richness of the guards' uniforms, the splendor of the gardens. There was more wealth and power here than in the whole of Sindhu. The king was mad, truly, utterly, completely mad, to even wish to stand against all this.

The two guards that had come with them from the outer walls led them down the broadest of the white paths through the paradisiacal gardens and around to the left side of the inner walls. There arched a gate of carved teak, and on the other side, as Madhu had assured her, waited the Audience Court.

Although it had been a day of strange and awesome sights, this was what made Radana stare slack-jawed.

The Audience Court was a broad stone expanse, open to the sun, and filled to the brim with people. People milled about aimlessly. They talked and argued and bargained with all the force and fervor of merchants in the market. Some carried wooden trays or buckets and shouted out that they had water and food for sale. Every caste and kind was there, from beggars hunching in the center of the court where there was no chance of shadow from the walls reaching them, to noblemen in silks with servants to hold fringed umbrellas over them.

While she stared, the arched doorway to the palace opened, just a crack. The crowd roared and surged forward up the steps. The soldiers were ready for this and leveled their spears, shoving the shouting mob back and away from the man in the long, green robe who emerged. Perhaps he spoke, but over the voice of the crowd, Radana could hear nothing. A single man scurried up the steps and made the salute of trust to the green-robed man, and fell into step behind him.

The doors closed, and the crowd fell back, each person who remained cursing in disappointment and trying to reclaim his or her little space on the stones to wait again.

Radana saw at once how it was. Probably you could bribe someone, if you knew the right palm to cross, but if you had no gold left, you could wait a hundred years and be no closer to that door.

Radana's shoulders slumped. All the strength that anger and righteousness had lent her fell away in a single instant. For the first time since she left King Kiet's chamber, tears threatened.

Her guide missed none of this.

"Now then, now then, pretty lady," Madhu chided. He ran his hand around her jaw so close that she could feel his heat, although he did not actually touch her. "Do you think I brought you here to abandon you to this mob? You must have patience, pretty lady. You must have faith."

His grin was sly and she had to resist curling in on herself against the heat of his gaze. She had been prepared for this too. If it was her body that would gain her entrance she would bargain with that too, but not until she was left with no other choice. That kind of use showed quickly on a woman, and Radana knew she must be seen as gold, not dross.

Radana lifted her head. "What can you do?" she asked sharply. "I have nothing left."

"What can I do?" Madhu pulled back, striking a gallant pose. "I am, after all, a sorcerer. You will see what I can do."

The bearers were getting impatient, eyeing one another, wondering when they might break in on this little conversation. Radana had only their fee left to her, and if they demanded more for having to wait . . .

"Very well."

She rose from the palanquin. The petitioners at the gate had watched her entrance with some interest. But as she was delayed, they turned back to their own conversations and schemes. Madhu paid off the bearers, who made their salutes to him, picked up their palanquin, and left without a backward glance. Now only Madhu was with her.

"What will you do?"

Madhu just grinned and tapped his long nose. "My pretty lady must be patient just a little while longer. Just a little and she will see what I can do. Have faith, pretty lady. Remember, I have got you this far."

With that, he slipped out of the gate and strode, grinning, down the white road, until he vanished behind the curve of the palace wall. Radana opened her mouth to call out, but she did not dare follow him. The sun was almost to its zenith and there were quarrels breaking out over the space in the shortening shadows. From the pitch of the voices, she could tell there would soon be open fights, and possibly betting on them. Some of the men had the right sort of gleam in their eyes to be interested in such a game.

Alone on the edge of a crowd of strangers, Radana wrapped her arms around herself and tried to calm herself enough to wait.

*H*amsa was loitering on the broad, curving stairs as Madhu hurried up, brushing fussily at the dust on his new coat sleeves. She took him in carefully, the new clothes, the intense air, and the small smile beneath his beard. He believed what he was doing was important, and that the reward would be great.

Hamsa stepped from the alcove into the sorcerer's path. "*Agnidh* Madhu," she said, making a respectful salute.

Madhu stared for a moment before making the full salute of trust. Whatever her reputation, Hamsa was bound sorcerer to the first prince and at least a show of respect was required. "Greetings, *Agnidh* Hamsa. Forgive me. My errand is urgent and I cannot delay."

But Hamsa did not move. "What errand might that be?"

"It is for _Agnidh_ Yamuna. You know well I cannot be late for such an important meeting." He looked up expectantly at her, and still Hamsa did not move.

Since Yamuna's threat and Natharie's adventure, Hamsa had begun to watch the traffic to Yamuna's rooms. If Yamuna knew she did this, he had said nothing. He seemed satisfied that she had not directly warned Samudra off his present course. Nor would she, but perhaps, just perhaps, there was something else she could do. Some straw or pebble she could shift to change the course of the dance Yamuna had set.

"What fine new clothes you are wearing." Hamsu gestured at Madhu's coat, trousers, and slippers. "Your errand has been most successful already." The runner who had told her Madhu was on his way up from the lower ring said he was barely even recognizable.

Madhu could not keep the grin from his face. "I will give much thanks to the Mother of Increase after I have made my report."

"Where was she from, your errand?" Hamsa asked slyly. Madhu was so famous for his love of women that even Hamsa had heard of it. "Perhaps I can find myself one."

With that, Madhu put aside all pretense of respect. "Ha! You would have to open your eyes for that, Hamsa!" She shared his chuckle, although the gibe dug near her heart, but what he said next made the pain vanish in an instant. "She was from Sindhu, if you must know, and now I must go tell this to the lord Yamuna."

Sindhu! Shock almost robbed Hamsa of her ability to playact. "Forgive me, Madhu." She stepped aside, saluting once more. "May your errand continue to be profitable."

He sketched a salute to her and all but ran down the corridor toward the winding stairs. Hamsa stared after him, twisting her staff in her hands.

Why is it Yamuna should wish to know about a woman of Sindhu arriving in the city? She gripped her staff. _Queen_

Bandhura, yes, the viceroys and the prince, yes, but Yamuna? What is happening here? And fast on the heels of this came the thought *Will anyone tell the prince?*

She did not waste another breath, but ran up the steps. The guards of the small domain knew her on sight and opened the ebon doors without issuing a challenge. Samudra was not in his rooms, nor was he with his mother, which left one last place to look.

She hurried to the viewing chambers and the garden terrace. She saw Natharie's Ekkadi sitting beneath the arch, busy repairing some bangle with tiny pliers. The maid was straining her ears to hear what her mistress might be saying, and trying hard not to show it. Ekkadi glanced up, ready to tell whoever approached to stay away, but when she saw who it was, she lowered her head. Hamsa knew she did not imagine the disappointment in the maid's eyes.

The late-afternoon sunlight streamed through the ivory lattice. The scent of citrus and greenery enveloped her. Before her, Princess Natharie sat on her favorite stone bench, and looked up at Samudra, who stood before her. Hamsa stopped dead, for here she saw plainly what she had only guessed at before.

Neither of them had so much as flinched at her approach, so intent they were on each other. Not even Samudra, with his soldier's instincts, noticed she was there. It was as if each sought to memorize and comprehend every detail of the other. She felt the air thrumming with their tension, their hope at such a fever pitch it was almost desperation. Hope that trust was not misplaced, hope that the heart did not lie, hope that love was not wrong.

She knew that Samudra bore a growing love for Natharie, but Hamsa was so bound up in her fears of Yamuna and her own weakness, she had not seen how strong that love had grown, nor had she seen how well it was answered.

And she felt her own heart break at the sight of even such tenuous freedom to love whom one would. In that instant, she understood how Yamuna could wish that his bound life might end so he could walk away, free forever. Loathing filled her at the notion, as one might feel loathing at the thought of eating rotted meat, but understanding remained. Could she take a lover? Yes, she was allowed. In fact, she could have as many as she pleased, if it did not interfere with her duties. She could even marry, but what husband would have her when she was not free to serve his house? She must follow Samudra in war and in peace. He was her first charge, and the only one to which she could be true, until the day one of them died.

Her eyes prickled and she had to close them to keep tears from spilling out. *No. No. I do not wish this. I will not wish it. This is the life I must live, and I will not betray. I will not do what Yamuna has done. I will not make myself as he is. If that is weakness, so be it.*

She moved forward, deliberately scraping her sandals against the floor tiles. The sound broke the moment between Samudra and Natharie, and they both saw her.

Samudra rubbed the back of his neck, a gesture he made when he was feeling particularly impatient. "What is it, Hamsa?"

Mindful of the listening Ekkadi, not to mention the whole of the small domain at her back, Hamsa stepped up close to him, to them.

"My prince. I have had word that a woman of Sindhu has arrived in the Audience Court."

She expected Princess Natharie to gasp, but the woman only sat back, her eyes wide. "Who is it?" she asked hoarsely.

Hamsa shook her head. "I do not know."

Natharie turned to Samudra, the pleading question plain in her eyes. Samudra remained silent for a long moment. Hamsa could see he was considering what few options he would have in such a situation. She wondered what Natharie saw.

"I'm sorry," Samudra said at last. "She will not be permitted to enter here."

Slowly, Natharie's fingers curled inward, making claws to rake against the silk of her skirt. "Why not? Builders and their sons come here, why not this woman from my home? Let your priests do whatever they will to purify her, but surely . . ."

"I cannot bring a stranger into the small domain without the emperor's permission." Samudra spoke softly, pleading with her to understand. Hamsa felt the skin on the back of her neck prickle and she glanced behind her. Ekkadi was staring at them, her bangle forgotten in her hands. The maid met the sorceress's eyes for a single heartbeat, and quickly picked up her work again.

"Please, Samudra," Natharie murmured. "She is from my home."

"I cannot ask that now."

Her clawed fingers knotted into her skirt. "Cannot or will not?"

Samudra flinched, something Hamsa had rarely seen him do before. "Cannot, Natharie. I ask you to believe this." He moved close again, a lover's stance. Did he know how easy it was to see this? As soon as she asked herself that question, Hamsa knew he did not care. "You know what is happening around us right now. I cannot add a suspicious action, even one this small."

They watched each other, each reading the other's silence. Hamsa had never felt so separate from Samudra or so angry at her own clumsiness with skill and word.

Natharie was the one who broke the silence. "I understand," she said.

"Do you accept it?" asked Samudra. Hamsa blinked and bowed her head, for she had heard the question differently. For a moment, she thought she heard, "Do you accept me?"

This time it was Natharie who shook her head. "No, Great Prince, I do not."

It was another blow and this one close to his heart. Samudra bore it like the soldier he was and replied with the salute
of trust. "I thank you for your honesty. I will find a way to
bring her to you as soon as I can, Natharie, I swear. Be but a
little patient."

Natharie made no answer, and Samudra's shoulders
slumped. He walked away without a word or backward
glance. Hamsa did look back, and she saw Natharie sitting
with her head bowed. Ekkadi picked herself up and hurried
to her mistress. She whispered urgently in Natharie's ear,
but Natharie did not move at all. There was nothing in her
attitude, though, that spoke of repose or resignation. The
princess of Sindhu hid her face so that her thoughts would
not show.

*She will not be patient. She will not wait a breath longer
than she must. Will Samudra let himself realize this?*

Samudra did not speak to Hamsa until they reached his
rooms and he had dismissed his servants with a scowl. Then,
he faced her and his expression was thunderous.

"How could you come to me with this news in front of
Natharie?" he demanded. "What were you thinking?"

*You do not want to know what I was thinking. Not all of
it.* She kept this to herself. "I wanted to see how she would
respond." This was at least part of the truth.

"Why?"

Hamsa planted her staff firmly, as if it would help anchor
her nerve. "Because I find it strange that this woman should
appear now, and I do not understand why Yamuna should
want to know that a woman from Sindhu was here."

"Yamuna? What business is it of Yamuna's who comes to
the Audience Court?"

"None, my prince. But he is making it his business." *Pay
attention, my prince,* she begged silently. *I am risking both
of us by saying this much.*

Samudra rubbed the back of his neck. "I can do nothing
now. Tonight I must . . . I must finish what I have begun.

Then my brother will understand my loyalty is strong. Then I will be able to speak with him about Divakesh and he will hear me. There are things that are stronger than Divakesh's ravings."

"I hope that is so, my prince. But it is not Divakesh who is playing now, it is Yamuna."

"Say it is the emperor. Yamuna is but a servant."

"Yes, my prince, but . . ."

Which was at last too much. "What would you have me do, Hamsa?" he cried, flinging out his hands. "What moves would you advise for this game? Come, you are so well versed in palace politics, you tell me what to do."

Hamsa was not prepared for the strength of his sudden anger, and it rocked her back. "I beg you understand, my prince," she said, nearly echoing words he had spoken to Natharie. "It matters because the princess will try to break seclusion again to find this woman, and even if she does not succeed, it matters because Divakesh is determined to make the emperor think some dishonorable thing is happening."

"The emperor will not believe that."

"How can you say such a thing, my prince? The emperor believes far greater lies already."

"Bandhura will not permit it. She has uses for Natharie."

"You are willing to trust Princess Natharie's safety to the tender mercies of the first of all queens?"

That stopped him cold. He knew the flint core of Queen Bandhura at least as well as she did. He knew how quickly she came to rule the small domain during his mother's illness. He knew how quickly she could break what she could not control.

Hamsa realized she'd been holding her breath, and released it slowly, softly. Samudra turned from her. He paced across the room to gaze out his open window at the green mountainside. Birds sang out there, unconcerned with troubles that broke hearts and empires. He touched the ivory window frame, running his fingers down it gently. For a moment her mind's eye saw him seize the carving to snap it in his fist. But in truth, he only turned toward her again. "You are hinting at something. What are you truly afraid of, Hamsa?"

Hamsa licked her lips. She could still see it, that image of him breaking the ivory, carelessly snapping strong bone in his rage. But she must speak. The bond between them compelled it as much as did her desperate desire to be true to her duty. "I am afraid that Princess Natharie did send for the woman," she whispered. *Look away, Yamuna, look away.* "And that there is another game happening here that neither of us has yet seen."

Slowly, so slowly Hamsa could see each separate motion, Samudra stalked toward her. "How can you even dream such a thing!" The words hissed through his teeth and she tensed, ready for the blow she was sure would land. "It is foul!"

She should have held her peace, but some vile demon in her soul would not let her. "What is foul, my prince? That I say it, or that you have already thought it?"

He raised his fist and Hamsa steeled herself. His fist swung down and she felt the air against her skin as it brushed past her. "You know nothing!" he bellowed. "I ask for your aid, and instead of straining your powers to their utmost, you remain an ignorant slave!"

It was too much. The sense of wrong, the helpless, heartbroken rage that she had kept dammed in her heart, burst out in a mindless flood.

"When have you allowed me to be anything else?" she shouted, but she could barely hear her own words for the drumming of her heart and the roar of her blood in her ears. "You care nothing for what battles I may have to fight! You will allow me no succor or aid. When I falter, you only draw farther away and leave me more alone. You would not treat the lowest peasant in your army as you have treated me!" She clutched her staff until it bit into her palms. "Yes, I am clumsy, and I am ignorant. It is all I have had a chance to become!"

Samudra stared, his eyes wide as her fury and her words sank slowly into his understanding. She was shaking. If it were not for her staff, she would not have been able to remain standing.

"Hamsa, I'm sorry," he said softly.

She dropped her gaze, breathing hard, trying to gain control of her shuddering frame. "No. I forget myself."

"No, you remembered yourself. Forgive me."

He left her there, and Hamsa felt her bond like a fetter on her soul. How much more did the prince feel it? She clenched her teeth against her curses. They would do no good. They never had.

Samudra paid no attention to Yamuna because he did not know the breadth of power of a true sorcerer. He only knew her weakness, her indecision. He saw Divakesh, who betrayed the Mothers, as the greatest danger of all to his brother. He saw nothing of Yamuna's bitterness at being forced to serve.

She should tell him this. She looked at the empty place where he had stood a moment ago. Why did she not follow and tell him?

Why not give the warning and then kill myself? She dug her fingers into her hair, trying to hold her mind and soul together when all the anger, all the doubt she felt threatened to tear her apart. *Free us both from this chain. Samudra needs someone who can be strong beside him. Not me. If I died there would be another.*

Yes, another chosen by Yamuna. Would Samudra be paired with a child? A half-dead old man? She bowed her head, clenching her eyes around tears as she had clenched her teeth around curses. *All is not written. The dance changes. It does. It must. I will not be only what Yamuna says I am. If the Mothers stand only because he has not toppled them yet, then I will see he pays the price for his delay, or I will die in the attempt and I will work my will from Hell if I must.*

But how? came the traitorous thought. *How?*

Hamsa set her jaw and turned on her heel. She would begin by discovering why Yamuna was interested in the arrival of one more woman of Sindhu. Samudra would listen to anything regarding Princess Natharie, that much was certain.

She needed to find Master Gauda. She would need an extra pair of hands to keep both Natharie and Samudra safe in Yamuna's game. He would have clothing that would disguise her, and he could be trusted to help Natharie when she needed it. It was impossible that Natharie should stay in the small domain knowing one of her own was outside, no matter what the danger.

You at least will not get us easily, Hamsa thought toward Yamuna, and toward Hell itself. *Not easily.*

Chapter Seventeen

"Mistress? Shall I go down for you? Mistress?" Ekkadi was whispering in Natharie's ear, and her words buzzed and bothered like a mosquito's whine.

"And what will you do if she does not speak Hastinapuran?" said Natharie more bitterly than she meant. "You know less of my language than I know of the Huni's."

"Yes, mistress," said Ekkadi with such proper humility that Natharie knew the maid was angered by that unfair snap. She made no apology, however. She had no room for it in her mind or heart. Someone from home was downstairs. Who was it? Was she from the palace, or was it someone here to undermine her parents? Was she trying to reach

Natharie, or reach past her? The questions swarmed around her head, leaving her breath short and her heart hammering.

She could not wait for her answers. She would not.

She was on her feet and crossing the terrace before she was aware she had moved. She did not slow her step or change her path, even as she realized every eye made note of her, and how white she must surely be. No doubt there was already a buzz of gossip behind her speculating what sort of quarrel she and the prince had just had. Let them gossip. They were nothing, they meant nothing. Home waited down below in the courtyard. She was not forgotten. It could be one of her sisters.

Master Gauda was in the performance alcove, watching slender Valandi kneel before an audience of her fellow students and lift her hands up to Heaven in ferverent prayer. "Very good," he was saying. "Hold, hold, and remember you are suffering, so take that smile off your face if you please . . ." But although his concentration seemed total, he did not miss Natharie as she came to stand beneath the archway, her hands knotted in her skirt to keep them from trembling.

His eyes narrowed. "Ah, Princess Natharie, you have decided to join us. Have you found the poem I sent you after?"

She opened her mouth, but could not force out a single word to fall in with the charade.

The drama master sighed heavily. "I thought not. I swear upon my eyes, they do not teach you to read in the south." He marched forward and took her firmly by the elbow. "Continue, Valandi," he said over his shoulder as he steered Natharie toward the library. "And the rest of you, I expect a detailed critique of the performance when I return."

With that, he led her out into the corridor. "What has happened?" he asked softly.

Finally Natharie's wits returned. "Be on guard, Ekkadi," she said, although Master Gauda frowned. Her maid nodded and fell back a pace, watching the corridor before and behind for listening ears. They would be far less conspicuous walking and talking, master and student, than they would be huddled together once more in the library.

"There is a woman of Sindhu in the Audience Court," she told him. "I cannot gain her admittance here. I must go out to her. Will you help us with the ruse again?"

Master Gauda was silent for five steps. "No."

Forgetting the need to be circumspect, Natharie stopped in her tracks. "Why not?"

Master Gauda rested his fingertips against his brow. Down the corridor drifted the babble of voices from the viewing chambers. The constant noise wrapped around Natharie, reminding her she was watched, reminding her how close the walls were and that all the windows were barred. Suddenly, she found it hard to breathe.

"Natharie, you are not thinking," Gauda murmured gently. "Divakesh is waiting for you to make a mistake he can bind you with, and this would be it. Whoever this woman is, whatever she wants, you will not be excused for breaking seclusion. You do not have the queen's protection this time." He lowered his hand and let her look directly into his eyes. Then, softly, so softly she might have imagined he spoke at all, he said, "It is a comfort to my soul to know the Awakened lands exist beyond these walls. Please, do not give Divakesh an excuse to make yet more war against them. You know Sindhu cannot stand against the Pearl Throne."

Natharie stood there, her lungs heaving as she tried to take in enough air to live. It could happen, just as Master Gauda said. Divakesh was mad enough to use any transgression of hers as an excuse for war. Against this was only the simple, terrible longing of homesickness. Out there waited someone who spoke her language, who had news of her family and her home, who might even be a beloved and familiar face. Someone who could prove to her that she was still herself at the roots of her soul and not lost to this strange grandeur and its cruel-eyed goddesses.

She took in a deep breath. "Then I will go to the queen."

"No, Natharie," said Gauda at once. "The queen is making use of you. She will protect you only as long as you are no trouble to her. This could become trouble. The instant it does, she will cast you aside."

"You and I are thinking of different queens, Master."

She pivoted on her heel and strode away. Ekkadi hurried behind her. Natharie still could not breathe. Master Gauda's words shook her resolve, but she told herself he did not understand, he could not. This place was a blessing and a haven to him. She would not wait in this cage until some bloodletting priest told her she might safely look on her own family.

"Mistress . . ." Ekkadi was saying, and there was a note of exasperation in the word.

Natharie ignored her. She just barely held herself to a walk as she headed for Queen Prishi's chamber. Inside, wrinkled, dignified Damman was on duty as usual.

"Damman, I must speak with your mistress. Will she see me?"

The serving woman hesitated, searching for a reason to refuse. In the end, she simply made obeisance and retreated into the curtained interior. After a moment, she reappeared, bowing and beckoning.

Somewhat to Natharie's surprise, Queen Prishi was not in her bed. Instead she lay on a low divan on her private terrace. The space was largely taken up by a sunken pool lined with lilies and lotus. In the shadow of the mountainside, the effect was of a forest glade. There were even a few bright butterflies that had found their way through the lattice.

The queen beckoned Natharie forward. "At last, my child. I've been waiting for you."

Natharie did come forward, her mouth open in wonder. Queen Prishi just smiled. "You think I do not have Samudra closely watched while he is here?" she asked. "I am still a mother, for all that I have been so many other things." With these last words, Natharie shivered, knowing the woman was seeing a distant past where she had no part. "You want to go to the Audience Court to find this Sindishi woman."

"Please help me, Majesty. I have no other friend here."

Queen Prishi shook her head heavily. "That is not true. However." She made a minute gesture and Damman was beside her, helping her to sit up straighter and piling more pillows behind her. "I will help you. It cannot be this moment, as you would wish." The last word came out as a gasp, and again, Damman was there immediately with a cup of nectar to moisten her mouth.

Natharie watched the old woman, knowing this weakness was the queen's own doing. For a moment, she felt small and selfish. She was risking so much for such a small thing, and here was a woman who fought for her life by bringing herself as close to death as she could come. Natharie bowed her head, and tried not to fidget like a child.

"Tonight I will send for you," said Queen Prishi. "You and your maid can exchange clothing, as you did before. You will be seen to sit with me, telling one of your stories, while your maid is seen to run an errand in the lower rings for us both."

Natharie bowed over her folded hands. "Thank you, Great Queen."

She could not read the emotion she saw in Queen Prishi's eyes, she only knew that it was deep and that the woman before her bore a pain she could barely begin to understand. "Do not thank me until it is done, Natharie. Go now, and cover up the gossip your tantrum has caused as best you can. Come again when it is fully dark." She closed her eyes, leaning back on the pillows, her exhaustion plain.

Natharie bowed again and slipped away as quietly and gracefully as she could.

Now there was nothing to do but wait, wait and pretend.

She did not look back to see how Ekkadi's eyes glittered

in the lamplight as they returned to the deep interior of the small domain.

*N*ight came swiftly to Queen Prishi's chambers. The poison she imbibed made her eyes sensitive to light, so she kept the curtains as close as she could without rendering the heat stifling. She had not seen the brightness of morning in . . . how long had it been? Years. Since Bandhura had married Chandra and she had seen the truth behind her daughter-in-law's cultivated manners. Since then there had been only pain, and plotting, and the metallic tang of the ointment she must rub into her burning skin every day to keep herself weak.

Damman helped her to her great bed, efficiently arranging her pillows and coverings while the girls and women Bandhura chose for her fluttered about uselessly, twittering and crooning platitudes. Sometimes she wondered if Damman did not suffer through these days even more than she did.

Oh, Rajan, I am sorry it should come to this. She closed her eyes. Damman dabbed her head with plain water and tipped some wine into her mouth. She felt these things distantly. Her mind was all with her husband, so far gone from her.

He had been a small man, fine-boned and delicate. His strength was well hidden behind his eyes so that only those who looked deeply could see it. She remembered that first, blushing, bashful, awkward night after their wedding, but more than that, she remembered the day afterward when he spoke to her so earnestly, already in love, seeking ways to bring love to her heart. And he did, for he had honored her and listened when she spoke. From that love she had worked from within, ordering the small domain and all who entered as best she could to aid the empire he ruled. She flattered, spied, and lied where necessary, and, yes, more than once, ensured that death came sooner than expected to a powerful man with ideas of his own about who the Mothers meant to hold the Pearl Throne.

Is Bandhura truly doing any different? Prishi's hands plucked at her covers. *Rajan, can I blame her for doing her best for our son?*

In her private darkness, she could see Rajan clearly. He sat cross-legged beside her, his eyes the color of northern amber, his wide mouth smiling fondly. In her mind, he sighed and reached for her hand. *Yes. Because she cares nothing for the empire. If she did, she would make Chandra strong, not indulge his weakness.*

I tried, Rajan. I tried to help them both.

I know, beloved.

I must do this one last thing, and then it is on Samudra's shoulders.

Yes, Prishi.

Is he strong enough? What she wanted to ask was *Will he forgive me?* But even in this waking dream she did not have strength to ask that.

The Rajan of her dream gave no answer, he only watched her with sad, fond eyes. The slip and slap of footsteps sounded on stone. Reluctantly, Prishi opened her eyes. Damman was holding back the curtains so that Natharie might enter. Behind her came little, bright-eyed Ekkadi who had made herself so essential to all plans that not even Gauda's warnings could separate them.

Natharie made her obeisance as respectfully as ever, but even in the light of the single lamp, Prishi could see how anxious she was.

If I were the friend you believe me to be, I would never let you do this, Natharie. But I fear it is not only Bandhura who must play on weakness to achieve her ends.

"I am in need of one of your stories, tonight, dear child," murmured Prishi, falling so easily into the character of the ailing dotard. "I think the one you first told us. The one of the woman king." She motioned for the girl to sit. Damman was already shooing out the other waiting women. Some of them would be off to report to Bandhura as soon as her back was turned, but that didn't matter. Not tonight.

"As you wish, Great Queen." Natharie's voice was steady despite the tension in her demeanor. In this much she had paid attention to Gauda, clever child.

She began the story gently, speaking in lilting cadences clearly meant to send an old woman toward sleep. Prishi looked over her head to see Damman standing by the curtains. Damman nodded to let her know the women were out of earshot, and would hear only the murmur of voices, not the words.

Prishi touched Natharie's hand. It was cold as ice. *As it should be, child.* Natharie understood the gesture. Moving with care, so that her words would not become breathy or strained, Natharie removed her veil and passed it to her maid. She had a great deal of grace for one so very tall. Clearly, her mother had taught her well. Prishi found herself wishing she could meet that other queen, and somehow explain that her daughter's sacrifice would not be in vain.

Slowly, cautiously, with Damman on watch the whole time, the transformation was achieved. Natharie sat dressed in her maid's plain clothes. Her height made it difficult to be inconspicuous, but if she hunched, and moved quickly and purposefully, she could be mistaken for one of the hundreds of servants who swarmed through the palace. And if Ekkadi kept her seat and bowed her head, any casual eye would see silver and silk in the flickering lamplight and assume that here was the princess, dutifully attending the dying queen.

It had, after all, worked once already. Why should it not work again?

Natharie knew enough by now to look to Damman for the sign that all was clear. Damman gave the barest of nods, and Natharie at last stopped the story.

"Good luck to you, daughter," said Prishi softly. "You

may believe . . ." But a gentle lie would not come and she made a flicking motion with her scabbed and gnarled fingers to send the girl away. "Go carefully."

Natharie made a hasty obeisance and was away without delay or further word.

With her mistress gone, Ekkadi had the grace to look awkward. Prishi, however, did not miss how the maid's hand kept lovingly stroking the new silks that covered her.

Prishi sighed. "Now, little maid. You may go to your master and tell him what has happened."

Ekkadi froze, her face showing nothing for the moment but utter surprise. Prishi felt herself smile, and a small laugh turned into a painful cough.

"But . . ." stammered the maid. Her mind was so well tuned for deception, she did not know what to do with the truth.

"But what?" snapped Prishi. She was tired. She wanted to sleep, to remember her husband instead of thinking on what she did now. "You do not have that much time. If the priest wants to catch Natharie in the fullness of her violation, he should be quick."

But still the maid hesitated. Her eyes narrowed to slits. For a moment she forgot rank, place, and courtesy and saw only another conspirator before her. "Why are you doing this?"

"That, little maid, is my own business."

Ekkadi frowned, but she accepted the answer. Perhaps she even remembered who and where she was. She made obeisance and turned, but Prishi snatched her wrist with one crabbed hand, holding her tightly. "Understand this, however, little maid," she said in a low and reasonable voice. "If you tell anyone of my part in this, now or ever, you had best be able to live on air and in the air, for you will never know when the poison, the needle, or the dagger will find you. Not even Divakesh will be able to save you from the ones who are still loyal to me. Do you understand?"

Prishi saw the fear in Ekkadi's eyes and knew that Ekkadi understood very well.

Prishi let her hand fall. "Go then."

The maid snatched up her skirts and ran, and Prishi closed her eyes, profoundly weary. *So, Rajan. The ending begins. May you and our sons one day forgive me for it.*

When Samudra saw the cruelty that Chandra and Bandhura would level against his love in partnership with Divakesh, his resistance would finally break and he would do what he must to take away the throne. It was thus Sindhu would be saved, and Hastinapura, and possibly even Natharie.

But it was a vile thing to set one brother against another. Justice would be meted out for that too. Prishi had accepted that when she set out on this course.

Queen Prishi turned to her woman. "It is time, Damman."

Damman's round, old face wrinkled in on itself as she struggled so hard to hold back her tears. Prishi took her hands. Damman had kept her roundness, but all the work she had done had given her thick calluses. *I would have given you ease if I could, my friend.* "You may go. I will not ask you to do this."

"And where would I go?" Damman shot back. "What would I do? Besides, if we are discovered, it will look very strange to see you preparing your own cup."

Prishi wanted to argue, but found she did not have the strength. "Very well. We do this together."

So Prishi sat on her pillows and watched. Damman knelt among the boxes and bottles, and lifted this powder and that syrup, and held the cup over the lamp, warming it, swirling the liquid that smelled richly of cardamom and ginger, and something else, something elusive and not unpleasant.

She had watched Damman do something very similar on her wedding night, while she was waiting for her imperial husband to come and make her his own. It would relax her, she had said, and warm her toward what was to come. Damman had prepared her cups to ward off the sickness that came with each of her children, the boys who survived and the girls who did not. Her cups had numbed Prishi when her husband, with his laughing eyes and warm hands, died, and she had considered the ways in which she might die too.

Damman's hands were shaking as she knelt and held out the gilded cup to Prishi.

Prishi took it. Her own hands were steady, if a little cold. "This releases you, Damman. You are free. Leave as quickly as you can, and go to the house of Lord Basdev. I've left some jewels there for you. You will want for nothing."

Damman nodded, her eyes brimming with tears.

Prishi looked into the depths of the last cup. *Forgive me. Natharie, Samudra, Mothers all. Forgive me.*

She drank. It was sweet and it was bitter, and she felt fear and freedom.

Before she had drained the dregs, her hand went numb. Prishi fell back, her eyes blind with the final darkness, so she did not see Damman raise the second cup to her own lips and drink it down to join her at the very last.

*N*atharie ran down the narrow servants' stair. The oil lamp she carried flickered violently with each step. In her other hand she clutched her hems up near her knees to keep them out of the way. Her mouth moved constantly, repeating Ekkadi's directions to the Audience Court, counting stairs and turnings, praying she did not get lost, praying she was not seen.

She emerged from the palace. The fresh night air was a balm after the closeness, heat, and dust. Her eyes, already used to the dark, took in the crowded yard spreading out before her, and she knew she had followed Ekkadi's directions correctly.

Thankfully, Ekkadi had warned her what to expect, or

Natharie's heart might have sunk at the sight of the enormous number of people. The yard was filled with little improvised camps complete with fires burning in clay stoves. The best off had pillows and blankets. Most people had lay down, and the sounds of snoring and heavy breathing rose on all sides. A few people were still upright, hunched near their lamps or their stoves, waiting for day, waiting to be noticed.

Natharie pushed back her veil. Holding her lamp high, she circled the yard, stepping over the sleeping bodies, which earned her a few curses and more than one kick to her ankle. She had only one real plan for her search. If the woman had arrived recently, she was probably in some spot closer to the gates than the stairs.

The gates were better guarded than the doors. These men were sharp-eyed and straight-backed, watching the yard. Watching her.

Already seen, stealth would do her no good, so Natharie pushed aside her fear and walked up to the three guards at the left-hand side of the gate, making the salute of trust with her free hand.

"Please, masters," she said, keeping her voice low. "I am sent from the small domain. Has anyone today come from Sindhu?"

The shortest and broadest of the three had a thin mustache on his lip. He blew out a great sigh. "What in the name of all the Mothers could the domain want to know for?"

Natharie risked a tiny smile. "Is it for any of us to question?"

That earned a chuckle from the guard on the mustached man's left. "As you say, sister." He dug his finger behind his ear, scratching and thinking. "I was coming on shift, and I heard something, over that way . . ." He pointed to the left. "Woman I think."

"She was talking with one of the rice sellers," volunteered the mustached man. "Pretty too. All in pinks. Silk, yet.

Thought of offering her a better bed for the night." He leered companionably at the others, forgetting Natharie for a moment's fantasy.

"You may be glad you didn't if she's wanted inside," answered the other. "Try over there," he said to Natharie and pointed again. "We don't want to start waking people if we don't have to."

Natharie made the salute again and picked her way across to the yard holding her lamp over her head, craning her neck, praying that the woman was not one of the anonymous forms under thin blankets.

There. The flickering light touched a flash of deep rose pink. Natharie stepped closer. There on her back, one hand resting on her belly, her hair spread out beneath her, lay her "Auntie" Radana.

Natharie stuffed her hand into her mouth to stifle her gasp. Kneeling at once, she shook the courtesan's shoulder.

"Radana. Radana."

Slowly, the woman stirred, blinked, and came awake. She saw Natharie and sat up at once.

"Princess Natharie. Thank all the blessed. Princess, I am come to warn . . ."

Natharie began to gesture her to silence, but even as she did, a hand touched her shoulder. She jumped, nearly out of her own skin and turned, and looked into Hamsa's wide eyes.

He knows, she thought, despairing that Samudra had found her, but relieved it was no one else.

"Who is this?" Radana demanded in a whisper.

"Hamsa. She serves the first prince."

Radana did not waste another heartbeat but threw herself at Hamsa's feet. "Great Lady, I am come with a warning to the Pearl Throne! I beg you hear me!"

Natharie stared, stunned. Hamsa recovered before Natharie did. "Quick." The sorceress forgot all rank and propriety and grabbed Natharie's hand. Natharie did not resist.

If Hamsa was already here, who knew who else might be coming to find them? The sorceress dragged her up to the gate with Radana following so closely behind she stepped on Natharie's heels. The soldiers all shifted their grips on their spears as they approached, ready to bar their way.

Hamsa stopped in front of the mustached guard and pushed the veil back from her face.

"*Agnidh?* What . . . ?"

She did not let him finish. "I'm on the prince's errand, Chintan. Let us through."

Chintan laid his free hand over his heart and then touched his forehead. "At once, *Agnidh.*"

The guards parted, but instead of opening the gate, Chintan stomped his foot down on what Natharie now saw was a wooden platform. A trapdoor lifted in it, and an angry eye glared in the lamplight. "*Agnidh* Hamsa on the prince's errand," said Chintan, and the anger turned to surprise. The eye and its owner disappeared, leaving the ladder leading down into the tunnels clear for Hamsa, then Natharie, and, more slowly, Radana.

The ladder ended in a square-cut tunnel of stone and earth. Lamps hung from chains and flickered in niches. Natharie could hear men's voices laughing or quarreling mildly, along with the rattle of dice and the tread of sandals. A pair of soldiers shouldered passed, stopping only momentarily when they saw Hamsa.

"Great Lady . . ." said Radana anxiously as her delicate sandals touched the earthen floor.

"Not here." Hamsa turned north and strode ahead, with the confidence of one who knew the dim route well. Of course she would. This was clearly a place of soldiers, and as such it would be Samudra's place.

Natharie found herself wondering how far the tunnels stretched. They passed ladders that led even farther down, and branch corridor marked with neatly etched plaques to keep new arrivals from becoming hopelessly lost.

Hamsa did not stop to consult these markings. She took the Sindishi women around a right-hand turning, and then another. Natharie thought she could sense the weight of the palace over them and the idea drained the blood from her cheeks. Did Hamsa mean to lead them straight into the heart of the mountain?

No. They came to another ladder, leading upward. Hamsa climbed this quickly. She unlatched the trapdoor overhead and paused a moment to watch. Then, she pushed it open and beckoned Natharie and Radana to follow her.

They emerged into a small, plain room. Its walls, where they could be seen, were adorned with friezes of the Mother of Increase with her sickle and round belly. But mostly, the room was taken up by shelves which were crammed with scrolls and tablets and sheafs of papers. Natharie realized it must be a records store, probably only one of many in this ancient palace.

The only furniture was a writing desk with an abacus and a lamp. Hamsa took Natharie's lamp from her hand, checked the other for oil and then lit the wick, setting the two lights side by side.

"Now." Hamsa turned fully to Radana, who immediately and humbly bowed.

"Forgive me, Great Lady," she said in her slow and clumsy Hastinapuran. "I see now that you are the sorceress who follows the Prince Samudra. I did not know you before. I . . ."

At this little speech, Natharie's frayed nerves gave way entirely. "Radana!" she shouted in Sindishi. "What is it? Why are you here?" *And why aren't you talking to me?*

Radana flicked her a glance full of scorn. "The news I have is for the Pearl Throne, not the child of traitors."

Natharie gaped. Hamsa had gone pale. "Who is this woman?" she asked Natharie.

"She is my father's chief concubine. Radana, you will tell me what is going on immediately."

But Radana just shrugged and turned again to Hamsa. "Take me to the Pearl Throne and I will tell all I know. You will be rewarded, I promise you, for I speak of grave treachery."

Natharie's hands curled into fists and she was a hairs-breadth from snatching Radana's shoulders and slapping her until her ears rang and the words tumbled freely from her, but Hamsa held up her hand.

"I cannot take you to the emperor until I know you have some truth to tell him. You will have to let me make a working upon you."

That, at last, made Radana hesitate and look toward Natharie. It was Natharie's turn to shrug. Impatience and anger boiled within her. Radana had never been at complete peace with her rank and all the world knew it. This could be some great lie. This could be . . . it could be true. Mother could have done something in her anger. It would be Mother. Father would not, could not break a treaty he had made, but Mother, Mother could.

Hamsa bit her lip. She snatched an ancient scroll off the nearest shelf and unrolled it. "Stand there," she ordered. Radana, clearly gathering her nerve, lifted her hems fussily and stepped onto the crackling parchment. Hamsa nodded and began to circle her, her staff tracing symbols in the dust of the floor. At the same time, Hamsa began to sing in a low, deep voice. Natharie could not understand a single word, but the relentless rhythm of the words made her shiver.

Nine times Hamsa circled Radana, drawing her signs over and again and singing her song without pause or hesitation. For a moment, Natharie had to admire Radana's courage. The concubine stood-stock still in the center of the faint circle, her hands folded together, never once flinching or betraying any emotion. Natharie found herself gritting her teeth against her impatience. Her thoughts darted between Sindhu and the palace above, where Ekkadi waited in her flimsy disguise beside a weak old woman. She had been gone too long already. Surely someone had noticed their ruse by now. She was a fool, a fool, a fool . . .

Hamsa let the last note of her song die away as she came once more to stand in front of Radana. She touched her palm briefly to the concubine's forehead and Natharie saw a single bead of perspiration trickle down Radana's temple. So. She was afraid after all.

"Speak now, and speak the truth," said Hamsa. "If you lie, I will know."

Radana licked her lips. "King Kiet and Queen Sitara have sent their spymaster to make common cause with the chief of the Huni who inhabit the Pillar of Heaven foothills. It is their intent to bring them down the river to Sindhu to do what they will from there."

Natharie's heart constricted and her hand flew to her mouth. No. No. They had not done this. Not even Mother in all her rage would doom Sindhu in this way. Father would not permit it. Mother would not . . . would not bring Natharie's death to her with such an act, because she would die, because she was hostage. Mother never would do this. This was a lie. But Hamsa stood before Radana completely silent. Not even the air stirred around them.

"So," breathed the sorceress. "You do not care, then, Radana, that your mistress will die when this becomes known."

Natharie choked on her own breath. She began to shake. Mother had done this. Father had done this. Her loving parents had condemned her to die, and Radana had come to carry the word that would bring them down, taking all of Sindhu down with them.

Radana lifted her chin. "I am loyal to the Pearl Throne."

Hatred blazed hard and sudden in Natharie and in that moment she wished hard for Divakesh's sword.

Hamsa was breathing hard and fast as if undergoing some great struggle. Natharie's glance darted to the door. Could she run? Could she escape to the walls and the gardens, maybe find a way into the city?

Then, Hamsa swung her staff around, touching it to the spot over Radana's heart. For a moment, the concubine stared at the sorceress, her eyes bulging with disbelief. Then, Radana's eyes closed in complete and utter peacefulness, and she slumped to the floor.

Natharie could not believe what she saw. "Is she . . . did she lie? Is that what this is?"

Hamsa went down on her knees. Her hands were shaking, her breath coming in ragged gasps. "No. No. She sleeps, that is all." She smiled a little. "Truth tellings are complex. They take hours to make. If you knew anything of the invisible workings you would know that. Sleep is much easier to weave, especially at night, especially when one is already tired."

Natharie's mind refused to encompass what was happening. "But you said . . ."

"I was the one who lied," Hamsa told her sharply. "But she believed, just as you did." Hamsa grimaced, and it came to Natharie that this working she spoke of was not finished. Hamsa by the force of will and soul that were the sorcerers' blessing held this spell over Radana. "Listen to me, Natharie. I cannot leave her like this. This working is light and will not hold. You must go find the prince immediately. He must be the one to know this."

"Yes . . . yes." Natharie shook herself. It was too much. Her mind dipped and spun, but she knew Hamsa was right. Samudra was the only help Sindhu had.

The only help she had.

"Where is he?"

Hamsa reeled off a series of directions to take her through the soldiers' tunnels into the gardens. Natharie forced herself to listen, and to repeat them, steadily and accurately, along with the passwords for the guards she would meet.

"What of Radana?" Natharie asked at last.

"I will take care of her."

Natharie met the sorceress's gaze. "Thank you," she whispered.

Hamsa nodded once. Natharie took up her lamp again and opened the door onto a corridor as narrow and as dark as any of the servants' ways. She looked sharply left and right and saw no one. Before she could forget the route Hamsa had given her, she ran ahead into darkness. For this moment, she needed only to worry about speed. For this blessed moment, she did not have to think about the message she carried.

Her heart breaking inside her, the princess of Sindhu ran on.

*A*s soon as Princess Natharie left her, Hamsa turned to the nearest records shelf. Most of the aging tallies were written on scrolls, and most of those scrolls were bound with colored cord, blue, green, red, yellow, black, or white. Hamsa went through the shelves, cutting the knots with her small knife, harvesting the cords, and sneezing as she raised great clouds of dust. Scrolls slithered to the floor, piling up around her ankles to be kicked aside and trod on carelessly in her hunt for what she needed.

It didn't matter. What mattered had already been done. Natharie carried the warning to Samudra. They would be able to escape ahead of the storm that was coming, and she would finally be able to obey her dream.

When she had a good handful of the silken strings, Hamsa sat cross-legged beside the fallen Radana. The sorceress was sweating, despite the fact that the room was quite cool. She could feel her working strain and begin to fray as Radana's self struggled to reassert its freedom and wake. She must be swift.

Setting the cords on the floor in front of her, Hamsa closed her eyes and drew in a deep breath, and another, and another.

She focused her mind, forming the task and its boundaries. Sleep. Deep, restful sleep. All care, all urgency, all need to be bound away. Just sleep. Only sleep. She knew how to do this. It was one of the first spells she had learned for healing, for nothing healed so well as blessed, blessed sleep.

She opened her eyes and looked down at the cords. She picked up a red one and a blue one and with careful fingers began to knot them together. She drew her magics up from within and down from without. She breathed them out onto the cords she wove one into the other making a loosely netted collar for Radana's pale throat.

Sleep. Healthful sleep. Sleep until the knots were undone and the spell was broken by the hand that wove it.

"Mothers give me strength to do this much, just this much," she murmured as she laid the net against Radana's skin. *Let it be strong enough to bring him here.*

"The Mothers may give you the strength, but you should have asked for time, little Hamsa."

Hamsa's head jerked up and the net she had woven so carefully slithered to the floor. Yamuna stood in front of her, three soldiers behind him, and the sorcerer Madhu in all his new finery, carrying the lamp for Yamuna and grinning to show all his dirty teeth.

Yamuna, however, only looked on her with scorn. "Did you think I would not know?" he asked, as he snatched the netting from the floor. "Did you think you could hide the least working from me?" He glanced at Radana where she lay and then turned to the soldiers. "Bring her. The emperor and the first of all queens need to hear what she has to say." He smiled at Hamsa in terrible mock hospitality. "Come, little Hamsa, it is time for you also to serve your true master."

Hamsa rose. She walked past him out in to the dark and narrow corridor. She did not look back. She did not want Yamuna to see her own tremulous smile.

Chapter Eighteen

Evening cast its long cloak over Samudra as he stood on the edge of the gardens, twisting his hunting spear restlessly in his hand.

It was the custom for the men of the imperial line from time to time to have some fearsome creature loosed in the gardens so they, and select intimates, could hunt. It was a good night for such sport. The air was warm, but dry and clear. Only a few stars lit up the sky, their brilliance making a setting for the white crescent moon that shone so brilliantly it was possible to see the new moon in its arms.

An omen, he thought as he gazed up at it, leaning on his hunting spear. *But of what?*

Out there, men waited beside a caged tiger, waiting for the signal to open that cage and retreat, leaving the garden empty for Samudra and Makul, and the others Makul brought with him. What would happen to the tiger tonight, Samudra could not say, but he would have his catch of men. Tonight, Chandra would understand the truth of his loyalty, and the loyalty of the others who would weaken the empire and drive brothers apart.

And Mother A-Kuha would understand that he honored her, but that he would remain Mother Indu's son.

Behind him, Samudra's groom held a restless Rupak, stroking the horse's neck and murmuring to him. Neither was happy about being kept from his rest, nor were the young men who held the lamps, but all here served as they must.

At last, the hoofbeats sounded on the shell road and Makul came riding up the gentle slope. He was alone, without even a man servant to attend him. Samudra straightened, warning tolling in his heart. When Makul reached them, he dismounted and handed his reins to Samudra's groom so that he could make his obeisance.

Samudra raised his teacher up and clasped his hand. "Thank you for coming, Makul," he said, and he meant it. They both knew what must be done, but after a sleepless night Samudra had seen how he might spare Makul the worst. The Mothers were kind, even Mother Vimala. He would not have to betray his oldest and best friend to save his brother. "Come, let us stretch our legs a bit."

"It is ever my pleasure to accompany my prince," replied Makul evenly. Side by side they walked, two friends who had seen much together, moving out of range of the lantern-light, and out of the hearing of the servants.

"It is a beautiful night," Makul murmured, looking up at the emerging stars.

"It is," Samudra agreed. His ears were straining for the sound of other horses, but he heard nothing except the nighttime sounds of the garden tempered by a muted roar from the tiger waiting for its freedom and its death.

"The others are coming soon?" Samudra asked softly.

"No, my prince."

Samudra stared at his teacher, and Makul returned his gaze with calm and ease. "I warned them. I told them you knew they wished you to take the Throne, and that you would not agree." Makul folded his hands behind his back and lifted his face to the stars. "Four have fled. One, at least, has taken his own life. Another, I believe is making sacrifice to Indu and Jalaja and praying this all will pass over." He gave a shrug and to show how likely he regarded that before he lowered his gaze to meet Samudra's. "If you wish to take anyone to the emperor, it will be me."

"No, Makul . . ." The unseen tiger roared. The night air felt suddenly close. Samudra couldn't breathe, couldn't speak. The world was filled with eyes watching and ears listening and knives everywhere, and Makul stood alone and unarmed before him.

"You were willing to sacrifice me when I was one of a handful, my prince, why not now?" Makul cocked his head toward Samudra. Then he went on more softly, and infinitely more sadly. "Or did you think to tell the emperor I aided you in your deception and so I should be spared while those who trusted me are gutted by Divakesh's sword?"

Samudra turned his face away. There was nothing he could say to that.

"Yes, you should be ashamed, my prince," said the old soldier harshly. "It was unworthy of you. You cannot be partially true to an oath." He spread his hands. "I am a traitor. You know that. I believe you should be emperor, not your brother who leaves us at the mercy of Pravan's idiocy and Divakesh's fanaticism. If your loyalty is to Hastinapura and the emperor, why do you hesitate to bring me to the justice I deserve?"

"I wanted only . . ."

At this, Makul spat. "What do you want, Samudra? Do you even know?"

Samudra bowed his head. He could not look at his teacher any longer. He could not look at anything. He squeezed his eyes closed and in his mind's eye he saw his brother. He saw the boys they had both been. He saw the fear in Chandra's eyes as the imperial crown was settled at last on his head. "I wanted to save him, Makul. That was all."

"You cannot. He has already doomed himself."

Samudra's head jerked up. What could he know of Chandra's doom? The Makul who stood before him in the silver light and thick shadows looked suddenly strange, scarcely human. The whites of his eyes shone too brightly and his skin shimmered with celestial light. "Who are you?" Samudra croaked.

But Makul just spread his hands. "I am your teacher and I am your servant, my prince," he said. "Who did you believe me to be?"

Samudra shook his head. "Nothing. I . . . she said she would come again when I was ready to speak from who I was. I thought for a moment . . ."

"What did you think?"

Samudra opened his mouth to tell him, but then, a sudden sound caught his ears. Someone ran toward them. Makul heard it too, and now they both saw a light carried by a figure in woman's dress bobbing above the grass as its bearer ran as if for her life. Samudra's mouth went suddenly dry. He might not know who stood with him, but he knew the tall form that raced toward him.

He thrust the hunting spear into Makul's hand and ran toward Natharie, leaving his startled teacher to trail behind him. Samudra grasped Natharie's arms to keep her from colliding with him and saw her eyes wide with fear beneath her plain veil.

"What is it?" he cried, half-afraid, half-despairing. How could she have left seclusion again, *again*. Would she never understand this could mean her death? What was she trying to do?

"Samudra . . ." she gasped, struggling for breath. "Word has . . . Radana . . . from my father . . ."

"Who is this?" hissed Makul, coming up behind them, the spear point lowered.

Natharie stared at the other man, the same question clearly in her own mind.

"This is Commander Makul, Natharie. He is my right arm." *Even now.* Samudra took back the spear. "Tell me what's happened."

She mastered herself with the strength that he had always seen in her, and she told him what had happened, of the woman Radana, of Hamsa's intervention, and the news of rebellion from the court of Sindhu.

"Mothers all," whispered Makul.

A thousand different thoughts tumbled through Samudra's mind, but one shone out clearly among all the others.

Even if Hamsa managed to delay word of this rebellion reaching the emperor, Natharie could not return to the small domain. To send her back there was to condemn her to death.

"You must take the great princess to the docks," he said to Makul. "Find a boat. She must go back to Sindhu and warn them what is coming." Makul nodded, accepting these strange orders with a soldier's discipline. "I will . . ." *What will I do? What can I do? Let her go and then go back and . . . and . . .*

Hamsa. Hamsa is alone with this now.

"I must go back inside." He was already two steps back toward his horse, when Natharie stopped him with his name.

"Samudra. If you go back, you'll . . . they'll send you to Sindhu . . ."

He also had thought of this. If his plans were not discovered, he would remain in command of all the emperor's forces. He would be sent to deal with the little rebellious Awakened protectorate as he had dealt with Lohit, and probably Divakesh would go with him. "Yes."

Natharie drew back. The lamp in her hand trembled, making the light across her face flicker so badly he could not tell which was stronger in her, anger or betrayal. "You cannot mean you would do this."

"Natharie, it must be me." *Understand, please understand.* "If I lead the army, there is a chance this will not be a slaughter. There will be a chance for honor and surrender, and a just peace. If it is left to Pravan and Divakesh"—*and Chandra*—"what do you think will happen to your family and your people?"

She winced, turning her face away. He heard the tiger roar again in the distance, and his hands shifted the spear to a ready hold before he knew what he had done. If he was to save any of them, he must move quickly. But he could not go until he was certain Natharie trusted him. He would not part from her while she believed he would betray her. He could not. She looked into his eyes and nodded, clearly holding back too many feelings and too many thoughts. But still he could see that she did understand, and, more, she believed.

"You must go now. You can trust Makul," he added to Natharie. "I owe him my life a hundred times over." *And perhaps one day he will forgive me for what I meant to do.*

But this time, it was Makul who hesitated. "My prince, it is dangerous for you to return."

Samudra felt a small smile forming. *My right arm. Even now.* "Hamsa is still inside, Makul. I cannot leave her to face this alone."

As Makul moved to her side, Samudra saw Natharie still watching him. There was fear in her eyes, for herself, but also for him, and some perverse part of himself found strength in that fear.

"Go with care, Natharie." It was nothing like what he wished to say, but he would not leave her with promises he might never be able to fulfill.

She nodded and let Makul lead her to the road that showed faint and grey in the starlight. Samudra did not stand to watch them vanish. Instead, he ran back to the grooms and his horse.

"Give the signal to start the hunt." He threw himself into Rupak's saddle.

The groom hesitated, and for a moment Samudra thought the man might break all discipline and question him. But no, he just turned to his junior, who thrust a bundle of reeds into the lamp he tended and when it kindled, raised it high, waving it back and forth.

Samudra sent Rupak cantering down the road a little ways before turning the horse's head toward the tiger's roar. The cage was open by now and the beast was free in the darkness. How had things come to such a pass that the great predator was the least of his worries? He gripped his spear tightly. When he could no longer see the grooms' lamps, he turned Rupak hard to the left, doubling back toward the palace. The horse was skittish underneath him, fearing what he scented on the wind.

So do I, old friend. So do I.

Samudra circled the palace as widely as he could, keeping always to the shadows and heading for the practice yard. Natharie had gotten out of the palace proper through the garrison tunnels; he would reenter it the same way. He would find Hamsa, and then return, gather up his grooms, and hunt down the tiger to keep his ruse whole. It would not last long, but it would give him time to question this woman Radana and decide what was best to do.

It would give him time to master his anger against the king and queen of Sindhu. How could they endanger their daughter who loved them so well that she had already given her life for the peace of her land?

Did they truly believe death would be better for her than life in the small domain?

Then, Samudra remembered the bright, contemptuous eyes of the king of Lohit when the man spoke of Hastinapura and the corruption of its priests and its soldiers.

Yes. Yes, they do believe that. We are so tightly walled in here in all our absolute purity and power that those we rule believe the worst of us.

Samudra cantered along the road at the edge of the practice yard. He raised his spear in salute to the men on the walls who could not help but see a form on horseback. He reined up Rupak in front of the stables. Leading the horse to an empty stall, he loosened the bridle and made sure there was hay. The grooms and their master snored in their lofts overhead, and Samudra made a note to reprimand the man for not keeping better watch, and to light incense to the Mothers as penance for allowing such a lapse.

Kindling a lamp from the coals banked in the stove, Samudra lifted the trapdoor and climbed down the ladder, blessing the ones who had realized that if trouble ever came to the palace, there should be a way to get to the horses.

More than one prince had used this low, dirt-scented tunnel as an escape route to adventure out beyond the walls. He himself had done so often enough in his youth. He tried to remember if Chandra had ever come out with him, and found to his shock he could not.

The stable tunnel joined up with the broader, brighter network beneath the walls. It was mostly storerooms down here, but there were always guards stationed in the ancient chambers and patrolling the corridors. He heard voices, and the steady tread of men's feet. He had one more reason to thank his teacher. Makul had insisted that young Samudra know the tunnels and their routine as he knew the corridors of the small domain, and Samudra now marched through them keeping just around the corner and just far enough ahead of the patrols to keep from being seen clearly.

As soon as he was underneath the palace proper, he found one of the servants' doors and raced up the winding stairs. When Hamsa had done what was needful with Radana, she would return to his rooms, as she had the night he met Mother A-Kuha. He was certain of that.

Samudra reached the seventh ring. He turned down one of the curving corridors that led into its heart. He held his lamp up high so he could pick out the faded symbols scratched on the stained and splintery doors. Here was a window, meaning this door opened on the viewing chamber, and here was a star, meaning he had found the chamber of the first prince.

Samudra pushed the door gently open. Light spilled through, but no sound accompanied it. He peered through the door and saw his attendant Amandad kneeling on the floor, his head in both hands. Fresh fear touched him and Samudra eased himself through the door, closing it carefully behind him.

Amandad heard the sound and jumped, spinning around. He was grey as a ghost.

"My prince!" Amandad rushed up to make his obeisance directly at Samudra's feet.

"What is it, Amandad?" he asked, his gaze darting around the room. Except for his man, the chamber was empty. "Have you seen Hamsa?"

"My prince . . ." Amandad began, then he choked as if suddenly realizing what question had been asked. "*Agnidh* Yamuna has taken *Agnidh* Hamsa to the emperor, with another woman, an outsider . . ."

Yamuna had Hamsa? And the other woman, that could only be this Radana, and they were being taken to the emperor. Hamsa had failed in her attempt to conceal the woman. Samudra brushed past Amandad. *I cannot leave Hamsa to this.*

"My prince, Queen Prishi is dead!"

Samudra froze in his tracks. Behind him he heard the man breathing hard and knew he was crying. But Samudra did not turn. He could not move. His will could no longer direct his limbs. He could only stand like a statue and hear Amandad's words echo in his mind.

Queen Prishi is dead.

"How . . . ?" He forced the word out. *Mother is dead.* "When . . . ?"

"My prince . . ." Amandad choked again, struggling to speak clearly. "She was found with her maid Damman. The first of all queens found her. She was poisoned, my prince. They . . . the . . . Princess Natharie has fled the small domain. She was the last to wait upon the queen. They are saying she did this thing."

Heat rushed back through Samudra and he could move again. He grasped Amandad by his shoulders and hauled him upright. "That is not true! How dare you speak such a vile lie to me!"

"I swear, my prince, I know it is not true. All the world knows it is not true, but it is the word of the first of all queens."

The consequences of these truths and lies began to unfurl in Samudra's mind. His mother, his mother was dead,

Natharie was gone. Word of rebellion in Sindhu would be out within moments. The gardens were surely being searched even now, and it would soon be discovered that there was no hunt, and that Makul, Samudra's teacher and ally, had left the gardens with a woman in maid's clothing.

Then they would be looking for him, and for Makul, and for Natharie.

They already had Hamsa.

He released Amandad and Amandad prostrated himself at once. Samudra looked down on him, trying to find room in his swollen heart to regret what had just happened. Amandad had done no wrong. If Samudra lived, he would make his apology.

If I live. If any of us live.

"Where have they taken Hamsa?"

"Divakesh insists all be heard before the Pearl Throne."

Divakesh as well. Mother A-Kuha, is this my punishment for denying you?

Samudra touched Amandad's shoulder. "When they come to question you, speak the truth," he said, which was all the protection he could offer the loyal man now. He darted back through the servants' door. Half-blind in the dim light, he raced up the stairs, past the eighth ring, to the ninth.

He had never entered the throne room from the servants' stairs. He did not even know for certain there was a door here. He made himself call to mind the map of the corridors he had walked as prince. The broad stair lay so that the halls circled the Throne's chamber and led to rooms for prayer, for waiting, for the emperor to robe himself. They ran this way, and this. This place where he stood was the dingy mirror for those bright and beautiful halls. Oriented now, he ran down the right-hand way, and found a door set in the wall, cut with the lotus, Mother Jalaja's sign, for it was she who had created the Pearl Throne.

He wanted to pray, but he did not know who would hear him. He felt the anger of the Mothers like a stone about his neck. The Mothers, who now held his own mother in their arms.

No. Don't think on that. Not yet.

As slowly, as gently as he could, Samudra opened the door the barest crack, profoundly grateful for its well-tended hinges. A thread of light fell across his skin. He pressed his eye to that opening and looked through.

He saw the Pearl Throne on its high dais of red-veined black marble. The pearls that gave it its name shone black, rose pink, and pure white in the glow of the few lamps the attendants had lit for this strange and hasty audience. Chandra sprawled, harshly undignified, on that sacred seat of emperors. Beside him stood the carved wooden screen. Bandhura was with him, then.

Chandra and the images of the Mothers behind him looked down on the huddle of figures at the base of the dais. Hamsa knelt there and Yamuna stood beside her. A second woman knelt beside the sorceress. She was clad in rose silks and Samudra thought she must be Radana. Beside her stood Divakesh, his great arms folded, and beside the priest prostrated in full obeisance huddled a third woman.

Who are you? He frowned at that third figure in her blue and silver silks.

All at once, Hamsa stiffened. She turned her head, just a little. Samudra sucked in a breath. She felt him. Perhaps by the bond between them, perhaps by her sorceress's instincts, but she knew that he was there.

No one else seemed to notice Hamsa's tiny gesture. All attention was on Chandra, who rose from the throne. Casually, as if he were doing no more than walking down a grassy slope, he descended the dais until he stood before the prostrated stranger beside Divakesh. Gently, he reached down and raised her up.

"Tell me again," said Chandra, smoothing her veil back. "Tell me what you say my brother did."

He lowered his arm, and Samudra's heart stopped. The woman was Ekkadi, Natharie's maid.

"I was not able to hear every word." Her voice shook badly, as well it might. Chandra stood so close, he could have kissed her with very little trouble, and struck her with even less. "But the prince spoke to her very urgently. He was most insistent in what he said. She was, I think, afraid a little, but . . ." Chandra touched Ekkadi's cheek, running one finger down her temple, a gentle caress. She faltered, looking back and up at Divakesh.

"Do not fear, Ekkadi," said the priest. "Tell your emperor all that you know."

"Yes," said Chandra, lightly, easily. "Tell me."

"We were summoned to Queen Prishi's chamber. She wanted to hear one of Princess Natharie's stories. She . . . she asked for a drink and Natharie prepared it and brought it to her. She, the queen, drank and, and . . ."

"Go on, Ekkadi. The Mothers are with you," boomed Divakesh.

"I thought she had just gone to sleep, I swear, Majesty, I swear it!" Ekkadi cried desperately. "Then, Natharie made me change clothes with her. I didn't know." She fell to her knees, weeping and put her hands between the emperor's feet. "I didn't know! I didn't know!"

But Chandra paid no more attention to her. He was looking at Divakesh. "Do you trust this girl, my lord?" he inquired.

"She is a true daughter of the Mothers."

"I see." Lightly, Chandra kicked Ekkadi's hands aside and stepped over to Yamuna. "And what is this you have brought me, sorcerer?"

"It is Radana of Sindhu," Yamuna answered.

The woman lifted her hands, pleading. "Please, Great Emperor, I am come . . ."

But Chandra had already walked on. Now he stood in

front of Hamsa. "And this, of course, is *Agnidh* Hamsa. Where is your master, Hamsa?"

"I do not know, Sovereign," answered Hamsa evenly. Her words raised all the hairs on the back of Samudra's neck, for she lied. She did know, and he felt her reaching toward him even while she strained to hold herself apart.

"And was it your hand that gave him the poison for our mother?" Chandra inquired.

Hamsa raised her eyes toward the emperor, a thing that was never done. "Prince Samudra did not poison the queen."

"No?" Chandra arched his brows, his voice full of mock surprise. "Then who did?"

"I do not know, Sovereign."

Chandra cocked an eye toward Yamuna. "Is this true?"

"I cannot yet tell, Sovereign," Yamuna answered. "I have had no time to work."

"Yes, these things do take time." Chandra sighed, his demeanor full of patience and understanding. Samudra ground his teeth together. "Now, you, from Sindhu, you say there is rebellion there?"

Plainly relieved, Radana spoke with a hasty eagerness. "Yes, Great Emperor. The king has brought the Huni down from the Iron Pillar mountains to aid him in his rebellion. I came as quickly as I was able to warn . . ."

"Yes, yes." Chandra waved her words away as if deeply bored by her recitation. "We have heard this much already. Have you nothing to add?"

Radana buried her face in her hands, her weeping muffled but still perfectly audible. "I have tried to serve, I swear it, Great Emperor. I . . ."

"If one more woman sheds a tear before me, I will have her eyes burned from her head," said Chandra. Radana fell instantly silent. Chandra rubbed his face hard and glanced backward at the screen. What was Bandhura thinking back there? What was her part in this madness?

And all at once, Samudra was sure whose hand had killed

his mother. It was just what Bandhura would do. She had feared Samudra's popularity with the soldiers and his influence on Chandra, and now . . . now Samudra was implicated in murder and rebellion. Behind her screen, Bandhura surely smiled.

"Now, we must consider how to reward those who have brought us these tidings," Chandra went on. He looked at each of the women before him. Every fiber of Samudra's body was as tight as a harp string, waiting for Chandra to speak. This was his brother at his very worst, when he wore this quiet, reasoned mask. There was nothing less than bloody murder in Chandra's mind, the only question was where the sword would fall.

"This one." Chandra moved to stand in front of Radana. "Since the princess cannot be found, this one will die in her place." He turned away, walking back to the dais, signaling the guards with a flick of his hand.

The woman dove forward, flinging herself full length at the emperor's feet, clutching at his heels. "Wait! Great Emperor! I came only to serve! I came to warn . . ."

Chandra rounded on her, his face distorted with fury. "You betrayed your king!" he roared. "Your lord whom the gods set over you! Why would I accept such service when I have treason enough in my house? Take her out of here!"

Radana screamed and leapt to her feet, to do what, Samudra could not guess. The guards seized her at once, and though she screamed and struggled, they hauled her between them out the great doors.

Chandra watched this little drama with his eyes half-closed and his face impassive.

"Now you, Hamsa," said Chandra, his voice once more casual and quiet. "I think we should give you to Yamuna's tender care so we may determine what you do and do not know of these things. Will you take this charge, my sorcerer?"

The sorcerer bowed over folded hands. "I stand ready to serve my emperor."

"Good." Chandra smiled. "When you are finished, I would have her punished for her part in my brother's treason." He glanced toward Divakesh. "That would be your duty, I believe, priest, would it not?"

"In betraying the Pearl Throne she betrayed the Mothers. It is for the sword of the Mothers to take her life."

Hamsa said nothing. Then, slowly, leaning like an old woman on her white staff, she stood and made the salute of trust, not to Chandra, but to the Mothers who watched all from behind the Throne. Then, one faltering step at a time, she began to cross the floor to the great double doors. The guards hesitated, uncertain what to do, and then she paused and turned to look over her shoulder.

"Well, *Agnidh*? Are you coming?"

It was a ludicrous, impossibly defiant gesture, and Samudra knew she would pay for it. Helpless, he watched Yamuna walk to Hamsa's side and bow, gesturing for her to lead the way, and Hamsa did. Samudra bit his tongue until the blood came to stop himself from crying out loud.

"And what for little Ekkadi?" said Chandra, looking down at the maid who still knelt beside the high priest. Chandra squatted down until his face was almost level with hers. "What for this maiden who says she has seen so much of my brother's treason?"

Divakesh rested one hand on the girl's shoulder. "I have sworn she will suffer no harm for what she has done in the Mothers' names."

"In the Mothers' names?" Chandra straightened up. "Tell me, Divakesh, did you order her to keep watch on Prince Samudra?"

If the priest had understood anything beyond his own heart he would have lied, but instead, he spoke the plain truth. "When she could, yes."

You ordered her to spy on Natharie. One of the few Natharie trusted, you turned against her. "So it is because of you that all this was witnessed." Chandra's stance had changed. He was no longer loose-limbed; he stood instead like the wrestler he was, balanced, ready to lash out at any instant.

Divakesh inclined his head once. "Yes."

Priest, you are going to wish I got to you before you had a chance to tell your emperor this, thought Samudra with a grim satisfaction that left him feeling soiled.

"I see. Well." Chandra sighed, a short, sharp sound. "Since you were obeying your masters, Ekkadi, I suppose there is nothing to reproach you for. You may return to the small domain."

Ekkadi hesitated for a heartbeat, probably stunned by her good fortune. She made obeisance and then, hiking her skirts up around her ankles, she fled the throne room. But no one watched her undignified, undisciplined departure. Chandra looked to Divakesh, and Samudra saw how his brother's eyes gleamed with tears he would never shed. "You made this, priest."

Only in part, Chandra. He had help from you and me. But even as he thought that, he knew it didn't matter. Divakesh had brought the evil news. To Chandra, that would make him responsible for it, and if Divakesh did not see his sovereign's fury, Samudra did. It was as palpable as fire against his skin. The question now was which would prove greater, Chandra's fear of the Mothers, or his anger at their priest?

"It is the will of the Mothers, my emperor," Divakesh was saying. "The dance must be held sacred. We have spoken of this many times," he added pointedly.

Chandra's face twisted. "So, you will join us on our great pilgrimage to Sindhu then?" He drawled the words. "To make sure we do all according to the Mothers' will in this glorious war we must now fight?"

Divakesh made the salute of trust. "Of course, my emperor."

Chandra smiled, slow, lazy, and sharp. Samudra shivered to see it. "Of course, priest. Of course." And with that Samudra understood what Divakesh's real mistake had been. He had broken the one promise he had made to Chandra. He had sworn that if the emperor followed his word, all would stay safe and steady, for all knew that misfortune was the sign of the Mothers' disapproval. But if Chandra obeyed Divakesh, that disapproval would never come. The dance would remain as it was, and Chandra would never have to stand before the Mothers and all the world.

Divakesh would protect Chandra as his father no longer could.

But Divakesh had failed. Bad news had come. Samudra had turned traitor, and the perfect world had cracked. Whatever else might come, Chandra would never forgive Divakesh that failure, and Chandra in his callous revenge could defy the Mothers themselves.

A foot brushed stone, and Samudra whirled. Out of arm's reach stood the drama master from the small domain, holding a lamp and bowing deeply, making the salute of trust with his free hand.

"My prince."

Samudra found himself panting. His whole body ached with the pain of all that he had just witnessed and his mind and heart were so full he could barely take in this new thing. "Master Gauda. What . . ."

The kohl-eyed eunuch did not wait for the question before straightening. "I am to show you the correct door out of this place."

"How . . ." It seemed he could do nothing but stammer. He was beginning to tremble. It was like after his first battle, he mused. During the fight he had been all fire and fury; afterward, he could do nothing but sit and shake for hours.

"Hamsa left me word earlier tonight in case things went wrong and Natharie did try to break seclusion."

"Why you?" Hamsa walked away so slowly with Yamuna, knowing she left him behind her, knowing he could do nothing at all to help her.

"Because I am a friend of Princess Natharie." Gauda dropped his voice, and Samudra was at last able to see that this one too was frightened. "And I am praying you will tell me she is still alive."

"Yes. She is away already."

"I give thanks." Samudra noted the strange wording of the prayer, and found himself wondering who Gauda gave thanks to, and how he came to be willing to risk his life for a student he had known for such a short time.

But Gauda was not going to give him any more time for contemplation or hesitation. "Come, please, my prince. Captain Pravan is already making sure his men are the ones on guard."

Of course he was. Pravan was probably already planning the sacrifices he would make to the Mothers in gratitude for this chance. Samudra could not have cleared the way for his ascendancy more completely.

In a daze, Samudra followed Gauda down the nearest staircase. "Do you know what is happening?"

"Everyone knows what is happening, my prince." Gauda held his lamp up high to light the way. Samudra realized belatedly he had left his own lamp behind. He had dropped it at some point. He didn't even remember it falling. "Sindhu is rebelling. The princess is being blamed for the death of the old queen. You are to be trampled to death as soon as you can be tried."

Ah. Is that how a prince is to die? "I have been very slow, Master Gauda, and naive."

"Yes, my prince."

They said nothing more as they hurried down the creaking stairs and through the dim corridors scented with dust and waste. Samudra could not navigate. He was no longer sure what level they were on. The few servants they encountered fell back at once, their eyes covered, not in obeisance but so they could say they had seen nothing.

At last, Samudra felt the weight of earth around him.

They were in the cellars again. He heard the distant sounds of soldiers, giving and accepting orders. He smelled spice and sugar. A rat skittered by, letting it be known how it resented his intrusion. His mind began to clear. They were not heading for the garrison tunnels, but through the food stores, kept down here in the cool earth.

Samudra had a heartbeat to see the door looming in front of them before Gauda blew out the lamp. He pulled himself up short in the abrupt darkness. There was the sound of fumbling, and then the creaking of a hinge. He felt fresh air on his face, but could see nothing.

"Here, my prince." Gauda's meaty hand fastened on his wrist and led him outside. In the dim moonlight, he saw Rupak. The horse shook his head in annoyance. Holding Rupak's reins was a slim, young soldier with a lieutenant's collar about his neck. This was Taru, Samudra remembered. He was a cousin of Makul's.

"The southeast gate is still watched by our men, my prince," Taru said, holding out the reins for Samudra.

The touch of the leathers shook the last of the confusion from Samudra. Here was something he could do. He could ride, and ride fast, down through the city to the docks to find Natharie. Surely she had not left yet. Not yet. It was too dark for her to have left yet.

Samudra swung himself into the saddle. "Lieutenant. They have taken Hamsa," he said. "You are to do what you can for her. Do you understand?"

Taru gave the soldier's salute. "Yes, my prince. Mothers guard you."

Mothers forgive me, you should say. Samudra nodded to the young man and to Guada, and wheeled his horse around, and galloped into the night without daring once to look back.

*F*rom behind her screen, Bandhura watched as Chandra dismissed the remaining attendants with a brisk word.

Alone, he stood at the foot of the dais, gazing up at the Mothers.

"Bandhura?" he said, and his voice shook.

She emerged at once. "I am here, Chandra."

She thought he would climb up to her, but as she watched he began to tremble with the force of the emotions he had held in check since his servants had roused him to this strange audience. She hurried down the stairs to wrap him at once in her arms. She expected him to melt into her embrace as he had done so many times before, but he remained apart, looking up at the Mothers, cold and afraid.

"Divakesh promised me all would be right," he said in a small voice.

Bandhura remained silent at that. What could she have said?

Chandra dragged in a long, ragged breath. "He swore that if he was high priest, all would be right. He would propitiate the Mothers and keep their wrath from me. He would be their servant and I would be free. He promised the dance would go on without their anger falling on me if only I did as he said."

She pulled away. She would be a pitiful queen indeed if she did not understand where these words led. "If he has failed in his office . . ."

"Oh yes. Yes. He has failed." He turned to her, master of himself again, and smiled his long, slow, lazy smile. Deliberately, he began to climb the dais. "He failed, and now we are at war, and I must go to the field myself to show that the Pearl Throne is strong." He reached the Throne, the ancient seat of power raised by Mother Jalaja herself. He stood beside it, contemplating it with that same slow covetous smile that masked so much anger and so much hatred.

"Yes, you must," said Bandhura firmly, pushing aside the fear that smile raised in her. "Now that Samudra is gone, you must show that you yourself are leader in war as well as in peace." For all her confident words, she found she could not make herself climb the steps to stand beside him.

Silently, his mouth shaped his brother's name, and his

hands curled into fists. "I tried, Bandhura. I tried to believe in him. Why did he insist on doing this to me?"

"Perhaps Divakesh was right in this much," she ventured carefully. "Perhaps the princess was pollution."

"I want to believe that." He gripped the Throne's arm as if he meant to break it off. "Then it is not his fault." A thought struck him. "Where is he now?"

"Yamuna will find him, my husband. He will receive justice for his treachery."

"Then what, Bandhura?" Chandra, her emperor, her husband, her love, faced her, spreading his hands wide. "When I am alone here without mother, without brother, without priest, then what?"

"You will not be alone, my husband," she said firmly. "I will be here."

"Yes." Now he stretched his hands out to her. Now she could run up those broad, black marble steps into his embrace and receive his hard kiss and give him hers and feel his heart beating against her breast. She could savor all these things and ask silently forgiveness for her moment of doubt.

It was a long time before his embrace loosened and she was able to pull away. But when she did, she saw love and assurance shining in his eyes. "You must pardon me, my husband. I need to return to the small domain for a moment. There is something I must see to personally."

"Yes." He nodded, folding his arms, gazing out across the empty throne room. "And then we will mourn . . ." His voice faltered as he remembered, but he rallied himself. "And then we will march out to war in the Mothers' names."

She laid her hand on his arm. "Then we will be safe, my husband."

Chandra covered his hand with hers and held it tightly. "Promise me, Bandhura," he whispered.

She smiled at his seriousness. "I promise, my husband. I promise."

She kissed him to seal her words, and left him staring up at the great image of Mother Jalaja. Outside the queen's door, her women waited, and she walked, stately and dignified, down the stairs to the small domain. So much remained to be done. The ceremony for Queen Prishi must be perfect in every respect. Once those preparations were well in order, she must send for the perfumer, who would have all the necessary ingredients for the potion Ekkadi would have to swallow.

Foolish girl. How can I trust you to be a good servant to me when I know you are Divakesh's creature? She shook her head in saddened amazement.

But even this could not diminish the triumph glowing warm within her. Chandra did not see it yet, but the Mothers had ordered all things as they should be. They had brought the woman Radana before the Pearl Throne. Because of her warning, the Sindishi and their allies would be taken by surprise and overcome with ease. Chandra would lead the army and this time it would be his name shouted in victory when they returned. Victory in a holy cause would cement Chandra's rule at long last. He would be safe. She would have fulfilled all the Mothers' purposes and they would reward her with his child.

Her women opened the door to the small domain. The kneeling, grieving women looked up to her and she smiled benevolently down on them. *I must be strong for them and for Chandra too,* she thought as she stepped inside the domain that was now hers alone.

There is, after all, much work left to do.

Chapter Nineteen

Like Samudra, Commander Makul was at first stunned to learn that Natharie could ride a horse. Also like Samudra, he accepted her declaration quickly and did not question the truth of it. Two friendly soldiers outside the walls supplied them with mounts, and despite the strange shape of the Hastinapuran saddle, Natharie managed to keep up with Makul as he set a brisk pace down the winding and increasingly foul streets of the city. Unlike when she had last traveled this way, though, those streets were sparsely populated, by fleeting, staggering shadows. Instead of stares and cheers, the pair of them drew only quick glances, or quick curses from those who had to dodge out of the way.

So, it was not very long before the docks opened up before them. Makul tied the horses, bribed a beggar drowsing nearby to keep watch on them, and led Natharie down to the river. He clearly knew this place well, and he scanned the clusters of boats moored by the wooden piers. Some had lit lamps hanging from their masts, and it was one of these that Makul finally approached. With a shake, he roused the half-naked man sleeping on the deck and began dickering for the price of the boat and his hire.

"Just the boat," said Natharie in Sindishi. Makul turned, his eyes wide with renewed surprise.

When the bargain was made and the man scampered off to get his newly filled purse somewhere out of reach of thieves, Natharie stepped on board. The river rocked the wooden deck, welcoming her.

She wanted to feel delight. She would go home. She was

free, but she could only look down the moonlit river and shudder. Her sacrifice had been for nothing. Her family had taken her offer of life and turned it to death.

"Should I offer you my sword as well?" inquired Makul behind her.

Natharie gave him a half-smile. "That art I never learned. I will content myself with readying the boat while you stand watch for us."

A muscle twitched in the commander's sunken cheek. "I must return."

Natharie stiffened. "They will kill you."

He shook his head. "Not yet. There will be many other things warring for their attention, and until the emperor gives the order, I am still commander over all, save the prince."

Where is that prince now? What is happening to him? Natharie looked southward again. For all she knew, the palace guards were already swarming the streets looking for her. *I should go at once.* There was just enough moonlight for her to read the river. It was broad here, and there was very little traffic this time of night. If she ran the boat out into the middle of the current, she should be safe from the worst of the shallows. Traveling by night would be safest anyway. If she was not hunted yet, she would be soon, and the longer start she had the better.

But she did not move toward rope or sail. Fear held her, and instinct. There had been so much betrayal already in this one night, there was sure to be more.

"I will wait here until dawn, Makul."

"Princess, the danger is great."

"I know, but hear me." The decision steadied her. "So much has gone so badly wrong that I may not be the only one who will need to escape. Should you return to the palace, tell any who need to go I am here until sunrise."

Gratitude shone plainly in Makul's eyes. He made the salute of trust and left her there without another word.

The idea of sleep seemed not only ridiculous, but dangerous. Natharie spent the rest of the night learning what she could of the little boat. It was river-worthy, but barely. Even as lightly loaded as it was, it rode low in the water. The tiller was sound, though, and the sail was whole, and there was a spare canvas in one of the two chests. The other held fishing tackle, flints for sparking a fire, a pair of knives, and man's loose tunic and pantaloons. Struggling under a stiff canvas blanket, Natharie shed her servant's costume and put those on, winding the cap of cloth around her head to hide her hair. It was a crude costume, and ill-fitting, but it gave her greater freedom of movement than her skirt, and from a distance it would help hide her from prying eyes.

At last, dawn sent its pale light across the sky, and the docks began to wake up. Those who lived on their boats roused themselves and shouted to one another. The smells of cooking rose over less savory scents. Porters, bearers, and traders emerged from the warehouses and shacks, ready to begin their working day. Gongs and bells rang out to greet the morning.

Natharie sat on the boat's single bench, alternately watching the shore and the river. Her stomach growled. Should she risk finding some food before she set sail?

No. I have delayed too long already. I will be able to barter for something farther down. She still had some bangles with her women's clothes. They would serve.

The thunder of hoofbeats scattered the gathering crowd. Natharie looked up in time to see Samudra ride into the dockyard, rein in his horse, and stand in the stirrups, staring over their heads.

Natharie leapt to her feet. She had been expecting Hamsa, or Ekkadi. If Samudra was here, either all was right, or all had gone far more wrong than she had imagined.

Then she realized that Samudra, a prince of Hastinapura, rode alone. Not even Hamsa or Makul was beside him. He dismounted his horse, and left it. He gave its reins to no one, he did not tie it. He simply waded through the crowd toward the docks.

She raised her arm, waving. He looked, looked away, and looked back again, before running down the docks to her little boat and clambering over the rail. He opened his mouth, then saw it was her face under the dirty cloth of her new cap.

You should not be so stunned, Great Prince, she thought as his eyes started out at her. *You've seen me in slave's clothes before.*

"Can you get us away?" he asked hoarsely.

You remembered I can sail. Something in this left her absurdly pleased in the middle of so much disaster. "Slip the mooring and push us off." She jumped up onto the tiller platform.

Samudra did as he was told, but clumsily. He had probably never before been aboard such a craft. It didn't matter. They were at the end of the dock, so once Natharie pushed them off with the long-handled oar, they had a clear passage. The water was deep in this season, and kind Liyoni's current was swift. It caught them up at once and Natharie was able to guide them out into the middle of her waters. Once she was sure they would not be snagged up, she raised the sail. The wind caught them, adding its speed to the current's, and they were truly away.

During the weeks of her seclusion she had imagined standing like this with the river breeze gliding over her skin and the rocking of a boat beneath her, and a thousand times she had told herself to put it out of her mind. Never once had she imagined that she might be flying from disaster to disaster. Nor had she imagined who would travel with her.

Samudra sat on the bench, straight-backed and still, which was a sensible posture for so small a boat.

"Samudra . . ." she began.

He turned toward her, and she saw the tears pouring down his haggard face.

Natharie gripped the tiller and concentrated all her mind

on steering the boat, trying hard not to see the man in front of her, trying with all her might to give him a little privacy, a little dignity, so he might grieve.

In silence they sailed away from the great city of Hastinapura, through the farmlands and on toward the wilderness, neither of them able to see what waited on the other side.

*W*hen Captain Anun came running across what was left of the gardens, King Kiet and Queen Sitara were standing together with the Huni's chief. Tapan Gol was showing them a demonstration of his archers, a mixed corps of men and women. Their black bows were deeply curved, and now a line of fifty of them knelt on the green grass. Two hundred paces away silk flags fluttered on wooden posts. The captain spoke a single word, and the archers knelt, drawing their bows, pointing their arrows high. The captain spoke another word, and together, they loosed. Those arrows flew into the air and rained down upon the silk, shredding the flags, pinning the scraps to the ground until there was not one bit of color remaining on the suddenly naked posts.

Tapan Gol was grinning, as much at the king's and queen's bland faces as at the accomplishment of his soldiers. Queen Sitara knew the Huni chief saw right through their façade. He knew his displays and exercises frightened them. He knew he could do as he pleased here and it was very likely they could not stop him. If they tried, and did succeed, they would most certainly lose the war to come.

So it was almost a relief to see Anun sprinting toward them to kneel at their feet.

"Hastinapura is on the move."

Sitara looked up at her husband. He stood there, heavy and solid, saying nothing. It was Tapan Gol who nodded with satisfaction. "It is good. My men are growing fat and lazy here in your sunshine. Come, King. You and I have much to discuss."

Kiet pressed his palms together. "With respect, Great Tapan Gol. There are matters I must put to my queen before any others. I will join you as soon as I am able."

Tapan Gol's long eyes shifted toward Sitara. What he thought she could not tell. If she had a thousand years she would not be able to read this closed-mouthed, closed-hearted man.

He shrugged. "As you wish, King." He turned away as if they had ceased to exist, and shouted to his people in his own language. In answer the Huni raised up a huge cheer, brandishing their weapons in the air and clapping one another on the back. Kiet watched all this for a long, tense moment before starting for the palace. Sitara followed him.

When they reached Kiet's private chambers, he went first to the altar. With careful motions, he lit one of the cones of incense that waited at the feet of the gilded image of the Awakened One. For a long time, he watched the scented smoke rise, and Sitara watched him. She had hoped that, as the time for the war grew closer, she would grow more distant from her life. She was certain what the price of her part in the plan must be, and she was ready to pay. But instead, she had grown closer to all that she loved. Each day was brighter, each moment with children and husband more vibrant and precious. She understood that her heart was savoring the life it must soon lose. She accepted that, even welcomed it. She would finally end all alone and in fear, and it would be good to have a store of love and beauty against that time.

His private meditations finished, Kiet bowed to Anidita's image and said to her, "Do we need to send word to the sorcerers?"

"Father Thanom said no. They are prepared for action. He said they would know when the time of need had come."

"Then we must pray they can do all they have said." Kiet took both her hands, looking down at them. His own hands were warm and strong as ever, the touch as dear. "It is my will that when the monks come, Sitara, you go with them."

She had expected this. It was not in Kiet to let her go without protest. "No," she said firmly. "I have begun this thing. I will end it."

"Just so, my queen." He squeezed her hands gently, willing her understanding and strength. "You will stand regent for our son until he is a man. You will be the strong spirit for our people until they are able to resume their lives again. You will stand in the face of Hastinapura and the Huni both."

A wave of cold swept across Sitara's heart. He meant it. He thought she could go through this life knowing all she was responsible for. "You will do all these things," she reminded him. "You are king."

But Kiet only shook his head. "And if I am not in the battle, at best, our people will believe me a coward, and never follow me again. At worst, our enemies will know this for the trick that it is."

No. No. It cannot be. It will not be. "Let me take your place then. Let me wear your armor and wield your sword." This was done by queens of legend. Had she not already done as much as they?

"No," he said again. "It is not possible."

"Kiet!" She grabbed his arms. She tried to shake him but it was like trying to shake a mountain. "You are not to die because of this thing I have done!"

"That you have done?" He laughed, a mirthless, heartrending sound. "Oh, my beloved." Kiet traced his thumb tenderly along her jaw. "That is too much arrogance. Do you truly believe that you could have done this without my consent from the beginning? I too am part of this, and I go to pay the price of it. It is my fate as king of Sindhu. Your fate is harder and my heart breaks . . ." His words faltered and his hand stroked her hair. Sitara closed her eyes, unable to look into his face and see the pain and determination there. "I may die for this, but you must live with what we have done."

Tears overflowed her eyes and ran hot down her cheeks.

She clapped her hands over her face to cover them, but she could not stop them. "What did I do in my past life that it should come to this?"

"Does it matter? This is where we are now and we both must do what is needed."

Sitara closed her mouth. She heard the break in his voice. He was near the end of his strength. She would not deny the courage that he had shown already by bringing him to tears as well. She folded her hands and bowed. "I hear the words of my king and lord."

"Sitara," he whispered.

Sitara threw her arms around him and kissed him hard, drinking him in. Then, she released him so she could go ready her children and to take up her future. With each step she left her heart farther behind.

*A*s ever, Divakesh *dva* Tingar Jalajapad, high priest of Hastinapura, sword of the Mothers, woke a few heartbeats before his acolyte, Asok, brought the flickering lamp that was the only sunrise ever to reach his cell in the mountain's stone heart. The young man silently set down the lamp, gave the salute of trust, and retreated. It was well known that when Divakesh woke he wanted no communion save with the Mothers.

Divakesh loved this moment. In the flickering light, it seemed as if his many images of Mother Jalaja truly did dance. Each aspect in its stone niche was different, each as perfect in its beauty as it was possible for an earthly thing to be. Each was only a pale reflection of the heavenly perfection of the goddess it represented.

She had been the whole of his existence since his childhood, since his mother and father had brought him to the temple, and made him kneel before the altar. They had handed over what little money they had to the priest to take him in as an acolyte. All his brothers and sisters were dead of the plague in the village. They had walked miles to find a temple that would not shut its doors against the illness that might follow them.

The last thing his father did for him was to kneel on the temple floor at his side.

"Look at her, Divakesh," his father had whispered hoarsely so only Divakesh could hear. "Love her with all your heart and you will understand, today and all the days to come. She will never desert you, not for hunger or any other need of flesh and bone. She is all the love there is."

Divakesh had gazed on that simple statue, not even turning around as he heard the tread of his parents' bare feet on the floor, leaving him. He saw how this was only a representation, a symbol of something greater. Since then, he had striven to understand, and to be worthy of that greater divinity.

As it did so often, Divakesh's heart swelled taut with his secret. His only desire, his only need in life was to look upon the true face of the goddess, to see Her true eyes and know he was worthy. He would work a lifetime and more, and knew he already had. All his being for each turn of the wheel, Divakesh was sure, had been honed for that moment, and that he had risen so high in this life was proof that he was close.

Today was a great day and it seemed to Divakesh the dance they danced was one of creation. Creating victory, creating blessing. The defiant and blasphemous princess was exposed for what she was and her influence on the small domain was ended. Within a few hours of the dawn sacrifice, the false sorceress would have her sentence publicly read. Then, she would come to stand on the great altar, and she would die. The shedding of her blood would purify the palace, and with that act, the army of the Mothers would march to war. Sindhu was the strongest and most arrogant of the protectorates that followed the vain Anidita. With Sindhu gone, that false worship would quickly crumble and true devotion to the Mothers would take its proper place.

Feeling the depths of his many blessings, Divakesh prostrated himself before Mother Jalaja for a long time. Then he washed, dressed in his scarlet robe, and went to the common room.

The common room, in the outer part of the temple living quarters, was quiet today. For once there was no conversation to be silenced when he appeared, only a hasty swallowing of rice and lentils by those who could not yet discipline themselves to perform the day's first dance before they had fed their bodies. All knew it was a great day and all knew how it was to begin.

It was still dark outside. Dawn was nothing more than a white line on the horizon and countless stars still shone overhead. The silhouette of the Queen of Heaven stood on her pedestal above the ever-burning flame. Divakesh mounted the steps and prostrated himself before her. All around him, the others lit incense and lamps. They made sure each of the Mothers had her due offering of saffron rice, and was properly anointed with oil and perfume. Divakesh's own task was worship, pure and entire. He emptied his thoughts of all but Heaven and Heaven's queen, so powerful, so beautiful in blessing, so terrible in wrath. It was her wrath he would embody today and all would know the cost of betraying Mother Jalaja.

Divakesh rose to his knees and made the salute of trust. Beside him, Asok waited, holding the white pillow where the sword rested. Divakesh lifted the great curving blade and kissed the flat. He tasted the steel and for a moment permitted himself to savor it.

He stood. All the others had repaired to the stairs below the altar platform. This place, this office, was his alone. Divakesh raised the sword, and began the dance.

Divakesh danced as he always did, with heart and mind full. He would give his best to the Mothers. He would hold nothing back. Praise, strength, breath, he would give all he had. If blood were demanded, he would give blood. He was the son of the Mothers. He was voice and heart and infinite soul. They were All, and he would show his understanding of this truth with each movement of his body, each beat of his quickened heart.

Slowly, Divakesh realized he did not dance alone. There was another with him, matching his movements, as he turned, as he knelt, as he swung the sword high. Outrage shook him, and yet he knew he could not stop. To stop would be to break the pattern, to allow imperfection into the dance of praise, and he would not permit that. He spun again, straining to catch a glimpse of the one who violated the sanctity of the dance.

It was a woman. She turned just at the edge of his vision. He glimpsed her before he made the bow. Gold flashed on her arms and about her waist. And more. He whirled again, and paused, holding the pose. He could not see her. Where had she gone? Pivot slow, kneel again. There. The flash of movement, the white flash . . .

The white flash of diamonds and gold. And Divakesh lifted his eyes to the pedestal before him.

The image of Heaven's Queen was gone. There was only the stone pedestal and the rising flame. And the woman who danced beside him. Divakesh prostrated himself instantly, fear and wonder rushing through his blood. It was Mother Jalaja with whom he danced. The Queen of Heaven was beside him now, not just in image, but in divine truth. Wonder dizzied him and he feared he would fall unconscious with the glory of it.

She moved without a sound, and yet Divakesh knew she came nearer. Some distant part of him was aware that all the others, the priests and the acolytes, had also dropped down in worship, but he could spare no real thought for them. Every fiber in him felt her approach as one felt the wind, the warm sun, or the nearness of fire.

"Look at me, Divakesh."

Trembling, Divakesh obeyed. She was glory itself. She

wore an aspect akin to that of the statue he had danced before. But on her living form the gold was crude and cold, an encumbrance more than adornment. She was the awesome purity of the night sky; the calm and the storm together were in her eyes. Before, he had thought he had seen her holding a sword. Now, he saw it was a delicate lotus she cupped in her hands.

"Divakesh, my priest. Do you know me?"

"I . . . Yes, Queen of Heaven. I know you."

"Yet you did not know me so recently."

As soon as she spoke the words, he was before the emperor again, within his own body and yet apart and watching himself. The other self was so proud, yet so afraid and weak, and his voice was as harsh as the vulture's when he said, "Oh, my sovereign, that was an evil dream. The woman was a devil, the temptation of sin calling you to forswear your purity and pollute yourself by mixing with the outcasts and the blooded."

Divakesh clapped his hands over his face in shame and fear. "I feared my emperor was deceived."

"How could any take my shape in deception, Divakesh?" Her voice was so mild, so sad, it wrung tears from his eyes. He looked up and saw her gentle sorrow and wished at once to grope for the sword at his feet so he might end himself and never cause even the slightest grief to her again.

"I . . . I spoke error. I beg forgiveness."

She smiled then and all the world was right in an instant. "You have it, my priest."

Such beauty, such wonder. There were no words. Not even the dance was praise enough. "I do not deserve it."

She cocked her head. "Why not?"

"I . . . I . . ."

She laughed, and there had never been music so pure. When it faded, Divakesh felt a stab of sorrow.

"You are taking my children to war, Divakesh. Why are you doing that?"

Divakesh found he did not understand. Why would She ask such a question? Was it a test? "I . . . it is the emperor . . ."

The Queen of Heaven frowned, and Divakesh prostrated himself again, his frame trembling as if it would shake apart. "It is you, Divakesh. Why?"

Confusion racked him. This was Her war. Her will. "But . . . surely you know, Mother of All. It is for your glory. To spread your worship and eliminate falsehood and show that your rule in Heaven is absolute." His tremors eased as he spoke and some measure of his confidence returned.

"Have I asked that my worship be increased?"

The question so stunned Divakesh that his head jerked up and for a moment he looked into the goddess's stormy eyes. "But . . ."

"I am who I am, Divakesh, have I ten worshippers or ten thousand." Her voice was great enough to shake the heavens and soft enough that he had to strain with all his might to hear a single word of it. "The stars know my name, the sun knows it and the earth sings it with each dawn. This is truth and will not change for your war. What great honor do the fires of forced worship bring me?"

"But . . ." He shook. He wanted nothing more than to bow before her, but he could not. He did not understand how this could be, and yet he knew he must understand. "The followers of Anidita teach falsehood . . ."

"Why do you believe there is only one path to Heaven, Divakesh?"

He could not look at her. She burned too brightly. He had to close his eyes, to put a shield of darkness between himself and Her. But it did no good. Her presence was not to be lessened by anything he could do.

"But . . . you . . . Hastinapura is your home."

"And within that house I will be secure, Divakesh. Believe this." She was closer now, and he could do nothing but lift his face and look at her, at the calm and the storm of her. She whispered now, words that only his deepest soul could hear. "Do not turn your eyes from this truth, or I will have no choice but to visit blessing upon others who see me more clearly."

"But, we are your children . . . and . . ."

"Yes. You are." She stepped back, lifting lotus and sword to the rising dawn. "Let that be enough for you."

And she was gone.

Divakesh blinked. The pedestal was still empty. The image and the substance of Jalaja both had left him.

Divakesh bowed his head and began to weep. He sobbed like a child, his despair complete. Priests and acolytes rushed up the stairs to the altar. Some began to ask questions, their voices a meaningless gabble in his ears.

"Did you see her?" He clutched the hand of the one nearest him without any idea who it might be. "Did you hear?"

"I saw only a great light, Holy One," answered a man. Asok. It was Asok. "And you danced with it, and it spoke . . ." He swallowed hard. "She spoke against the march to Sindhu." Asok's voice broke and tears shone in his eyes. "Master, what have we done?"

What have we done? What have I done? Divakesh stared at the empty pedestal from which the Queen of Heaven had vanished. He tried to recall the perfection of her form, but could not do so clearly. It was too much for his mortal mind. He remembered her light, her warmth, the intensity of her presence as she spoke. She said . . . she told him . . .

Within that house I will be secure, Divakesh. Believe this.

"We must go to the emperor at once, Holy One," whispered Asok hoarsely. He was still shaking. All the priests were. Some wept tears of fear and wonder. Most were still on their knees, unable, it seemed, to move from this spot, this moment. "We must tell him to stand down the army and go no further with this war."

Divakesh bowed his head. Beside the burning light of Mother Jalaja, he saw Natharie of Sindhu facing him down, her own blood dripping from her throat, unafraid before him and before the Queen of Heaven though he could strike her down as due sacrifice. She knelt, but remained defiant in her vanity and blasphemy. He thought of the king and queen who brought her into this life, of their whole country, thousands upon thousands of souls equally blasphemous, equally defiant and unafraid before the great light that had come down to him. It could not be that Mother Jalaja meant this unspeakable, galling pride to continue. It was incomprehensible that the Mother of all that was true and perfect should permit error and blasphemy to reign inside her borders.

Within that house I will be secure.

It could not be true that the little foreign princess with her beads and her unashamed eyes understood better than he did. It could not be that his understanding that he had worked so hard for, the austerities to which he had pushed himself, the sleep and food and love denied and sacrifice in the service of the Mothers had been in error.

"Holy One?" said Asok again, his voice trembling as badly as his hands. "Holy One? Should we not go to the emperor now?"

But it was a different voice Divakesh attended. A different phrase, that was the heart of all she had said.

Within that house I will be secure.

Yes. That was what she meant. Of course. It was his flawed understanding that had confused him for a moment. Divakesh raised his head. He looked at Asok, and Asok jerked backward. Divakesh felt the holy light burning brightly inside him, and knew it was that which made his acolyte afraid. Asok did not understand yet. That was all right. It was his role as high priest to make all things clear.

One motion at a time, Divakesh stood. "Lohit was not of

itself formally part of Hastinapura," he explained patiently to those around him, who had heard and not understood. They could not have understood what had confused him. "The treaty had been differently worded, and the nature of the tribute was separate from that paid by Sindhu. It had been wrong to punish Lohit, which was not truly a part of the realm of the Mothers." He must accept that sin and do proper penance to right the balance again. "But Sindhu *is* a part of the empire, and so must be brought into proper worship and be made pure."

They stared at him, the priests on their knees, the young men on their bellies. Their mouths gaped, showing how stunned they were at the clarity of his perception. Asok had gone white in shock.

"Holy One . . ." Asok began.

"Have you a question?" inquired Divakesh coldly. "Speak. I will tell you the truth. Mother Jalaja has shown it to me."

Asok's mouth opened and closed several times, as understanding of what had truly happened sank into him. Divakesh thought perhaps his acolyte should have shown more wonder and less fear, but fear was appropriate. Wonder would come later, when this first flush of feeling had faded. "No, Holy One," Asok whispered, and his voice shook, although Divakesh could tell he was trying very hard to keep it calm and steady. "I have no question."

"It is well." Divakesh turned back to the empty pedestal. There was no need for Mother Jalaja to be there anymore. She had filled him with her Essence, and her Truth, and it shone in him so clearly as to make her lesser servants shake in his shadow, and Asok, his face taut and pale, could no longer stand to meet his burning eyes.

All his work, all his sacrifice and study and denial, had finally brought reward. Divakesh made the salute of trust to the pedestal. *Thank you, Queen of Heaven, for your blessing upon this great task. I will show you I am worthy of the charge you have laid before me.*

With his new and greater understanding shining in his eyes, Divakesh lifted the great sword once more, and as those around him fell back, he began to dance.

Chapter Twenty

Below the Palace of the Pearl Throne, Hamsa waited in the dark, and tried to keep breathing.

She had known about the warren of cells that lay below the garrison tunnels. She had known it was a filthy, stinking place without hope, that it was forever cold and dark in a land of heat and light. She had never in her worst imaginings thought she would find herself cast into one of those cells, where the ceiling was too low to allow her to stand up, where the rats got to her scanty scraps of bread before she, groping in the blackness, could find them. She had never dreamed of iron fetters on her wrists and ankles tearing into her skin until each became a ring of fire eating into her flesh, or that there would come a time when each ragged heartbeat made the arrival of death that much more welcome.

She would have forsaken her final mission and lain down to die if it were not for the soldiers.

They came whenever they could steal past their compatriots whose loyalties were to their new commander, Pravan. They knelt with her in the darkness, slipping her a little clean water, a slice of orange, a piece of fresh flat bread. They whispered to her the news. "They've not found the prince yet," they would say, or "Makul is still free. Pravan needs him to order the troops." Or, "We'll free you if we can."

They meant it, that last promise, but she knew with dull certainty that it was impossible.

She heard the creak of hinges, and she cringed. She could not help it. But no light came to blind her as it did when her wardens entered. There was only the sound of shuffling cloth against filth and straw.

"It's me, *Agnidh*," whispered a young man's voice. "Taru."

"Taru," she breathed. Her throat was dry and her lips were split. "Did you . . ."

"I did." Clumsily, their flailing hands found each other. He opened her fingers, and placed in them a small knife. It was not even as long as her palm, a delicate thing for splitting open the tiniest of fruits. But it would do. It would do.

"Hamsa. Forgive me, forgive me, but there is no more time. I am . . . we are come to take you to . . ."

So. It had come then. It was time to take her before the sword of the Mothers. She had thought Yamuna would come to gloat over her before this happened. But no, why should he? He held her soul tight in his jar. What could she do against that?

"*Agnidh? Agnidh*, do you hear me?"

It was Taru speaking, the frightened and heart-sore boy come to do a difficult thing with what mercy he could offer. How long had her little reverie lasted? She didn't know. She tried to smile at Taru, and then remembered he couldn't see her. It seemed now she could see in the dark. She saw her mother and her father. She saw the old woman who taught her in her home village. She saw Samudra as a long-legged boy, running races while his brother cheered him on. She saw Samudra as a grown man looking at Natharie with his heart in his eyes. She gripped the little knife.

I will buy you both a blessing, Samudra. Even if I am Yamuna's prisoner, I can still pray.

"*Agnidh* . . ." began Taru again. "There's something . . . I must tell you. Something's happened with the priests. They're all afraid."

This last word penetrated Hamsa's dulled mind. "Afraid? What could Divakesh's priests be afraid of?"

"They will not speak openly, but there are whispers that there was a vision, maybe of one of the Mothers, and it spoke against war with Sindhu. But Divakesh says it spoke in favor of it, and now he walks through the palace telling everyone that it is a holy cause."

"He did this before."

"Not like this, *Agnidh*. I've seen him. His eyes . . . I've seen madness, *Agnidh*. It takes men in battle sometimes. It's not the holy breath that makes Divakesh look like that, I swear it."

Hamsa swallowed several times. If she had not known that Divakesh had already lied about Mother Jalaja's appearance to the emperor, she would never have believed it. Again the goddess had come to him, and again he had lied? No wonder he had gone mad. Such a thing would break a mortal mind in two. She thought this almost idly. It didn't really matter. The one who held her here was not Divakesh. He was just the one who would kill her.

"If he is mad then why do any still follow him?" she managed to ask.

"Because the emperor says we go forward. He says none are to question or oppose Divakesh. I think some tried to tell him, but . . . we set out tomorrow at dawn."

Hamsa could picture it, a trembling priest, or perhaps even Asok, Divakesh's acolyte, kneeling before Chandra, and him listening to every word with a small smile on his face. The petitioner would look up hopefully at that sly and lazy countenance, and would hear the emperor say on no account would their plans change. All would go just as Divakesh had said.

And they would not understand. They would not understand that the emperor had made up his mind to destroy

Divakesh, whom he in his own twisted understanding blamed for Samudra's betrayal. And he would use his entire army, his entire empire to do it. He would let Divakesh's madness take the fore until Divakesh understood how badly he had failed. Only then would Chandra let him die.

So, Divakesh would be defeated. That was good to know. But until the emperor's slow, cruel vengeance could take hold, there were so many other things that could happen, and in all that time, Divakesh still ruled and Yamuna still held her chain. That chain led only one place.

"Well then," she sighed. "We had best not keep the Sword of the Mothers waiting."

"Agnidh . . ." said Taru again.

"No." She stopped him. "You have done what you can. Now we will both do as we must." She tightened her grip ever so slightly on her knife. "It would be a great kindness if I could pray before I die."

"If you wish, you are allowed to go to the temple before . . ." His voice trailed away. She smiled to let him know it was all right, before she remembered he could not see her.

Taru's touch led her out of the cell and raised her up. Her legs were weak as water and the chains dragged at her joints, stretching them almost to the breaking point, and even the dim, greasy light of the corridor burned her eyes. Taru led her out into the main corridor. The air still stank, but it was fresher here than in her cell, and Hamsa breathed it deeply. Her chains did not allow her to do more than shuffle along. Two other soldiers walked behind her. Were they also Samudra's men? They were silent and their eyes were hard. She could read nothing in them. Not that she had much strength or thought to spare. She must bend all her thoughts to the temple, and to what must happen next. Her focus must be strong, her will all on a single point, her heart as undivided as her sorcerer's soul.

They walked down empty corridors. Not even the slaves were to be allowed to look on her, or to touch so much as her shadow, lest her impurity and rebellion infect them. The soldiers who accompanied her would be carefully cleansed when their task was done. Divakesh would make sure of that.

She was not, of course, taken to the imperial temple where she was used to worshipping with Samudra and his family. There was a little place set aside for slaves and those who were to die. It was behind a door carved with only a single lotus, and the nave was barely large enough to allow three people space to kneel. But it was still a temple of the Mothers, and their images danced here, each statue life-sized and carved with loving detail, the red stone gleaming like warm, living flesh in the lamplight. Someone had lit the sacred fire and even spared her some incense. Its perfume was heady after the stench of prison.

Hamsa looked at the Mothers arrayed before her. She felt the weight of the chains on her wrists and ankles, and the warmth of the blade against her curled fingers.

"Please," she said to the guard. "Let me make my prayers alone."

Taru nodded, but the taller of the other two soldiers looked uncertain. "And what will I do if you work some magic to escape?"

She looked the man right in his eyes. His heart showed plainly in them. He might not like what was happening, he might even be Samudra's man, but he was loyal to the Throne. He would not betray its servant, not without orders from a captain he trusted. She certainly did not qualify as that.

"I am bound by the will of the sorcerer Yamuna," Hamsa said quietly. She lifted her hands. "And these chains. I can do nothing." It was true, and it was not true. Would he choose to believe? "I go to stand before the Mothers. Let me make the last sacrifice I can."

He nodded slowly. Did he understand what her words

meant? Taru did, and she could see it was hard for him to hold steady. "Very well," said the other. "But we can give you only a moment."

Taru led the others out, closing the door behind them, and Hamsa was alone with the burning fire, the Mothers, and her knife. She uncurled her fist. It was stiff. There was a hard red line on her hand where the blade had pressed, almost cutting her skin.

Clumsily she knelt before the fire. She lifted the knife in her left hand and laid it against her right wrist. Her fingers shook, even now her heart wavered.

No. There was no time for doubt. She would do this. Even if it meant only her death, it would be her hand and her own actions that brought her end, not Yamuna's will and Divakesh's arm.

Hamsa exhaled. She called up the magic from inside her hollow heart and soul. She pushed the iron shackle up on her arm as far as it would go. She breathed onto her festering wrist. She leaned forward and kissed her wounded flesh, leaving a wet and shining circle on the blue vein visible just below the brown skin. She pressed down with the silver blade and cut a red line, long, swift and deep.

The blood welled up rich and red-black at once. She stared at it, stupid and dizzy from the sight. The pain of the wound followed a moment later, and she bit her lips hard to keep from screaming. She squeezed her eyes shut, clutched her arm, and rose to her feet. Spilling out her life's blood, Hamsa began to dance.

She danced with wavering, drunken steps tracing a circle around the fire. She danced, expelling with the blood all the magic in her. She danced, weaving breath and blood, fire and pain and life. She danced in prayer and sacrifice. She danced in desperate silence as the hot blood ran down her arm and spattered onto the floor. She danced in her own blood and danced in silence.

Mother Jalaja, Queen of Heaven, hear me, hear me. I am the least of your children. I do not deserve my single soul. But I beg you come to me, hear me. I have nowhere else to turn. This last thing I offer, I make sacrifice of all I am. Come to me. Hear me. Mother Jalaja, hear me . . .

Her foot came down wrong in the path of her blood, and Hamsa crashed to her knees. She heard the hiss as blood met fire. The world swam and spun.

Mother Jalaja, hear me . . . I am the least of your children . . . This last thing I offer . . .

"I hear you, daughter."

Hamsa opened her eyes. The temple had faded away into blackness. There was only the fire, and herself, and the woman before her. She shone like the sun, crowned in gold and diamonds. A garland of lotus flowers hung around Her neck and flowed across Her bare breasts. Another garland girdled Her waist.

Hamsa was still bleeding freely, but it did not seem to mean much now. Perhaps she had already died. Hamsa prostrated herself before the goddess.

"Mother Jalaja, Queen of Heaven, I . . ."

"I know." She shook her head, and her face was stern. "You should have come before. You should not have waited for Divakesh to bring me here."

Hamsa was beyond shame, even in the face of the goddess's reproof. "I know. I am unworthy."

"You think too much on what you are, daughter, and not on what you must be."

"Mother, it is only you who can make me what I must be." She did not want to have to speak these words but there was only honesty left to her. Only truth would help this thing be done. "I have lived too long in my fear and now the wheel has turned and left me no time. I have come to beg for Prince Samudra. I plead with you. I offer up my life to you. Do not let my weakness doom him."

For a moment, Hamsa thought the goddess's face grew gentle. "Samudra does not ask this of you."

Shame crawled out from Hamsa's belly, draining the last of her strength. "He puts little faith in me."

"He knows nothing of your true power. But he is a soldier. If your power were fully at his command, he would use it. He will use up your power and life, and he will not regret that moment until it is done, for that is what commanders must do. Would you live long enough for him to give you such an order?"

Hamsa remained silent for a long moment. She had been ready to die a moment ago, but this was new. Was it possible that she might live? The Queen of Heaven was here. All things were possible.

Live in service to her prince, the service Yamuna mocked, that he rejected with such abhorrence that he would destroy empires to escape it. Live and serve, until Samudra ordered her death.

Then Hamsa realized something was missing. The bond. The working that tied her to Samudra. It had vanished and no longer weighed on her heart. She was herself alone here in Mother Jalaja's darkness, and it was only her soul that would decide.

She spoke slowly and from her laboring heart. "If that is the way it must be, I accept." Certainty grew in her. This was herself that spoke and none other. "I too am of the land and a child of the Mothers. I do not wish my home to fall because I refused to help it flourish."

Mother Jalaja nodded. "Then, so be it. You will have power now. The power that is your own, and the secrets your other half has learned watching the sorcerer Yamuna. But this is your doom. When you next look on us, it will be on your lord's command. At that time, you will forfeit your place on the wheel."

Those words sank like lead into Hamsa's soul. Mother

Jalaja did not mean she would die. She meant that Hamsa would no more be reborn. This life, this time would be her last. If she accepted this she would have more than she had ever dreamed, but it would be an end more final than that of other souls.

Hamsa made the salute of trust. "So be it, Mother."

Mother Jalaja nodded her head, and Hamsa felt approval and sorrow wash over her. "Stand."

Hamsa stood, amazed that there was still strength in her limbs to do so. Mother Jalaja laid her palm over Hamsa's wounded arm. Her touch burned as if Hamsa had laid her arm in the fire, but Hamsa stood and she held and encompassed the holy pain.

"Open is your heart. Open is your soul. Receive the power that is your gift, your right, and your doom."

The fire of the Mother's touch sank through her skin. It ran into her blood, igniting her veins and her bones beneath them. It was pain, blinding white like the heart of a star. It was ecstasy. It was the pinnacle of hope and it was despair. It was the key to her soul. It was the seal on her future, and she felt the coming days close tight about her.

Last of all, it was strength and understanding. All that she had struggled to learn, all that her mind had been unable to compass before, she now knew. She knew where her heart was and she felt the center of her soul. Never again would her own magics slip away from her. They were hers forever.

Hamsa opened her eyes.

Around her she saw the temple, and she breathed in the smoke and scent of the sacred fire, and she was alone. Her knife lay at her feet in a circle of her blood that was drying rapidly on the stone floor. Her arm was healed and whole, save for a red circle about the size of a woman's palm that showed beneath the shackle. It was laid over the place where the veins ran closest to the surface, and she knew it would be there until the day she died.

She did not know how long she had been gone. It did not

matter. She must act swiftly. The blood already spilled gave her the beginning. She picked up the knife and knelt, steadying herself.

She drew up the magic within and without. It surged in her, remembering the Queen of Heaven's promise and her touch. Words came to Hamsa, and she sketched them in the blood she had spilled. Singing softly under her breath, she brought the magic in and poured it out, weaving its pattern in blood and steel and song. She laid the knife blade, annointed with her blood and enchanted by her working, on the shackles at her wrist. They snapped open at once, and she caught them before they could fall. She treated the shackles on her ankle the same way and caught them too.

"Mothers forgive me," she said as she walked to the statue of A-Kuha the Deceiver. She no longer felt the fear of blasphemy. She had made her bargain. A holy life would not save her from it. Now she had power enough and more. This life was the only one she would ever know. There was a sharp kind of freedom in having neither reward nor punishment to consider, and it made her reckless.

Hamsa snapped the shackles around Mother Destruction's wrists, and wound the chain around her ankles. With the last of her blood, she drew a symbol on the head of the statue, breathing on it and kissing it, tasting clay and iron as she did, breathing her magic out, weaving it into the magic without.

Then she cast the knife onto the floor, grasped the shackled statue, and tipped it over.

The crash was loud, and it brought her guards running, as she had known it would. They walked into the circle of her spell and saw the statues of the Mothers, all as they should be, caught in their dance. They also saw Hamsa, or what they took to be Hamsa, sprawled on the floor, weeping in her despair. They saw the blood and the knife, and Taru, tears shining in his young eyes lifted her to her feet, walking her slowly toward the door. Her chains rattled and dragged and her head sagged down from shame and weariness.

They did not see they walked with a stone. They did not see Hamsa standing in the empty place left by the goddess's statue. Nor would any other. Not even Yamuna. Not this time.

The door closed behind her. She was free. She was dizzy, exultant, drunk with the proof of this new power. Oh, she would have to take care as she never had before. This was the lure of the sorcerer's power, the bane on all of them, the one to which Yamuna had succumbed. Power they had and power they would scrabble for if they were allowed. She felt the taste of it now, wondering already what heights she could reach.

Leave it for now. You are not yet truly free. Neither is Samudra.

That thought steadied her and she stepped from her borrowed place. She would be visible now. Only speed would save her. She undid the red ribbon that bundled her braids and shook them out. She dipped her head down so they became a screen for her face, and calmly she walked out of the temple. The priests had preceded the guard to witness and bless her execution. There was none here to notice her. She snatched down several saffron mantles from their pegs by the door and folded them over her arms in an imitation of laundry to be delivered. She was filthy, but no longer bloody, so she would not attract much attention. Out in the corridor, she hunched herself over further, and walked with determination, one more servant in the palace of servants, invisible in plain sight.

She must hurry. Her illusion would last until Divakesh's sword came down. Fortunately, there was much dance and ritual, many blessings, and a reading of the charges to come before the sword did. She watched the corridor walls for a door that would take her down into the garrison tunnels and scurried ahead.

*I*n his private workroom, Yamuna lifted his head. He felt . . . something. A quiver in the air, a wrongness in the pattern that was the dance. It had a familiar touch to it.

The fool. She's trying again.

With a disgusted sigh, he set aside the scroll he was studying and reached for the jar that held her shadow. Impatiently, he went through the ritual that would draw up the correct magic to make the working, and opened the jar.

And nothing came forth.

Startled, Yamuna drew down the magics more deeply. He faced the opened the jar and held his hand over it, concentrating all the force of his will on his silent command.

And nothing happened. Before him stood an empty jar of dead clay. It held nothing, nothing at all.

Yamuna stared, unable to believe what was before him for a long moment. Then, crying aloud in his fury, he flung the useless vessel across the room. It smashed hard against the wall, but before the shards fell, Yamuna was running down corridor and stairway.

Hamsa had escaped. Somehow, pathetic, weak, cowardly Hamsa had escaped.

*I*n a small wardroom off the garrison tunnels, Makul paced back and forth. He should not be here. He should be up at the altar, standing witness to Hamsa's execution, letting her know that there was at least one friend left to her. But he could not make himself go. Of all the things he had faced in his soldier's life, this failure was too much for him. Samudra had fled, heading toward Sindhu and all that was there. To prevent disaster, Makul had to help the fool Pravan lead a holy war that would only mean the death of innocents and secure the Pearl Throne for an unworthy son.

And there was nothing he could do but hide in the earth like a snake and curse himself.

"Makul." A woman's soft whisper cut through his bitter self-castigation.

Makul whirled around and saw Hamsa standing in front of him, a heap of saffron cloth in her arms. He felt his eyes start from his head and his blood run cold for a foolish moment, as if she were already a ghost. "*Agnidh!* How is this . . . ?"

She smiled. "There's no time, Commander. If you would help the prince we both love, I need a favor of you."

"Whatever I can do."

"Thank you." She came forward, looking over her shoulder to make sure none followed. "Listen." She spoke softly, quickly. "They will soon discover what they execute is an illusion. There will be a great cry and a search. You must be the first to my rooms. There, you will find a black arrow. Do not let anyone take it from you. As soon as you can, you must shoot that arrow due south toward Sindhu. Do you understand?"

"No," said Makul frankly. "But I will do as you say."

"Thank you." She touched his hand, and in return he gripped her fingers for a moment.

"What has happened, Hamsa? Your eyes burn. What demon . . ."

She smiled a little. "No demon, Makul, I swear it. But I must go now. Remember your part and all will be well."

Hamsa was gone in an instant, her bare feet making no sound on the floor. Makul stared at the place where she had been, wondering for a moment if he had imagined the meeting. No. He still felt the warmth of her skin against his fingers. She was alive and had found a way to escape.

Makul smiled and in an instant was running down the corridors, hope filling his heart and propelling him onward. The fight for Hastinapura was not over yet.

Yamuna found the three soldiers leading Hamsa up to the great altar at the foot of Indu's stair. Daylight streamed in through the open door that led from the courtyard.

"Stop!" he bellowed. The three soldiers halted at once. Between them, Hamsa, filthy and trembling, ducked her head.

Yamuna stalked up to her. "What have you done?" he cried. "You created a working to try to escape. Who helped you? What was done?"

Hamsa remained silent.

"Tell me!" Yamuna clouted her hard across the ear. Pain shot up his arm. Hamsa reeled backward but made no cry.

"Tell me!"

Hamsa only shook her head.

Yamuna smashed his fist against the other side of her face, and again the pain was harsh.

This time Hamsa sprawled on the floor. She struggled to her knees, her chains scraping and rattling. She bowed her head again, but still said nothing. Yamuna stood there, his chest heaving. Slowly, with the force of years of discipline, he collected himself. Silence in pain, hiding her face . . .

He seized Hamsa's chin and dragged her head up so she had to look at him, and he saw that the pupils of her wide and frightened eyes were not black, but they were red, red as polished stone.

"Give me your sword," he ordered the nearest soldier.

"But, sir . . ." began the youth.

"Give me your sword!"

The youth gave way and drew his sword, handing it to Yamuna hilt first. He grabbed it and swung it over his head. The thing that wore Hamsa's shape looked up at him with its red eyes, and grinned.

Yamuna cried out again, and brought the sword down on her neck. The head rolled away and the illusion shattered, and the broken image of Mother A-Kuha lay on the floor at his feet.

The guards gaped, first at the broken goddess, and then at Yamuna.

"Find her," he said, his fist tightening around the sword hilt. "Find her!"

The soldiers scrambled to obey, running back into the heart of the palace. Yamuna stayed where he was, his hand clenching the sword and his teeth grinding together. It was not possible and yet it was happening. It occurred vaguely to him that Divakesh would be waiting for his sacrifice. Well, he could wait. He, Yamuna, had told Hamsa her place in the way of things and he would be the one to punish her for breaking the order he had set. When he was done, she would wish she had accepted the priest's sword on her neck.

*W*hen Hamsa felt her illusion shatter, she was already back in her own chamber in front of the dual-goddess altar where she had knelt so many times to contemplate her own despair. So. Yamuna had uncovered her deception a little early. She shook off the thought. She could not afford to dwell on it now.

Hamsa opened one of her few chests of tools. Inside waited skeins of colored silks, cards of needles, and a pair of delicate scissors made of silver and bronze. She caught them up, and with her other hand she seized the bundle of her hair. She had a hundred braids. Each one was a spell, woven during her apprenticeship, woven with clumsy fingers and weak resolve. In the ordinary way, she would have released them one at a time as she received orders or found need. Now, instead, she lifted the scissors and she began to cut away at them, making her hair into a ragged cap, and filling her hand with the tightly made braids. When at last she held all her braids loose in her fist, she laid them on the floor. Her head felt strangely light. A breeze blew against her scalp and shoulders, making her shiver. She laid the scissors aside, picked up the shorn locks of hair, and began to weave them together. She drew her magic out and drew it in, and bound her braids together, making a great spell of so many weaker spells, taking the magic she had shaped so clumsily in her youth, and bending it to a new shape, burning up life and future, all the futures that could ever be. It was wonderful and it was terrible and she could not stop. Sweat poured down her forehead and her hands began to shake, but still she worked, concentrating on her breathing, focusing on each movement of her fingers, feeling the forces within and without slip into place and seal together.

When she was finished, she held a girdle before her. Swiftly, she looped the black netting around her waist and tied it with the red silk band that had once pulled these braids back from her face. For an instant, she felt the prick and itch of her own hair against her skin. Then, her heart labored for three beats and stopped. She fell to the floor, stiff as wood. Pain racked her as her arms slapped against her side, and her legs squeezed together, pressing, fusing, binding, sealing. Her throat closed, sight left her, and pain and all sensation followed, and then there was only peace, and slow, slow patience.

Yamuna strode underneath the archway when the blow of the working reached him and sent him reeling back against the wall. It was as if the whole of the palace had been shaken and turned. Servants and guards scurried past, eyes down, intent on their own errands, and trying their hardest not to notice him.

Yamuna found his stride again and continued to his rooms. Who was doing this? It could not be Hamsa. She was not strong enough to even dream of such power.

When he arrived in his chamber, about half the palace sorcerers were already assembled, their eyes wide with fear and confusion. They had felt it too. Even sheep could feel a windstorm, and of course they had come here to find out what it meant. They were well trained, all of them.

"Where is this done?" he shouted at them. "Find the worker!"

Now that they had orders, they moved quickly, forming themselves into a circle. Threads of silk were removed from pockets and satchels, and cast out onto the floor with ancient chants washing over all, as the magic was drawn in and drawn out. The air in the room went cold at once with magic and fear, catching up the threads, directing their fall, forming them into the required symbol. The threads drifted to the floor, and Yamuna stared in pure, stupefied disbelief.

This working that shook the air around them came from the small domain. Only one sorcerer resided there, and it was Hamsa. In her own chamber. It was she who bent all the dance of the palace to her own needs.

Without another word Yamuna turned and ran, and all the stunned sorcerers stayed where they were. Without orders from their master, not one of them dared move.

*I*t was truth that got Makul into the small domain. The eunuch guards crossed their pole arms to bar his way as he came tearing up the stairs, sword at his hip and bow slung across his shoulder.

"The sorceress has escaped!" he cried. "The prince's rooms must be secured at once!"

Startled soldiers would frequently obey the loudest order. These four were no different. He ran ahead through the gates, and they formed up at once to follow him.

As a boy, Makul had lived for a time in the small domain, and he still remembered its ways, so he did not have to waste time wandering the gilt and ivory maze. The prince's rooms stood behind the queen's suite, and the sorceress's next to those. The door was closed, but not locked. Makul burst in. At first glance, the chambers were empty and silent, but there on the floor in front of the shrine lay the black arrow, as Hamsa had promised.

"Search the room," he ordered. He did not want to give them time to think they had let a whole man into this most protected of all places. "And the prince's rooms. Hurry!"

Still bewildered and obedient, the guards scattered. Makul scooped the arrow up from the floor. The shaft was strangely warm, almost as if it were living flesh. That idea worried him and he pushed it aside. He too had his orders and his duty.

He stowed the arrow in the empty quiver hanging at his waist. One of the eunuchs had come back, to report, or to challenge him. He did not give the guard time to speak.

"Alert the others. The ring must be made secure."

His orders held once more. Outside he could hear the babble of women's voices, a blur of questions growing increasingly urgent and fearful. Bandhura would be down from the imperial ring in a moment and he would no longer remain unchallenged. Makul hurried through the door that connected Hamsa's rooms with the prince's. There was one terrace in this ring that had no lattice covering it, and that was the one that belonged to the prince's private rooms. He could carry out Hamsa's directive from there.

"Makul!" a harsh voice shouted at his back. Yamuna.

Makul did not break stride or turn. He strode through the empty rooms and out onto the balcony. The cool bulk of the mountain rose up green behind him, making a ragged living wall, but to the south there was a narrow gap through which shone a sliver of blue sky.

Makul unslung his bow and tested the string. He had gotten no further than that when Yamuna stalked through the archway. Makul had never paid the sorcerer much attention. He was a special sort of servant—a tool, an aide, and that was all. This once, though, Makul saw the man fully. He saw the concealed menace in his lean form and the hunger and anger blazing in his eyes. Makul cursed himself for a fool. A soldier should know who the enemy was.

"Commander Makul, give me that arrow," said Yamuna softly, reasonably. "It is to be used for betrayal. Surely such a loyal servant of the Throne as yourself cannot now betray it."

"No, *Agnidh*." Makul took up the black arrow.

"Then you are a traitor, Makul." The sorcerer stepped forward. He wound his fingers around one of the hundred braids in his hair. A hundred braids, every one a working of protection for the emperor, so Makul had heard, and his heart thudded shamefully. "Give me the arrow, and you will have an easier death than you should."

Makul did not waste breath on a reply. He fitted the arrow into the string.

With one swift yank, Yamuna tore the braid from his scalp and held the bloody thing up for Makul to see for a moment before he cast it to the floor, where it lay, its grey strands unraveling.

All at once, Makul felt his heart laboring to beat, and he knew what spell of protection Yamuna had loosed on him. Sweat sprung out on his skin, and the world began to blur before his eyes.

No. Not my eyes. I must see. He blinked hard.

Pain. It licked at him like a flame, creeping up his shins, through his groin, into his belly and his chest. He heard sounds of struggle behind him. Weakness took his knees, and again the world blurred.

No. He shook his head, and bent his leg under him, raising the bow high, pointing the arrow south toward Sindhu.

His heart and breath froze. His hands shuddered.

Mother Jalaja guide my hand.

Yamuna snickered and lunged forward, but even though his eyes could not see, Makul's arm remembered what to do. His fingers let go, and he felt the arrow fly. For one dazzling moment, he saw a line of fire traced across the blackness that was his world.

With that burning image before him, and Yamuna's screams in his ears, Makul fell to the floor and died.

Chapter Twenty-one

For seven nights of the waxing moon, Natharie and Samudra sailed down the sacred river. Shadows of cities gave way to farmland, which in turn gave way to the crooked shadows of trees as they passed into the deep forest. During the day, they came to shore and hid their boat as best they could and snatched some sleep beneath the sheltering arms of the banyans and mangroves. Twice, Natharie in her man's guise went into tiny villages to barter for rice and salt. The rest of the time they relied on what Samudra could catch from the river with line and hook. He seemed confused by the fact that the ban on eating flesh did not extend to fish, and Natharie did not have the nimbleness of mind left to explain the reasoning behind it.

In truth, they did not speak much. Both were locked in their silent sorrows. Each tried to give the other some room to grieve the betrayals that had been committed against them, as well as those they had been forced to commit. The river remained kind, and what boats they did see in the night either were benign or were also on clandestine errands and their owners had no heart to make trouble for others.

Strangely, instead of keeping them separate, their silence seemed to be bringing them closer together. By the seventh day, Natharie found she could understand the meaning in a glance of Samudra's, and that he could do the same with her. She knew she could pick out his silhouette in the dark, and she found herself watching him more and more often. The way he sat, the way he scrubbed at his neck when he did not like the tenor of his own thoughts. Sometimes, he swam alongside the boat, to get clean or exercise himself, and he was as strong and graceful as a porpoise in the ocean. One day while they slept, her faint dreams grew restless, and when she opened her eyes, she was looking directly into Samudra's. His breath was fast and shallow and she knew he had been watching her sleep for some long time. It was the weight of his gaze that had touched her heart and woke her.

She did not forget that every day they drew nearer to her home, where Samudra was the enemy, or that behind them an army was advancing to attack and destroy all she knew. But for this space of time on the sacred river, it did not seem to matter as much. Sindhu and Hastinapura were elsewhere. Here were only Samudra and Natharie, and Samudra was kind and honorable and when he looked on Natharie a warmth spread from her heart into her veins, a warmth that she was less and less willing to deny.

Dawn came on the eighth day, and as was their custom they scanned the shores for a place to beach the boat. They found a shallow, muddy bank between two great palms. The vegetation had been changing, as had the touch of the air. It was heavier here, a more comfortable garment to wear than the thin stuff up in Hastinapura's mountains. Palms and other familiar trees grew more closely together. All these things told Natharie that if they had not yet crossed Sindhu's borders, they would soon. Still, she could not bring herself to say this to Samudra. She did not want to face home and family and war. Not yet.

Samudra drew the boat up onto the bank and unstepped the mast, something at which he had become quite good over the past days. While he gathered branches, leaves, and fronds with which to cover the tiny vessel and hide it from any passing boats, Natharie started inland, looking both for signs of habitation and for a place where they could spend the day in some semblance of safety.

The forest was thick here, and the songs of insects, birds, and frogs blended into a never-ending cacophony. Ferns towered higher than her head. Green snakes hung like ripe fruits in the trees and watched her with beady, black eyes as she passed. She walked carefully, for her overly delicate sandals had broken days ago and she now went barefoot. So when one sole brushed something strange, she drew back at once. Underneath the forest litter, she saw a flat, black stone. Ahead of it was another, and there was another after that, leading in a straight line away from her.

Natharie took the knife from her trouser sash and notched two nearby trees with arrows pointing the way back to the shore. Then, moving as cautiously as she knew how, she followed the sporadic path of stones, stopping occasionally to mark her way.

She nearly stumbled over the temple. The rains and the forest had had their way with it. The wall beams had fallen. Ferns and moss and bright white shelves of fungus had overgrown them. Leaves and old palm fronds made a carpet for the floor, which sprouted a few mushrooms of its own. The stone and clay altar had fared a little better. Moss grew here too, turning it a uniform green and obscuring any words or symbols that once might have been written there. The visage of the god or goddess was all but worn away. All that remained was a cross-legged torso with a few shreds of gilding clinging to its robes. A broken hand lay at its feet. One moss-green finger pointed at Natharie.

Natharie made obeisance out of respect to whatever power this shrine had been made to honor. Her first thought was to leave the place, but the floor was smoother than the surrounding ground, and the branches were thinner overhead, meaning there was less danger here from either snakes or the great cats that stalked from branch to branch.

Samudra, when she fetched him to the place, agreed.

"I think whatever god was here must have found other worshippers now, or perhaps taken another aspect," he said. "There are ancient temples all over Hastinapura. Some of them are carved from whole cliffs, and are a wonder to look on." He made the salute of trust to the remains of the altar god. "We are travelers asking shelter in this place. We honor the memory of what is holy here."

No answer came, but neither did any sense of foreboding. This place was simply a place. Soon they were gathering dried litter, sticks, and branches to light a fire to hold back the mosquitoes and other predators so that they could sleep.

But sleep would not come to Natharie. She could not even lie down. She hunched by their meager fire watching the flames dance and hearing the warning song of the insects that flew close enough to investigate. Samudra stretched out and she hoped he would sleep, but he did not. After only a few moments, he sat up. He was so close, she could have reached out to touch him. But of course she did not. She could not.

"What is it, Natharie?" he asked softly.

She sighed and tugged at the winding cloth of her cap. The thing itched. She itched. "We are nearly to my home," she said, in a tone almost petulant, as if she were a child who did not want her outing to end.

"I know it."

She should say something. She must say something. She would burst if she did not. But which of the thousand things in her could she say? "You have . . . you have behaved kindly toward me and with honor since we met, and I have never thanked you for these things."

Samudra smiled at this. It was a soft, real smile that warmed his eyes. "You did. You waited for me when I needed you to."

There were so many answers to that—polite, innocuous, pious answers—but somehow she could not draw breath to utter any of them. In this place, if never again, only the truth would come to her. "I wanted to."

"I'm glad," he whispered.

Their gazes met, as they had countless times on this strange, silent journey, and she saw the weariness in him. He was as tired as she was. Tired of duty, tired of trying again and again to accomplish something, anything, only to have that effort fall to ashes because of the plots and plans of others. He too had been abandoned by his family and in his loneliness had reached out to a soul that he prayed might understand.

She did understand. In that moment by the fire, looking into his dark eyes, she understood perfectly. She leaned forward, and she kissed him.

His response was warm and immediate and it went through her like the pure light of the sun at midday.

It was a stupid, blind, unreasoning thing she did now, and part of her mind tried to stop her, but stronger and more urgent was the heat of his mouth, the salt taste of his skin, the warmth of that skin beneath her hands, the shape of arms and shoulders and chest. She wanted nothing else, not future, not love, not life itself. She wanted this, and this, and this and she would have it. She would have all she wanted, all they wanted, this once, and she would rejoice in it.

And so their night passed in alternating moments of desire and sleep, and neither felt the eyes of the gods or the turn of the wheel around them.

*T*hanom, the father abbot of the monks of Sindhu, lifted his head. He sat in the monastery garden beneath fronds of green bamboo, breathing in the peace of sunlight and shadow, and allowing himself a little regret for having to leave this ancient and beautiful grove. The wheel was turning. He felt it in the movement of the air, in the fall of the sunlight. He felt it in the power that hummed constantly through the air.

It is time. The words spoke themselves calmly in his mind. They might have been his own thoughts, or those of some entity outside. To Thanom at that moment, it did not much matter. They were the truth. He could feel it in every particle of himself.

What those such as Queen Sitara could not feel when they came here was the thousand thousand threads that wove through the ether, binding each sorcerer to the whole of Sindhu. The mandala she had seen was nothing but a way to make those threads visible, distilling and concentrating the awareness that each sorcerer here carried. This was how they lived out the Great Teacher's edict, with constant awareness of all the land around them, of all lives and all actions. This was why their meditation must be so deep and so profound, so that all the awareness did not overwhelm mind and soul. They were apart here, yes, but they were not isolated as most thought. For it was one of the truths of sorcery that when one knew, one was also known, wholly and completely and forever, and there was nowhere to hide, not even inside one's own soul. As a result, they were terribly, constantly exposed.

This was what he could not find words to explain to the queen; that it was to escape the trepidation and responsibility brought by constant awareness that might drive some of the cloistered to betray Sindhu and Anidita's teaching and join with Hastinapura. The worship of the Mothers could lead to extremes of action, but those actions were voluntary. Here, there was no choice. A sorcerer must give all of himself, or herself, and if they broke under the strain, that was as it must be.

Well, now we act with all that we have known and with all that has come to know us. Thanom stood, folding his hands. *And it has yet to be judged whether we act correctly.*

Thanom was not the only one to feel the shift in the ethereal weaving around them. The other monks filed into the garden. Even the cook, his hands still white with rice flour, left his kitchen, nodding to the abbot as he passed. The meal no longer mattered. It would not be needed.

On the other side of the wall, the nuns followed the same path, all moving toward the mandala house.

Was the mother abbess also afraid? Thanom felt the fine sheen of perspiration on his brow. He had hoped he would be more composed for this day, but now that it had come, doubt crept into his heart.

It does not matter, he told himself. *A forest of doubts would not matter. We have set this wheel in motion and we can do nothing but turn with it.*

Thanom joined the procession, walking with measured tread to the mandala house. It was the center of all life here, and as they drew nearer, the threads that bound them all grew tighter tying each sorcerer's heartbeat, each breath together with the world around them. He sensed the ones within the mandala house, whom he could not yet see with eyes. They stood in their circle, their great song rising up and filling the air. One by one the monks in their procession joined in the great chant, swelling it with their voices and supporting it with their will, with their trained minds, and the magic they drew up from their own souls. Over the wall, the lighter voices of the nuns lifted up in chorus and that which was female joined with that which was male. The threads spun and twined together, and their weaving became whole.

The pitch of the song changed, and the winding and touch of the threads changed with it. They loosened, looped around to the winds and the world at large, to gain consent and cooperation and blessing for what must come. The monks moved forward and with great care, unfastened the panels of paper and wood that made up the walls of the mandala house and laid them aside. The nuns did the same, and now there was only a wooden roof supported by four poles. The song from within melded that of without as they stood and joined the ring of their fellows that circled the stone floor where the great mandala waited.

Again the song changed, and again the threads shifted, catching up song and sand, intention and acceptance, and at their feet, the mandala that was Sindhu made with countless days of work, discipline, and song.

Tears sprang into his eyes. Thanom knelt and reached out

his hand. With one swipe, he scooped up a handful of sand, and the mandala was torn open.

He tossed the sand into the air, and the power of the song caught it, whirling it around, drawing the remaining sand up behind it, making a swirl of color in the air now, turning and blooming and stretching out into a blanket in all the colors of earth and sky. It surrounded the singers, wrapping them in its folds, pushing the old world, the other world, away. At its heart was a road of shimmering silver. It stretched into the rings and swirls and ripples of color and none could see its end.

Still singing, Father Thanom set foot upon the silver road. In ordered lines behind him came the monks and nuns. They would walk the shifting lands and here they would create a haven for the innocent and helpless. All those who could not or would not take up arms in this war would be sheltered by the workings of the sorcerers. It would take all their strength to create that haven and hold it safe. One by one, just as they had entered, they would falter and their souls be borne away to the next life. Perhaps some would return to this life before them, but Thanom did not believe it likely. It was all right. An ending could be as sweet as a beginning, and an ending that preserved and nurtured life was the sweetest one of all.

Their song settled about them, holding back the swirl of chaos all around and solidifying the road beneath them. All the sorcerers of Sindhu walked into the lands between life and death on that road of song, which carried them forward to the work they had chosen.

*T*hen, the great miracle happened across Sindhu.

It happened in each town, in each farming village, beside each fishing boat that floated on the sacred river. In the rice paddies and the workshops and the prisons. In each place, a monk and a nun appeared, always a pair together. They came from nowhere. They came with folded hands and serene faces, and the people who saw them fell to their knees in wonder.

"Come with us," they sang. "Come with us, for the war is come to the land and we will take you to safety. Come with us."

Women and children came, driving the smallest of the livestock with them, men came with the cows and bulls, the oldest and the youngest came, and the sorcerers went before them, singing the words of praise, of making and of binding, and as they sang the people saw the silver road from beneath their feet and they stepped onto it, their faces slack with wonder. The world opened before them and closed behind them, and it was the song that kept them from fear, and from thinking to look behind.

They came to the palace and gathered up all those who were not soldiers there, walking the weeping queen and her wide-eyed children onto the silver road, singing to soothe the heart, singing to pause the life of form and of fear so all that was seen and all that was felt was as a distant dream to those who now ran onto the silver road to escape the nightmare of war. Singing so that the road would hold and safely harbor all the lives they took into their charge. Sindhu's sorcerers walked singing from the world, and they took Sindhu's people with them. Behind them, the ethereal gateways closed and left no trace of their being.

Chapter Twenty-two

"Natharie." Samudra's voice was so gentle, her waking mind heard it only as a playful whisper. She opened her eyes and saw the world around them grey with evening. Their fire was only a few smoldering ashes. Samudra propped up on his elbow, leaning over her, but not looking at her. He stared at the altar. She turned to follow his gaze with her own, and saw the snake.

It was huge, rearing back to expose its death-pale belly. Its hood was spread wide and its tongue flicked in and out, tasting the air, tasting the fear that welled up in Natharie as she saw its shining black eyes.

Samudra's gaze flicked down, and Natharie's did the same. The snake was not alone. Its mate lay full-length on the temple floor, twined in intimate communion with its fellow, who towered protectively over it, even as Samudra had risen over Natharie.

Move, and I strike, the serpent seemed to say. *Do not move, and I strike.*

"My sword," breathed Samudra. "Your cap."

Natharie understood. She did not lift herself. On her belly, as if she were a snake herself, she slowly eased backward, moving less than an inch at a time. The serpents watched unblinking. The risen one swayed as if uncertain what this meant. Its mate also watched, tongue flicking impatiently. Did it taste the quality of the fear? Natharie stretched her hand out, slowly, slowly, slowly to reclaim the length of linen she had cast aside carelessly.

You kin of the nagas, *you children of earth, we meant no disrespect. We wished only shelter. We will depart if you will but permit.* Her fingers clutched the cloth and pulled it toward her, slowly, slowly, slowly.

Samudra stayed where he was, still as stone, matching his gaze with the serpent's. The cobra swayed and opened its mouth, displaying its great fangs. Samudra drew back, just a little. This seemed to satisfy the snake, and it shut its mouth, but it did not close its great hood or drop down beside its mate.

Where is the sword? Sweat stung Natharie's eyes. Her hair fell across her face, a black curtain tickling cheek, nose, and chin. She was terrified she would sneeze, and bit her lips so hard she tasted blood.

She spotted the sword hilt not far away to her right. Still flat on her belly, she inched her hand toward it. She wore her tunic, but her legs were naked and the sharp edges of the palm fronds cut into her skin. The serpent's mate hissed loud and sudden, and jerked back. Samudra started, and the serpent lunged faster than sight, and sank its fangs into his arm.

Samudra screamed in pain and horror and Natharie's cry echoed his. She snatched up the sword, but it was too late. The serpents were already gone, and on Samudra's forearm, two beads of scarlet blood formed.

Natharie raised the blade at once, ready to bring it down, to sever his arm and cut the poison off, but Samudra lifted his hand, which was already shaking.

"No. Not with the bite of these snakes," he said quietly. "We have no way to bind or burn the wound before this poison reaches my breath. I would just die from the loss of blood."

The sword fell clattering to the broken stones and Natharie's arms dropped useless to her sides.

"What can we do?"

"Sit with me," said Samudra. "Be . . . be here."

She knelt. She felt . . . she felt too many things. She wanted to scream, to cry, to snatch Samudra up in her arms and love him with all the fervor that filled her pounding heart. Instead, her trembling hands took up the length of linen and wiped his blood away.

Samudra also knelt. He had gone as pale as the serpent's belly. Sweat beaded his brow, but that would not last. Soon, he would be cold. Then, his breath would leave him, dried away by the poison that now coursed through his blood.

"This is what you must do," he said quietly. "You must gather what food you can and take to the river. You must not come ashore again until you reach safety . . ."

"Stop." Natharie choked out the word. *Compose yourself. You cannot let his last sight be of you suffering.* "Save your breath. If you must speak, you should pray."

Samudra smiled weakly. "From the Awakened woman I get this advice?"

She swallowed hard. She would be strong. Although her whole soul screamed because the last resting place for heart and hope was being torn from her, she would not break. Not yet.

"We are neither of us fit for this death," she answered him, wondering at the steadiness in her own voice. "Think on Heaven, my prince. Let what powers will come know you died in what holiness you could find."

He closed his eyes and nodded his head. The first of the spasms shook him, and he coughed. "Then, let me ask this one thing of you."

"What is it, Samudra?"

"Marry me."

Her hand flew to her mouth to stop the hysterical laugh that threatened to bubble out. "Samudra, don't . . ." But his face was strained, the paleness already giving way to deathly grey. The sweat dripped from his brow to his bare chest. She could see his ribs laboring to rise and fall.

"How can we marry?" she asked, trying to stay calm. "We have no one to officiate."

His smile was pained, but real. "As first prince, I can make any marriage my brother does not contradict."

She swallowed again. This was ludicrous. Samudra's life could be measured in heartbeats. There was no time for such a sham.

But would it be a sham? She had given herself to him. She had felt love as well as passion. She felt it now, in her sickened heart, and in the way the tears pressed behind her eyes as he coughed again. She wanted him to live. She wanted to talk with him and walk and fight beside him. She wanted to see him on the Pearl Throne where he belonged, and she wanted to stand with him in front of her parents and show them that all was right, for Sindhu, for her.

She was wasting time. "Yes, Samudra. I will marry you."

He closed his eyes, and she saw his mouth shape words of thanks. Then he coughed, hard, and his eyes opened, startled and in pain.

"We . . ." He drew in a ragged breath. "We need a circle around the fire."

Natharie fed the coals until the flames rose once more. Then, using a charred stick, she scraped the black circle as Samudra directed, adding clumsy symbols of blessing and fertility at the cardinal points. By the time she had finished, the sweat had dried on Samudra's brow. His skin drew tight across his cheeks and his fingers were thin and sharp.

"Kneel beside me," he whispered, and Natharie did. His skin gave off no warmth. She picked up her wrap and laid it across his shoulders. He clutched it to his chest, and his hand shook, and it shook again as he raised his palm over the dying fire.

"By the blessing of the Mothers, I Samudra *tya* Achin Ireshpad do beg Mother Harsha who is the Queen of Increase and Mother Jalaja who is the Queen of Heaven, to witness and bless what I do now say." His voice quavered and his words were lost in a fit of coughing that sapped his strength for a moment and left him leaning against her, gasping for air. Then, with apology in his eyes, he straightened himself up and went on. "That I, Son of the Moon and First Prince of Hastinapura, do give Samudra *tya* Achin Ireshpad to the great princess, Natharie Somchai of Sindhu. I'm sorry," he added in a whisper. "I . . . have forgotten any words of the Awakened One."

"All is right, Samudra," she whispered in answer, cradling his head against her shoulder. "It is enough."

Samudra kissed her. Natharie returned the kiss, willing the heat of her blood and body into him, willing the pain and poison to pass into her own, stronger flesh. When at last they could each bear it, they separated. Samudra met her eyes. He was trembling. His breath wheezed in his throat, but his face was calm.

"Now I can pray."

Natharie helped him turn toward the altar. She lifted his hands and helped him press them together. He was so cold. He trembled like a plucked string. He bowed his head, in reverence or because he no longer had the strength to hold it upright, Natharie couldn't tell.

"Forgive me, Mother Vimala," he whispered. "These are your creatures, I know . . . I . . . I was too weak. Forgive me."

Tears in her eyes, Natharie sat cross-legged beside him, cupping one hand inside the other. She strove to calm her mind. This was now her husband beside her. She loved him. She did love him. Whether she should or she should not, the wheel had turned and this was her place. It was her last duty to help bring him as close to Heaven as she could. She could not do that filled with rage and tormented disdain at this injustice, or carrying the fear that this was just punishment for her all her sins and failings.

Where water, earth, heat, air no footing find. She heard the words of the benediction clearly in her heart.

There burns not any light, nor shines the Sun.
The Moon sheds not her radiant beams.
The home of Darkness is not there.

Her fingers moved, telling the beads that had been gone so long. In her heart she heard them, clicking back and forth, counting heartbeats, counting breaths, sending the world slipping away.

When deep in silent hours of thought
The holy sage to Truth attains.
He is free from joy and pain,
From form and formless worlds released.

Over and over she repeated the words in the silence of her mind. All other awareness fell away. Her breath grew deep and easy. Warmth rose from the center of her being, cradling her heart and mind, relaxing her, driving out fear and anger, leaving only peace and strength.

Distantly, she heard a cough, and the shuffling thump as Samudra fell. She was not startled. She opened her eyes, and rose to come by his head, which she lifted and cradled in her lap. He shook. His lips were blue. It was a miracle he had not fallen before. He looked up at her in fear.

"Peace, peace, my husband," she whispered. "Think on Heaven. It is here. I am here."

"I do not want to leave you." She could barely hear the words for the wheezing and straining. His breath was cold and foul. Her heart, so calm, so poised in its meditations, quietly and surely broke in two.

"It's all right," she told him softly, covering his cold hands with her warm ones. "Just rest a little. I'll be right here."

Hope dawned in his pain-racked eyes. "Just rest a little."

"Yes, husband. Close your eyes." She laid her palm over his eyes, shutting out the cruel beams of the setting sun, the sight of the whining, stinging insects gathering like vultures at the scent of death. "It's all right."

She felt the gentle brush of Samudra's lashes against her palm as his eyelids, trembling, closed.

"I . . ." His breath was coming hard now, his whole frame straining. Natharie held him hard and tight, trying to ease the shudders. "I love . . ." But the words were lost in retching and whooping gasps that did no good. His chest no longer moved, his mouth gaped, his eyes stared in horror at death and his throat choked for air that it could not draw. Natharie held him close and hard. His shudders racked her, and his flailing hand clawed her face, and she felt the blood run free but she did not let go.

Between one heartbeat and the next, Samudra relaxed so completely that Natharie was pulled forward by the sudden weight and fell gracelessly across him. When she scrambled back, she saw his eyes were closed. As she watched, they opened again, slowly, smoothly. Samudra's eyes stared out at Heaven, and Natharie knew she was alone.

Natharie screamed. She beat the rotting floor with her fists. All the strength, all the peace she had been able to call upon fled with Samudra's life. There was only the weakness and rage of an animal that has lost its mate. Tears mixed with blood on her face as she pounded her own breast, babbling her inconsolate grief to Heaven.

In her rage she leapt up and grabbed a branch and hammered on the altar. "Come out! Come out!" she screamed to the hidden serpents. "Come take me! I'll crush your skulls with my bare feet before I join him! Come out!"

But her strength had already been sorely taxed, and her stinging hands had to drop the branch and her weakened knees had to collapse and she could do nothing but weep. At last, even her tears ran dry, and she crouched there in the shadow of the altar, dry and hollow. Gently, the peace that death had stolen came back to her.

She stood. She bowed toward the altar. She walked calmly back to the river and carried water in a bowl to wash Samudra's body. She closed his eyes and laid him out straight and neat. She lacked the strength to dress him properly, so she drew his loose trouser-wrappings over him like a blanket so that he was decently covered.

The soul of those who have just died was a heavy thing, the sages taught. It carried its weight of earthly concerns and hatreds. It would cling to the world of form for three days, while such things drained away into the earth from which they came. Only then could the soul become light enough for death to carry to the other world to be joined with itself in the Land of Death and Spirit. Until then, the dead one could not be left alone, lest the soul, terrified and heavy, sink back into the body and try to live again, creating a foul ghoul.

To prevent this, someone, ideally a monk, had to sit with body and soul, and soothe them by singing of peace and Heaven. There was no monk here, there was only herself.

She crossed her legs and rested her hands on her knees, and she began to sing.

When deep in silent hours of thought
The holy sage to Truth attains.
He is free from joy and pain,
From form and formless worlds released.

Be at peace, my husband. Be free. Be free.

Twilight closed over on the living and the dead, and Natharie began the hymn again.

*P*onderously, the great army of Hastinapura marched across Sindhu's plain.

It was a grand and glittering sight, moving to the sound of horns and drums and the endless tramping of thousands of feet on the clear, dry roads. The elephants were painted red with symbols of death and fortune. Their gilded tusks shone in the fierce sunlight. Banners fluttered in the humid breeze, showing themselves red, blue, saffron, and green, all proclaiming that the emperor came as warrior, that the Mothers looked down from Heaven and the earth should tremble. Before all, the priests carried the image of Queen Indu, Mother of War, riding on her tiger's back, brandishing her sword and shield, her head thrown back so that she might howl out triumph over all enemies.

Behind her came the emperor's golden chariot, drawn by four horses, two snow white and two obsidian black. Chandra, in the gilded armor and golden crown surmounted by the great ruby that pulsed like a living thing when sunlight touched it, stood behind his driver.

But to witness all this strength and glory, there was no one at all.

Pravan sent ahead outrider after outrider and all came back with the same news. The countryside was abandoned.

What little livestock there was wandered freely about the fields. Doors hung open and wild animals had already been scavenging in pantries and storage pits left full and unsecured. It was clear that the land had been empty of humanity for at least several days.

Pravan reported all this to the emperor as they camped for the night beside a silent pilgrims' hostel. The imperial party took over what had been the main common room, a plain, square chamber with worn wooden floors and bare walls. When they had arrived, those walls had been covered with tapestries and banners, all of which Divakesh had immediately declared anathema and ordered to be burnt. His underpriests, an increasingly nervous and pale cadre, had hurried to obey.

"So!" cried Divakesh when Pravan finished delivering his latest report. "All the Awakened could do when the Mothers came to them was run!"

Pravan risked a glance up. The emperor was sitting crosslegged on the elaborate divan that had been set up for him, and in contrast to Divakesh, he looked thoughtful. "Are you sure, my lord Divakesh?" Emperor Chandra asked.

"What else could it be?" The priest's eyes shone as he looked out the open window and across the silent, empty countryside. "It is a sign from the Mothers. We will not even meet any resistance as we carry their will forward. It is the final sign that we have done right."

The emperor nodded and turned to his sorcerer. "What do you say, Yamuna?"

Instead of the sorcerer's usual tart reply Yamuna pressed his lips together, making a thin, straight line of his mouth. "Some great thing has happened here, my emperor. What it is, I cannot say." He also looked toward one of the open windows, but instead of declaring triumph, his nostrils flared as if he caught some scent the rest of them could not detect. "It should also be remembered that it was a great thing that allowed *Agnidh* Hamsa to escape."

"You say it was great only because you were unable to prevent it," sneered Divakesh.

"Yes," said Yamuna calmly, but his eyes promised payment. "Yes, that is why I say it was great."

"It was the Mothers teaching you humility in your power, *Agnidh*." Divakesh raised his hand. "It is another sign that they walk close to us during this time of destiny."

Pravan shifted his weight. He had seen men look like the high priest before. It came when the battle had been too hard and too long and yet they must be sent into the fray again. It was the look of a man who had traveled so far beyond his own fear that he was no longer fully within his own soul. There were rumors murmured around the fires, that the Queen of Heaven had come down to look on her priest, and she had been displeased with what she saw. They said that was why Mother Jalaja had spirited away *Agnidh* Hamsa. They said *Agnidh* Yamuna had gone to the emperor in a rage and demanded he delay the march until Hamsa could be found, and that the emperor, gripped by Divakesh's madness, had refused.

Pravan silenced these whenever he heard them. He had even killed three men for speaking treason and blasphemy. But the rumors persisted, and when Pravan stood beside the priest and looked into Divakesh's shining eyes, in his heart he believed them.

For this moment, though, Pravan envied Divakesh. He wanted his certainty back, even if it came at the price of madness. When they found Makul dead on the prince's terrace and heard Yamuna telling the full tale of the old commander's treachery, Pravan had felt triumphant. Now he had the rank he had always desired. There was none over him save the emperor, and the emperor listened to his opinion in all things. Now the wealth would come, and the wives and the lands. All things would come as soon as this very little war was over.

But the farther they marched into this ghost of a country,

the more worried Pravan became. Right now he would have given his sword and his right arm to speak with Makul, whom he'd spurned before as cautious to the point of cowardice. But Makul was dead, and the officers he had carefully chosen to command the ranks underneath him responded to his fear with fear of their own and looked to him for orders.

Pravan made the soldier's salute to his emperor and the Mothers' priest and turned away, heading for the small city of tents where the soldiers were quartered. He would not sleep tonight, he knew. He would send out more outriders, and they would come back with the same news, but he would send them anyway, because it was all he could do.

Chapter Twenty-three

The water bowl was dry. It was the third day since Samudra had died. Natharie no longer had the strength to chant. She needed to concentrate on breathing. The heat was a weight, pressing against her head and chest. Even filtered by the forest's branches, the sun burned where it touched her. The welts raised by the biting insects were beginning to ooze. Her lips had begun to crack. Sometimes she thought she heard voices, whispering and buzzing in the trees. Sometimes she wanted to go and find them, but she did not think she could move. She had long ago ceased to feel her legs. There was only a painful tingle now and then.

She pulled her thoughts back to the hymns. That was all that mattered. When the sun went down, it would be the last night. When the sun came up, it would be over. It would be all over.

She is free from joy and pain,
From form and formless worlds released.

There was something wrong with that repetition, but Natharie could not think what it was. There was something else wrong, something outside, something beside her, but she could not think what that might be. Samudra still lay beside her, as peaceful beneath his cloak as if he were asleep. For two days he had lain there and she had sat here, and she had seen what she had seen and done what she had done, and something was wrong.

It didn't matter. All that mattered was releasing her husband's soul to the next world. That was her task. All else had to wait.

She is free from joy and pain,
From form and formless worlds released.

"She sleeps, she sleeps," hissed a voice.

Painfully, Natharie opened her eyes. She did not realize she had closed them. Dully, she saw her death in front of her.

The serpents had returned.

One rose up in the noble pose, its hood unspread. Just looking about, seeing what was there. The other, the female, for she was the smaller of the two, slid forward, her tongue tasting the air.

"She sleeps, but she wakes," said the male. "But she sleeps."

The female gave a series of short hisses that might have been laughter and glided up to Natharie, circling her. The snake's hide grazed her toes. Natharie could only watch it. Her heart hammered hard in her chest, but it seemed a thousand miles away. She could feel nothing of the snake's caress at all and that only increased her fear.

"And this one?" said the female, slipping up to Samudra, and raising herself up as her mate did to inspect him. "What of this one?"

Natharie tried to speak, and failed, and tried again. "No," she croaked. Her lips split painfully as she formed the word. "You have killed him already. Leave us be."

"We have killed him?" The male pulled back, his tongue flickering fast. "Who came to our home? Who built the fire that called to us with its warmth?"

Natharie closed her eyes again. Her throat was swollen with thirst. She could not think. She could not understand why the serpents would speak to her now when they had said so little before.

She made herself open her eyes again. The female leaned forward and glided across Samudra's chest. Natharie cried out wordlessly and raised her numb hand. The male hissed his warning, but not to his mate, to Natharie. She froze, and to her shame let her hand fall.

"I like this one," said the female, flicking her tongue against Samudra's cheek. "I want it."

"No," croaked Natharie again. Her mouth was bleeding. She could taste it. Her tongue was like leather. "I beg you."

The male's hood spread out, just a little, just another gentle warning, and he slipped forward. "And who are you to deny my wife this?" he asked, his voice full of quiet danger.

"He is my husband," said Natharie. "I am his wife. Leave us in peace."

"Ahhhhh!" sighed the male. The female continued her trek across Samudra's chest, slipping off his body on the near side, and gliding around his head, stroking him with her long, lithe body. "Perhaps you will make a bargain for him, then."

"Why do you do this?" Her voice cracked, high and sharp. "He is dead too long, you can't . . ." Her words fell away, and the snakes looked up at Natharie, suddenly perfectly still.

Dead. Dead three days in the heat and the damp of the forest. Dead with the flies and mosquitoes drinking her blood, but not his. Around him, there were no flies. There was no stench. The body had not corrupted at all.

Natharie's breath was suddenly coming hard and fast. A buzzing began in her ears and the world swam in front of her eyes. That was what was wrong. Samudra lay beside her as perfect and whole as he had been when he fell. If he was dead, how could this be?

And what had the serpent said, she was asleep, but she was awake but she was asleep . . . what power, what enchantment surrounded her? This was not the madness of thirst. This was more. This was the gods or the demons, come to taunt, to tempt. Samudra had called the snakes the creatures of Mother Vimala. This was the other world brought to the opening made by the passage of Samudra's soul.

"A bargain," said the male snake again. Flick, flick, went his tongue, tasting the thoughts that thronged so thickly through the air around Natharie. "A wish for you, in return for him."

"A wish," repeated Natharie dully.

"Any wish," said the serpent, gliding still closer. "Any wish at all."

Natharie swallowed. It hurt. She looked at Samudra. The female glided across his throat and rose up, her tongue touching his cheek.

"You fear so many things other than the two of us." The male's tongue touched Natharie's hand. Slowly, sensuously, he slipped up her arm. His skin was dry and scratched against her own. She wanted to scream. He climbed her slowly, taking his time, knowing she did not dare move. He curved around her throat, and raised up his head to whisper in her ear. "Would you destroy the land of the Mothers? Would you have revenge for all the wrong done to you and yours? Give us the man. Speak your wish, and it is done."

"How . . . ?" Natharie's skin prickled. It wanted to sweat out her fear, but there was no water left within her.

"Was it not our kind who came to your Awakened One in his need and brought him shelter and succor? Were we not blessed because of it? The earth is our home, and no secret can be kept from the earth. Come." He was moving again, gilding down her other arm, caressing her slowly with the whole length of his body. The serpent's touch made her think of Samudra's. Arousal and revulsion both rose in her, and she did not know which was worse.

"Give my wife this son of the Mothers, and you will have what you want most."

If he had been dead, she might have given in. She was so thirsty. She was so tired. If she said yes, Samudra would be gone and her duty to him would be gone as well. With a few words, she could save Sindhu and all she loved. She could rest. She could drink. She could die.

Die. She could be dead very soon. But Samudra was not dead, and that was a very, very important thing.

The snake was in her lap now. He lifted himself up so Natharie looked into his burning eyes. "We served the Awakened One, why should we not serve you? Give us the man and let all be done."

His tongue flicked in and out, so quick, so strangely graceful. He had a scent, a dry, spicy scent that reminded her of something she could not name.

Give us the man and let all be done. Give us the man and let all be done.

All.

She could give, and wish, and die.

But Samudra was not dead, and that was still important.

Now Natharie remembered why. "No," she said.

The snake pulled back and its hood began to spread, slowly, oh, so slowly. "Why refuse us?"

"Because he is not dead."

The snake was silent for a long moment, as if conceding the point. "But he is still yours. He is your man."

"No," said Natharie again. She was so tired, it was so hard. "If he were dead, I might give you his body, and it would be . . . a lesser sin, but he is not dead, so he is not mine to give. I would be enslaving him and that I will not do." She closed her eyes. There. That was what she had been trying to remember. She would not give Samudra over to these two. If he were awake to give himself . . . that would be one thing. But he was not, and there was only her here to speak, and if this was the last thing she did, she would not act incorrectly. Not here at the very end.

"What is he to you?" asked the female. "You feel the spark of love in him, but what is that? He is the son of your enemies. He is a soldier and has already tasted his own death a hundred times. What is this last death to him or to you?"

"He is not mine to give. His life is his own." *Father, Mother, oh, Bailo, forgive me. Forgive me. Awakened One, watch over them, I cannot do this.*

"Then we will take you instead."

"No," she said quietly.

The serpent drew back, hissing in anger at this outrage, but Natharie knew she spoke the truth. In this place, at this time, surrounded by these horrors and these miracles, her heart was open and she understood.

"You cannot take me. I have done nothing wrong. You told me yourself. You are servants of the divine. The divine is not selfish. You cannot take me because it is not for myself that I refuse you."

The serpent opened her mouth and Natharie saw her fangs, and to her surprise the serpent threw back its head and laughed. While she stared, the cobras doubled back along their own bodies and slipped away, back under the altar, back to the forest, leaving her alone with Samudra.

Shaking with starvation and relief, she crawled closer to him. She had not touched him for any of the three days, but she did now, laying a trembling hand against his cheek. His flesh was cool, but not cold. Not deathly. He did not breathe, but the scent of him was still sweet.

"Samudra," she whispered. "Samudra, come back to me. Come back, my husband, my love. Come back."

She leaned over him, breathing her words over and over again into his mouth. "Come back, Samudra. Come back."

Still calling, she kissed him, breathing her new hymn into his still body. *Come back, my husband.*

Come back.

Come back.

*S*amudra woke, refreshed. After a moment, he realized he was no longer lying on forest litter and rotting wood, but on a slope of soft grass. His body that had been so heavy and cold before was now warm and light. He sat up and looked about him.

A green hill rose before him, to meet the gates of a great, white city. Even the Palace of the Pearl Throne would have been dwarfed by the size and magnificence of this place. Its many towers rose like trees in a forest. Its walls gleamed as if light emanated from within. Perhaps it did, for the sky overhead had a strange, greenish cast to it, and he could see no sun. In the gentle wind that wafted from it he smelled many strange and delicate scents. There was nothing he could put a name to, but they all made him feel strong and quiet, hungry and aroused all at once.

In all the world, there was no sound. He could not even hear his own breathing.

In the next moment, he realized he was alone.

Samudra scrambled to his feet, looking all about for Natharie. As he did, he remembered the ruined temple, their love, and the shock of pain as the serpent sank its teeth into his arm, and took his life.

Took his life. He was dead.

First, he was angry. His work was unfinished, the empire was now wholly in the hands of Divakesh and Pravan. And Natharie, oh, Natharie, his wife, his love, was abandoned in the wild forest while he was here on this hillside whole and healed of his pain.

He raised his fist to the strange, green Heaven and shook it. "What is the good of leaving me my mind and will if I cannot act!" he shouted, his words ringing through the silent world.

"Many ask that question."

Samudra spun on his heel. Behind him stood a small, slim figure in a loose, long robe of pure white. He could not tell whether this was man or woman. Its face was as smooth and big-eyed as a child, its hair was black and pulled back in a neat queue, and its hands were unlined by work and un-roughened by weather. It wore no rings or jewels that spoke of rank or status.

"For most it fades away with time." The voice was light and soft, and yet it vibrated strangely in Samudra's mind, almost as if it were not one voice but a chorus of them. It could have belonged to no one, or everyone.

Samudra knelt at once, bowing his head and folding his hands. "Forgive me, Father Death."

Death touched Samudra's head, and the touch was as cold as the poison had been and as gentle as his mother's kiss. "You are forgiven. You are also summoned. Come with me."

Samudra swallowed his questions. He was dead. He could only follow.

Death led him up the green hill to the white walls of the city. Their feet (Death's feet were bare, Samudra saw them as they appeared and disappeared beneath the white robe) made no noise on the cool grass.

The walls cast no shadow and the gates of the city stood open. A thousand different images decorated their sides: doves, swords, blooming lotus, raging fires, and, he shuddered to see, snakes with their mouths agape and their fangs bared.

"Where is my wife?" he asked.

"It is not for me to know the business of the living," said Death, and they walked under the archway into the city.

The city was as fabulous as its gates. Its streets were broad and gleamed like veinless marble. There were no hovels, no garbage, no waste or dirt of any kind. Each building was a magnificent temple, and Samudra realized the scents he had smelled before were those of incense rising from sacrificial fires. Trees grew green and vibrant from the marble, spreading flower laden branches which added their scents to the perfumed air. Birds were everywhere. They sat on the temple roofs, they roosted in the branches. They were all colors; scarlet, veridian, royal purple, vibrant blue. They opened their beaks and stretched out their throats, and Samudra knew they sang, but his ears heard nothing.

"Why am I deaf to the bird's song?" he asked his guide.

"That is for your host to answer," said Death, and they kept walking.

In a little while, they began to pass people. Samudra had heard tales all his life of the beauty of celestial beings, and now that beauty surrounded him. No two were the same. There were men of soft and sensual beauty, women whose beauty was hard as a sword. They were white as the moon, black as the night. Some were tall and slender, some as round and comfortable as the image of motherhood. Some had great wings hanging from their shoulders, some had feet or hands like bird's claws, some had jewels where their eyes should have been, and still others had the black and white bodies of serpents, and yet even they were as beautiful as they were terrible.

"Who are they?" he managed to croak.

"Children of the Mother," answered Death. "Even as you yourself."

On and on they walked through the midst of all the unbearable beauty. Fear racked Samudra, but he could neither tremble nor sweat, nor find any physical release. He could only look on the bright, inhuman beauty and fear it as he had never feared an enemy in battle.

They came at last to the summit of the city, and there was another temple. But for all the grandeur around them, this place was strangely simple. Marble pillars supported its peaked marble roof. Nine steps led up to an open place where a sacred fire burned. Behind the fire was a low, wide altar, and on that altar sat a woman. She was robed simply, and was more beautiful than any of the unearthly creatures he had yet seen. Samudra looked into Her eyes and he knew Her at once.

"Mother A-Kuha." He knelt, kissing the smooth street before him.

"Samudra," she answered mildly. "You are late."

He looked down at the white marble between his hands, not understanding.

Mother A-Kuha sighed. "Come here."

He could not even conceive of disobeying. He stood and mounted the steps. He passed the fire that burned with such sweet scent, but without any heat at all, and stood before her.

"You have failed me, Samudra. Do you understand that?"

"I . . ." he began, but he fell silent. "Yes."

He did understand. She had come to take him by the hand, and he had turned away. He did not wish to see her aspect or hear the words. Because he did not wish to face the tasks his own life set before him. He wanted to say that he thought he acted out of honor. He wanted to say that he meant to save his brother, but he realized she already knew these things, and not one of them mattered. He had acted from anger and selfish pride, without thought and without control and these things had undone all the others.

"You are fortunate my sister loves a wager. It is she who gave you this second chance. I am allowed to test you once more, my prince. If you fail this time, there is no return for you. Turn around."

Samudra turned. He looked first at the altar fire, and this time saw there was no wood beneath it, there was only a golden flame. On either side of the fire, in the place where there had a moment before been only open air, waited a door. Both were exactly alike: pure white and unadorned.

"What is this?" he breathed.

"Your choice," said Mother A-Kuha. "What happens next depends on which door you walk through."

"How can anything happen to me?" he asked wonderingly. "I am dead."

He felt warmth at his back and knew that the goddess smiled. "The dance does not cease because you are dead, Samudra. Behind one door is your old life. Your tasks are the same, your duties, your pain. Nothing is changed. Behind the other is your next life. In it, you will have all you have wished for. You will have no burden of imperial duty. Your brother will not fall because of your action or inaction. You will live long and free, and die in peace, and never have to fear failing those you love."

With Her words, great hope sprang up in him. A new life, the next life. He would no longer be the nexus for treason, no more have to guard himself against those he trusted and loved.

And yet, and yet, was that not the coward's way? He stared at the doors. They were flat and featureless, arched and white and unmarred. Between them, the fire burned, bright and sweet and utterly silent. What honor was there in tasks half-finished, in abandoning duty?

What do I care now for honor? I am dead and all matters of honor surely are settled.

"You must choose now, Samudra," said Mother A-Kuha gently.

What choice was he making? To what was he being called? He knew nothing, nothing at all. He did not even have breath or heartbeat to steady himself.

What do I do?

But no answer came to this silent prayer. There were the doors. There was the fire. There was the goddess behind him. Or was She gone? He heard no sound, saw no shadow. He itched to turn, but something deep in his being told him he must not. He must look at the doors. He thought for a rebellious moment to pick one at random and throw it open, but that was not right. He had not been brought to this place just to act like a child in a moment of anger. He must, somehow, someway, make a true choice. To never fail those who loved him, to be able to fulfill all his duty with a full heart. Surely that was better. To move on, to begin again, wiser and stronger. That was what he had wanted all along, and that was what Mother A-Kuha offered him. She knew his heart as She knew his fate.

But what of Natharie? Samudra bowed his head. She would be better off. What had he done except fail her? In thought and deed, he had sworn he revered her, but he had not. When she had broken seclusion, he had been revolted. He had even married her in shame and in weakness, shame for the act of taking her in love, shame for succumbing to the poison, and for not wanting to leave her alone to tell her family that she was spoiled by a man other than her husband. Widowhood gave her purity. He realized he had been as ashamed of her act as he had been of his own. She came to him willingly when he was in need, and he had believed it lessened her, even more than the acceptance of her gift lessened him.

I have been wrong, wrong, in so many ways. Natharie? Can the living hear the prayers of the dead? Forgive me if you can, my love.

Even as he thought this, he heard the whisper of a voice. It was strong but it was faint, as if coming from a long way away. He knew the pitch and timbre of it at once. It was Natharie, calling out. Calling him.

Come back, my husband. Come back.

Without thought, he ran forward and tore open the right-hand door. For a startled instant, he saw Natharie bending over his own body, and he was pulled forward and the world around him spun and he was raising himself up whole in himself once more, kissing Natharie and she was kissing him back in wonder and delight, using the last of her strength to breathe him back into the world before she fell fainting into his arms.

In the home of the gods, A-Kuha observed all, and she grinned.

"I win, Sister."

Chapter Twenty-four

When morning came, Samudra carried Natharie down to the river as gently as he could, grateful for the careful signs she had made when they walked this way before. Once he reached Liyoni's bank, he laid her on a bed of fresh palm fronds and trickled a little water into her parched mouth once more. He washed her with a scrap of sailcloth, wiping away the blood and grime that covered her, cooling the burning of her skin, wetting her lips. He wished desperately that Hamsa were beside him with her greater knowledge of the healing arts.

As he dabbed the cloth on Natharie's face, her eyes fluttered open. He tensed, fearing to see fever there. But no, she recognized him and lifted a trembling hand toward his face. He caught it, kissing back and palm, pressing it to his heart, letting her feel the beat of life within him. She smiled then, and closed her eyes, sliding into blissful, healing sleep.

He did not want to move her again, but they could not stay here. If she was not ill now, another day in this wilderness would surely make her so. The mosquitoes and river flies were already rising with the warming morning. He needed to get her home to Sindhu and to the care of her own people.

So he uncovered the boat, raised the mast, and laid her on the remaining sailcloth. He pushed off with the long oar, into the middle of the river, and, saying a prayer to Mother Chitrani, Queen of Waters, he hoisted the sail and took hold of the tiller.

They made slow progress. He could not read the river as Natharie could and twice beached them on sandbars. He had to drop the anchor frequently to bathe Natharie's skin with cool water and make sure she drank again. He had no bread or rice for her. He scanned the banks anxiously, looking for sign of habitation. About midday he saw the carved pillar that marked the border of Sindhu and he breathed his thanks to the Mothers and the Awakened One.

But as they sailed on into the afternoon, Samudra began to grow uneasy. There were no other boats on the river, and there should have been. The Sindishi were great fishers and the river was their highway for all trade and cargo. He thought he glimpsed a few farmsteads through the trees, but since he saw no sign of people or animals he could not be sure.

Natharie, perhaps sensing something amiss, struggled to sit up. Samudra's first thought was to urge her to lie still, but he did not. This was her country. She would know where they were and where they would find hospitality.

As she stared out at the riverbanks, welcome, gratitude, and deep hunger all flickered across her ravaged face.

"I have seen no people, Natharie," he told her. "I am not certain what to do."

"It may be . . . because of the war they have been moved to the city." She studied the bank a while longer, looking at the lay of the land, the shape and thickness of the forest. "I think we should reach the monastery before dark. The monks will shelter us."

Will they? Both of us? Samudra did not voice that thought. They would shelter Natharie, and that was what mattered. He could strike inland, find the army . . .

And then what?

They sailed on. The riverbanks grew closer, forcing the

river current to move faster. Still the thick forest lined their way. Still they traveled with only the sounds of the birds and the animals for company. As the light was finally beginning to fade, Natharie pointed toward the left bank and Samudra saw the long timber pier stretching out into the river.

Breathing a prayer of thanks to the Mothers, and to the Awakened One for good measure, Samudra steered them to the dock. The boat's bow drove under the pier with a loud crunch and Samudra endured Natharie's pained look. He leapt out to secure the boat before the river could bear her away. When he helped Natharie from the boat, they both smiled to find she had strength enough to stand. Still, he did not let go of her arm, but supported her as they walked toward the monastery walls, which bore the the leering faces of demon hunters. These figures glowered down on them, as if daring them to enter.

These carved presences seemed to be the only guardians of this place, though. The monastery gates were wide open, but the place was absolutely silent. Not so much as a goat bleated to announce their presence.

"This is not right," whispered Natharie.

"Could they have abandoned it because of the war? If the farmers would have gone to the city . . ."

She shook her head. "The monks are all sorcerers. They must live apart. It is the law."

"Then they will have their own way of protecting themselves, and surely they will not mind if we make use of the shelter they abandoned." Natharie was beginning to sway on her feet. "Come, we must find someplace for you to rest."

She nodded and Samudra led her forward. Despite his calm words, every nerve in his body was alert, straining to feel a stray breath of air, or hear the snap of a twig that would warn they were not alone. But there was nothing.

Natharie directed them to a long, low building with green eaves that proved to be living quarters. Neat rolls of sleeping mats lined the walls alongside plain chests for clothing and whatever personal possessions the monks were permitted. Samudra unrolled one of the mats for Natharie, and she lay down on it without protest.

"I'm going to find the kitchens. Perhaps the monks were so good as to leave us some food."

Natharie nodded, already halfway toward sleep again. *Watch over her,* Samudra thought to the serene image of the Awakened One in the shrine at the end of the dormitory. As he hurried back out into the gardens again, he had the unsettling feeling that Anidita was smiling indulgently behind him.

The living quarters were one of a set of three buildings that made a U-shape around a green yard. The building directly opposite held the kitchens and the stores. Samudra found quantities of rice, lentils, roots, cabbages, and a variety of fruits. The cool room in the cellar stored pots of powerful pickles, urns of coconut milk, eggs, and loaves of bread gone only slightly stale.

He brought bread and milk back to Natharie and roused her to eat and drink. While she did, he went back to the kitchen several more times, ferrying back a small clay stove, pots, a bag of rice and another of millet and one of tea, a quern, and a satchel full of other supplies.

Natharie smiled at him as he neatly set up the supplies and lit the stove.

"You cannot sail a boat, but you can create a whole kitchen?" she teased. Her voice was no longer so hoarse as it had been, and that alone made him smile.

"You forget, my wife, I am a soldier," he said, laying tinder on the blossoming flames. "I have made camp under much less luxurious conditions."

She smiled at him, and even in the dimming light he could see how health and strength were returning to her. He felt his tension ease, and allowed himself the small hope that all would yet be well, if only for this brief space of time.

But even as he thought that, the soldier in him grew restless.

He did not like this quiet. He could not fully trust a deserted place where there was no sign of how it came to be deserted. He was already prepared for a sleepless night on watch, but something nagged at him. Something seen or not seen.

Samudra stood. "I am going to walk around the walls once," he said. "Before the light fades." His eyes swept the dormitory. The windows were all firmly shuttered. There was only one door. "Can you bolt the door behind me?"

Natharie nodded, and Samudra kissed her swiftly. As he stepped out into the thick evening air, the feeling inside him grew more certain. There was something, someone, else here.

Unsheathing his sword, Samudra moved forward.

A circuit of the walls at first yielded nothing beyond an appreciation for the simple gardens they encompassed. But as he walked up the farthest right wall, he found an open pavilion built right into a gap in the wall. What had once been panels of paper had been laid aside on the grass. On the polished floor lay swirls of colored sands, and something else.

Exactly in the center of the floor, an arrow's black shaft stuck out of the floorboards.

Samudra's head jerked up. He turned a full circle, but there was no one, and yet, and yet, there was something. It galled him. He stepped up onto the pavilion floor and walked toward the arrow. It was a strange thing. Both shaft and feathers were solid black, but the shaft was not smooth as on a normal arrow. Instead, it was deeply carved with a repeating pattern that made it look as if the wood had been braided together. A red ribbon had been tied around the shaft. It reminded him of something and in a heartbeat he knew what. It was like the red band that pulled Hamsa's braids back from her face.

Her braids. He looked again at the pattern in the wood. He reached his hand out and he felt a strange warmth against his palm, as if he held it near the flesh of another living being.

Was it possible? Had she found a way? Samudra laid

aside his sword and took out his knife. He dug its tip into the planking around the arrowhead until he was able to lift the arrow free. Holding the shaft in his hand, Samudra knew what it was he felt. It was as familiar as the rhythm of his own breath but far less noticed. It was the bond that tied him to Hamsa, and it was strong and unsevered. He held in his hand a greater magic than he had dreamed possible.

Samudra reclaimed his sword and reverently carried the arrow back to the dormitory. Natharie let him in when he called to her.

"What is it?" she asked, watching him with wide eyes as he carried the arrow past her.

"Hamsa."

He carefully laid the arrow down on the floor and with fingers that trembled with the wonder of it, he undid the knot in the red thread.

As soon as the thread fell away, the arrow was gone. Instead, Hamsa lay before him, but not as she had been when he last saw her. Hamsa had always been a round woman. This Hamsa had not a spare ounce of flesh on her. The bones at her wrist and collar stood out stiffly. Her hair, all her braids had been shorn roughly from her head, leaving only ragged stubble behind.

Despite this, Hamsa's eyes opened and she saw clearly. "You are late, my prince."

"I have been told that before," he whispered. His mind was dizzy with wonder and awe, and all he could give voice to was the least of sentiments. "It is good to see you, Hamsa."

Her gaze drifted over to Natharie. "And you too, Great Princess. I am glad. We may begin the last work." She took in a deep breath and let it out again. "But first I fear you must let me rest a little."

"As long as you need, Hamsa," said Samudra. But the sorceress's eyes were already closed and her breath had slowed and deepened, carrying her into sleep.

Natharie unrolled a second mat and Samudra laid Hamsa upon it.

"You will grow bored with caring for weary women," she said softly, lightly.

Samudra grinned at her. "I think not." He felt strangely buoyant, as if some new world had opened up in front of him. He could not have said why this was, and yet it was so. Perhaps it was finding life where he had expected only death, or perhaps that he had not betrayed Hamsa after all. It was much like the sudden joy in the midst of battle when he looked up and saw not the enemy advancing, but allies.

Natharie looked down at the starved, sleeping sorceress.

"How is it she is here?"

He shook his head. "I don't know. However she came, it was a great working she made. Mothers forgive me, I would not have believed her capable of such a feat." He was grinning and he knew it, but Natharie was not. She rubbed her arms as if despite the sultry heat of the evening she grew cold.

"I fear the morning, Samudra," she whispered.

He came to kneel beside her, wrapping her in his embrace and savoring his right to do so. "Do not. The wheel is turning that is all, and whatever comes we will meet it."

He held her like that until sleep came for her too. Then, Samudra laid his wife down and settled himself cross-legged between the two women sleeping on their mats, his back to the wall, his face to the door. He laid his naked sword across his lap and with a better will than he had known in so many bleak days, he set himself to wait, and to watch.

*H*amsa woke with the dawn and sat up at once. For all her starveling appearance and cropped hair, Samudra could not remember ever seeing her so filled with vibrant energy. Her eyes sparkled mischievously as she made formal obeisance to him.

"None of that!" he whispered sharply, pulling her to him. "Embrace me as a sister! Mothers All, Hamsa! What have you done?"

"Almost as much as you, I think," she said, holding him at arm's length and looking him up and down. "Yes," she said with sudden sobriety. "You too have walked farther shores."

"We all have." Samudra nodded toward Natharie, still sleeping on her mat, disheveled and utterly beautiful.

"And I fear we are not done yet," said Hamsa softly.

Samudra nodded in agreement. "But that is not all you have done, Hamsa. I saw the arrow. How is it you could make such a working? Why have you never done so before?"

Her mouth twisted into a tight and mirthless smile. "I couldn't." And she told him with careful words the story of how Yamuna had held half her soul captive in a jar of red clay. All the while she spoke, Samudra felt his eyes widen and his heartbeat grow heavy, like that of a child at a story of demons and ghosts.

"Mothers All," he exclaimed again, this time in a choked whisper. "I do not know where to begin to speak my apologies, Hamsa. You were right in so many things . . . and I could not hear."

She just shook her shorn head. "It does not matter, my prince. All that matters is what we do next. We have no time to waste." He met her eyes and saw there the one he had missed for all the long years, the strong and steady counselor, the protector he was meant to have, and Samudra smiled, feeling the doubled strength, the safety that came only from knowing there was a loyal friend to guard his back.

With some small guilt, Samudra shook Natharie's shoulder. She quickly came awake, showing how much her strength had returned after a night of safety and a filling meal. In the small hours of the morning, Samudra had set about turning milk and rice into porridge, which was now ready, and before anything else, he insisted the women eat.

They both had two bowls and Natharie laughingly vowed he would be the one in charge of the kitchen wherever they made their home.

"Yes, wherever that may be." Samudra laid his bowl aside. "Hamsa, we have had no news for days. What can you tell us of how things now stand between Hastinapura and Sindhu?" *While I have fled down the sacred river and been the guest of the Mothers, what has my brother done?*

Hamsa crossed her legs and sipped at a cup of tea. "Some of this I heard from your soldiers, Samudra. Some . . . I came to understand through other means. Great magic was worked here across many years." Her gaze grew dim. "Some is here still. The rest . . . it has left echoes."

She told them of the preparations for war, of Divakesh's manic insistence that the fight go forward despite those who whispered that he, Samudra, was wrongly accused and that Hamsa's disappearance was an omen. She told them that Makul had died ensuring her escape and Samudra wept unashamed at this hard news.

Then she told them the story that had come to her during the slow, patient dreaming of her other form; how the monks had gathered all the people of Sindhu together and walked them beyond the borders of the world so they might be safe from the war to come.

"It is a thing I never heard of, even in legend," whispered Hamsa, clearly awestruck. "To walk even one divided soul . . . one who is not a sorcerer through the Land of Death and Shadow is a monumental task. To take thousands . . . it is a miracle."

"They are there now?"

Hamsa nodded. "And safe as if they slept in their own beds."

"Is my family with them?" asked Natharie. She had clenched her hands together until her knuckles turned white.

Hamsa only shook her head. "I do not know. I'm sorry."

"Where is the army now?" asked Samudra quickly. Neither of them had the time for sorrow anymore.

"They are in Sindhu," said Hamsa without hesitation. It was strange to hear so much certainty from her and yet it lifted Samudra's heart almost as much as the prospect of action. "More than that, I cannot say."

This time it was Samudra who hesitated. Ordinarily, he would not have considered asking such a question, but there had been so many miracles in the past few days, what was one more? "Is there a way you can send me to them?"

The sorceress considered for a long moment. "No. Not as you would wish. I fear, my prince, I must save my strength."

"For what?" cried Samudra, surprised, and a little irritated.

"For Yamuna," she answered. "Do you want to end this fight, Samudra? We must draw Yamuna from the battlefield."

"You are certain?"

Hamsa nodded. "Yes."

She was watching him closely, waiting to see if he remembered his earlier words. How could he forget, when this utterly transformed Hamsa sat in front of him speaking with a confidence that he was used to in great generals?

He said none of this. He only asked, "How may it be done?"

"Easily enough." Hamsa smiled grimly. "I will let him know where I am." Samudra opened his mouth to ask how that could be enough, but Hamsa anticipated his question. "I dared to crack his plans in two. In his mind there is no greater sin. He will come as soon as I call, and then . . ."

"Then what?" asked Natharie.

"Then we will see whether I have truly understood the way of things or not." Hamsa's eyes went distant, seeing something invisible to him. "But you cannot be here when this happens," she went on and she unfolded her legs. "Come. We will go ask Liyoni if she will speed you on your way."

Samudra glanced at Natharie, and together they stood and followed Hamsa down to the dock. She stood at the end of the pier and raised her hands. She called out three words that Samudra did not understand, and then she stood still, close enough to touch and yet a thousand leagues away. Moments passed away and all the morning went still. Not even a mosquito sang.

"Get in the boat," said Hamsa, not looking at either of them. "She will carry you."

Natharie did not question, but climbed aboard and slipped the rope at once. Samudra stepped in beside her, but turned back.

"Hamsa . . ." he began.

"This is my fight, my prince," she answered. The new light in her eye grew briefly dangerous, and for the first time in his life, Samudra felt his skin shiver as he looked upon his sorceress. "You must go to your own."

Samudra made the salute of trust to Hamsa, and then picked up the pole and pushed the boat into the current. It caught them up immediately, swiftly bearing them away.

*H*amsa stood on the long pier and watched Samudra and Natharie's little boat riding on Liyoni's great current until she could see them no more. Then she turned and walked back toward the monastery. She was tired. She wanted rest, but there was no time. This was the fight she had wished for, she could not refuse it.

She did miss her walking stick.

She reached the open gates and turned. The air was still and heavy with the scents of the forest. The insects chirruped lazily and the birds could not be bothered to call out at all.

Hamsa lifted her face. "Yamuna? Yamuna, where are you?"

As she spoke his name, in her mind's eye she saw him. He

was in the emperor's pavilion, crouched beside the emperor's throne. No one heeded him, least of all his master, who was watching the high priest in front of him with his lazy, dangerous gaze. Hamsa felt the emperor's hate and fear of Divakesh vibrating through the world almost as strong as Yamuna's working. The sorcerer hunched over a square of white silk drawn with inks, earths, and bloods. Beside him waited a jar of black glass. Her name had been woven into the circle nine times. Some of the earth was ash from things belonging to her burnt in special fires. The blood was his own. He sought her with every iota of his strength. His eyes burned with this intent and no other, and only the lingering protections of the monastery kept his malice from her.

"It is time, Yamuna," said Hamsa. "You want me. Here I am."

With those words, the invisible gates flew open wide. Away in that pavilion, Yamuna's head jerked up. He saw her now, with the eyes of his own mind. He knew just where she was and he leapt to his feet, triumph blazing through him. He snatched up the glittering black bottle. Without stopping to consult priest or emperor, he strode out into the open air. While soldiers stared and shrank away, he cast the bottle to the ground. It shattered and countless pieces of night flew in every direction, but they did not fall. They whirled together like a swarm of black flies, buzzing and cutting through the wind. They swirled around Yamuna, lifting him up into the sky, making the wind visible with their shining blackness, and they bore the grinning sorcerer away.

Her inner vision faded. The wind blew gently through her ragged hair. Hamsa turned and walked back into the deserted gardens to wait.

Chapter Twenty-five

Pravan stared out at the the rice fields that surrounded Sindhu's capital city. The land was so flat that by standing in his stirrups, Pravan could see the sacred river snaking through the countryside a quarter league away. The rice was green and waving in its flooded paddies, and these fields were as abandoned as all the others had been. The city walls were massive wooden palisades atop earthen banks rising up five times a man's height, their battlements painted red, green, and gold. They looked sound, but the stout gates hung open, and beyond them Pravan saw no smoke rising. He heard none of the sounds that must come from a large city, no voices human or animal, no sound of cart or foot. Whatever had taken away the people of Sindhu had not spared this place.

"Was it plague, Captain?" murmured his lieutenant, Vikas, who brought his horse up beside him.

"I wish it was," he said softly. *If it was plague we could turn around and even Divakesh could not contradict us.* "Is there word from the outriders yet?" He'd sent men into the forest, and into the fields, to search for ambush, for cowering farmers, for someone, anyone, who could tell them what was happening in this ghost of a place.

Vikas, forgetful of proper respect, only shook his head, and Pravan could not find it in him to rebuke the man. "We will need to send others," he said, his eyes scanning the country around them again, and again. "See to it."

And if they do not come back? We should turn around. We should go all the way back to the Pearl Throne. He pictured

himself trying to say this to the emperor, and his whole being curdled with fear and revulsion. They had to find some
witness to what happened here. It was the only way the emperor might hear reason.

"They say," Vikas began, then he stopped, looking around
to make sure no one overheard. "Sindhu's Awakened One is
really a sorcerer and that he lifted them all into Heaven.
They say he is even now readying an army of demons to rain
down on us."

"Worry about the Huni, Vikas, not demons," Pravan
snapped with more confidence than he felt. He wheeled his
horse around. "We will halt here while I get our orders from
the emperor!" he shouted to the officers behind him. "I want
good watch kept! Now is not the time to be caught napping!"
*Not with open gates and an empty city before us and the for-
est behind.* "And when the outriders come back see they are
brought to me at once!"

Pravan gathered his nerve and rode back to where the imperial chariot waited.

Divakesh, however, had beaten him to the emperor's
chariot. The man had walked all the way to Sindhu, like
the lowliest foot soldier, preparing the way for the image
of the Mother carried on her golden palanquin behind
him.

"Here comes Captain Pravan," the emperor was saying as
he approached. "You can ask him."

Pravan dismounted at once, making the salute of trust.

"Why have we stopped, Captain?" demanded Divakesh.
"Why do we not seize this city and carry Mother Indu to its
heart?"

Pravan licked his lips and prayed to Mother Vimala, who
oversaw traders and others who lived by their tongues, to
send him persuasive words. "The city may appear empty,
Lord Divakesh, but this may yet be a trap. It may be the
Sindishi and their allies have all withdrawn to some hidden
spot within the walls and they are waiting for us to walk in.

Caution will lose us but a few hours, perhaps as much as a day, but may gain us the victory."

"How dare you!" Divakesh stalked forward, his chin quivering with the force of his rage. Behind him, Pravan saw the emperor smile his lazy smile, and the fear he had been keeping at bay bit deep into his heart. "How dare you suggest the Mothers have not brought us victory!" shouted Divakesh. "How dare you suggest we have done wrong in their names!"

Pravan took a step backward. "My lord, I did not suggest wrong, only caution." All the rumors that he had heard about the high priest, the rumors which had cost men their lives, came flooding back to him now.

"Caution!" roared the priest. "Cowardice! The Queen of Heaven has commanded this war and it is our duty to follow Her without hesitation or question!"

"Divakesh," said the emperor quietly.

Divakesh turned in place, and for a moment Pravan thought the priest meant to rebuke the emperor for interrupting him. Emperor Chandra handed his spear to one of his personal army of attendants, then lifted off his crown and gave it to another. He scratched his scalp vigorously and swung his arms over his head, stretching, and all the time watching the walls of the city.

"You tell us it is the Mothers who created this victory, my lord Divakesh," the emperor said at last. "Is it not then right and proper that you should take Mother Indu into the city and consecrate it to her before any of us enters? Would that not purify the confines and render them fit for the First Son of the Mothers?"

Pravan felt himself tensing to hear what *Agnidh* Yamuna would say about all this, but the sorcerer was gone already and none knew where. Some said he fled in the face of a bad omen, and the men were growing more nervous because of it. Pravan tried to accept the story that Yamuna had gone to root out whatever curse emptied the country and hid the enemy, but his heart did not believe.

Divakesh's eyes gleamed. "It will be as you say, my emperor," he bowed. "I will take my priests and a hundred of the soldiers, with trumpeters and drummers. The Mother of War must have a worthy escort." Without waiting for Pravan to give counsel, let alone permission, the high priest strode off, bellowing his orders to whoever was nearest. Men scattered out of his path, to hurry to obey him, or just to get out of his way, Pravan could not tell.

Beside him, the emperor whispered, "So now, you old devil, now we will see. If you truly know the will of the Mothers, you should have no trouble doing this thing."

"My emperor . . ." began Pravan carefully.

"No, Pravan." The emperor shook his head, his attention all on the city walls before them. "We must wait now and see."

"Yes, my emperor." A hundred men. *It won't matter,* he told himself. Even if the Sindishi had somehow managed to bring every Huni out of the mountains, the Hastinapurans still would outnumber them three to one. "But . . . should we not withdraw, just in case?"

Emperor Chandra reclaimed his crown, settling it back on his head to cover his oiled curls. "In case the high priest Lord Divakesh is mistaken about the holy will of the Mothers?"

"Forgive me, I meant no . . ."

"But you did." The emperor gestured for the attendant to hand him his gilt-tipped spear, which he cradled in the crook of his arm. He measured the city walls with his gaze once more. "Yes. We will withdraw until we hear the priest's bells ring out joyfully over the city."

Pravan gave the salute of trust. A rush of relief flooded through him. He reclaimed his mount and returned to his officers to give his own orders. Slowly, as it did all things, the great army gathered itself, turned, and began to back away, withdrawing toward the treeline. All except Divakesh's priests and his hundred men. They marched in a neat double column through the rice paddies, on the narrow raised roads that ran between the pools thick with tall, green grain, across the arched bridges over the irrigation canals, carrying Mother Indu on her palanquin. The great drums thundered, the conchs and ivory horns blared, and the little troop marched through the city gates.

Pravan stood in his stirrups, shading his eyes. He imagined Divakesh's eyes blazing in triumph, his priests carrying Mother Indu directly to Sindhu's royal palace where the main temple of Anidita surely lay. Would he stop and behead all the images of the Awakened One on the way? Pravan wondered idly. Or would he save that exercise for later, once the city was reconsecrated?

A distant flash caught his eye, but it was gone before Pravan could focus his attention on it. Then, there came another. It arched up from the rice paddies and fell inside the city walls. It was followed by another.

Pravan stood in his stirrups "The fields!" he shouted. "To the fields!"

Runners scattered. Men surged forward. Pravan kicked his horse's ribs and the beast leapt onto the road, galloping full-speed to the nearest dike.

Before him, the Huni rose up, water sluicing from their black, lacquered armor. Their spears and axes were bright and their orders were clearly given, because they stepped onto the roads and the bridges.

Behind them, the first flames rose up in the city, and Pravan heard the war horns blow behind. Wheeling his horse in a tight circle, Pravan looked about him wildly, to see the army of the Sindishi pouring from the forest straight into the still disordered camp.

They were trapped. Burning city and enemy before, river to the right, and yet more enemy behind.

I was right, thought Pravan ridiculously. *This once, I was right.*

It didn't matter, for he was also dead. There was nothing to do. Pravan raised his sword and cried out, madly, word-lessly, and charged.

And so the rout began.

Chapter Twenty-six

The river current propelled the little boat forward at undreamed-of speed. The rushing air stung Natharie's eyes and blew her hair back. It was like riding the wind itself. She did not even attempt to raise the sail or hold the tiller. Liyoni carried them, and she would trust the river. Natharie stayed on the bench, clutching Samudra's hand with one of hers, and the rail of the boat with the other. She did not try to speak. Even if she could have found the words, the wind around her ears was so loud she did not think she would be heard.

All the world around them was a blur of greens giving way gradually to browns as they left the forest lands for the open plain. Only the sun overhead was unchanged, patiently tracing its course across the cloudless sky. Gradually, though, the blue above them dimmed. At first, Natharie thought it must be the evening beginning, but no, the sun was still a good hand span above the horizon. Still, the sky dark-ened.

Then, the rough wind of their passage took up something new. It was the scent of burning, and Natharie realized that what dimmed the sky ahead of them was smoke.

Reflex jerked Natharie to her feet, but the speed of their passage knocked her back down. Samudra caught her and she saw he had smelled the smoke as well. Sindhu was burning. The battle had begun.

As if the river realized their fear, the unnatural current that carried them fell away. Once more they were just a small boat on Liyoni's broad back. They had left the fields behind and now the gently sloping banks were covered only with brown reeds. Natharie's heart constricted as she stood to raise the sail. They were almost to the place of her womanhood ceremony, the place where she had first seen the horse, and Samudra, where this turn of the wheel had begun.

She looked past that place, toward the city walls. Something was very wrong. The air was full of the scent of burning, and it stung her eyes. The distant walls of the city were . . . wrong, empty, smudged black by the smoke. There was something else too, a sweet smell that brought the taste of corruption.

Samudra at once leapt onto the tiller platform, shading his eyes from the sun, staring out across the shore. "Mothers All," he breathed. "We're too late."

Natharie scrambled up beside him. Bodies sprawled on the top of the bank where the sacrificial horse had once stood. Tufted arrows stuck out of their throats and the blood had already dried on their faces.

Natharie sat down, turning her face away for a hard moment, willing herself not to be sick.

"Hastinapuran," said Samudra beside her, his voice flat and cold. "They are all Hastinapuran. And the arrows are Huni." He paused. "I see the Huni flag. I see Sindhu's. I do not see ours."

Natharie's heart skipped a beat. She had been so terrified of the Hastinapurans in their might overrunning Sindhu, it had not occurred to her that Hastinapura might be defeated by Sindhu. She saw how grim and white-faced Samudra had become and realized he had not truly believed it could happen either.

What now? She stared out at the river. *What now?*

A bump appeared in the river's rippling brown surface. She thought for a moment it was a log caught in the current, but then she saw the arm curve over and the feet kick up.

"Samudra!"

He turned, crouching low, instantly, his hand on his knife hilt. The swimmer came closer, flailing in the water. He lifted his head, and saw them both staring at him.

Then Samudra cried, "Taru!" He lunged forward so far Natharie feared he would tip the boat. Samudra grasped the swimmer with both hands, hauling him over the rail and, coughing and gasping, onto the deck.

"My prince!" the swimmer, Taru, cried, trying simultaneously to wipe the water out of his face and make some kind of salute. "I knew it was you! I saw . . . I . . . Oh . . . Thank the Mothers you are safe!"

Samudra crouched beside him in the bottom of the boat, helping him sit. "Taru, what happened here?"

Taru turned his face away. He was young, Natharie saw as he pushed his black hair back from his face. Little more than a boy.

"What happened, Lieutenant?" Samudra snapped.

His prince's barked question swung the boy's head back around. He struggled to speak clearly. "We came to the city plain in the midmorning." He turned his face toward the smoke rising from the darkened walls. "It . . . they were waiting for us. They were waiting in the forest and in the rice fields. Divakesh took a hundred men into the empty city, saying the Mothers had already won the battle for us but . . . they had soaked the streets with oil, we think, and they set fire to it, the whole city. The men inside burned. Oh, Mothers . . ." he wailed. "We heard them scream, and we could do nothing. We were caught between the fire and the forest and they rose up from the rice paddies." He shook his head slowly, his eyes distant, seeing it all again.

They set fire to it. Natharie sat and gaped at the boy. *They* set fire to it. It wasn't Hastinapura that had burned the home she dreamt of and prayed for. It was her father, for he would lead the army. Her father had destroyed their home.

"Captain Pravan had warned us to keep good watch, but he did not watch the patrollers well enough, and they were lazy and we . . . it never would have happened if you were with us, my prince," Taru was saying. Water still ran down his face and he angrily wiped it away as if it were tears. "Never. But, we were unready and they cut us down. Captain Pravan died defending the emperor, I saw that, before . . . before . . ." He bowed in his shame. "Before I ran. A few of us made it to the river, but the current was so strong, the others were swept away. I held on to a tangle for a time . . ." He gulped. "And then I saw you, my prince, and I knew I had to try to reach you . . ."

But Samudra was not listening to this. Natharie doubted he heard anything after Taru spoke of the soldier who died defending his brother. "Where is the emperor now?" Samudra asked. "I don't see his flag."

"The emperor is captured. The Huni have him."

Samudra sat back hard, as if he had been struck. "He is alive?"

Taru hesitated. "He was taken alive. That is all I know."

The boat was still rocking on the current, carrying them closer to the city with every heartbeat. Natharie shook herself. She picked up the anchor stone and heaved it overboard. Samudra didn't even glance up at her movement. "And where is Yamuna who was supposed to keep him safe?"

"He fled," murmured Taru.

"What!"

"I did not see it, but I heard. It was early in the day, just as Divakesh and the others were walking toward the city. I heard *Agnidh* Yamuna give a great shout. 'She's here! She's here!' They say he leapt up in the midst of his workings, and rose into the sky and vanished."

Hamsa. She had called Yamuna, and he had gone to her, as she said he would. But it was more than that. She had lured him away when his protection was most needed. Natharie wondered if Samudra thought of that at all. His face was flushed and his hand still clutched the hilt of his knife. Feeling a coward, she looked away from the murder in his eyes, scanning the shore, telling herself she was looking for soldiers, for Huni who might spot their boat and decide to loose a few arrows into it, in case the crew was Hastinapuran.

As we are.

"That is all I know," Taru said again. "I am sorry, my prince."

Samudra laid his hand on the boy's arm. "It's all right, Taru."

But Natharie had questions of her own. "What of Sindhu's king?"

The glance Taru flashed her was pure poison. "He can rot in hell for all I care," he muttered.

Samudra, control stretched to breaking by all this news, lifted his hand to strike the boy, but Natharie caught his wrist. "No. He is only heartsore." Samudra grunted, acquiescing if not agreeing, and let his arm fall.

"What shall we do then?" he asked, bitterly, almost mockingly, his gaze on the shore.

"It is plain, my husband," answered Natharie, keeping her own voice calm. "We must go to the camp and do what we can."

Samudra twisted around, disbelief plain on his face. "You would have me walk up to the Huni?"

"No. To the Sindishi. You must go to my people and my family, as I went to yours."

He laughed once, anger still clouding judgment. "What will your father say when he sees who you bring him?"

"I do not know," she answered. "But what can you do floating on the river here?"

Samudra stared at the shore yet again. She watched him weighing and judging all that he saw, considering the situation with his soldier's eyes, calculating cost and gain. He wanted to find his broken and scattered army, she was sure. He wanted to rally his men to to his side and sweep down on the Huni like divine vengeance, but his shoulders began to slump slowly, and she knew he saw no way to do so.

"Very well," he said. "But we wait until dark. This is more than I can do in daylight."

"As you wish."

"I will come with you," said Taru at once.

But Samudra shook his head. "You must go find our men, gather them in the forest. Tell them I am here, and they must wait on my orders." It would not do to renew the battle while he was in the enemy camp, Natharie realized, especially while he went to negotiate with the enemy king.

Taru accepted his orders with the soldier's salute, touching heart and brow. Now that he had purpose, he was calmer, his fears wiped away by the prospect of useful action. It no longer mattered what the danger was. Here was something he could *do*. Natharie knew exactly how he felt.

Taru slipped once more into the river, and silently swam away. Keeping as low as she could, Natharie picked up the oar, ready to ease them toward the shore, but Samudra shook his head and instead hauled on the anchor rope. Natharie saw what he meant to do, and nodded her agreement. If the boat was found, it should be well away from them.

When the boat was floating freely again, they both slipped over the rail into the cool silty waters. *I salute you, Liyoni. Do you remember the woman you made?* thought Natharie as she swam against the now sluggish current to the mud and the reeds of the shore. With Samudra beside her, she stretched herself out in the blood-warm mud. They watched the smoke rise over them, and waited for darkness.

Yamuna came to the monastery on a hurricane wind, broken glass making his train upon the tempest. His storm bent the treetops down. It whipped Hamsa's borrowed robe tight against her legs and breasts.

Hamsa stood in the middle of the open pavilion, in the place where she had landed in her arrow form. She had found a white staff very like her own. As she watched Yamuna arrive like one of the gods, she clutched it as if it were an anchor. Fear and doubt assailed her, old habits of her old self, not yet quite washed away. She felt Jalaja's sign on her wrist and calm purpose returned, though Yamuna's glass shards fell like hail, clattering and clinking as they rained down around her. They slit the cloth of her robe and sliced her scalp, stinging like flies.

It was nothing. A show of power, meant to distract and distress; meant to make the girl whose soul he had divided be afraid.

Arms spread wide, Yamuna landed on the garden lawn as neatly as an eagle on its perch. He grinned like death itself. Memory of long years of weakness made Hamsa tremble. Fear and anger washed through her, but neither would serve her now. She must be calm. She must remember the truth and the blessing of this place, and of the temple. If she forgot, he could still be her demise. Summoning all the discipline she had, she pushed that fear away.

"Little Hamsa," Yamuna said in a soft voice that might have been a lover's greeting.

She watched the death's-head grin that spread across his face. He still thought he owned her. He had seen her escape, but he did not know how much her soul had taken when it fled him. He did not know how much she had seen: all his sweating and planning and cursing, all his striving and his own fear. He did not know she could see his weakness here and now, as if he was nothing more than a dark shell hollowed out by his own constant plotting.

He stalked toward her, a tiger moving up to wounded prey. "I did not think you would be so foolish as to send for your death."

Hamsa simply shrugged. "You did not think I could escape you, either, Yamuna, but here we are."

Anger contorted his face, but he remembered he was supposed to be above the taunts of such as she and he smoothed his expression out swiftly. "Yes. You will tell me how you managed this remarkable thing. Then, you will die." He spoke with utter certainty. He could not be wrong. He had held her life in his hands for so long, it must still be there. A ripple of strange emotion ran through her, and to her shock, Hamsa recognized it was pity.

"No, Yamuna," replied Hamsa. "You are mistaken. I will do neither."

She thought this would provoke another of his mad outbursts, but Yamuna just cocked his head. He studied her for a long moment, looking at the way she stood and the place she held.

Looking for the working she might have laid down against his coming.

"There was great power here," he remarked. "But it is almost drained away now. Perhaps you thought to use it against me." He stepped onto the edge of the platform.

How is it you do not feel the threads around you? She had thought him blind before, but now she knew that was wrong. Yamuna was numb. He had wrapped himself so tightly in his own cloak of power and pride, he could feel nothing beyond it.

"There is still great power here," said Hamsa. "It was laid here by generations of sorcerers following the teachings of the Awakened One. It's quite amazing. It is as strong as the magics laid in the foundation of the Pearl Throne."

"Is it?" Yamuna arched his brows, and took one more step forward. "Well, they had so little to do, these exiled sorcerers."

"I must disagree, *Agnidh*. I believe they kept themselves very busy."

Yamuna sighed. "It will be a point of contention between us then. Now. Tell me how you escaped now, Hamsa. Spare yourself the pain before you die."

Before you die. The words slid through her mind. Her spirit remembered its confinement, all the time in the dark, unable to fight, unable to act, unable to do anything but wait for the next command. If he had told her to die, she would die. So many years of commands and helplessness. She should lie down now. She should do as she was told.

Oh, no, Yamuna. Not anymore. "You cannot kill me here, Yamuna," said Hamsa quietly. "Feel the air around you. Touch the workings. They're in the boards of the floor and the shadows of the garden. You cannot kill me."

His brows arched higher yet. "You think to frighten me with the old workings of absent monks? Hamsa, I preferred it when you screamed."

He raised his hand and she felt the chill that came as he drew up his power. She knew she witnessed the rarest of sights as his arm circled wide. Yamuna could weave a working of air and will and nothing more. It was the greatest display of power there was. She could not do such a thing, even now.

"Listen to me, Yamuna," Hamsa said, feeling little more than regret as the air trembled around her and grew thin with cold. "You are in a sacred place. Violence is not permitted here. Not by knife or sword. Not by magic. You cannot do this."

He heard her, she was sure of it, but he did not listen. Yamuna drew the power of air and wind into himself to mingle with the power of his own blood, of his bitter, fractious soul, binding together into a curse with which to ensnare her. He knotted his fist tightly, holding all his power with the hard grasp of flesh and bone. His eyes burned with his fire and his contempt.

Slowly, as if offering a fragile gift, he held out his hand and opened his crooked fingers. He meant to release the curse, for it to waft toward her, its invisible, intangible threads wrapping around her new-made soul, to throttle and smother her, to crush her down.

Hamsa reached out and covered his hand with her own. "No, Yamuna. It cannot be done."

His eyes bulged in their sockets. He would have snatched his hand away, but she held it fast. Air and wind tightened around them, becoming like ice, like glass. Holding the curse contained within itself, holding all the power Yamuna tried to pour out in him.

Yamuna's whole frame shook with the force of his will. She felt his pent-up power, flooding blood and sinew, swelling heart and lung.

"Stop, Yamuna," she warned. His hand was cold and calloused and his fingers clawed at her palm, digging into her flesh, but she held on. "You can still stop."

But he would not stop. He dragged up more power from the depths, hot and swollen with anger, and now with fear. Oh, yes, with fear, for the pain must be beginning, and she was still untouched by his working. She saw it in the fever-brightness of his gaze, in the way his jaw trembled and in the trickle of sweat that ran down his brow.

Then his skin, tight and shining, began to split.

A small red thread appeared on his cheek. Another snaked up his arm, and yet another across his bare chest, and still he drew in the power and strove to cast it out to her. He strove to capture her in his net woven of nothing but his hatred, to force her to bow to him, to die kneeling before him. But none of it could reach her. The fire burned only within him. She stood cool and composed, holding his hand, letting him claw at her. But even that was a futile scrabbling. The work of years had broken his nails and left nothing which could harm her. Nothing at all.

Yamuna clenched his teeth against his pain, and another split opened in his skin, and another, leg and arm and hand and face tore open and his blood ran freely down his trembling body, and still he raised his magics, still he struggled to throw them outward and weave her death around her.

Revulsion flooded Hamsa. When would this end? How long could he stand the pain of it? His brow opened now, and blood ran down his cheeks in shining scarlet rivulets. So much pain, all for nothing. Strangely, absurdly, she felt tears prick the back of her own eyes at such waste of life and power.

End this, she prayed. *End this.*

Whether it was because her prayers were heard, or because Yamuna's flesh was at last overwhelmed, Hamsa could not tell. But at last, Yamuna collapsed. His blood dripped out onto the pavilion floor, staining what remained of the colored sands and flowing across the varnished boards.

Hamsa knelt beside him. He was panting, his skin ashen grey. His eyes, so bloodshot the whites were pure red, stared up at her, unable to comprehend the limits of his own power. She had never even dreamed of such a moment, when she would be whole and well, and he would be broken by his own working. It was triumph. She had beaten him. She should feel joyous, exultant, but all she felt was sick with shame and pity. It must have shown on her face, because Yamuna gave out a bark of bitter laughter. Pink foam bubbled from his lips and Hamsa shivered to see the cold light in his eyes. "Well Hamsa, will you kill me, here, now, as we are, slave and slave, sorcerer and sorcerer?" He tried to spread his arms, but they flopped down at his sides, weak and lifeless, oozing blood from dozens of splits. "Do it, little Hamsa. Kill me, send me into my next life so we all can begin this charade again!"

She saw the terrible hope in him. He did want to die. He

wanted to walk into his next life, but not to make amends.
No. He wanted to be able to try again, to build power once
more, to spend another lifetime breaking those who thought
they might master him.

And she knew with a cold and awful certainty what his
doom must be. "No." She shook her head slowly. "I will not
give you that release. Your master yet lives. Can you not feel
it, Yamuna? So this will be your punishment."

"You have no power to pronounce sentence on me," he
croaked. "You cannot even raise your staff to strike me
down!"

She ignored him. "You will live, bound to service, as you
have been. Nothing will change for you, *Agnidh* Yamuna,
save that if he lives, you will serve the man you helped to
break." She leaned close to him. "And hear this, Yamuna.
You may be the serpent, but I am the mongoose, and I know
where your hole is. From this day forward, I will be watching for you."

She touched his forehead, drawing up her own magics
laid carefully by for this moment. "Sleep now, *Agnidh,* until
it is time for you to resume your duties."

He looked at her with such pure hatred she was surprised
the world did not darken, but a moment later those shining,
mad eyes closed, and the lean form slumped down into
sleep.

Hamsa sat beside him, turning her face south. It would all
be over soon. She could feel it in the air, in the threads of
fate that still hung in this place. One way or another, freedom would come.

*T*here was, in truth, not much time to wait in the reeds
and the mud, for which Natharie was grateful. The flies were
gathering in their millions to feast on the dead bodies nearby
and the stink of death and decay rising from the mud was
overwhelming.

Natharie was hungry. She was thirsty, and the river rippled at her back, but to move was to risk being seen by the Huni patrols that marched by so close on the top of the banks. She itched. She chafed to be so close to her father, and yet unable to go to him. Samudra, on the other hand, barely seemed to breathe. This was his home, she realized. He did not truly live in the small domain. He lived on the battlefield, with the scent of burning and death around him. This was the game he had spent his life mastering.

At last, the sun, bloodred from haze and smoke, dipped down below the horizon. The last few fingers of light stretched out to meet the first of the stars and the rising moon.

"This way," whispered Samudra, cautiously rising into a crouch.

Bent double, Natharie followed him, keeping her movements as quiet as she could. She was stiff from lying flat in the mud, and she was as filthy as she had ever been, but compared with the suffering the axes of the Huni would inflict, this was nothing and she knew it. Those hard-eyed men and sharp women might not hold their fire long enough to realize she was King Kiet's eldest daughter.

The shadows thickened as Natharie and Samudra traced their slow circle around the camps. Shouts and barks of laughter lifted above the groans of the wounded and the murmurs of the prisoners. Fires sprang up, scattering the flies just a little, and driving her and Samudra away with them. The fires also illuminated the flags, however, and they were able to tell that the Huni flags were clustered by the river, and the Sindishi were farther inland.

At last they came to the edge of a dirt track, and Samudra lowered himself full-length on the ground again. Natharie stretched out beside him. Ahead, two soldiers dressed in scaled armor stood at the edge of the camp, swatting at flies and mumbling to each other.

"Do you know them?" breathed Samudra.

Natharie peered at them, trying to see clearly in the faint firelight. Their dimly lit faces brought no names to her. "I do not," she told Samudra. "But they wear the royal badge on their helmets. They are my father's men."

Samudra nodded then, and touched her hand. It was a kiss, that touch, and a signal that her time was now.

Slowly, carefully, Natharie stood, raising her hands up before her, showing them to be empty. The guards lowered their spears at once, and the one on the right came swiftly forward while his friend guarded his back.

"Who is that?" shouted that nearest guard.

"The princess Natharie Somchai!" she called, letting her voice ring out. It felt so fine to say her name in her own tongue, she wanted the world to hear it.

The guard's eyes went wide and he gripped his spear more tightly. "It cannot be!"

"It is." Natharie stepped onto the road to move closer to the firelight. Not that it would help much. In men's clothes and coated in mud, she did not look much like herself. "If you do not know me, bring me to Captain Anun of the women's guard. She will say who I am."

That caused the man to go off his guard, just a little, and raise his spear. "Captain Anun is dead."

The words thudded straight into Natharie's heart. There had been so much else to worry her, she had not stopped to think that strong, quick, clever, loyal Anun might not be here. "No!" she cried.

The guard straightened up now. "It was she who wielded the torch inside the palace to help spread the fires from the center of the city."

Natharie saw how it would be. Anun would have waited at the garden gates for Divakesh and his hundred men, and looking them right in the eye, she would have tossed her burning torch onto the palace roof. Grinning, she would have stood there while they ran. A few probably fell with her arrows in their back. Natharie lifted her eyes toward the city walls, no more than a black mound in the darkness. The whole city was Anun's funeral pyre.

"She would not permit any other hand to do such a thing," Natharie murmured. Then, she shook herself, holding back her tears for another time. *How much more practice will I get at this?* "Does the king live?"

"He does."

There is some mercy in the world. "Then take me to him. Take me to my father, and let him see who I am."

Wariness returned to the soldier's stance, but still he said, "Very well, but you must stay close to me."

"I will," she agreed. "And you must know I am not alone." She beckoned, and with exceeding care Samudra stood up.

At once, the spears were leveled at his heart, and at hers. "Who is that?"

"A soldier of Hastinapura," said Natharie. "With valuable news for King Kiet. I vouch for him on my life," she added, hoping they did at least in part believe she was who she claimed to be.

The soldier looked Samudra up and down. He saw a Hastinapuran, filthy, lightly clothed, and completely without armor. He did not like this, but neither, it seemed, did he want the responsibility for it. "You will hand over your sword and knife," he barked.

Samudra did so without comment. The soldier took them and unceremoniously dumped them beside the fire. He and the other four surrounded her and Samudra to walk them through the sprawling settlement of tents and fires. Natharie saw startled glances and open mouths as she passed by. Clearly, some here did recognize her. Their escort, however, did not allow them to stop until they reached the scarlet and saffron pavilion that belonged to the king. The four guards who stood there challenged them at once with lowered spears, but Natharie was in no mood for another scene such as they had just endured.

"Father!" she called out. "Father!"

The tent flap flew open and King Kiet bolted out, staring around him. He saw Natharie in the darkness, covered in mud, her hair hanging loose about her face. His mouth shaped her name silently.

In the next moment, Natharie was in her father's arms, all but crushed by the strength of his embrace. She did not care, she just hugged him back as he said her name over and over.

"But how is this?" he asked when he could finally bear to step back a pace, his hands remaining on her shoulders.

"It is because of a good friend." Natharie gestured for Samudra to come forward. He did, and he bowed correctly over his folded hands.

In return, the king inclined his head. "What is your name, man? Who do I thank for my daughter's life and freedom?"

"Father," said Natharie softly. "This is the first prince Samudra."

Even as the soldiers had done, Father drew up short at this. Samudra did not move, so the least gesture could not be taken as a threat.

"Father, let us go inside. What we have to say is not for all the world to hear."

Slowly, King Kiet nodded. He stepped back to let them walk into the pavilion, but not once did his gaze leave Samudra.

The pavilion was simply furnished with a few mats for sitting and some low tables. Soldiers performed the servants' roles, setting out bowls of food and filling cups of tea. The king dismissed them all with a word.

"You must be hungry," he said to Natharie. "Please eat, and tell me what has happened." But Natharie did not move until her father added, "You also, Great Prince."

They all knelt at the table, and Natharie worked hard not to fall on the food like a starving beggar. Belatedly, her father thought to call for water so they might wash at least their hands and faces, and that also helped her to feel less the wild woman. Between bouts of eating, drinking, and washing, Natharie told her father all that had happened since she had left her home. He listened in stony silence, not once interrupting until her narrative was done.

Then, he looked down in his hands. "If I have to endure one more miracle, I swear I will break in two."

She smiled wearily. "Father, I feel the same." She poured some tea into the cup he had not touched and handed it to him, an echo of simpler days.

He smiled a little, and sipped. The familiar ritual seemed to steady him and he was able to look up at Samudra. "So, Great Prince, you are married to my daughter."

"By the laws of Hastinapura, Great King, I am."

Her father turned his weary face to Natharie. "Daughter?"

All the long, muddy afternoon she had thought about how she might say this thing. "Father, he is my husband in all ways that matter, but most of all because he is husband in my heart."

The king watched the steam rising from his cup for a while. "Very well," he said at last, and Natharie saw how much it cost him to accept what she had done. *I'm sorry, Father. I did not mean for it to be this way.* "Since you are son to me now, Prince Samudra, I suppose should ask what is it you want?"

"I want your help, Great King," said Samudra flatly. "For it is your allies who hold my brother."

"So they do." Kiet nodded. "And they are already sending out notice of this, along with the demands for his ransom."

Samudra winced. "Great King." He set his own cup down and rested his hands on his knees. "If the Huni are given ransom, they will only carry this war farther into Hastinapura. It is their goal to topple the whole of the empire and leave it open for their cousins in Hung-Tse to the north to come and pick up what pieces they do not claim for themselves."

"Why should this worry me? Hung-Tse does not threaten Sindhu. Hastinapura does."

"No. My brother Chandra and his high priest threatened

Sindhu. One is dead. The other a prisoner. It is left to me to speak for Hastinapura, and I say to you that my only wish is to end the conflict between us, and then take what remains of my men home and to never return here with them."

"Other lands have heard such words from you before," replied the king. "Why should Sindhu believe them now?"

"Because now they are given by my husband," said Natharie.

Her father sat silent for a long moment, and Natharie found herself suddenly afraid he meant to refuse. "Father," she said gently. "Consider. If Hastinapura falls, there will be nothing but war on our borders for generations. It will engulf us as surely as the emperor Chandra meant to do."

"You make many promises it will be difficult for one who is only a prince to keep. Will you leave your brother to die?"

"No, Great King."

"Then you will set him on the Throne again?"

Samudra hesitated only the length of a single heartbeat. "No, Great King."

The king's mouth twitched, as if he could not settle on what words to say. "I will not deny I would far rather it was you who held the Pearl Throne, Great Prince." He sighed, running his hand through his hair. "But it is out of my hands. Tapan Gol is determined to have his ransom and will not release the Hastinapuran emperor at my urging."

"Then I will go free him," said Samudra calmly.

"How? I cannot be seen to help you in this," he added sternly. "If you fail, I must still deal with Tapan Gol."

Samudra smiled. "I will take an image from the epics. They will not let Chandra's brother in to see him, but I do not believe they will refuse his weeping bride."

The king straightened one muscle at a time as Samudra's words sank in. "You will not put this deed on Natharie's head."

"You misunderstand me, Great King. Natharie will not play the weeping bride. I will."

Now the king stared in frank disbelief. *Oh, Father, so many great things have happened, how is it you cannot accept this little thing?* "You would meet your enemy dressed as a woman?"

"Great King, to end this nonsensical war, I would get down on all fours and howl like a dog," said Samudra frankly. "My personal pride is the least sacrifice to make for peace now." Kiet opened his mouth again, but this time Samudra did not let him speak. "King Kiet, it is my intention to save my wife's life and kingdom. You know the Huni are not safe allies, especially when they believe you to be weaker than they."

"There are signs already that they will turn on us as soon as it convenient." The king sighed and said softly, "I would not have done this had there been any other choice."

Samudra leaned forward. "The choice is before you now."

Kiet looked at Samudra, but he was seeing something else, something far away. Perhaps he was even seeing his son, Natharie's brother, grown and sitting before him.

"How will you practice this deception?" the king asked.

It was Natharie who answered. "It will be simple, once we have found some women's clothes. I will play one of the court sorcerers, and we will say I brought Queen Bandhura here by magic to plead for her husband's life."

Her father looked at her, and blinked, as if not quite certain who stood before him. "You have grown bold, Natharie."

She smiled. "I have grown desperate, Great Father. I too want to end this thing we have created between us." *And may the Awakened One forgive me, but just perhaps I want to be sure you do not change your mind about aiding Samudra once this deception is begun.*

If her father saw this thought in her, he gave no sign. "Very well. We will do this, and may Anidita bless it for the right thing."

Natharie embraced her father, and Samudra bowed to

him. King Kiet looked from one of them to the other. "But first you will have proper baths."

*F*inding the women's clothes was easier than Natharie had supposed. Being unfamiliar with the ways of armies, she had not immediately thought of the little force that followed the soldiers, which included many women who made their living in various ways from the soldiers and their needs. These supplied some bright linens and cheap bangles that might pass for gold in the darkness, and an opaque, fuchsia veil trimmed with gold that would hide Samudra's face and hair. For her own disguise, she found a clean serving woman's dress, a comb, and a piece of red ribbon. While Samudra drew on a skirt over his trousers and a tight, padded breastband over his bare chest, Natharie divided her hair into neat sections, binding them up into a passing imitation of a Hastinapuran sorcerer's hundred braids. With each detail that strengthened the flimsy disguise, Natharie blessed Master Gauda and swore to herself that she would see him able to practice his art and his worship openly.

While they readied themselves, the king spoke a few words to his guards and sent them out into the camp. Gossip spread fast among soldiers. By the time Samudra pulled the gaudy veil around his bowed head, the camp was buzzing with the rumor. Queen Bandhura was here, brought by magic because she could not bear the thought of her husband languishing in captivity.

"I'll take your hand," said Natharie to Samudra. "Remember to keep your head down." She looked to her father, seeking courage, and confirmation of all that they had planned. His face was twisted tightly. He wanted to make her stay. He wanted her to be safe in that other world with the monks and her brothers and sisters. But all he did was stand aside and let her lead Samudra out into the camp.

The soldiers stood as they passed, showing her at once

that the rumors had indeed done their work. Flickering firelight lit a hundred staring eyes. Men's whispers filled the
night air like smoke. Remembering her part, Natharie threw
her arm around Samudra's shoulders, as if sheltering a delicate lady from the harsh attention of so many men. This action also helped disguise her height as they hurried forward.
It was so absurd, part of her wanted to laugh, but they
crossed quickly into the Huni section of the camp, and those
long-eyed men watched their passage silently, and the light
of their fires fell on knives and black-tipped spears, and the
laughter died cold in Natharie's breast.

It was not hard to find Tapan Gol's pavilion. It was a plain
canvas thing, but half a dozen colored pennants fluttered
from the tops of its poles. Probably they all meant something, but Natharie had no time to wonder what, because
four guards stepped up to her. Samudra made himself tremble and shrink back in her arms, turning his face into her
shoulder.

"I am *Agnidh* Hamsa," said Natharie, barely remembering
to speak Hastinapuran. "I bring the first of all queens to her
husband the emperor Chandra, unlawfully held by the thief
and murderer Tapan Gol!"

As she hoped, her little outpouring raised a shout of spiteful laughter from one of the guards. He translated quickly
for his compatriots, who joined in his mirth.

"Please," whispered Samudra tremulously, peeping over
the edge of his veil. "Please, let me see my husband. I beg of
you."

This earned a snort of derision. Then, the pavilion's flaps
parted, and a lean man in a plain, black coat emerged. He
folded his hands and walked calmly up to Natharie. Samudra shrank back again, hiding beneath his veil again.

"I am the voice of the great Tapan Gol," said the man.
"Who is here to negotiate for the release of the hostage?"

Natharie contorted her face into a mask of outrage, and
then let it slip, little by little. *Master Gauda, you should see*

how well I learned your lessons. "This is Queen Bandhura, First of All Queens of Hastinapura, wife of the emperor Chandra."

The lean man looked down his nose at Natharie. "And you are the sorceress."

"I am."

His mouth twitched. "Be aware, sorceress, that if you begin any working, I will know, and your master will be killed at once." Then the lean man turned his back, as if to show he did not fear to do so, and returned to the tent.

Natharie bit her tongue. Still supporting the sagging Samudra in the circle of her arms, she walked into the tent. One guard followed them. The remainder stationed themselves outside.

The only concessions to luxury here were the piles of beautiful carpets that softened the ground, and a carved wooden chair where sat Tapan Gol, solid as a mountain and with eyes that reminded her of the serpents in the forest. Beside him on one of the carpets sat the emperor Chandra, his hands bound together, and hunching in on himself as if he hoped not to be seen.

Chandra straightened when they came in, his jaw hanging slack. Samudra did not give him any chance to speak, but threw himself at his brother's feet, weeping hysterically.

"So, this is the queen?" mused Tapan Gol. "Your woman is very fond of you, Emperor Chandra."

"You can do as you will to me, Tapan Gol, but do not insult my wife," said Chandra, his voice dangerous despite his helpless appearance. He leaned forward, lowering his face to his "wife's." He froze, but just for an instant, and clumsily raised his bound hands as if to stroke a beloved face. Samudra looked up at him, letting his brother clearly see his face, but at the same time, keeping his veil between himself and Tapan Gol. The lean man beside him shifted his weight.

He suspects. Samudra, be quick, that one suspects.

Out loud, Natharie said, "This is dishonorable, Tapan Gol.

How dare you hold one of imperial blood in these conditions?"

Tapan Gol glanced sideways at her. "It took five of my men to bring him to me alive. I prefer not to let him out of my sight."

"But I fear you must, Tapan Gol," said Samudra softly.

The Huni chief froze for just long enough for Samudra to turn on his knees and cast off his veil. Tapan Gol's hand was on his knife in an instant, but Samudra's knife was already out, and as the Huni chief leapt down on him, he brought the blade up swift and sure. Natharie did not even see what happened. She just saw the Huni chief slump forward and fall, Samudra's knife in his throat. The guard behind them gaped, giving Natharie the moment she needed. She snatched the pole arm from the man's hand. With one sweeping blow she knocked his feet out from under him and brought the butt crashing down on the base of his skull. He grunted once, and lay still.

By the time she looked up, Samudra had already retrieved his knife, and he crouched before the black-coated man. Outside, a voice called, "Mighty Chief, is all well?"

Samudra nodded to the man, the question plain in his eyes. The man could answer with the truth, and die, or he could choose to live. The man looked down at Tapan Gol, his heart's black blood still oozing from his throat, a raw, grisly sight.

"Tapan Gol is dead!" he cried out. "Tapan Gol is dead!"

In one swift motion, Samudra slit the man's throat and he toppled down beside his master, their blood running together, but it was too late. Outside a mighty howl rose, and immediately a crowd of Huni rushed into the tent, but they were not ready for Natharie and her pole arm. She tripped them as they ran in, dodging them as they fell, leaving them to Samudra and his knife, the sight of so much blood making her own run cold.

This is what I am become. This is what I am become.

This is what I must become. Her father was a soldier. Captain Anun had died in violence. She could not hold back and undo all their sacrifices. Her only real fear now was that someone would think to cut the tent ropes and trap them all beneath the fallen canvas.

But a new cry went up outside, accompanied by the sound of running feet and the clash of steel. Sindishi shouts mixed with the Huni. Samudra pushed back the tent flap and they saw that Natharie's father had not been idle. In the sporadic light of trampled fires they saw the Sindishi with staffs and swords beating back the startled Huni, driving their former allies down toward Liyoni's banks. And all was noise and confusion, and the only thing Natharie knew clearly was that Samudra shoved her behind him and faced the tent flap, his bloody knife in his fist, waiting for anyone who might to run in and renew the attack, but none did.

Gradually, the noise outside fell away, and it once more became possible to make out individual voices. One of them was Father's. "Prince Samudra? Is all secure?"

"All is secure, Great King," Samudra answered, wiping his brow. "I require a moment, and then I will join you."

"Very well."

Samudra reached out with bloody hand toward Natharie, and she nodded, letting him know she was well, although she could not seem to catch her breath or put down the pole arm. Still, Samudra accepted her silent assurance, and turned to his brother.

The emperor Chandra had rolled off his pile of carpets at some point during the fight, and now crouched behind it, his hands up, ready to defend himself as best he could. Natharie looked at the ruler of the empire that threatened to bring her home to ruin, the one who had almost taken her life from her, and thought he looked like nothing in that moment so much as a cornered rat.

"Natharie," said Samudra softly. "I must speak with my brother."

"How dare you bring her here?" spat Chandra. "She killed our mother!"

Still clutching the pole arm, Natharie stalked forward. Fear widened Chandra's eyes and he scooted backward from her approach. "No, Great Emperor," she said. "Queen Prishi's death is far more yours than mine." She had so much more she wanted to say to this man, curses and taunts and accusations, and all of them merely spiteful now. "She poisoned herself to bring on illness and senility so that your wife would not kill her to keep her from influencing you."

All blood drained from Chandra's face. "You lie!" he cried out.

Natharie did not bother to answer. She turned her back to the former emperor. "I will await your word, my husband," she said. Then, she walked out into the night, and there with the aftermath of the fight boiling around her, she stationed herself outside the pavilion like a guard, leaned on her stolen weapon, and tried with all her might to stop shaking.

"*H*usband?"

Samudra turned to face his brother. The trappings of empire had been stripped away from Chandra, and he had been left only a plain vest and trousers, his hands lying useless in his lap.

You are a wrestler and a fighter, and we're in a tent full of stray blades, and all you could do at this time was sit there, thought Samudra wearily. It seemed to him that even with all that had happened, he did not know the depths of his brother's weakness until this moment, because now he understood that Chandra had been waiting to see if he, Samudra, would conquer or be killed.

Chandra lifted his bound hands and Samudra gave an impatient grunt, and knelt to cut the cords.

"Will you kill me now, Brother?" asked Chandra casually as the thongs parted.

Samudra felt the knife in his hand. It was slick and warm. The odor of blood filled his nose and the taste of it was harsh in his mouth. He looked at his brother sitting before him, who had been the cause of this slaughter, who had driven him from his path and place where he had been happy and safe. Samudra looked at Chandra sitting there, calm and defeated and splattered with the blood of the enemy Samudra had killed.

Samudra stood up. "No."

Chandra lifted his head, and Samudra swore he saw contempt in the other man's eyes. "Squeamish?"

Samudra just stared at him. *How can you do this? Here and now after all you have done and I have done, how can you?* "Brother, I swear, even now, I would give you back all that has been taken if you would just acknowledge that you have done wrong."

"You know nothing," said Chandra contemptuously. He picked himself up off the carpet and stepped over the body of Tapan Gol. To Samudra's utter surprise, Chandra threw himself into the Huni chief's great chair, sprawling on the carved seat as if he had all the right in the world to be there, and rubbing his wrists to bring the feeling back to them. "You know nothing of the burdens of the Mothers or what it is to be betrayed by those who should uphold you." He looked up at Samudra with jaded eyes. "Kill me, Brother. Rid yourself of me and seal your guilt."

All at once, Samudra knew what his brother was doing. Chandra was trying to shame him. Chandra believed if he heaped enough of the blame on Samudra, Samudra would accept it, would believe that it was his own weakness that had borne his brother down into defeat and with his heart breaking he would embrace Chandra and swear never to doubt him again.

Oh, my brother, I am not the only son of Mother Deception in this place.

"I will not kill you, Chandra," he said. "You will stand

before the men outside and give me the Throne, and then you will retire to the small domain."

Their gazes locked, and Chandra slowly straightened up in the bloody seat where he had dropped himself. This time, Samudra saw fear, and this time it might just have been real. He also thought somewhere in there he saw sorrow, for their mother's death, and perhaps even guilt for his part in it.

"Brother, please, do not do this thing," said Chandra softly. "Have mercy. Do not leave me humiliated like this."

Samudra turned the knife over in his fingers. His brother ducked, cringing. Kill him. It made sense. *Don't leave him alive to challenge what had been done. Don't leave him alive to betray.*

Kill my brother. Let the fear win. Let destruction win over creation. Let death win over life.

But if he chooses death over this dishonor, can I deny it to him? He is still my brother. He is still of royal blood.

"Brother, I'm going outside and give my orders. If you truly wish to die, that is between you and the Mothers." Samudra laid down the knife and walked out of the tent.

Outside, in the heavy air of the false dawn, he took a deep breath. Natharie stood there, the only still figure in a milling ring of soldiers, all being directed by her father. Of course she was. She would never leave him alone at such a time. Wordlessly, he took her into his arms and held her close, savoring her warmth and her strength. He needed that strength so much now. His legs were about to give out under him. So many had died so needlessly already, and one more might die yet. He did not look back. His ears strained. He wanted to run back inside and strike the blow himself. He wanted to run back inside and snatch the knife away and embrace his brother and swear never to doubt him again. He wanted . . . Mothers All, he wanted to lie down and go to sleep.

Cloth rustled. Samudra loosened his hold on Natharie just enough to turn and see Chandra walking from the tent, his hands empty and loose at his side. Their eyes met, and Samudra knew, without any joy at all, that he had been right. His brother did not have the strength to take his own life with his own hand.

"Well." Chandra smiled a ghastly, ghoulish smile. "It appears you win, my brother." He raised his voice and all around them voices went still. "I Chandra *tya* Achin Harihamapad, who was the Beloved of the Mother and Protector of the Pearl Throne, do hereby renounce that throne in favor of my brother who was the first prince Samudra." Smoothly he made the salute of trust, but he peered over the tips of his fingers. "You have what you want, Brother. I hope you enjoy it more than I."

Samudra reached forward, but Chandra backed away, retreating beyond his reach. With his old, slow, lazy smile, Chandra knelt to his brother, pressing his brow against the muddy ground. Then he stood and turned, and walked into a fold of uncertain Sindishi soldiers, who closed around him, protecting him and preventing the escape Samdura knew he had no intention of making, yet.

Samudra made to step forward, but all at once, Natharie was beside him. "Let him go," she said, laying a hand on his shoulder. "Let him also breathe for a space."

But even as he spoke those words, a new shout went up. A dozen different arms were pointing toward the river where the darkness roiled and then opened like a flower. Light spilled out, solidifying into the form of a silver road shining so brightly that the firelight dimmed. Shadows moved on that road, accompanied by a great singing that lifted his heart even as it drew tears from his eyes.

Then the shadows poured off the silver road, spreading out to the sound of cheering and crying. Samudra's heart swelled with relief and he wiped the fresh sweat from his face. A final small cluster of shadows stepped from that road onto the earthly soil. Samudra's first thought was to kneel, for surely these were celestial beings come to set seal on this time of miracles. But even as the silver road faded away, taking the beautiful droning song with it, that sound was replaced by human voices. Human voices crying aloud in praise and wonder, in fear and dismay. Samudra realized that these were the Sindishi being returned to their home. The last few shadows stepped onto the riverbank and beside him Natharie stiffened.

Then she ran.

She ran with her skirts hiked up around her knees. Pushing past soldiers, cursing and pounding on them when they did not get out of her way fast enough, she ran toward the shadows. Someone else ran beside her. It took Samudra's dazzled eyes a long moment to see this other was King Kiet.

A man nearby lifted a torch. Samudra snatched it from him and raised it high. He felt the pavilion's door move at his back, and Hamsa came to stand beside him and witness the unfolding joy and chaos. The newcomers ran into the crowd of soldiers, shouting out names, receiving embraces of brothers, husbands, and sons. King Kiet held a woman in his arms, kissing her as if he never meant to stop and Natharie . . . Natharie was engulfed by a crowd of children as she tried to embrace them all at once. While he watched, she looked over the top of their heads at the woman, her mother, who had stepped a little away from the king.

They did not move toward each other, Natharie and her mother, but neither did they look away. It would be a long time before there was peace between them. Samudra understood that, just as it would be a long time before he fully understood and forgave what his own mother had done. But at least now they would both have that time, as she and he would have time to remake their lives and their lands and make good on the promise of the debts and wagers and miracles that had brought them to this place. Then she and he would return to the Palace of the Pearl Throne. Bandhura still waited in the small domain. What would she do when she found her husband had fallen? Would she stand by him? Samudra found himself inclined to believe she would. In her own way she loved him and he did not believe she would forsake him now.

What then would he do with the both of them? And what would he do with the whole of Hastinapura, which was now his to guide and guard until Death came once again to stand him before Mother A-Kuha?

Samudra sighed. He had been wrong before. This was not the end.

It was the beginning.

About the Author

Sarah Zettel, author of seven fantasy and five science fiction novels, won the Locus Award for the Best First Novel for *Reclamation*, and was runner-up for the Philip K. Dick Award for the best paperback original SF novel for *Fool's War*. Her fantasy work includes three Arthurian novels, *In Camelot's Shadow, For Camelot's Honor*, and *Under Camelot's Banner*. *Sword of the Deceiver* is the fourth novel in her Isavalta series. She lives with her husband and young son outside Ann Arbor, Michigan.